ENTER THE MULTI-VERS

C. ROCHELLE

CONTENTS

ISBN:

Cover design by divineconception
Character art by @biggsboi_ and @lemonade_doodles

TYPOS & LANGUAGES

While many people have gone over this book to find typos and other mistakes, we are only human. **If you spot an error, please do NOT report it to Amazon.**

I *want* **to hear from you if there's an issue, so I can fix it.** Send me an email at **crochelle.author@gmail.com** or **use the form** found pinned in my FB group or in my link in bio on TT & IG.

GLOSSARY NOTE: As there are a handful of non-English & scientific words in this one, including bastardized French from our favorite Mafia Queen, I've included a short glossary in the back for your convenience.

SLANG NOTE: There is always a bit of slang peppered into my writing—**and there is** *extra* **slang this time, because of how young/ingrained in normie society the twins are.** When in doubt, use Google, or contact me using the methods above if you truly believe it's a typo.

KINK CONTENT NOTE

Greetings, super smut lovers!

Before we begin the filthy fun, I wanted to include a quick note about the kink content you'll find within Enter the Multi-Vers. (And yes, the infamous mile-long **Content, Tropes, Kinks & Triggers List** can be found on the following pages.)

It's safe to say that if you've read my previous books (Villainous Things and otherwise), you've already met some kinky fuckers. One of my favorite things is to write characters who experiment, who are unapologetic about what turns them on, and who don't take things too seriously in the bedroom.

Readers often tell me I make kink accessible for them—that the welcoming way I write it gives them permission to explore it for themselves.

That warms my heart to hear, even if I would call my books before this one 'kink lite.' I may be a kinky fucker myself, but I've never been a part of the community. Therefore, I've never felt comfortable writing a character who was living the kink lifestyle, practicing BDSM instead of just enjoying some good kinky fun. Until now.

I knew going into this book that Dre was a Dom—a sadist, specifically—but realized that would create challenges for a supe who was strong enough to tear someone in half if they played too rough. If this was me, I would get myself educated, to make sure no one got hurt.

So that's what I did. I brought in a kink consultant—someone with years of experience in the community, including as an educator—and I had them read along with my other alphas as I wrote Dre (and Gabe's!) journeys.

Having this support was invaluable. While I already possessed an innate understanding of kink dynamics (plus, I *always* research what I write), I learned so much by having this person in my corner coaching me along the way.

I learned the rules so I could break them.

You see, Dre *wants* to play too rough. He wants someone he can't kill—someone who can handle the pain he needs to give. Someone like Theo.

Meanwhile, Dre's also doing his best to guide his twin through a sub-awakening—to encourage Gabe to explore his darkest desires safely. But not too safely.

Because Gabe is the bait, and Theo is the prey. Extremely dangerous prey. Exactly how Dre likes it. How they *all* like it.

What I'm getting at, in my usual wordy way, is that you will see both *safe* and *unsafe* kink practices in this book, but neither should be seen as a guide.

Yes, I did my due diligence to write responsible kink—to show it being practiced in a club environment. But I did this knowing full well that what my characters wanted, what they *needed,* was anything but.

Please remember: These three men are *supernatural creatures,* with abnormally high pain thresholds, and barely any limits. This is my darkest book to date, but it is *fiction.* Therefore, much of what happens on these pages should remain fictional.

I repeat this sentiment in the content and trigger warnings on the next few pages, but I hope the care I put into these pages shines through the darker content.

That being said, my first concern is that my readers are safe. If you spot something that is wildly inaccurate *(even after taking into account how these men are not human)*, or feel a trigger needs an additional warning, please do not hesitate to reach out.

I hope you enjoy my kinky little (thicc) book! This one took me on a journey.

XXX
-C

WARNINGS, CONTENT & TRIGGERS

Enter the Multi-Verse is an MMM romance between twin villains and a very villainous alien. Our men find other men in tight supersuits—and with fancy accessories—incredibly attractive.

This is not your kid's superhero book. This is *Sin City* and *The Boys* having a love child with extra spicy Spideypool and is **meant for 18+ adults** who can handle such things.

The **Villainous Things** series contains standalone books (each with HEAs) that feature interconnected characters and an overarching plot. You should read them in order (starting with **Not All Himbos Wear Capes**).

Please do not hesitate to email the author directly with any questions or suggestions for adding to the TWs.

NOW THE GOOD STUFF

Content, Tropes & Kinks:

- MMM supervillains x intergalactic villain romance.

- POVs from all three MCs.
- Spy vs. Spy (hidden identities).
- Control x Controlled Chaos x Batshit Cray.
- A BIG age gap + different worlds.
- Forced proximity (they were roommates).
- Hot alien accessories hidden beneath a(n equally hot) skinsuit.
- Lifestyle BDSM **(please see Author's Note in the previous pages).**
- A technically non-binary alien who happens to be inhabiting a male presenting skin suit this time around (which he/him personally prefers).
- A side character who uses they/them pronouns.
- **The two points above are NOT triggers. I'm simply including them in the content list so that anyone who gets bunched up about it can take their ball and GTFO.**
- Completely unhinged possessiveness from almost the first chapter (including between our codependent twins).
- *Mine, mine, mine.*
- A frustrated Dom who stubbornly thinks his perfect match doesn't exist (even when it's dangling right in front of him).
- A repressed sub who is finally living his best "good boy/needy slut" life (with zero sense of self-preservation… but better hair for bottoming).
- A bratty, TSTL at times, alien who truly just wants to throw chaos grenades and watch the world burn (preferably without pesky emotions getting in the way). Just accept Theo is a hot mess and enjoy it.
- An "I will punish you until you start acting right" brat/brat tamer dynamic.

- A former ho of an alien being forced to experience feelings and examine things and being VERY GRUMPY ABOUT IT.
- Tendrils—NOT tentacles—that can be used for pain or pleasure.
- "What a pretty little skinsuit you'd make" (fr).
- "I want to fucking devour you" (fr fr).
- Threatening behavior doing nothing to discourage boners.
- Consensual somnophilia aided by sleepy-time powers.
- Pain. Sluts. Just sluts in general, really.
- Impact play to the extreme (see Triggers).
- SO much dirty talk, praise, and degradation—just bucket loads.
- Biting, marking, territorial cum play, and knife play (in a way…).
- Restraints (the sexy, intergalactic kind).
- Voyeurism + exhibitionism (both in a kink club environment and between the twins, in their mind-bond, when their sammich filling alien is even remotely involved).
- Some very public playtime where all three of them (plus various unruly tendrils) "behave like animals in human clothing, seeing what [they can] get away with in polite society."
- Mild threats, followed by facefucking. Rinse, repeat.
- Begging, edging, orgasm denial.
- Cock and ball torture.
- A bit of blood play. Just a tasty smidge.
- BREEDING KINK(S) (plural).
- So many schmoopy feelings. Gross.
- Star Wars references and Space Daddy sightings (the author is Mandalorian obsessed. Deal with it).

- All the stretching, blow jobs, frotting, dicks (and other appendages) in asses (and other openings), etc, because this is an MM+ romance.
- The pesky overarching plot being all wrapped up— *even though there WILL be a just-for-funsies book 5…*
- …but not before the author rips the rug out from you at least a half a dozen more times (some of this was a surprise to me too, trust).
- Some interesting formatting to differentiate between the infamous **Rabble** group chat, inner thoughts, twin mind-speak, and a few flashbacks/visions. *Please see the following pages for a guide.*

Possible triggers (please also check above list and note this may contain SPOILERS):

- ****Kink being explored and negotiated in both safe and unsafe ways (please see Author's Note in the previous pages)****
- Sweary dialogue.
- Naughty, medium-dark humor.
- Pet names, used as both nicknames and honorifics.
- Using religious phrases in an overtly sexual context (oh, my God/Jesus Christ), along with the use of the words slut/cockslut/brat/whore/slave/cum-dumpster/etc… (both with family and in the bedroom). The word bitch is also used in a derogatory way.
- Pompous artists, art school stereotypes, and the art scene being absolutely fucking ROASTED by an author who has survived all of the above.
- Fear and violence (against each other and others) as foreplay.
- Morally gray characters with psychotic ideation all around.

- **No 'cest** (outside of Theo's fanfic), although the lines are very blurred. Those of you opposed to it will be happy and those of you who WANT it won't be disappointed either, trust.
- Self-administered post-battle medical care with related on-page mention of mild gore.
- Questionable consent with the twins entering the minds of others (including their own family).
- Manipulation by a certain controlling family member, for supposedly noble reasons (one guess as to who…).
- Deception from the start from all sides (including unexpected players in the game).
- Age gap-related behavior that could come across as predatory… until you remember that these are actual predators (and time is relative, space travelers).
- A slightly graphic description of body suspension in a classroom-like environment.
- Theo and Dre violently poking at one another (partially to antagonize, partially to flirt). It's a love language.
- A serious battle for dominance. Like… furniture—and bones—get broken. **For real. This is EXTREME sado-masochist play, at a level that would be not only inappropriate/dangerous for humans, but abusive.** But these are supernatural creatures who make it clear ahead of time that they are WAY into it, so we cool.
- A very non-consensual (but boner inducing) intergalactic kidnapping.
- A very non-consensual (but equally boner inducing) imprisonment of the one responsible for the kidnapping.
- Jokes about making lampshades out of human skin. It's just jokes. We're totally joking.

- A "tourist" in the kink scene being gently shot down by a more experienced Dom (for his own good and safety).
- Casual drinking and drug use (please note: weed is legal in the author's home state for both rec and medical use).
- ***SPOILER ALERT TW FOR GUN VIOLENCE, FORCED SUICIDE & MILD GORE IN CHAPTER 16.*** We have a mentally unstable stalker/intruder forced to unalive herself with a gun through the use of superpowers. I promise, there is a reason for it (I don't believe in using blood and guts for shock value purposes). **If this might trigger you, skip to the next chapter once the guys hear footsteps approaching.** The spice kicks in with Chapter 17, anyway.
- An aneurysm used as a coverup in a coroners report.
- An awkward family dinner amidst a fresh crime scene. Some very flippant attitudes about death & murder in general (again, these are supernaturals we're talking about).
- A safe word actually being used.
- Some rather important conversations happening while balls deep, but otherwise, things usually get discussed when everyone's in the correct state of mind.
- An interrogation/torture scene where a bad guy (as opposed to our baddie MCs) gets his fingers cut off before his brain is melted.
- Societal pressure (and requirements) to have children that results in both irresponsible sexual activity (prior to formation of throuple) and child abandonment.
- Resulting daddy issues (not the fun kind) and continued indifference/disrespect to the (now all grown up) abandoned child(ren).

- Supes and aliens behaving as if they have the biggest dick (in theory - we all know Violentia claims that title).
- A cutthroat, dubious moral code for supes that isn't meant to be understood by normies. "It's how the game is played."

(Please also see the following pages for more on supe identities and additional notes on the Multi-Vers timeline and formatting)

A NOTE ON SUPERHERO & VILLAIN IDENTITIES

A SUPE'S IDENTITY IS SACRED!

In this world I've created, superheroes and villains are supposed to guard ALL secret identities from normies—including their own, that of their family / clan, and even their enemies. When one supe addresses another as their supe name, that is a not-so-subtle way of saying they are considered the enemy at that moment. (Siblings may also do this to show the battle has begun—like during notoriously cutthroat White Elephant gift exchanges.)

To further clarify:
Shock = Supe name
Andre Acosta = Civilian name (for use around normies)
Andre Suarez = Secret identity

Awe = Supe name
Gabriel Acosta = Civilian name (for use around normies)
Gabriel Suarez = Secret identity

NOTES ON TIMELINE & FORMATTING

TIMELINE

Enter the Multi-Vers takes place on a *parallel timeline* to Putting Out for a Hero. For example, when the twins arrive on Theo's doorstep, Balty (along with Wolfy and Simon) are flying to the Salah's East Coast mansion.

I did my best to line things up correctly throughout this book, and hope readers enjoy reliving certain scenes/events from the twins' and Theo's POVs. That being said, if you eagle-eyed lovelies spot something that doesn't seem correct, send me an email at **crochelle.author@gmail.com** so I can check.

FORMATTING

Enter the Multi-Vers not only features the infamous **Rabble** group chat and the usual internal monologue, but twin mind-speak and a few flashbacks/visions.

Below is how I formatted each, to try to avoid confusion:

GROUP CHAT (with extra spaces above and below text segment):

Name Bolded: *Left-aligned and italicized for others.*

Right-aligned, italicized & bolded for POV texter.

INTERNAL MONOLOGUE:
Left-aligned and italicized.

TWIN MIND-SPEAK:

"Left-aligned, italicized with quotation marks for other twin."

"Right-aligned, italicized with quotation marks for POV mind-speaker."

NOTE: Mind-speak is italicized, in quotation marks, and bolded when sent to an outsider's head.

FLASHBACKS & VISIONS:

Left indented.

STALK C. ROCHELLE

Stalk me in all the places!
(by joining my Clubhouse of Smut on Patreon, my Little
Sinners FB Group, and subscribing to my newsletter)

For everyone who felt like they were from a different planet.

Ugh. Why must your dedication be so tragic? You need something that will titillate the masses… Something like,

"Tendrils are hot, tentacles are NOT!"

—*Theo Coatl, world (and beyond) famous artist*

PROLOGUE

Kill.

I'm going to kill him.

I'm going to kill them all.

Killkillkillkill…

CHAPTER 1
GABRIEL

"What the fuck is this bougie shit?"

Dre snorted in agreement with my blatant saltiness, but otherwise didn't respond. He didn't need to. My twin's mind was an open book to me—as mine was to him—and the concrete monstrosity we were both gazing up at was *not* to our liking.

Even if it is our new 'home.'

Until we get the intel we need, anyway.

We were here to spy, even if—on paper—Dre and I were simply two recent graduates, arriving for the first day of our new live-in internship. But what our clueless, yet potentially dangerous, host didn't know was that Wolfy had sent us.

And when Wolfy says 'jump,' we say, 'however high, we'll go higher.'

This wasn't because we feared him, although any supe with half a brain would. It was because our eldest brother deserved every ounce of our family's loyalty. He deserved our lives to be laid down for him in tribute.

After all, blood is thicker than murder.

The powers my twin and I had possessed since birth made us the crown jewels of our parents' arsenal. Never mind that we were two villains who could read—and, to some extent, control—minds. When our powers combined, we could literally *melt* someone's brain out of their skull from hundreds of miles away.

And what supe clan wouldn't want an ace like that in their pocket?

Despite this, Dre and I had been spared from the nightmarish childhood Wolfy endured, thanks to *him*. While we were occasionally utilized against our parents' enemies, Wolfy convinced them to keep us out of the fray—to save us as a boss battle threat for anyone who defeated *him*.

But nobody survived Wolfgang Suarez—not even our formidable parents—even if he did come home bloodied and barely clinging to life a few times in his younger days.

One of my earliest memories involved peeking into the bathroom as Wolfy stitched up a nasty post-battle gash on his forearm. It had looked like a fucking crime scene in there, and the cut was deep enough to see the bone, but my brother hadn't made a sound as he worked.

Completely unmedicated.

> *I* was the one who'd whimpered, which snapped his attention to me. His gaze had softened—as it only ever did for Dre and me—and he'd beckoned me closer.
>
> *But not too close.*
>
> "This is our life, young *Padawan,*" he sighed, returning his focus to his self-taught first-aid. "And the sooner you get used to it, the better clan leader you'll be someday."

I barely managed to tamp down the panic that shot through me at his statement. Instead, I kept my gaze riveted to Wolfy's wound and focused on covertly entering his mind—so I could *feel* every stitch along with him.

It was the least I could do.

"But I'm the baby!" I exclaimed, ready to point out how Dre was born twenty minutes before me. *"You're* the one who's gonna be our clan leader someday. Not me."

"Yes," Wolfy murmured. "That's the plan." A secretive smile twitched his lips—despite the searing pain I knew he was feeling—before he sobered and met my gaze again. "But if something goes wrong, *you'll* need to step up and take my place."

I'd probably only been seven at the time—meaning Wolfy was nineteen, if that. But even then, he'd seemed invincible to me. The idea of not only Glacial Girl and Apocalypto Man falling, but *my hero* as well was unfathomable. And the thought of ruling our clan— even with Dre by my side—had me dangerously close to puking all over the blood and gore-covered bath- room floor.

"W-we do?" I stuttered, pure terror causing my powers to falter as I slipped from Wolfy's mind.

My brother's gaze drifted to the open doorway, presumably looking for Dre. I knew he wouldn't find him. After we'd snuck out of bed, my twin had veered off to go watch *The Empire Strikes Back* with Vi and

Xanny while I followed the scent of blood. I could still *feel* Dre's presence in my mind, but his attention was focused on the 'grown up' movie, uncaring what we were up to on the far side of the family compound.

"No," Wolfy quietly replied, refocusing his attention on me with signature unwavering intensity. "Just you."

My jaw had dropped. Telling me to do *anything* without Dre was unthinkable, especially as our powers were so intrinsically linked.

How would I even survive it?

But Wolfy hadn't given me a chance to argue. "Can you be brave for me, Gabriel?" he hissed, almost desperately. "If the day comes when you need to step up for our family, will you have the balls to do it?"

I'd straightened at that. My brother had always spoken to me as if I were at his level, despite the age gap, and at that moment, he *needed* to know he could count on me.

And the last thing I ever wanted to do was let Wolfy down.

"Yes." I nodded once, my voice only wavering slightly. "I can be brave. I can have the… balls."

I'd whispered the last bit, with a nervous glance over my shoulder in case our terrifying mother chose that moment to walk by and wash my mouth out with soap.

When I turned to face Wolfy again, he was obviously

fighting back a laugh, even as he dipped his head in thanks. "Well done, *Padawan.* I knew you had it in you." His smile faltered as a rare glimpse of pain flashed over his face. "Why don't you go watch the movie with the others, before you miss the big plot twist about Darth Vader."

When I still hesitated to leave, Wolfy cleared his throat and shifted awkwardly in place. "I'm about to… remove some shrapnel, and you don't need to see that. You've had enough exposure therapy for one day, Gabe."

I still might have dragged my feet about leaving if I hadn't suddenly felt an insistent tug on my awareness.

From Dre.

Checking in.

Nodding again, I dutifully walked out of the bath-room, but not before glancing back in time to catch Wolfy pulling his shirt over his head.

Revealing a sight I'll never forget.

What I saw remained seared into my brain for hours afterward. Even when Darth Vader uttered his legendary words—and Dre gasped in shock from where his head rested on my shoulder—all I could think about was my eldest brother's extensive injuries.

If someone had taken a cheese grater to Wolfy's chest, it couldn't have looked any worse. There'd been so much blood, I'd morbidly wondered how he'd made it home without passing out.

Or how the other supe looked when he was done with him.

It wasn't until years later that I learned Wolfy repeatedly offered himself up for hand-to-hand combat—for battles Dre and I could have easily won without ever leaving the house. *That* was how badly he wanted to shield us from how awful our family was.

Until he could finally make it better.

Back in the present, I refocused on glaring up at the offensive new construction in Big City's bougie—yes, *bougie*—Teal Coast neighborhood.

It might have seemed classist of me to turn up my nose at the *nouveau riche*, especially since the *obscene* amount of generational money my family possessed had been acquired through questionable means. But it wasn't about that.

My main issue with the building—which I would be stuck existing in for the foreseeable future—was that it was making my well-trained design sensibilities twitch.

Yes, Dre and I had BFAs in *industrial design,* not architecture, but we therefore knew the ideal qualities of form and function, inside and out.

And this corner lot mansion overlooking the Bay is not it.

In my research for the job, some blowhard local journalist had praised the building for having "whimsical craftsmanship—unlike so many other homes in the city with their sleek, even sterile design."

Barf.

Because he was the other half of my soul, Dre chose that moment to pipe in with exactly what I needed to hear. "This is for Wolfy," he wryly reminded me, followed by the ghost of a smile. "We can endure this neo-classical Georgian trash for him, right?"

Damn straight, we can.

"I suppose." I dramatically sighed while adjusting the body bag-sized duffel slung over my shoulder. "But also for our Mafia Queen—long may he fucking reign."

Dre nodded once in response, back to his signature brevity.

Because who could argue with pint-sized perfection?

Simon Alarie was the tiny, yet terrifying yin to Wolfy's yang, even without their *inventus* connection. Anyone less tyrannical or bloodthirsty wouldn't have survived the villainous Suarez clan, and Simon had stepped into the role of co-leader with ease.

I would have considered bending the knee for his inherent psychoticness alone, but as far as I was concerned, Simon's unprecedented ability—and desire—to *touch* Wolfy had earned him our protection for life.

Because if anyone deserves love, it's the secretly soft boi Hand of Death.

"Are you planning on loitering on my doorstep indefinitely? Or are you two arguing over who gets to put a finger on my doorbell and ring it?"

Busted.

Dre and I craned our necks, squinting four stories up to where an enormous figure was peering down at us over the grotesquely ornate terrace railing. Since he was backlit by the unrelenting California sun, I couldn't get a clear ID, but judging by his air of audacity, the man shouting down at us was our mark.

Our prey.

"Theo Coatl?" I hollered back, like a jackass, since *this* was apparently how we were doing the fucking meet and greet.

"The one and only," he chuckled, raising a glass of what I prayed wasn't goddamn rosé. "And the door's always unlocked. Take the elevator to the top, boys—I've been waiting for you."

CHAPTER 2

ANDRE

Is this guy actually invincible or just too stupid to live?

I shook this thought from my head as I followed Gabe through the *unlocked door*. It wasn't like anyone in this part of town needed to worry about crime, but the rich stayed that way by keeping their shit locked down—not by giving would-be thieves free rein.

This job's gonna be way too easy.

And boring.

With a huff, I sternly reminded myself Theo Coatl wasn't human, or a supe. We actually didn't know *what* he was—yet. All we had to go on was that he was an obscenely wealthy artist who'd potentially stuck his dick in a gold-digging Parisian normie 25 years ago to produce a terrifying individual.

Our Mafia Queen.

Simon didn't know *he* was the reason we'd been sent here— only that we were gathering intel on our clan's behalf. It was unusual for Wolfy to keep secrets from his *inventus*, but apparently our brother didn't want to get Simon's hopes up about his heritage, in case we were wrong.

As usual, I had to hear this salacious gossip *secondhand.* While Wolfy had briefed both my twin and me on the overall mission and potential risks, only *Gabe* got the behind-the-scenes director's cut.

This didn't surprise me. The two of them always had a unique connection, and I'd simply learned to bury any jealousy I felt about it. Gabe and I already got preferential treatment from Wolfy compared to our other siblings, and—in the end—no one could ever come between me and my twin.

And heaven help anyone who tries.

A comforting mental nudge from Gabe had me refocusing on our present task—and present personas. As far as Theo knew, we were just a couple of starving artists looking for a prestigious internship after spending the last month drunk and high off our asses in the Berlin club scene.

The last part is true, at least...

It wasn't difficult to look stunned by post-graduation reality, especially as the formal entry we'd just walked into resembled something out of Liberace's personal style guide for wealthy eccentrics.

The gold-veined white marble floors and 20-foot mural covered ceilings were nothing but a prelude to the grand staircase dominating the space. It snaked its way up to the second level on either side, carpeted in zebra print and featuring iron railings so over the top, they were probably crafted by Italian angels.

Have mercy.

"Breathe, Dre," Gabe hissed through his teeth, leading me around a massive arrangement of hot pink roses to an antique elevator closed with an accordion-style brass grate.

Once inside the vintage compartment, I exhaled and ran a hand down my face. "I'm trying, dude," I huffed, annoyed I hadn't prepared for the negative effect this chaotic environment would have on my nerves. "It just feels like we've died and gone to maximalist hell."

Where more is more is MORE!

Gabe snorted, his gaze lifting to watch the numbers light up as we headed to the fourth floor. "Yeah, well… we knew what we were getting into by taking an internship with Big City's Renaissance Man himself."

Theo Coatl was the Teal Coast neighborhood's premier interior designer—and abstract sculptor, among other things—known for being just as comfortable in a corporate boardroom as he was in an opium den.

He was also notorious for *never* taking on lowly interns.

But nobody says no to Bunny Alarie.

If anyone scared Wolfy, it was Simon's socialite mother, but they both just wanted what was best for their little monster. So—in the interest of her precious baby learning who, and what, his father was—Bunny reached out to Theo through his agent to secure this coveted opportunity.

It probably hadn't hurt that *our* family was paying *him* to take us on through one of Wolfy's untraceable offshore accounts. Bunny had also, drunkenly, mentioned she'd made sure Theo knew we were twins—claiming it would seal the deal.

So he has a twin fetish.

Awesome.

That insight probably should have freaked me out more than it did, but I had too many kinky skeletons parading out of my own closet to judge what *anyone* else was into. Plus, we'd gone to *art school.* Our classmates had dressed in bondage suits with gimp masks because it was Thursday… or performed live nipple piercings in the dark as their senior projects. Weird was relative in the world of artists.

If Theo wanted to treat us like pretty little acquisitions in his eclectic collection, so be it. Role play was nothing new to me, and both of us had experience blending in where we didn't belong.

Since we don't seem to belong anywhere…

Thanks to Wolfy, Gabe and I had attended school with normies since we were old enough to defend ourselves. I still wasn't sure *how* he'd convinced our parents to let us loose among the unwashed masses, but I assumed it somehow fit into their villainous plan for eventual world domination.

Wolfy claimed he was trying to protect us from being used for nefarious means.

At least by anyone other than him.

I didn't shy away from violence the way my twin did, but I still—begrudgingly—appreciated Wolfy's interference, if only for abstract reasons. Thanks to our continued exposure to the outside world, Gabe and I were now skilled enough to hide our powers from not only normies, but the most lethal supes. The hope was that this sharply honed skill would also work on whatever kind of creature Theo was.

If not, I'll just kill him.

If the decor doesn't kill me first…

"Dre…" Gabe's voice in my head grounded my buzzing nerves as the slow ass elevator finally groaned to a halt. *"Remember, I've got you. No matter what."*

No matter what.

I nodded—sending the sentiment right back to him through our mind-bond—as the elevator chimed and the doors opened.

Revealing the stuff of nightmares.

It was nice, if your taste was terrible. Since mine *wasn't,* I had to momentarily rest my weight on a garish Doric column to avoid collapsing in despair.

The coffee and side tables were gleaming marble and gold, while the floor was no doubt some endangered rainforest wood. Seating was a dizzying menagerie of crushed velvet and animal prints. I spotted tufted ottomans, fainting couches, and other low-lying furniture options that promised you'd be down for the count if you ever made the mistake of taking a seat.

Death by pretension.

I blinked rapidly, attempting to lessen the glare coming off the high-gloss peacock-blue walls—but there was no mercy to be found, no matter where I looked. The long banquet table at the far end was mirrored and the nearby kitchen was stainless steel, with stark white milk glass countertops and black lacquered cabinetry. All reflective. All polished by invisible staff to shine until the viewers' eyes were burning.

The main living area stretched the entire length of the building's footprint—perfect for entertaining large numbers of brown-nosers at once. No less than 10 sets of French doors were flung open to the terrace where Theo had called down to us. Another set of four along the opposite wall led to a private turf yard—walled in on three sides by perfectly mani-cured shrubbery.

Desperate for relief, I peered over a hideous arrangement of cloying lilies and beyond the terrace—feeling my tension immediately lift at the sight of the calm Pacific a few blocks away.

At least I'll have somewhere to escape to decompress…

Unfortunately, a pretentious asshole-shaped silhouette appeared in one of the many terrace doorways, obscuring my glimpse of Zen. Whatever tenuous grip on control I still possessed faltered as our host stepped further into the room —allowing the natural light streaming in from the backyard to illuminate his perfection in startling detail.

Well, fuck.

Of course, I already knew what Theo Coatl looked like. Like the good little covert operatives we were, Gabe and I had poured over every interview we could find—memorizing our mark until we knew him as well as we could outside of slip-ping into his head.

Last month's *Avant-Garde in the Bay* described Theo as being in his late forties, of Chilean descent, and one of Big City's most eligible, and perpetual, bachelors.

He'd recently unveiled a temporary installation on the Teal Coast pier, titled *Flotsam,* which was an abstract representa-tion of a mob of tourists blocking the view while taking self-ies. I'd actually been mildly interested to learn more, but the reporter seemed singularly intent on discussing how Theo's home was the setting for notoriously debauched play parties.

Just another reason to never sit down.

Since nothing here can be easily sterilized.

Theo hadn't been fazed by the invasive line of questioning—unsurprising, since he seemed to live for the drama. He'd smoothly steered the conversation back to his recent exhibits and current interior design client list, while hinting at a collaboration with a perfume manufacturer near Sunrise City, but then the reporter veered right back to who Theo was supposedly fucking.

Half of Big City's art scene, apparently.

The photo shoot paired with the article had revealed a handsome man with mischievous dark-brown eyes, a roguish smile with suspiciously perfect teeth, and just enough silver in his jet-black hair and neatly trimmed beard to wander into hot fox territory.

So what if I saved a few choice shots to my phone?

I need to keep a visual of our mark handy.

The problem was that a handful of lifeless photos hadn't done him justice. Theo Coatl was blindingly attractive in the flesh, and the pure sex appeal emanating from his pores was dizzying.

He was also wearing nothing but a thin, floral print kimono robe. And the overt sluttiness of greeting strangers dressed like that was… doing things to me.

Lord. Have. Mercy.

"Andre and Gabriel Acosta," he purred—our civilian names sliding off his tongue like warm butter. "Welcome to my *modest* home."

The way he said 'modest' at least told me he had a sense of humor, but then he paused expectantly, his gaze roaming over us as he awaited our reply.

Which I was too tongue-tied to deliver.

What the actual fuck?

I maintained the aloof expression I was known for, even if the unexpected effect this man was having on me felt more insulting than the maximalist hellscape surrounding us.

The only saving grace was that my reaction fit nicely with the role I'd trained myself to play—at least, out in public. Supposedly, I was the quiet one—the twin you didn't have to worry about—and I often let Gabe take the lead in interactions with others.

Including family.

In reality, I could own everyone in the room if I wanted to. I just *chose* not to, and didn't give a fuck if anyone got the wrong impression. Most people didn't interest me enough to waste words on, anyway.

Most of the time…

"It's nice to meet you," Gabe blessedly stepped up, gesturing between us. "I'm Gabriel and that's Andre, and we're both really looking forward to this opportunity… Sir."

Theo's gaze darkened at my twin's accidental honorific, and I had to forcibly stop myself from thinking about someone calling me that—especially the obvious brat standing in front of us. The last thing I needed was to act on the inexplicable urge I was feeling to spank a stranger's ass raw.

There's a time and a place for that.

And I need to sneak away to the club the first chance I get.

Shaking off whatever the fuck had come over me, I refocused on the conversation—and my prey.

"So polite," our host cooed, giving my twin the lecherous appreciation we often received. "But please, call me Theo… in this instance, at least." Before I could wonder if Gabe was getting propositioned on his first day, Theo switched gears. "And while I appreciate the visual introductions, I *doubly* appreciate your drastically different hairstyles. Otherwise, you are… perfectly identical." He punctuated this statement with a contented sigh, confirming we were most likely here for the aesthetics.

And the fetish.

Gabe pushed a strand of hair out of his face from where it had fallen loose from his short man bun—a sharp contrast to the disconnected fade I preferred. Then he chuckled low.

Here it comes…

"Well, our *dicks* are different, too." His tone was casual, but I *felt* his ingrained need to assert dominance with our host. "Mine curves to the left while Dre's goes right. In case you were wondering."

Let the dick measuring contest begin.

I slowly blew out a breath, preparing to rally if I needed to actually form words and smooth things over.

Theo slow-blinked at Gabe before a wide grin stretched across his stupidly attractive face. "I *was* wondering, in fact, so thank you for that salacious mental image. Now!" He briskly clapped his hands and swept past us toward the stairs, leaving a cloud of intoxicating cologne in his wake. "Allow me to show you to your rooms—assuming that's where you want to sleep."

Brat status confirmed.

Gabe shot me an incredulous look before turning to follow, and I couldn't help smirking behind his back. My twin reveled in throwing people off their game, but Theo had clapped back—which told me everything I needed to know.

Things suddenly got a hell of a lot more interesting.

Being two of the most powerful supes in existence meant we rarely encountered a challenge, so the tease of a worthy opponent made my synapses fire all the way up.

Despite the danger.

Or… because of it.

Not even being surrounded by questionable decor could discourage the predator hungrily pacing beneath my skin. If Theo wanted to put up a fight during our mission to extract intel for Wolfy, he was going to find a fight waiting for him in return.

Game fucking on.

CHAPTER 3
THEO

How could I refuse such a gift?

This situation had turned into an unexpected windfall, which more than made up for how it began.

Initially, I'd been annoyed to learn one of my countless human conquests was reaching out, and this irritation had morphed into dangerous displeasure when my agent added she was asking for a *favor*.

Some people have a death wish.

The instant I'd heard the demanding voice of Claire 'Bunny' Alarie on the line—with her unmistakably curt Parisian accent—I remembered the force of nature that she was.

And how arguing with her was near impossible.

My first assumption was that she was after my money, and when she mentioned two young men looking for work, I'd even braced myself for the inevitable accusations of an accidental pregnancy.

As if spreading my seed was an accident.

But then, Bunny surprised me. She'd clarified that the men were simply the sons of an old friend, graduates of Big City's most prestigious art school, and from a family so wealthy, they made the 1% look like filthy peasants.

And they were *twins*.

It's as if they were made for me!

I refocused on my pretty prey. As mentioned, Gabriel's longer hair helped immensely in telling them apart, especially since they were both dressed in tragic black. I was sure other factors would help differentiate them eventually—like how they sounded when they came—but, for now, I simply drank in their almost ethereal beauty.

Height-wise, they were only slightly shorter than me, but more leanly built. With their strong jawlines, straight noses, tawny skin a few shades darker than mine, and striking blue eyes, they could easily make a living as fashion models.

Instead, they were *all mine*.

At least… they will be soon enough.

Twins were apparently a rarity—with identical twins being the rarest of all—and their existence had always fascinated me.

One of the first things that caught my attention when I first arrived on this planet was how *unique* its inhabitants looked, even those related to each other. Most intergalactic species had fairly standard appearances, with minute variations only discernible to those closest to them. The true forms of my kind were so similar, we recognized each other by frequency alone, so being set loose here—among such endless visual variety—felt illicit and thrilling. It had actually made deciding on a skinsuit difficult at times.

So what if I didn't have to decide on only one?

Knowing how our enemies, the *Lacertus,* first conquered humans—not through war but *breeding*—had me wondering if *twins* were more likely to possess remnants of these otherworldly genes. These random, often late-night musings only made me even more determined to play around with Earthling genetics. After all, I'd originally been sent here to investigate what exactly made humans tick.

So what if I've gone a little off-script in the centuries since?

Supes were the missing piece of this evolutionary puzzle— the results of *Lacertus* powers co-mingling with select human DNA—but I generally steered clear of taking them to bed. Thanks to politics, most were oddly clueless about their own heritage, but that ignorance allowed me to play freely, right under their supposedly all-powerful noses.

Not that any of them are powerful enough to stop me.

Out of morbid curiosity, I'd 'partnered' with a prominent supe family on the East Coast whose eldest offspring had unusually high levels of *Lacertus* DNA. The matriarch was insufferable—and truly thought our initial meeting in Argentina was an accident—but I appreciated her loose morals.

Since this experiment is anything but ethical.

The Salahs offering their unwitting heir as my lab rat was helpful, but so was their designation as so-called 'heroes.' I knew they'd protect their investment should the authorities start sniffing around, especially as—at the time our project began—they were more beholden to human laws than 'villains' were.

Even if they were too stupid to know how arbitrary those designations were.

But then Big City's Captain Masculine and Doctor Antihero had to pull back the curtain on that entire idiotic farce, forcing me to speed up the production of the DNA-enhancing serum I'd been developing—

"Is this our room?" Gabriel's raspy voice brought me out of my reverie.

How sweet he'll sound when he begs.

Wait…

I blinked in confusion before peering into the unused staff dorm he was gesturing toward. While I had a personal chef, a housekeeper, and the occasional groundskeeper, none lived on site—mostly because of the salacious nature of my extracurricular activities. I trusted them as much as someone like me could, but money talked, and there were *many* who could easily pay for juicy details and incriminating photos.

Although the occasional rumor only strengthens my brand.

"That… wasn't the plan," I mumbled, wondering why on earth he'd want to sleep *here.*

My studio was also located on this floor, and while that space vibrated with possibility, this room felt… lifeless. It was unadorned—an eyesore of beige walls and simple Shaker-style furnishings. There wasn't any visual texture or accent colors to be found.

The thread count on the beds is under 300, for Stellaria's sake!

"This looks fine to us." Gabriel shrugged, breezing past me and unceremoniously dropping his duffel bag to the floor with a thud.

The idea of *any* guests of mine existing in such a hovel made my human shell sweat—even those whose fates were already sealed, like these two. "Surely, you will want to see the guest suites one level down before deciding," I calmly replied, even as my smile began to crack. "I personally decorated them in the same style as upstairs—"

"No," Andre cut in with a voice that was quiet yet firm, and strangely made me stand up a little straighter. "We agree. This looks fine to us," he calmly repeated his brother's words as he followed his twin into the bedroom.

Are they… communicating with each other?

I'd heard twins had a language all their own, and that some supposedly exhibited occasional signs of telepathy. With what I had in mind for this pair, I certainly hoped that wasn't the case.

Unable to resist, I sent out the faintest tendril from my true form—so thin you would have to be at a certain angle to catch the unusual shimmer in the air. Coiling it around Andre's neck, I tightened my grip incrementally. Just enough to constrict his breathing.

Just enough to make him choke.

Oddly, it was *Gabriel* who hissed before glancing at his twin in alarm. *Andre* didn't react at all. He was maddeningly impassive as he maintained unwavering eye contact—as if he hadn't felt a thing.

Fascinating.

"Are you sure?" I continued, casually winding my tendril back into my borrowed form. "There's plenty of room on the second floor."

Andre's upper lip twitched. "But where would your *other* guests stay?"

Ah, so they've done their homework.

I laughed and waved a hand dismissively. "For my parties, you mean? Most spend the night in my bed… which is *more* than big enough for a crowd. In case you were wondering."

This time, Gabriel choked so abruptly, I quickly checked that I hadn't mistakenly unleashed another tendril.

Since they do occasionally have minds of their own.

His skin had pinked deliciously as he clearly fought against his own reaction to my words—making my true form writhe beneath my skin.

I can't wait to make him squirm.

When my attention returned to Andre, I found his irises had darkened to almost black. Before I could determine whether the change was from anger or lust, he simply turned and tossed his bag on one of the two narrow beds—unwisely leaving his back unprotected and open to attack.

Humans possess such stunted survival instincts.

"I hope that's not a required part of our *internship?*" Gabriel gritted out, back to his role of combative, angry angel as he crossed his arms and glared at me full-force.

Instead of immediately replying, I allowed my gaze to lazily drag over him. These humans may have only been in their early twenties, but they'd clearly found time for the gym during their schooling. I'd purposefully chosen a vessel that could visually intimidate—and believably hold its own in an altercation—but neither Andre nor Gabriel looked like they'd go down without a fight.

How thrilling!

"That remains to be seen," I murmured, calmly meeting his seething gaze. "I've never had an *intern* before, let alone a pretty little matched set."

Gabriel swallowed thickly, once again looking adorably lost for words. Unfortunately for him, all this did was encourage my lecherous behavior. While I *knew* I was wandering into dangerous territory by shamelessly flirting with these young men, my reputation had already preceded me.

So, what the hell?

It's not like I have an HR department to worry about.

With a slow exhale, Andre turned to face me—his expression still intriguingly unreadable. "Will you be showing us your studio next, Theo? I assume it's on this floor."

I tilted my head, intrigued by the sureness of his statement— how even the question wasn't truly a question. "What makes you say that?"

Andre shrugged. "The upper level is curated for the public eye. It's what you've chosen to share with the world… or your exclusive guest-list, at least. One level down from here, and the grand entryway, are still more interactive exhibits meant to wow your audience. But all this"—he gestured broadly to include the entire third floor—"is just for you."

It was my turn to be lost for words, and not only because the less talkative twin suddenly had a lot to say, but because he said it better than I could have myself.

I'd traipsed countless reporters and photographers through my home over the years, since it *was* a showpiece. Yet I was infamous for never allowing them into my studio. My reason had always been that I needed to keep my creations under wraps until they were ready to be unveiled, but now I wondered—much to my annoyance—if there was more to it than that.

How dare *this human make me… contemplate!*

I scoffed and plastered on a cocky smirk. "So astute. And an appropriate observation, given that you're both so intent on inhabiting this floor…"

Where everything is just for me.

Andre's eyes narrowed momentarily before he smoothed out his expression again. "Yes. We *are* here to assist you with your work, correct?"

Among other things.

"Of course," I lightly replied, beckoning them closer. "Keep in mind, however, if you reveal my secrets, I'll have to kill you—"

An unexpected change in the air pressure had me biting off my words. I quickly sent exploratory tendrils down the hallway and service stairs to the first floor—attempting to locate the reason for the disturbance.

Only to come up empty-handed.

That's… odd.

"Are you all right?"

With a start, I realized Andre was now standing less than a foot away, his gaze raking over me almost clinically.

How the fuck did he sneak up on me?!

"Yes," I snapped, aggravatingly caught off guard thanks to whatever false frequency I'd picked up. "I thought I heard my housekeeper, Lupe, come in, that's all. Let's head to my studio. I'm eager for you to become involved in my latest project."

Andre's mouth twisted in what looked like a smirk, but I was already spinning on my heel and hurriedly leading the way.

Yes, I *had* partly taken on these two graduates to do some grunt work for me—assuming the NDAs I required would scare them into silence. But I couldn't help noticing how *eager* I was to share my sacred space with them.

It means nothing.

They're simply a pair of useful tools—like palette knives.

Or grenades.

Naturally, I'd done my homework on Andre and Gabriel as well. It was a fairly standard resume for any artist who came from money—expensive boarding schools, drool-worthy connections, international exhibitions immediately after graduation—but the biggest gap in public record surrounded their *family.*

I wonder why that is…

Shaking my head, I flung open the door to my studio with a dramatic flourish. In the end, it didn't matter *who* was paying their way. These two belonged to me now, and they were never leaving this house again.

Not alive anyway.

"Step right up!" I announced, waving them inside my lair like a carnival barker. "Let the fun begin."

CHAPTER 4
GABRIEL

I guess I'm just gonna have a perma-chub now…

Theo Coatl was *doing things to me,* and it wasn't just because he was the hottest man I'd ever seen. My well-contained powers were trying to fight their way out of me to get to him —to do what, I couldn't guess. But the more pressing issue was that my proximity to our potentially dangerous mark was threatening to give me a raging hard-on.

Why does he smell so goddamn good?

I couldn't even pinpoint what exactly he smelled like. There was an undercurrent of electricity—probably related to whatever his powers were—but the rest was some sort of primal lizard-brain mating juice that was making my eyes cross.

If he asked me to drop to my knees right now, I would hit the ground, no questions asked.

Fuck.

This was definitely not *part of the plan…*

Besides my unruly libido, the biggest problem was how *Dre* was looking at him. My twin hadn't blinked once since Theo first sashayed into the room in the very kimono that was now permanently filed away in my spank bank.

When Theo had done… *something* to my twin—without even touching him—he'd barely flinched. *I'd* felt that shit, but the only reaction from Dre was a steady chant of *"mine, mine, mine"* through our mind-bond. In supe-speak, this could just as easily mean dibs on a fight or a fuck.

Or both.

Dre was little more than a scope locked on a target at this point—a hawk perched on a limb staring at a mouse in the field below. This unwavering intent was not only a threat to our cover, but to the promise I'd given Wolfy when taking this assignment.

To keep my twin on a short leash.

For everyone's safety.

Theo seemed blissfully oblivious to the danger as he rambled on about the various workstations in his ridiculously lavish studio. I waited until he'd turned his back to us—too busy waxing poetic about the rotating platform he'd constructed for his nude models—before creeping into my twin's head to scold.

"What the fuck are you doing, Dre? Was that you *poking him back there?"*

"I'm just trying to figure out what we're up against."

"Yeah, well, we're gonna figure it out real quick if you alert him to the fact we're supes, dude. Chill."

That motherfucker *snorted* in reply. Not dismissively—we would never condescend each other—but like he didn't believe that our opponent was worth worrying about.

I wouldn't be so sure…

I couldn't tell if Theo was fully aware of what he was doing, but the pure power rolling off him was nearly suffocating. Normies couldn't pick up on these vibes—not unless we wanted them to—so I couldn't help wondering if he was testing how responsive we were… or baiting us into showing our cards.

Neither is good.

Whichever it was, I absolutely could *not* have Dre baiting him in return, so I did the only thing I could think of in this situation.

I tattled to Wolfy.

"YOU NEED TO CALL DRE IMMEDIATELY!!!"

Not two seconds later, *my* phone rang. My twin had his own phone, but notoriously never answered it—much to Wolfy's annoyance. In the end, we were rarely apart, so my phone had become the best way to get a hold of either of us.

Unfortunately, I was already regretting my decision. Theo was frowning at my pocket as if the phone itself had consciously interrupted his tour, while Dre—rightfully—glared at *me* accusingly. But the person whose disapproval I dreaded the most was on the other end of the line.

"Excuse me," I mumbled politely to our tour guide before doing my best to sound confused as I answered the phone. "H-hello?"

"I thought you had things under control." Wolfy's voice was barely audible, but still dripping with disappointment. "Did we not discuss your responsibilities in this situation?"

Ah, fuck.

"I…" I stuttered, not wanting to say too much in front of Theo —or Dre—but also not sure what I would have said, anyway.

I've already fucked this up.

Wolfy sighed, his gooey center showing through as his tone softened. "Let me talk to him, *Padawan.* I'll handle this."

He always does.

Wolfy handles everything.

"Big bro wants to talk to you," I mumbled, handing the phone to my other half while simultaneously locking down my mind so he couldn't immediately rage at me.

Or see why I called Wolfy in the first place…

"That's *weird*," Dre deadpanned, snatching it out of my hand while continuing to stare me down.

"I dunno." I shrugged, already scheming how to hide from him for the rest of the day if need be. "He said it had something to do with the dirty laundry."

As in, stop fucking airing it, dude!

With one last glare, Dre stalked from the room with the phone held to his ear—no doubt plotting his revenge while Wolfy ripped him a new one.

And leaving me alone with our mark.

Okay, maybe this wasn't the best idea…

"Are you close with your family, Gabriel?"

Theo's voice was like honey being poured through my veins —making me feel languid and insubstantial.

And safe.

No.

Not safe.

"Um…" I replied, rapidly blinking to snap myself out of whatever goofy spell I'd fallen under. "Well, our parents are both dead, so our older brother takes care of us now."

Although, he did that when they were still alive, too…

Theo hummed, but not sympathetically. It was more like he was absorbing the info and filing it away as future leverage.

Just like a supe.

It may have sounded like I was just handing him intel, but Dre and I had been strictly instructed on what to share—and what to guard with our lives. Obviously, our true identities were a no-fly zone, along with anything that might unmask our infamous family. But with deception, it was always easiest to tell *most* of the truth alongside the lies.

And Glacial Girl and Apocalypto Man are both dead and burned to ash.

Good riddance.

"But you're no longer a child in need of coddling and care." Theo's hypnotizing voice returned as he advanced, forcing me to retreat. "You're a *man* with his own agenda—his own wants and desires. You don't need your *big bro* controlling you from afar. Not when you can handle yourself."

I ain't handling shit right now.

Now my body was *vibrating* from his proximity, along with his scent. Even though it made absolutely no sense, all I could focus on was why the fuck we weren't both naked and rolling around on the ridiculous Persian rugs layered all over the floor.

Where the hell did that *come from?*

Weird insta-lust aside, Theo was right about one thing. I most definitely *was* a man with wants and desires, and not one of them currently aligned with what Wolfy had tasked me with.

Get in his head.

Get the intel.

Get out.

Get a fucking hold of yourself, Gabe!

"Nobody controls me," I growled, more annoyed with my traitorous body than anything. My words ended with a gasp as my back met the worn edge of a wooden worktable— rattling the small glass bottles lined up along its surface.

Theo hummed again as he loomed over me, but it was more like a purr that had my toes curling in my boots. "You wish someone would, though, don't you?"

I actually stopped breathing. It was as if Theo had found a way into *my* head, and there was nowhere for me to hide. Even though this kimono-wearing asshole had known me for barely ten minutes, he'd somehow zeroed in on my darkest desire and held it up to the harsh daylight pouring through the floor-to-ceiling windows. Forcing me to *look.*

Offering me what I wanted more than anything.

But I can't.

I can't fuck this up.

"Your face is perfectly symmetrical," he murmured, blessedly switching gears as he mapped me with his deceptively warm brown eyes. Deceptive because—this close—I could tell there was no actual warmth behind them. This close, they glittered like stars in a far off galaxy. Mesmerizing. "I bet you don't possess a single unflattering angle—"

We *both* hissed in a breath as he absently cupped my chin, sending a harsh jolt of electricity shooting down my spine.

Straight to my dick.

What the FUCK?!

Apparently just as surprised as me, Theo snatched his hand away and stumbled backward. This action revealed Dre standing in the doorway—looking exactly as disgusted with me as I would have expected.

Bro, same.

"Are you measuring my brother's skin for a lampshade?" he muttered, tossing me my phone without waiting to see if I was ready. "Or was that last season's home decor line?"

I almost fumbled the catch as Theo glanced at my twin over his shoulder. "Lampshade?" he absently echoed—his gaze drifting to the industrial sewing machine across the room. "I hadn't considered that…"

Dre met my gaze, and we didn't need our mind-bond to come to the same conclusion.

Dude is 1000 percent gonna make a lampshade from someone's skin.

Why is that so hot?

That last thought was 1000 percent *all mine,* but before I could descend into another shame spiral, Theo cleared his throat.

"As pretty as Gabriel would look, lit up next to my bed…"

What?!

"…you both have the ideal background to assist me with my latest endeavor," he casually continued, as if he wasn't threatening to go full Buffalo Bill on me.

It took my half-horny brain a moment to realize Theo was gesturing toward the table I was still plastered against. I turned, finding nothing but a few dozen nondescript brown bottles—like what you'd see in an old pharmacy.

"Selling out for Big Pharma?" I snarked, still salty over my uncontrollable reaction to this man.

Theo was aggravatingly unbothered, openly laughing in the same way he had when I gave him the report on our dicks.

Even though I haven't seen Dre's since we were young enough to take baths together.

People loved to assume that being twins meant we were spit-roasting bitches left and right, but our *very* separate sex lives were exactly that. Separate. The unspoken agreement had always been that we closed off our mind-bond while fucking —or even just jerking off—and even though Dre's absence still felt like a presence in my head, it worked for us.

We're close enough as it is.

"Not pharmaceuticals. Cosmetics, rather…" Theo joined me at the worktable, although he notably kept his distance. "It's all very top secret, of course, which is why I keep *this* area of the house locked and off-limits to anyone who hasn't signed a lengthy NDA—in blood. Speaking of which…" He glanced at his pricey as fuck Omega Moonwatch. "I'm hosting a gathering tonight, so you'll need to access this floor again afterwards… assuming you decide to join us."

It wasn't a question. Theo reached into the pocket of his kimono and pulled out his phone, which he briskly tapped against mine. An alert chimed and my screen lit up with instructions on how to download an app I'd never heard of before.

Along with a shit ton of notifications from the Suarez family group chat.

The Rabble.

Sigh.

"It's funny how you keep your studio locked down, yet anyone off the street can just walk in your front door." Dre appeared at my side, shocking me once again by saying more words to a relative stranger than most heard from him in a month.

Theo chuckled, even as he gracefully stepped away from my twin—as if not wanting to risk another electricity-induced boner.

I really need to unpack that one.

"Yes, well, material objects are... impermanent. Much like human life," our host mused as he headed for the door. "But art!" He dramatically gestured around the space before spinning and pointing to the little brown bottles behind us. "Art has the power to *improve* humanity for generations to come, and this priceless permanence must be protected at all costs."

With that slightly unnecessary—but completely on-brand—declaration, Theo Coatl swept from the room, leaving me to wonder why he was inviting us to his gathering tonight.

And what kind of party it is...

"We need to talk, Gabe," my twin bluntly stated after we heard the service stairwell door slam shut. He picked up a bottle and inspected the liquid inside through the glass before meeting my gaze—his expression as serious as I'd ever seen it. "There's been a change of plans."

CHAPTER 5
ANDRE

When the 'news'—heavy on the air quotes—broke that heroes and villains were the same, no one was *less* surprised than me.

Maybe it was because we'd had two of the shittiest villains as parents and one of the kindest—Luca Meier, aka The Kinetic Assassin—as a mentor, but 'evil' had always seemed kind of relative.

And anyone who'd seen our **Token Hero** in action knew heroes were just as bloodthirsty as the rest of us. Butch was part of the family now, but for many years, Captain Masculine was the Suarez clan's biggest enemy.

And numero uno *on Wolfy's hit list.*

Gabe and I had always been off the Captain's radar—undercover normies that we were—but while our classmates obsessed over Big City's *savior,* we clocked him as the threat he was. One thing I'd consistently noticed how the cameras were always rolling when he pummeled a hapless villain into a bloody pile of mush. It turned out, this was Biggs Enterprises controlling the narrative on our hero's carefully curated reputation.

And the *heroic* Salah clan—whom Balty was currently en route to marry into—were more than happy to agree to an alliance with Wolfy. Anything to keep their dirt swept under the rug.

Fucking opportunists.

Just like the rest of us.

While Wolfy's motives for sending us here could be seen as noble—at least, toward his *inventus*—I knew there had to be another angle. Now that we were *all* more involved in the family business, thanks to Simon, I'd started picking up enough intel to be dangerous.

Enough to find opportunities of my own.

"We should definitely attend Theo's party tonight," I blurted out the instant we were back in our dorm-style room.

It was hard to say how good our opponent's hearing was, but that he'd obviously not been planning on bunking us in here had me believing it wasn't bugged. Yet.

As long as he's not a mind reader, we'll be all set.

Gabe blinked at me while his brain momentarily fizzled, his tell that he was sneakily trying to hide something. "Oh? Uh, sure… Yeah, we could do that…"

Dude needs lessons in deception.

"Theo obviously has his sights set on you," I continued, immediately burying the stab of jealousy I felt at that statement—not wanting *him* to pick up on *my* fizzle. "And what better way to sneak into his mind than while you're fucking?"

"Jesus, Dre!" Gabe choked out, his eyes nearly bugging out of his pretty little head. "Warn a guy before offering to turn 'em out. *Jesussss…*"

I cackled and strode to the bed I'd claimed—upending my duffel bag to unpack. "Oh, calm down. You're no blushing virgin and I assume you've figured out how hot it is to get into someone's head when your dick's inside them... or vice versa, in your case."

Since you're obviously a bottom.

"I..." The uncertainty in my twin's voice had me slowly turning to face him.

My other half was sitting on the opposite bed, his cheeks bright red as he gnawed at his bottom lip. While he was still bravely maintaining eye contact, he spilled the tea where he felt safest.

In our heads.

"I've... never been on the receiving end of that before..."

Oh.

That complicates things.

I blew out a breath and walked closer, crouching in front of him so he'd feel more in control with us at the same level. "Okay, well, I definitely don't want you doing anything you're not comfortable with, but... my plan was to use your fine ass as bait. Sorry, not sorry."

That got a laugh out of him, as intended. "I look exactly the same as you, dude," he huffed. "Just with better hair."

Yeah... better hair for bottoming.

I kept that observation to myself since this apparently *was* virgin territory for him. But while I was now one percent *less* sure about my strategy, I still thought it was the best plan we had.

Better than Wolfy's, at least.

"You can take it slow…" I rose and sat on the bed next to him. "Just lead the guy on. Fuck around a little to keep him interested—whatever gets him to let down his guard enough to slip in there and find… *whatever* we're after…"

Which we both know you *know more about than me.*

As usual.

As skilled as I was at locking *my* shit down, Gabe clearly caught the underlying bitterness of my statement. But just as he opened his mouth to reply, his phone dinged with a familiar sound.

*The fucking **Rabble** group chat.*

I shamelessly spied on the action over his shoulder, even as I slipped my hand into my pocket, in case I needed to jump in with damage control on my phone.

Since I can guess what's coming.

The Dumb One: *You fuckers should have seen Wolfy's face just now as he laid into Dre [volcano emoji] [gravestone emoji]. RIP, little bro.*

The Mafia Queen: *Was it any worse than the terrified expression you've been wearing this entire flight, Baby Hulk?*

Simon does not play.

The Dumb One: *I'm not terrified. I'm deep in thought.*

Okay, but I can't let that *go.*

Cranking up my supe speed, I pulled out my phone, determined to get in with the burn before Simon stole my thunder. Even though they were currently flying across the country together in Wolfy's private plane, I knew our

Mafia Queen preferred the audience **The Rabble** provided.

> *Careful, Balty. You don't want to exhaust yourself before Dahlia Salah gets her icy claws on your dick.*

Talk about RIP.

Clan Daddy: *The only one who needs to be careful right now is you, Dre.*

Try me.

I snorted and tucked my phone away, knowing a complete lack of response would piss off Wolfy the most. Glancing at Gabe again, I found him still staring down at his phone with his brow furrowed, but when I followed his gaze, I saw the screen had gone dark.

Shit.

"This… new plan… to use me as bait." He swallowed thickly. "It didn't come from Wolfy, did it?"

With a heavy sigh, I slung my arm around his shoulders and pulled him close. The tension in both of us lessened the instant we touched, and I took a moment to simply absorb the steadiness of our bond before replying.

"I've *got* you," I fervently repeated his words from earlier, meaning them with my entire soul. "No matter what. The instant you need me to step in, I will fucking end this guy."

Although, I would love to play with him first.

Bat him around a bit.

Gabe tensed like he always did when I went dark. "No," he blurted out before smiling warily. "I've got this. Let's… go to the party, like you suggested. I'm totally fine with watching random strangers fuck all over Theo's hideous furniture. I mean... I'm assuming that's what will happen tonight..."

My lips twitched in a return smile, even as I internally acknowledged we probably should have talked about this kind of shit before now, especially before walking into Theo's notoriously hedonistic environment. I could have taken Gabe to the club with me—exposed him to the lifestyle so he wouldn't be such easy prey...

Stop it.

He's prey in appearance only.

We're the predators here.

Theo had a shit ton of power pulsing beneath his skin—enough to choke me out earlier. But I'd had no trouble spooking him in return with the tiniest tap on his amygdala.

He has no clue who he's dealing with.

This man thought we were nothing but two fresh-faced college grads willing to do *anything* to make a good impression during our once-in-a-lifetime internship opportunity. In reality, the two of us could easily take him, and if turning our opponent into a mindless vegetable was what it took to scrape his skull for intel, so be it.

Even though it would be such a waste...

I huffed, annoyed that the thing pissing me off the most about Theo—besides his *terrible* design sense and singular focus on my identical twin—was that I wanted him so badly I could practically taste it. My sex life was the one area where *no one* told me what to do, so being forced to hold myself back was putting me in a foul mood.

Worse than usual.

I debated mentioning how we might witness random strangers doing a lot more than *fuck* tonight, but I was feeling a little bratty myself. Getting to see the scandalized expression on Gabe's face once he realized what a play party actually was would do wonders to lift my mood.

After all, roasting each other is the Suarez family's love language.

In the end, my vanilla twin would survive, and our eccentric host was going to be too distracted by whoever was up his ass—figuratively and possibly literally—to pay attention to us. It would be easy enough to keep an eye on both of them while also testing just how much I could get away with before Theo suspected anything was amiss.

Let the games begin.

———

It was easy to blame the decor.

An hour in and I could already tell nothing was going to happen that might endanger the painstakingly upholstered furniture, aside from one of the vapid elite spilling their wine. And with the guests being more interested in keeping their fashionable outfits intact than letting their inhibitions go for a scene, Theo's gathering was closer to a sexually charged pretension-fest than a genuine play party.

Sigh…

Besides the amazing spread of food—which no one besides us was eating—the only perk was that the lights were turned down low. This lessened the effects of my maximalist migraine, even if it meant drunken normies kept accidentally on purpose stumbling into us in the dark.

Apparently, basic no-touching etiquette isn't the standard at Theo's parties…

After a tipsy woman wearing a slinky black cutout dress practically fell onto my dick, I found my gaze searching the room —searching for what I needed to take the edge off.

For who *I wanted to take it out on.*

To no one's surprise, our host was holding court several feet away, lounging in a cobalt blue wingback like the king of rizz, surrounded by his adoring subjects.

I was one of them, apparently, as I couldn't tear my eyes away from him. Specifically, I couldn't stop eyeing how the fabric of his cadmium-red suit stretched over his enormous thighs like a beacon. The color—combined with the low light and his devilish smirk—had the man resembling Satan himself.

Fuck, I wanna make him bleed.

Theo looked goddamn edible, and he damn well knew it. He also knew I was watching him. Every time my attention drifted in his direction, he was waiting smugly to meet my gaze.

Dude had nothing to be smug about. This gathering was lame as fuck, so either *Theo* started the rampant rumors of debauchery himself or he'd purposefully orchestrated a toned-down version tonight to mess with us.

From what I've seen, it could probably go either way.

Just as I was about to ask Gabe if he wanted to ghost and go out to a bar instead, a lithe man approached Theo and immediately sank to his knees in front of him.

WHAT THE FUCK?!

The jolt of unexpected *rage* that shot through me was almost blinding. I had to grip the edge of the buffet-laden credenza I was leaning against to stop myself from immediately stalking over to rip the trespasser's hands off Theo's thighs.

Maybe rip them off completely.

"I… need some air," Gabe choked out, and when I sharply glanced at him, I found him staring at Theo with a look of anguish painted across his face.

Interesting…

Before I could ask if *he* was experiencing the same weird possessiveness, my twin had hustled outside to the turf yard.

I could *feel* Theo's gaze on me, but I refused to give him the satisfaction of making eye contact again. Instead, I grabbed the next guy who walked by—some beefy specimen of himbohood—and violently crashed his lips to mine. Normally, I would have enjoyed how sloppy and desperate he was, even tasting like some fruity-ass drink, but my aware-ness was still annoyingly on King Rizz in the wingback.

Fucking hell.

With a growl, I pushed the himbo away, deciding to take out my fury on the idiot who'd touched what my brain had decided was mine. But when I turned to make my move, I found my target with his tongue down some random woman's throat instead.

And Theo was nowhere to be seen.

CHAPTER 6
THEO

It had been so long since I'd enjoyed a proper *hunt*. I was nearly giddy with excitement.

What delightful prey I've found!

Andre was obviously an expert in playing his cards close, but the way he'd just reacted to a random art blogger thinking he could suck me off for an exclusive told me I'd finally found someone as possessive as me. The more mysterious twin was a present I couldn't wait to unwrap in a myriad of ways— some more painful than others.

Because only one of us can come out on top.

Me.

And Gabriel couldn't be more perfect. He was clearly the more innocent one—like an angel I wanted to help fall from grace. He was so broody, so dreadfully restrained, even as he practically *vibrated* with the need to be set free from whatever psychological shackles were keeping him bound.

I know what will loosen you up, baby boy.

Again… me.

I had an agenda, however—as loose as it was—one that the twins could legitimately assist me with. So, while I couldn't wait to make a pretty pair of puppets, I knew I should at least *try* to take it slow with luring them into my bed.

Really savor the experience.

Since it will probably kill them in the end.

Sadly, humans weren't built to play with me, which was one of the main reasons I maintained this form while fucking. Well… *that,* and to avoid the pesky mass hysteria that a glimpse of me would inspire.

This planet is so touchy.

Plus, I *enjoyed* feeling human. I'd inhabited both male and female skinsuits since my arrival, but there was just something about impaling someone on my cock that truly blew my skirt up.

I should write a poem about it.

"Don't be fooled by how far away the stars appear," I crooned, materializing next to where Gabriel was gazing skyward at the far corner of my artificial lawn. "The cosmos are truly within us."

He huffed, adorably attempting to hide how badly I'd startled him. "Are you referencing Carl Sagan or hitting on me?"

Oh, you're cute.

"A little of both." I grinned cheerfully, unleashing a few tendrils of *star stuff* to not-so-gently nudge any nearby guests back inside and shut the doors behind them. "But the second option shouldn't surprise you, given tonight's gathering."

Gabriel stiffened, but I somehow sensed it wasn't because my advances were *unwanted.* He truly seemed to be holding himself back from being more responsive than he already was.

What will it take to make you snap?

"Yeah… I don't really think this…"—he turned to glance through the French doors to the party inside—"is my thing."

He grimaced as his gaze met mine, clearly believing I'd take issue with the fact he hadn't initiated an orgy on my polar bear skin rug. As if I hadn't wanted to maim every drunken idiot who'd stumbled too close to *my* new toys since the night began.

As if the one who kissed Andre won't be blacklisted forever.

Or black bagged.

I slowly released a breath, willing myself to calm down. My meathead personal trainer was blameless for getting caught in the crossfire between two alphas. And his slobbering *had* provided the perfect cover for me to sneak out and corner Gabriel without Andre noticing.

Divide and conquer.

"You are under no obligation to socialize with these sycophants." I waved a hand dismissively, earning me a tentative smile in return.

I stepped closer, lightly skimming the back of his neck with a near-invisible tendril—making him shiver. Curiously, I didn't experience the same strange blast of electricity I'd felt earlier when we'd touched skin-to-skin, although my chest felt oddly tight.

It was probably a fluke.

"Besides…" I purred, refocusing on my seduction and loving how his long eyelashes fluttered in response. "I'd rather not share my new protégés with anyone else."

To put it mildly.

Gabriel snapped himself out of his trance before rolling his eyes good-naturedly—as if I hadn't thoroughly reviewed the twins' portfolio before agreeing to take them on. My work was quite literally the *only* thing I cared about here on Earth. The last thing I needed was a pair of amateurs sullying my genius with their unskilled labor.

"Yeah, on that note…" Gabriel rubbed the back of his neck, his hand brushing against my tendril, making *me* shiver this time. "How can Dre and I help with this… *cosmetics* project of yours?"

He's so desperate to keep things professional between us.

I nodded, willing to humor the man if it helped him to fucking *relax*. "Very well. I've been developing a revolutionary perfume for decades, but require bright young minds like yours to package it properly."

His brow furrowed. "I mean, we have *some* package design skills… but that's not exactly our wheelhouse—"

"Oh, this won't be sold to the mass-market," I interrupted. "It's invite-only. What I need from you two is a dispenser—a way to discreetly apply the scent while out in public."

Gabriel tilted his head and quietly observed me. For a moment, I wondered if he was already suspecting my intentions with this project were less than honorable.

Rightfully so.

But then his expression changed—his gaze growing distant as the creative well bubbled to the surface.

He truly is perfect.

I meant what I'd said by calling tonight's crowd a bunch of sycophants. While my guest list always included some of the biggest names in modern art, they weren't *true* artists. These fools didn't understand how it felt to be *compelled* to create— for the muse to fully take the wheel until nothing else mattered besides scratching the itch that burned beneath their skin.

Like star stuff forming new life in the vast universe.

All at once, I felt a pang of what could be called homesickness, even though I hadn't set foot on Stellaria in centuries. Visually, my home planet was gorgeous, but the singular focus my kind had on strategic, territorial expansion left much to be desired.

Anarchy is a far superior mindset.

"I guess we could create an atomizer with a timed release," Gabriel mused, his pretty gaze lifting to the sky once again. "That way, the scent stays fresh on whoever's wearing it—"

"You misunderstand," I murmured, stepping closer still— unable to resist the pull this man had on me. "The scent will be applied to *others*… by the one carrying the dispenser."

There was no mistaking Gabriel's suspicion this time. "Why the hell would people need to put perfume on someone *else?*" His eyes narrowed. "Discreetly…"

Time to backpedal!

"Consider it a performance piece," I chuckled, returning my focus to the hunt. "Like scent marking between two animals."

Like one of the many ways I intend to mark you.

"B-but we're not animals," he choked out, backing away from me.

With nowhere to run.

The way his voice caught in his throat fired up my predatory instincts, and I aggressively advanced until he was trapped against the hedge. When our human forms made contact, I once again experienced that unexpected jolt of *something* I was determined to decode.

What are you made of, little angel?

Besides the universe.

"*I* am," I countered, dipping my head to drag my nose up his neck—breathing him in and groaning at how incredible he smelled.

Gabriel was an intoxicatingly *human* mix of vanilla and chamomile tea, with an undercurrent of acrylic paint and crumbling paper from secondhand books. This combination was both soothing and seductive—making my true form vibrate with approval.

I can't wait to smell your fear.

All I could think about was stripping off this man's all-black ensemble before spreading him on the stage in my studio— like a meal to be enjoyed. Of fucking him slow and deep, while biting every inch of his skin until he was bleeding and begging for release.

I'm going to eat you alive.

Gabriel's *whimper* snapped me out of my thrall at the same instant I felt a preternatural tap on my awareness. Lifting my head, I glanced sideways to find Andre leaning against the doorframe leading back into my house, quietly observing us.

Do you want to watch?

As usual, his expression was blank, but the intensity roiling off him felt oppressive—like the air before a thunderstorm.

"Fuck." Gabriel tensed as he caught sight of his twin, drawing my attention back to my prey.

My pretty little prize.

"What's the matter, *angel?*" I murmured, brushing my lips over his—relishing the tingling sensation that danced over this point of contact. "Do you not want to be my muse?"

"I can't," he growled, his delicious kitty claws reappearing once again as he pushed me away. "This isn't…" He shot a glare at the now empty doorway. "This wasn't the plan."

He muttered that last bit almost to himself, but I couldn't help laughing. "The *plan?* Oh, Gabriel. I'll gladly show you how fun life can be when it goes completely off the rails."

Climb aboard this crazy train!

"I'm here for a *job,* Theo," Gabriel hissed. "I can't do"—he angrily gestured between us—*"this!"*

I stepped closer again, invading his space. "Can't or *won't?*" I hummed, feeding off the anxiety I could feel emanating from his pores. "Or won't *allow* yourself? To be specific…"

He sharply inhaled, suggesting I was getting closer to the truth. "I just *can't,* Theo," he gritted out. *"Please…"*

The "please" caught my attention. While I felt compelled to claim him as mine, I dutifully backed off—although not without a heavy sigh. "Very well. I'm certainly not going to force you into anything… as enjoyable as that might be for both of us."

As expected, his pupils dilated, but then he rapidly blinked, as if to hide the evidence of his arousal.

You can't hide from me.

Gabriel's agonized gaze tracked my hand as I ran it down the front of my designer suit. Reaching my throbbing cock, I gave myself a rough squeeze, smirking when his plump little lips parted on a soundless gasp.

"I need to go take care of this, angel, with the help of a more *willing* participant." When he growled, I arched an eyebrow—instantly silencing his protests.

Any of tonight's guests touching my cock sounded less than appealing, but all I needed was a hot hole and the memory of how Gabriel was looking at me.

With barely contained desire.

Whether or not he realizes it.

"And here's what *you're* going to do," I continued, using a firm tone to make it clear this was a command, not a request. "There's a small room off my studio with a single bed. You're going to lock yourself in there and get undressed. Then I want you to take out your *aching* cock and fuck your fist, like the desperate slut you are. And I want you to pay attention to exactly *what* you're thinking about when you soak my very expensive sheets with your cum."

Gabriel had half-collapsed against the hedge, his mouth hanging open and chest heaving—apparently too over-whelmed by what I was saying to even respond.

Oh, I'm just getting started with you.

I canted my chin toward a nearby tool shed. "There's access to the staff stairwell through there. I don't want you going back inside because I don't want *any* of these people to see you like this. From now on, *no one* gets to see you wrecked, besides me. Do you understand?"

You're my *slut now.*

This was the moment of truth. My angry little angel could continue to resist, or he could give in to what he so plainly— so *painfully*—wanted.

Either way, I'll get what I want.

Eventually.

To my absolute delight, Gabriel's shoulders drooped—the fight visibly leaving his body as he slowly nodded once. "Yes," he whispered, barely audible, but I still heard it loud and clear. "I understand."

Good boy.

With a purr of approval, I spun on my heel and strolled away to rejoin my guests, confident Gabriel would follow through with my instructions.

The thought of him *shaking* on the studio mattress—so close to my objects of creation—had me keeping a firm grip on my cock as I searched the party for easy prey. It wouldn't be nearly as satisfying as claiming the twins, but I could bide my time.

Especially when victory will taste so sweet.

CHAPTER 7
GABRIEL

Of course, I went straight to Theo's studio.

Like a little bitch.

Like a desperate slut.

It hadn't taken much for me to stumble down the staff stairwell with his words echoing in my head, creating a loop of lust that made every inch of me feel raw and oversensitive.

"From now on, no one gets to see you wrecked, besides me. Do you understand?"

The only fucking thing I understood at the moment was that when Theo talked to me like that, my brain stopped functioning. If he'd followed up that sorcery by asking me to confirm I was from the infamous Suarez clan and then demanded I give him Wolfy's home address, I might have actually said, "Yes. Yes, Sir."

Jesus, I'm fucked.

Even though this was playing out exactly how Dre wanted—and how *I* wanted, if I was going to be honest—it wasn't what I *should* be doing. It wasn't what Wolfy *trusted* me to do.

But why does it matter how *I get the intel, as long as I get it?*

With a growl, I shook that rebellious thought from my head as I practically booted my way into Theo's studio. Asking for forgiveness, not permission, was more Dre's style, even if my twin didn't give a fuck if anyone forgave him for anything.

That's because he can afford to act that way.

Dre didn't have the responsibility of carrying this clan should our leader fall. He was free to do whatever he wanted, while I was expected to live up to a destiny that should never be mine.

At least, not mine alone.

I just don't want to fucking think anymore.

My frantic gaze snagged on a door near the worktable Theo had trapped me against earlier. Part of me was expecting—possibly hoping—to discover a sex dungeon on the other side, but when I nudged open the door, I found a walk-in closet converted to what looked like a dressing room for the nude art models.

This was surprising, since Theo seemed like the type to leer creepily at his models as they disrobed in front of him.

Like most of my art school professors…

My gaze fell on the narrow twin bed—neatly made up with 'very expensive sheets'—and suddenly, the idea of Theo watching me while I undressed didn't sound half bad.

"I want you to take out your aching cock and fuck your fist."

Yes, Sir.

Never mind that I'd *never* responded to something like this in my goddamn life. At the memory of Theo's filthy command, I was wrestling my dick free from my dress pants like I'd die if I didn't come in the next five minutes.

Assuming I even last that long…

With a sigh of relief, I climbed onto the bed and kneeled with my back to the wall. My dick was *throbbing* in my hands—the need to get off making me lightheaded—but I forced myself to take a breath and focus.

No… not focus.

Feel.

Because *that's* what Theo's words were offering me. If I did what he said, I wouldn't have to *think*. I could simply enjoy the sensations without worrying about the consequences.

Fucking bliss.

The ragged moan that escaped me on my first stroke would have been humiliating if anyone was around to hear it. But I was alone and allowed to be as *desperately slutty* as I wanted.

As I was given permission to be.

I lifted my gaze to find my crazed reflection staring back at me in the mirrored vanity against the opposite wall. My first instinct was to avert my gaze, as it felt like *Dre* was watching, but then I realized I didn't mind so much.

Not if it's Theo making me unravel…

Deciding to save the psychoanalysis on *that* combination for another day, I spit on my hand, and began thrusting into my fist—just like he'd told me to do.

Like a good boy.

Nah, fuck that.

Like a Desperate. Fucking. Slut.

"Fuck, yes…" I choked out, not even caring that I was apparently way more into degradation than I ever would've guessed.

It's fine.

Totally fine.

Just me and my reflection that I'm projecting all my darkest desires onto.

"Look how fucking needy you are…" I whispered, pretending I could *feel* Theo's breath on my sweaty skin as I shuttled my hand faster over my spit-covered dick. "Look at you, wishing I was stuffed in your ass so you could come on my cock."

What would it feel like to have Theo inside me?

Because that's what I want…

My thoughts strayed to how Dre had apparently been assuming I was a bottom all this time, even though I'd never told him about my secret subby desires. I knew my twin was a gold card member at Big City's premiere kink club—The Refinery—but that was only because we both kept constant tabs on each other out of habit.

And a bit of codependency.

A lot, actually.

While Dre wasn't *wrong,* it wasn't something I'd ever taken the time to explore—not with everything else I had to worry about.

I just can't fit a sub-awakening into my schedule.

    "Can't or won't?"

Fuck.

Am I really that easy to read?

That Theo also seemed to have me pegged only made my thoughts simultaneously clearer *and* more convoluted. The one rule in this house was obviously *anything goes,* so there was no good reason for me to *not* take this opportunity to figure out what I wanted.

What I needed.

I fucking can't, *though.*

I won't.

"Shut up and take it," I growled at my reflection, exhausted by my indecision. "You'll take everything I give you, and you'll fucking thank me for it."

Yes, please!

I could almost feel his large hand around my throat, squeezing until I was fighting for air. But it didn't matter how much I struggled. Fantasy Theo pinned me down while forcing orgasm after orgasm out of me until I was sobbing. Drained dry of everything I had to give.

Including my soul.

The idea of being completely consumed was all I needed to careen off the edge. My balls drew up tight as white-hot pleasure raced down my spine—electrifying me from the inside out.

"Fuuuuck…" I breathlessly gasped as hot cum splashed over my hand and onto the sheets. "Thank you for letting me be your slut."

Sweet. Jesus.

With a curse, I dropped onto my back on the mattress, careful to avoid the incriminating wet spot of shame. I felt like I'd just run a marathon twice over—wrecked beyond belief—but also weirdly *calm…*

Until Dre's voice sounded in my head.

"Well, that was… educational."

FUCK!!!

In my horny haste to obey Theo's command, I'd somehow forgotten to lock down my mind from my twin.

I will never hear the end of this.

"Uh… sorry, dude…"

Sorry for traumatizing you forever.

Dre's warm chuckle somewhat soothed my humiliation.

"It's fine. I'm just… finishing up. I'll be—fuck—down in a few."

I sat up so fast I almost fell off the goddamn bed. Dre was clearly in the middle of a hookup… which meant I needed to respect his space and get the hell out of his head.

But what if it's…

"It's not Theo on my dick right now. I promise."

With that, the proverbial line went dead as Dre abruptly shut down our bond.

Why didn't he boot me out before, though?

Stranger still was that the idea of Theo being on Dre's dick didn't bother me one bit. I actually would have preferred *that* to knowing the object of my obsession had left me on the lawn so he could go find some rando to use as a cock sleeve.

I wanna be his cock sleeve…

Tensing, I double—triple—checked that my connection to Dre was still *off* before easing off the bed and tucking my dick away. Then I stared at the cum puddle I'd left behind, wondering what to do about the sheets.

With the evidence…

A full-body shudder ran through me at the thought of Theo approving of the mess, even as I scowled over how I'd let him herd me into this situation. That fucker got me all worked up and then told me to *pay attention* to what made me come—because he *knew* that would make me think of *him.*

Sure, buddy.

Believe that all you want.

With a huff, I ripped the sheets off the bed and marched them to the laundry basket I'd spotted in the staff stairwell. But then I couldn't find any clean ones to replace them with, so I stomped back to my room, annoyed that Theo was now going to know what I'd done.

As if he doesn't already know.

Just like Dre knows.

With a groan, I dropped my face into my hands and I sat heavily on my bed, wondering how the fuck I was supposed to face either of them ever again.

What the hell is wrong with me?

"Hey, hey… none of that." Dre was suddenly standing in front of me, moving my hands and gripping my chin—forcing me to look up at him. "Why are you so upset?"

I was wrecked in every way possible while my twin still looked as slick as when he'd gotten dressed hours earlier. Not a single hair was out of place, even as he exuded the self-satisfied vibe of a man who'd just gotten off and wasn't conflicted about it at all.

Asshole.

"Why the fuck do you think I'm upset?" I snapped, close to tears for no goddamn good reason. I was all twisted up and embarrassed, but I also knew that if anyone could bring me back to baseline, it was my other half.

Even if I'm acting like a fucking toddler.

Dre's jaw ticked as his grip on my chin tightened. This instantly settled me while also stirring up a fresh wave of confusion over how my body was reacting to all the things.

I'm such a fucking freak.

"How *dare* you?" he hissed, making my eyes widen in surprise. "I know our family feeds off busting each other's balls, but one thing we *don't* do is kink-shame. Ever. So how fucking dare you think I would ever do that to you?!"

Well, fuck.

Dre was absolutely right. He'd *never* taken a low blow at me —despite knowing most of my secrets—and kink-shaming was usually absent from **The Rabble** group chat.

Probably because it would be like shooting fish in a barrel.

"We *are* related to some kinky fuckers, huh?" I joked, hoping my olive branch of humor would lighten the mood. When he cracked a smile in return, I added, "Well, except for Balty."

My twin gave me a flat look before releasing my chin and sitting next to me on the bed. "Just because someone hasn't figured out their shit yet doesn't mean it's not there, Gabe."

Case in point, I guess.

We sat in a silence that was weirdly comfortable considering we both knew what the other had been up to twenty minutes ago. And even though it was cringe to talk about my repressed sex life with my twin, I knew I should take advantage of having an expert on hand.

Because I need to figure out my shit.

"How did you know what you liked?" I asked, tentatively peeking at him.

Dre smiled softly, even as he kept his mind firmly locked down—probably to keep things from getting any weirder. "It was a slow process. I noticed recurring themes in both the porn I watched and what was creeping into my extracurricular activities." He paused and eyed me cautiously. "And since fragile normies were who I was fucking, I knew I'd better get my ass educated before I accidentally hurt someone… or worse."

Jesus.

That concern had never crossed my mind—probably because what *I'd* been doing with these fragile normies was tame compared to what my fantasies actually involved.

Fantasies where I'm *the one on the receiving end, anyway…*

But we weren't dealing with a human here, so it would probably be best if I got *my* ass educated as well.

Before I'm the one getting hurt.

Or worse…

Even *more* confusing was how the idea of Theo causing me pain only made me more interested.

I really *need to figure out my shit.*

Not knowing where to even *begin,* I politely tapped on the door to Dre's mind until he let me in.

"Can you — ?"

"Yes," he replied immediately—out loud—turning his entire body to face me on the bed. Giving me his full attention. "I'll share everything I know."

CHAPTER 8
ANDRE

I decided to take Gabe to the club with me on a Thursday night.

This was for a few reasons—the first being that themed events happened on the weekend. Based on how bunched up my twin got over Theo's lame gathering, I was guessing he wouldn't feel comfortable being surrounded by a large crowd who were mostly there to fuck.

The next reason was that Thursdays were education nights, and I assumed the clinical nature of the demos might be *less* weird for him than watching strangers go at it in the semi-private rooms.

I sighed and handed Gabe back his version of the atomizer prototype to continue tinkering. Theo had set us up with space to work side-by-side in his studio, and while my twin's proximity usually helped, lately, I was having trouble concentrating.

If I was going to be honest, the main reason I'd made Gabe wait a few days before experiencing the wide world of kink was because I needed a chance to wrap *my* head around the situation.

Because this is weird for me, too.

I didn't *mind* talking about this kind of shit with Gabe, but it was jarring to suddenly be monitoring his sex life so closely after years of staying as far away as possible.

But tonight's the night.

Ready or not.

On cue, my phone lit up with a text, letting me know Gabe's application to The Refinery had been approved.

As if Madam Sinistre could ever say no to me.

"We're all set for later," I quietly said, noticing Gabe press his lips into a thin line as he tried not to let his nerves show through.

I've got you, dude.

"Big plans for tonight, boys?" Theo called out from where he was rendering schematics for Big City's sewer system on his laptop.

Lord knows why.

Knowing him, it's probably for an 'underground' performance piece.

I swiveled on my metal stool to face the eccentric artist, stifling a smirk at the fact we'd been here for almost a week and hadn't caught him wearing the same kimono twice.

At first, I'd assumed it was part of his not-so-subtle seduction of my twin, but soon realized this was just how the guy felt comfortable dressing at home when he wasn't entertaining would-be swingers.

And who am I to judge about having a signature look?

Today's kimono was '80s teal with a pattern of coral hibiscus entwined with grass-green snakes. Since the walls of Theo's studio were neutral eggshell white—*thank god*—I could actually appreciate how the colors popped against his skin.

"I *see* you eyeing me over there. Do you like it? This old thing?" he teased, striking a ridiculous pin-up pose that almost had me breaking character. "It's from my leisure collection, two seasons ago—but the design has aged well since it's a classic."

Yeah.

Floridian Nana Classic.

"Do you have any in black?" I deadpanned, eager to see how he'd react to our funereal preferences.

Modeled after Wolfy, of course.

Since we're his minions.

Gabe snorted in amusement, snapping Theo's attention to where he sat beside me. "I *do*, actually," he smoothly replied, laser-focused on my twin. "They can be found in the dressing room behind Gabriel. You're familiar with the layout in there, right, angel?"

"Asshole," Gabe muttered, but didn't look up from where he was fiddling with the atomizer. His face gave nothing away, but his knuckles were so white from gripping the screwdriver, I wondered if it was about to snap.

Or if he *is.*

The tension between Gabe and Theo this week had been insufferable. The older man was clearly trying to control the situation by only giving my brother crumbs of attention, and Gabe's response had been to ignore these crumbs completely.

Unfortunately, all that accomplished was encouraging a brat like Theo to poke at him more, and it had taken an incredible amount of restraint for me to not correct the behavior.

73

Since brat taming is my favorite thing.

Despite the personal issues, the three of us had fallen into a comfortable working routine. We started each day together with a gloriously greasy breakfast at the kitchen island, prepared by Theo's personal chef, Jensen. While we ate, Theo trolled his socials for art world drama—which he shared with us, along with salacious insider gossip—before discussing what he needed from us for the day.

Our ongoing project was the development of inexplicably discreet perfume dispensers, but there were plenty of 'other duties as assigned' tasks to keep us busy. From running upstairs for more coffee or downstairs to sign for deliveries, to being an extra set of hands on one of Theo's sculptures or scheduling interviews, it felt like an actual internship.

Aside from the sexual undertones.

Although, that's also par for the course…

The more time I spent around Theo, the more I realized he was more playful than predatory. At least… he wasn't predatory in the way one might expect with such a large age gap between us. He treated both Gabe and me like adults who'd been deemed worthy enough to exist in his sphere—to the point where I wondered if us being only twenty-three even registered with him at all compared to whatever other factors he was judging us by.

To put it simply, Theo behaved like a supe.

This meant that no matter who else was present, he was simultaneously the smartest guy in the room *and* the one with the biggest dick. This had nothing to do with gender and everything to do with confidently knowing your powers could eliminate any obstacles in your path—including other supernatural beings.

We'll see about that…

I squinted at my opponent, wishing I could make a move and get inside his head already. But I didn't want to alert him to the fact that we were more than a 'pretty matched set' of normies.

Patience, Dre.

This was where Gabe came in. He was the perfect temptation, and his complete cluelessness about kink only made him more enticing to a man like Theo. But I wasn't about to use my twin as bait without making sure he had a basic understanding of what he was walking into.

Gotta give my boy a fighting chance.

Personally, I could've handled Theo with my eyes closed and both hands tied behind my back. Hell, I could dominate him while gagged and bound with wrist and ankle restraints—not that I was into that.

I preferred to be in charge, and even though Theo had clearly set his sights on topping my twin, I couldn't help fantasizing about what might have been had I met him under different circumstances.

Like at the club.

"We're going out for some bro bonding time," I finally replied to Theo's question about our plans. "Assuming that's okay with you?"

Not that it fucking matters.

Theo cocked his head and, for a moment, I thought he was going to have the balls to tell me no.

"Of course it's okay," he purred. "Going anywhere special?" He casually tacked on the question, even as his gaze sharpened.

We don't belong to you.

"The Refinery," I replied, matching his feigned nonchalance with an *actual* don't give a fuck vibe.

I expected more of the same casually taunting banter Theo and I had enjoyed over the past few days. Instead, his entire face momentarily flickered, like old television static, revealing something *inhuman* underneath.

WHAT THE FUCK WAS THAT?!

Gabe must have seen it, too, judging by the choking sound he released behind me. But Theo either didn't realize he'd slipped up or he did it on purpose as an intimidation tactic, because he simply nodded and returned his attention to his laptop.

"Well, try not to stay out past midnight," he absently murmured, although it was less a suggestion and more a command. "It's when we all turn into pumpkins, you know."

Or ghosts in the machine…

"Dude. What the hell *is he?"*

I huffed a laugh as Gabe's question echoed inside my head, tinged with barely veiled *curiosity.* Before I replied, I turned to face the worktable again. Partly turned. I would probably never turn my back on Theo Coatl again.

I may have slightly underestimated what we're dealing with here…

Talk about behaving like a supe.

Of course, the last thing I wanted to do was admit he'd rattled me—especially to the one person I needed to keep calm at all costs.

"Nothing we can't handle. Trust."

The instant I said it, my guts twisted. I still wanted to educate Gabe on the lifestyle—to help prepare him for his future beyond this job—but tossing him into bed with a literal *monster* for his first time felt… irresponsible.

"But maybe we should come up with a Plan B, so you don't have to — "

"No. I want *to do this. Wolfy needs the intel."*

I sharply glanced at my twin, surprised by the conviction in his voice. He resolutely stared back at me for a moment before his gaze drifted over my shoulder to where Theo sat.

The change that came over him was instantaneous. His gaze grew distant and hooded as his body practically melted off the stool. Gabe looked *thirsty* for whatever Theo wanted to give him—just like a good little sub.

Well, fuck.

I guess we're doing this.

A few hours later, we were in an Uber, wearing black suits, and headed for The Refinery. I was doing my best to exude enough calm to counteract Gabe's anxiety, but my mind kept drifting to the threat we'd left behind.

Who could be anywhere in the city at this point…

Theo hadn't joined us for dinner, as he usually insisted on doing. Instead, he'd appeared—dressed in a distractingly sexy plum-colored suit—as Jensen was dishing out, curtly informing us he had to "meet with an associate" before breezing into the elevator.

The immediate urge to search Theo's bedroom was strong, but Gabe and I agreed that his leaving may have been a test to see what we'd do when given the chance. It was also tempting to follow him—to see *who* he associated with—but I decided my twin's Sex Ed was more important.

Because knowledge is power.

When Gabe wiped his sweaty hands on his pants for the umpteenth time, I finally spoke.

"You don't have to *do* anything tonight, you know," I sighed, even as I shot him an encouraging smile. "We're just gonna watch a demo or two. See if anything sticks."

See what kind of kinky fucker you are.

Gabe nodded, gnawing at his bottom lip. "W-what are the demos tonight?"

Keeping my tone neutral, I began reading off the members-only section of the website. "Looks like there's a suspension workshop, wax play, flogging…" I trailed off as he tensed, unsure if that was a good thing or not.

He needs to let me in.

Never mind that my reasons for wanting *full* access weren't entirely noble. The instant I saw Theo cornering him on the lawn the other night—with so much delicious tension between them I could taste it from where I stood—I knew I would go insane if I wasn't as involved as possible. So when Gabe accidentally left our connection open while jerking off to thoughts of Theo, I couldn't resist eavesdropping, especially once I realized the kind of games he wanted to play with our opponent.

My *kind of games.*

All that aside, my twin's comfort and safety were still my top priority, so I didn't force my way into his head. I took it slow —carefully watching Gabe's reaction as I knocked on the door to his mind. The one he only shut on me for *this* kind of situation.

Too bad.

We're open-door now, bro.

Just as I'd hoped, Gabe blew out a slow breath and let his mental doors swing wide, wordlessly submitting to my request for unfiltered access to everything he desired.

Namely, Theo.

"It's just for now," I promised, even as I wondered how willingly I'd ever let this connection go. "As soon as you want me gone, you can boot my ass out."

At least, you can try…

He nodded once, already looking more relaxed as the Uber pulled up in front of our destination.

"Okay," he murmured, smoothing his hands down the front of his suit and slipping behind the impassive mask we'd been conditioned to wear in public. "I'm ready."

CHAPTER 9
GABRIEL

I was so not ready.

Yes, I'd made my twin describe the club to me in detail—down to the brand of faucets in the restroom—but nothing would have prepared me for how it *felt* to walk into The Refinery.

Even though the foyer was just a waiting area, the theme was established. Two low-hanging fixtures with Edison bulbs were the only light source and did little to brighten the matte black walls in the weirdly cozy space. A heavy velvet curtain separated this entryway from the rest of the club, muffling the moody sound of ambient music coming from inside.

It's definitely a vibe.

The elegantly dressed hostess who greeted us was flanked by two beefy, emotionless bodyguards, but her smile for Dre was genuine.

"Mr. Acosta, it's always a pleasure to see you…" Her warm voice trailed off as her gaze drifted to me. "And you have a twin, I see. How intriguing…"

Here we go.

While the hostess—Fay, according to the neat stack of bone-colored business cards printed in Silian Rail at her podium—wasn't being overtly inappropriate, she was clearly *very* intrigued. And while I had no idea how much access she had to our member files, I hoped she could tell she was barking up the wrong tree.

Not that some people care either way.

Although, maybe she's just being friendly…

What is the flirting etiquette with the staff here, again?

Or the fucking *etiquette?*

My senses were a jumbled mess at the moment, and I realized the cloud of *lust* permeating The Refinery's atmosphere wasn't helping. Usually, I had no problem blocking out the internal chatter from everyone else except Dre, but I was so keyed up with nerves and anticipation, I felt like a broken compass, swinging wildly in every direction.

But not in girlfriend's *direction.*

Sorry, Fay.

Before I could do something dumb—like turn down someone who might not be interested in me in the first place, Dre came to my rescue.

"Yes, my brother, Gabe, is visiting from out of town," he crooned with an uncharacteristically friendly tone that caught me off guard. "So I decided to show him my home away from home. Is Sin around?"

Does Dre have… friends?

A smirk twitched Fay's perfectly painted lips as I contemplated this formerly hidden area of my twin's life. "Oh, you know where to find them. I'm assuming you perused tonight's workshops?"

"Of course," Dre replied, gripping my elbow and steering me through the curtain. "I wouldn't want to end up on the receiving end of Sin's flogger again by daring to miss a performance... I mean, an educational presentation..."

Fay tittered as we passed through the curtain, but my brain was still catching up with the conversation.

Again?

I was grateful Dre hadn't outed me as a local newb, but couldn't help being confused by his almost flirty friendliness —not with a woman but *anyone*—and by what his offhand comments about 'Sin' had implied.

There's no way I'm letting this intel go.

I'd always assumed my twin was dominant, beyond how most supes naturally behaved. It was in the way he carried himself—with absolutely nothing to prove—and how he effortlessly took control of a situation when given the chance.

Even if he allows me to take the lead at times...

For better or worse.

Usually worse...

He would make such a better clan leader than me.

This stark contrast in our strengths had resulted in a strange divide between us over the years, which was compounded by Wolfy's singular focus on *me.* It was because of my supposed destiny that I maintained an aura of big dick energy, even as I'd rather kneel for someone else than expect others to bend the knee for me.

But since we're laying it all on the table now...

"You've been *flogged*, dude?" I whispered as we reached the lacquered walnut bar.

Dre ordered us both whiskeys—neat—before turning to me with an amused expression on his face.

"A good Dom needs to fully understand the perspective of the submissive—preferably by experiencing a scene first-hand." His face fell as he switched to speaking in my head.

"In my case, I also needed to know how hard I could go—how much pain normies could take before I… broke them."

My eyes widened, but not because the idea of accidentally tearing a normie in half during sex was anything new. Since the USN hadn't explicitly forbidden supes from *fucking* humans, we all had it hammered into our heads since birth to hold our punches, so to speak.

And our dicks.

"You like to… break people?" I asked, because *that* was the part that interested me.

For… reasons.

Dre hummed as he accepted his whiskey from the bartender and brought the tumbler of rich amber liquid to his lips. "I do. I enjoy inflicting pain when it's warranted and wanted." He cleared his throat, as if he was about to say more on that subject, before shrugging. "I just love putting a brat in their place."

My breath caught as a fresh wave of chaotic emotions swept in. Yes, the idea of Dre doing this to someone else was hot—*especially a certain someone*—but the excitement now buzzing under my skin was more about wondering how *I* would respond to being 'put in my place' by my own Dom.

"Do you think *I'm* a brat?" I whispered, knowing I didn't have to keep my voice down in this environment, but doing it anyway.

He smiled softly. "You definitely have your bratty moments, but no, you're not a brat in the grand scheme of things. What I think…"—his gaze absently drifted over the crowd—"is that you want to give up control, *without* the fight."

Well, shit.

Theo said the same thing…

I took a sip of my whiskey as my gaze followed my twin's. Ignoring the well-dressed patrons—many of whom were staring at the two of us with barely concealed hunger—I took in the dark academia-meets-modern decor. The black walls and low lighting from the foyer continued inside, with burnished steel and walnut surfaces for the bar and surrounding tables. Embellishments were sparse, but each piece was ornate and meant to invoke emotions and start conversations.

Overall, it was both homey and luxe. I could see why Dre thought of The Refinery as a relaxing second home, even with the sexually charged atmosphere.

Or maybe because of it.

It was always odd to not be at the same level in our areas of expertise. Besides Dre's endless supply of confidence, we were closely matched in almost everything we did—from our traditional schooling among normies to our general supe training with Luca—but this kink journey was brand new territory for me. And I knew from experience that feeling inadequate in my twin's presence was… dangerous.

"You know, Gabe…" Dre's tone was light, but the way he was looking at me made it seem like he was gauging my reaction.

"I could take on more responsibilities for you. Not just with this"—he waved his hand—"but with family shit."

Danger, danger, danger!

"Nah, I'm good. I've got it, dude." I lightly laughed, even as I internally sweated bullets at the idea.

Wolfy was already going to be royally pissed at me for getting into our mark's *bed* instead of just into his *head.* The last thing I needed was to shatter his trust completely by letting my twin get his hands on the reins.

Dre observed me quietly, while casually poking around inside my head to figure out what was bothering me. I allowed it, knowing full well the secrets I kept on Wolfy's behalf were buried where he'd never find them.

Which I hate.

But it's for his own good.

I think…

Clearing my throat, I peered at the empty stage across the room. "Okay, so when do these demos start?"

Dre smirked before downing the rest of his whiskey like a shot. "I'm sure they're already underway. I was just letting you get a little liquid courage in ya first."

Waiting for me to throw back my drink, he grabbed my elbow again and dragged me down a dark hallway off the main bar area. I didn't mind the manhandling, but people were oddly loitering, forcing us to awkwardly weave our way around them as we headed for our destination.

It wasn't until I looked closer that I realized they were all facing large windows along one wall—with rapt attention to whatever was going on beyond the glass.

"These are the semi-private rooms," Dre murmured in my head as he slowed our pace. *"For those who like to watch and be watched."*

Oh.

I cautiously peered around the couple in front of us, and my jaw *dropped*. A woman was naked, blindfolded, and tied to a wooden cross-shaped apparatus while another woman teased her with a whip. I probably looked like a tourist gaping in Times Square, but I screeched to a halt—wanting to see what happened next.

Needing *to see.*

The Domme whispered something in the other woman's ear and waited for a verbal response before stepping back. After a few smacks of the whip on the floor—either for practice or to ramp up anticipation—she refocused on her willing target with the collected cool of a supe.

I wonder if there are other supes here...

My wandering thoughts were snapped back to the present scene when the whip was brought down to snap against the bound woman's chest. A red mark immediately blossomed on her skin, but that was only the beginning. Next came a blow to her thighs, followed by one directly across her nipples. The Domme then fell into an expert rhythm, cycling through locations and leaving a perfect path of pain as she worked.

And leaving me *wanting.*

"Do you like this?" Dre whispered in my head, either to not disturb the surrounding voyeurs or for my privacy.

I could only nod, my gaze fixed on the submissive's half-covered face, documenting her every reaction to what she was experiencing. Wishing it was me.

"Which part?"

I almost responded with "all of it," but then took a moment to consider. It definitely wasn't her nudity, as I'd known from a young age that I was gay. I also didn't think it was the exhibitionist aspect, as the idea of being on display did nothing for me.

At least not in the presence of strangers…

The pleasure-pain the sub was experiencing was definitely a huge draw—and being *marked* by someone else was high on my list—but it was more than that.

Something… intangible.

My gaze drifted from the woman's ecstatic face to where her wrists were tied to the cross with leather straps. Her hands twitched with every blow, but she didn't struggle against her restraints. Instead, she seemed to *melt* into the wood that was holding her upright—fully trusting in both the structure she was tied to *and* the woman in charge of the situation.

That part.

Dre hummed thoughtfully, absorbing everything I was showing him. I shifted in place—feeling as if I were on display after all, but weirdly okay with it.

Because it's him.

"You want to give up control, without the fight…" he repeated his earlier assessment before elaborating, *"but you still want to feel as if you have no choice."*

Fuck.

The choked sound I made drew a few glances our way, but Dre smoothly grabbed my elbow again and moved us further down the hall. I was thankful for how he was dragging me onward, since my head was now *spinning* with this new—and eerily accurate—information, but my twin didn't give me time to spiral.

"C'mon. It's time for you to watch Sinistre in action," he chuckled in my ear, his natural confidence grounding me, as always. "And I think you're gonna *love* what you're about to see."

CHAPTER 10
THEO

To say I was displeased with what I saw would be an understatement.

It wasn't the human sitting across from me, per se. I'd been doing business with Ward long enough to know his extremely low bar on ethics and legality matched my own.

And that alone excuses other offenses.

Usually.

However, it was *his* guest who was earning my ire. The tipsy woman sitting next to him in the dusty pizzeria Ward ran his business out of. The one intruding on our meeting with her breathy giggles and errant wine sloshing on the schematics we were discussing.

The one Ward was finger fucking under the table.

Much to my displeasure.

I assumed it was a sad show of dominance on his part. As if I would become insanely jealous over the fact that *his* fingers were buried in her cunt instead of mine.

I'd rather gnaw mine off, to be honest.

"As you can see…" I did my best to keep the irritation out of my voice. "This junction in the main sewer line provides direct routes to downtown, the waterfront, and the uphill neighborhoods, like Teal Coast—"

My report was interrupted as Little Miss Tipsy threw her head back and groaned, convulsing her way through an orgasm that was in no way discreet.

Or appetizing.

The idea of instantly star hopping away from this hot mess was tempting. But I was so close to distributing a serum that could permanently alter life on Earth—starting with Big City —and I needed this idiot and his human minions to do the grunt work for me.

Possibly at their own peril…

Oh, well!

"Wanna taste?" Ward's wannabe gangster cadence snapped me out of my scheming.

To my *extreme* displeasure, he'd reached across the table to hover his slick-covered fingers above my wine glass—ready to stir in some extra flavor if I so chose.

I can't think of anything worse.

On a different day, I may have taken him up on the offer, if for no other reason than to encourage his disgusting behavior. I'd also never been a stickler for germs—since earthly diseases didn't affect me—and I'd never had a preference between what humans considered male and female.

Usually.

However, ever since the Acosta twins had walked into my home, the idea of touching anyone, or their sex juices, was making me cringe.

And normally, I fully embrace the cringe.

It had physically *pained* me to leave Gabriel on the lawn the other night—shaking and on the precipice of surrender. The need to claim him felt imperative, and normally, I might have pushed a little more, just to see if he would tumble over the edge. But with how sweetly he'd said *please,* I'd found myself powerless to do anything but respect his wishes.

Since when am I a gentleman?

Luckily, I'd discovered an orgy-in-progress happening in one of my guest bedrooms on the second floor—although I couldn't seem to bring myself to join in the fun.

Nearly blinded with unfulfilled desire, I'd done the only thing I could think of. Unleashing a tendril, I'd investigated the studio bedroom, curious if my angry angel had obeyed my instructions. Finding him there, chasing his release so desperately, settled something inside me, and his climax a few minutes later luckily fed my own.

Because there's nothing better than coming all over my guests.

Usually…

Unfortunately, all that less-than-satisfying encounter had done was make me want *my* twins even more.

Mine.

Both of them.

Knowing Gabriel and Andre were both at the notorious *Refinery* tonight was causing my present irritation to reach near homicidal levels. Of course, I was a gold card-carrying member of the most exclusive kink club in town, but I rarely bothered stepping through the doors.

Too many pesky rules…

But I'll make an exception for tonight.

The mental images I was suffering through—of Andre and Gabriel making themselves available for someone *else's* cock —were almost more than I could bear. I needed to wrap up this meeting before I murdered my associate and was forced to start from scratch.

I simply don't have the patience.

"The atomizers we discussed are in the prototype stage," I brusquely stated as I hurriedly gathered the wine-spattered schematics back into my briefcase. "And the serum trials have proven their effectiveness—"

"Yeah, I know," Ward huffed, as if offended I hadn't taken him up on his offer of secondhand cunt bitters. "My man on the inside with the Salahs has kept me informed over the years."

I froze, my focus narrowing on my prey. "What do you mean?"

The Salahs were the East Coast hero family I'd partnered with for the past couple of decades. Ward was the only other person who knew their identities, because—as a self-proclaimed leader in the silly anti-supe resistance—he claimed it was his right to know which enemies he was in bed with.

But apparently, he didn't think I deserved the same respect.

"What do you mean by an *inside man?*" I elaborated, enunci-ating every word like the stab of a knife as I forcefully restrained my tendrils from snapping this human's head off.

As satisfying as that would be…

Ward shifted nervously in his seat, looking everywhere *except* at me. Our unwanted witness caught on to my mood, snapping to drunken attention long enough to mumble something unintelligible and slither away.

At least the trash took itself out.

"I'm certain I told you about him," Ward muttered, trying—and failing—to sound unconcerned as he shakily brought a glass of wine to his lips. "His name is Joshual Preek, and he's a lesser supe with persuasion powers. The perfect mole to pose as a director of publicity for such a self-important family."

I was certain Ward had *not* shared this extremely vital information with me—nor asked for my permission to involve someone else in our schemes. However, I could also appreciate the logic of having eyes on the ground, and knew a single supe—lesser or otherwise—was no match for me.

So for that, you shall live another day.

"It must have slipped my mind," I coolly replied, relishing the way Ward swallowed thickly. "Perhaps you could arrange a meeting early next week between the two of us. I prefer knowing who exactly I'm working with."

And this Preek should know who exactly he answers to.

Ward nodded once, keeping his wary gaze locked on me and wisely choosing not to argue. I'd purposefully exhibited enough of my powers over the years for him to know I was something 'other,' although his pea-brain was incapable of comprehending what he was actually in bed with.

Not that I'd ever give him the pleasure.

For all he knew, I was a disgraced supe with a bone to pick against my own kind, and that misconception was fine with me.

I'm just here for a good time.

And a fun little science experiment…

In testing my serum on the Salah family heir, I'd determined that, over time, exposure to even a synthetic version of *Lacertus* DNA made the beast rise to the surface of the genetic code.

My plan for Earth—if you could call it that—was fairly loose. Infect the general population with my serum, inevitably catch supes in the crossfire, and unleash a race of mutant alien lizards on the world. Humans would then respond like they always did when eliminating a foreign threat.

By rolling out the big guns.

Never mind that my initial pitch to Ward had ended there. He didn't need to know supes would most likely respond in kind to any act of war—protecting their own, regardless of the politically motivated hero and villain divide. It would be an absolute bloodbath.

I can't wait!

Ward and his resistance didn't deserve this intel. All they wanted to hear was that supes would be eliminated, anyway, so I confirmed they would be. Probably. Maybe. It was no skin off my back either way. I mostly wanted to throw a chaos grenade into the heart of Big City to see what might happen.

To sit back and watch the world burn.

The thought of planetary destruction brought a smile back to my stolen face—and Ward recoiling from the display made it sweeter still. With my good humor restored, I snapped my briefcase closed and exited the restaurant, knowing exactly where I was headed next.

The Refinery.

CHAPTER 11
THEO

Once outside, I accessed my star hopping powers to dematerialize, quickly drop off my briefcase in my studio, and then reappear outside the club across town. This all took less than twenty seconds, and in only another minute, I was checked in and breezing through the velvet curtain.

Ready to reclaim my property.

There was no logical explanation for the level of possessiveness I felt for the twins—aside from my naturally covetous tendencies going haywire.

Or Mercury being in retrograde.

I didn't mind bloodshed one bit, but was momentarily concerned about how I might react should I find either of them otherwise engaged.

A massacre certainly wouldn't help me remain under the radar…

Everyone was spared a messy end when I tracked down both my prizes—blessedly *not* coming on someone else's cock. Instead, Andre and Gabriel were in a well-lit room, sitting on one of a dozen black vinyl benches facing a small stage. Others in the audience were studiously taking notes, and I realized this was one of the educational programs The Refinery was known for.

And what are we learning about today, boys?

My gaze drifted toward the stage to find the intriguingly androgynous human who owned the club standing beside a man lying facedown on a massage table. They hadn't noticed my late arrival, as their entire focus was on carefully sliding a pair of hooks through the skin of the man's upper back.

"The ritual of suspension dates back thousands of years in many cultures," they explained before moving to place another set on his lower back, and one in each thigh. "So while many of us who practice do so for similar reasons—to transcend the body *through* the body—we should take care to not stray into the territory of appropriation."

I was exceedingly more interested in how cleanly the hooks pierced human skin than in the lesson being taught. That my twins had chosen *this* demonstration interested me the most.

Sluts for pain, are we?

I sure hope so.

While I knew enough about body suspension to understand there was a cathartic aspect involved for most humans, I'd never explored the act myself. I simply didn't see the point of using inorganic *hooks* for something my tendrils could easily achieve on their own.

How fabulous it would be to capture my new prey in this way…

Unable to resist, I unfurled a tendril and snaked it toward where the twins were seated. Gabriel was closest to me, with his suit jacket removed and his shirt sleeves conveniently rolled up to expose his forearms.

I brushed my tendril over his skin, loving how prettily my angel shivered. He glanced down in confusion, but upon finding nothing amiss, returned his attention to the stage.

"The position we're exploring today is called Superman, for reasons that will become obvious in just a moment." The androgynous teacher—who I vaguely recalled was named Sin —was now looping a rope from the rig hanging above through the six hooks on their subject. "And while it's important for experienced professionals to be the ones placing each hook, human skin is much stretchier and resilient than we realize."

Don't I know it?

All at once, I remembered Andre's offhand suggestion of creating a lampshade from human skin. This caused my tendril to go rogue, and before I could stop myself, I'd scratched a thin line onto Gabriel's skin—scenting the air with a mouthwatering hint of blood.

Gabriel reacted far more subtly than I would have expected— hissing so faintly, only Andre noticed. Instead of checking on the welfare of his twin, he snapped his blue eyes to where I was leaning in the doorway, glaring at me suspiciously.

How fascinating.

Not only were these two incredibly responsive—when they weren't hiding their reactions, as I suspected Andre of doing —but I was now convinced they could register the other's pain.

I wonder if they can also feel each other's pleasure…

Before I could test that theory, Andre raised a hand and placed it on the back of Gabriel's neck—gripping his twin possessively. He maintained eye contact with me while doing so, and I recognized a delicious dare when I saw one.

Interestingly, I didn't feel as murderous as I normally would, seeing someone else touch *my* things. Similar to how I enjoyed Gabriel pretending to resist—practically begging me to take what I wanted anyway—I *liked* Andre challenging me to defy him. It made me want to misbehave even more… again, just to see what might happen.

Chaos grenades galore!

Keeping his gaze locked on me, Andre leaned closer to his twin and whispered in his ear. Gabriel's eyes widened before he turned his head to face me, his expression a mix of shock, wariness, and conflicted desire.

All of which is like catnip to a creature like me.

Not for the first time, I wished my tendrils picked up on more than just vibrations, so I could *hear* what Andre was saying. But all I could register from both men was the cloud of lust and anger radiating outward in equal amounts.

Tasty.

A collective gasp arose from the audience as Sin used the rig to lift their subject off the table. While I could appreciate the way the man's skin stretched to its limit, calling the pose 'Superman' had me rolling my eyes.

The literal hero worship this society had—outside of the resistance, of course—was pathetic. And while I recognized the pop culture reference, I had *never* witnessed a supe fly in the way this demonstration was suggesting.

It usually looks more like a hawk descending on its prey.

Talons first.

"What are you doing here?" Gabriel hissed, his body suddenly blocking my view of the stage.

His tasty muscles were tense with what I'd realized was more repression than anger, but more pressing was how the twins kept sneaking up on me.

Even if my angel did just give himself away by willingly *approaching.*

Like the good boy he is.

"My meeting finished early, and I was curious about what you were up to," I replied. "Nosey, if you will." I laughed in delight when he looked surprised by my honesty and took that as an invitation to step closer. To keep pushing. "Not to mention, I wanted to ensure no one was touching what belongs to me."

Gabriel's breath hitched, his mouth falling open to match the dazed expression on his beautiful face.

Gotcha.

A smirk curled my lip when he snapped out of his body's natural reaction to growl at me like a cornered dog. "I don't... I don't fucking belong to you."

Luckily, no one was paying any mind to our confrontation. The audience had been invited to crowd the stage for a closer look, and Andre was engaged in a conversation with Sin—his attention momentarily diverted from his twin.

Big mistake.

"You will," I smoothly replied. "And you like the idea, so I'm baffled why you're denying yourself what you know I can give you."

Gabriel licked his lips. "Because I ca—"

"Don't you *dare* say you *can't* again," I hissed, advancing until I loomed over him. Remembering we were in public, I instantly backed off, not wanting any concerned bystanders to get involved. "At least, not without explaining *why.*"

To my utter shock, I was extremely invested in his answer. I knew the internship itself wasn't an obstacle—or else he would have used that as an excuse already—so the idea that something about *me* might be abhorrent to him was... *upsetting.*

What the fuck is wrong with me?!

Gabriel's gaze drifted to his twin, who still wasn't looking our way, before meeting mine again. "It's a matter of... control," he quietly replied, his cheeks pinking deliciously. "I-I don't know how to let it go, even though I..."

Even though he wants *to.*

The predator within me purred in satisfaction. If there was something I loved, it was taking control—whether of a situation or the people in it. I couldn't think of anything more enjoyable than overpowering my angel and using him for my pleasure.

For both *our pleasures.*

"Mmm..." I thoughtfully hummed, unleashing a few tendrils to invisibly cage him in. "I may have a solution for that."

"Oh, yeah?" Gabriel whispered, his body vibrating with a resonance that almost felt familiar.

Like home...

"Yes." I nodded, noticing Andre was now watching us closely. His expression was more curious than anything, but when our eyes briefly met, he glowered, which only encouraged me to continue. "I want you to sleep in my studio's spare room tonight as an invitation."

"An invitation?" Gabriel shakily released a breath, his subconscious already catching on to what I was suggesting.

"Yes," I repeated, holding his gaze so he understood this was an agreement between us. "An invitation for me to enjoy you however I want—regardless of whether you're awake and able to tell me yes or no."

This was another moment of truth. Gabriel had proven himself to be obedient when he dropped the angry angel act, but giving me *carte blanche* access to his body was a level of surrender he'd only agree to if he was fully on board.

Will you defy your twin for me, angel?

His gaze slid to Andre, and once again, I wondered if they could communicate telepathically.

He can't give you what you need.

Only I can.

"Yes," Gabriel rasped, his eyes wild with an almost unhinged level of desire when he looked at me again. "Yes, *please.*"

There was that *'please'* again—the word that did strange things to me when coming from his lips.

What is wrong with me, indeed?

Before I could respond, he jolted, as if suddenly remembering something.

Or suddenly receiving a message…

"I need a safe word," he mumbled in a rush. "In case I want you to stop."

Even though I doubted he'd end up using it given his obvious desire for this to happen, I would gladly give this man anything he wanted to make him mine. "Of course. What safe word would you like? Mine is *Stellaria.*"

Not that I ever use it.

"Stellaria," he murmured, and I almost groaned at how beautiful the name of my home planet sounded on his tongue. "Ok, mine is… Shock."

"Perfect," I praised, lightly brushing the back of my knuckles along his jawline and shivering at the now expected electricity between us. "I'll see you later, angel. Don't wait up."

With that, I shot a smug smile at Andre before spinning on my heel and striding from the room, leaving my willing prey trembling behind me.

CHAPTER 12
ANDRE

There was no better way to flush out a brat than to delay gratification.

If I'd thought the sexual tension in this house was bad before The Refinery, it was nothing compared to the cloud of lust I was now wading through every damn day.

It's glorious.

I knew Gabe was dying to obey Theo's orders—that he would have scampered off to do exactly that the same night if given the chance. But I convinced him to sleep in our room instead. Then I did it again the next night.

And the next.

It wasn't because I was trying to cockblock my twin. Far from it. I was equally eager to get him—and therefore, *me*, by proxy —in a room alone with our mark.

But I didn't want it to happen just yet. I wanted to wait until Theo was frothing at the mouth—mindless with lust. Until he was so obsessively focused on getting inside my twin that he didn't notice me inside of *him*.

Sure, I also wanted to make sure Gabe was in the right state of mind to consent to this situation, but it was mostly about power.

Because I'm *the one in control here.*

"Spread your legs for me," Theo crooned from across the room. "That's a good boy."

Gabe appeared to be calmly putting the finishing touches on his version of the dispenser prototype, but I could feel the pressure in *my* head as he clenched his teeth in frustration.

Too bad I'm nowhere near as passive.

Swiveling my stool resulted in an eyeful of ass. Not Theo's, sadly, but the nude model he'd hired for the day.

Who's spreading his legs like he's auditioning for Moulin Rouge.

"Gabe and I are heading out," I bluntly interrupted the figure drawing session Theo had scheduled for today. "We're gonna do some field tests down by the pier."

Away from this performance.

Because that's what it was. Theo wasn't getting what he wanted, so he was acting out—shamelessly flirting with his model to get a reaction out of Gabe.

Except I'm *the one who's hard as steel over his little tantrum.*

If Theo was *mine,* he would have already been over my knee —age gap be damned. He wouldn't be the first older man I'd disciplined, and a good spanking would have cleared the air.

Unfortunately, that wasn't part of the plan. Our mark needed to believe *he* was the one on top here, and Gabe was the perfect subby distraction.

Theo frowned, no doubt noticing how I wasn't asking for permission. Instead of acknowledging my words, he cranked up his too-white smile to a moon landing level of brightness and addressed his model. "Javier, why don't you take five in the dressing room? I'll be in shortly to *assist* in any way needed."

What a slut.

Fuck, I want him to be my slut.

"Done!" Gabe slammed his tools down on the worktable so hard *Javier* almost tripped as he stepped off the stage. "I'm ready when you are, Dre. Let's blow this joint."

With that, he leaped from his stool and stalked toward the door—keeping his gaze stubbornly averted from the model scurrying into the dressing room and the kimono-clad man leering after him.

"Blow, huh?" Theo thoughtfully hummed as my twin reached the threshold. "Good idea… See you in a few, Javier!"

It was my turn to grit my teeth. The violent *jealousy* emanating from Gabe through his wide-open bond was mixing with mine until my vision started going red.

Calm the fuck down, Dre.

You can't kill the human.

I took my sweet time following Gabe out the door, giving Theo a *look* laced with maximum disappointment.

As expected, he held my gaze. "You can't stop the inevitable, you know," he lazily drawled, uncrossing and recrossing his legs like he was Sharon Stone in goddamn *Basic Instinct*.

Suarez clan movie marathons for the win.

I stopped directly in front of him and crossed my arms. "And just what do you think is inevitable, Theo? Your dick buried in my brother's ass?"

"Yes," he sighed dreamily—his eyelashes fluttering before he snapped to focus again. "Among other things."

I had no idea if Theo meant various appendages were destined for various holes, or if he was about to launch into an unrelated villain monologue. Either way, I needed to cut this conversation short, for both our sakes. My palms were *itching* to grab him by the hair and force him to his knees—to fuck his throat until my dick was covered in his spit and tears.

Wrecked would look so pretty on him…

"Well, that's not what Gabe's here for," I huffed, having no trouble behaving like the possessive asshole he expected me to be.

Although just who *I'm feeling more possessive of is unclear.*

If Theo thought I truly didn't want him pursuing my twin, he'd only try harder to bag him—and fall right into our hands.

Checkmate, bitch.

"What about *you,* Andre?" he murmured, a lecherous smile stretching across his face. "Is that what *you're* here for?"

My jaw dropped. I didn't believe for a second that he was actually interested in me. And the only place this brat's cock would ever end up was down my throat as I edged him for hours.

Punk.

With one last glare, I turned and strode for the door. "Tell Jensen he's cooking for one tonight. We'll be back late."

The inhuman growl Theo released added an extra spring to my step, and I whistled obnoxiously all the way down the hideous zebra-print stairs before skipping out the front door.

Smell ya later!

"Fuck, Dre, I'm a mess," Gabe muttered as we walked side by side toward the waterfront. "No one has *ever* made me this fucking thirsty before. It's not natural…"

I frowned. While my twin had never been this twisted up over anyone, his current state was probably because he was also teetering on the edge of a sub-awakening.

And I can't have him thinking there's anything wrong *with that…*

"It's okay to like what we like, dude," I carefully replied, noticing he was sweating, despite the overcast weather. "I mean, you saw how it was at The Refinery. People there are into wild shit."

Including me.

"Yeah, well, how many of them want to get fucked while they're asleep, huh?"

Even in my head, Gabe's self-loathing was clear. His gaze was fixed on the wooden planks of the boardwalk as he picked up his pace, practically spitting the rest of his words out loud. "What the fuck do you call *that?*"

I couldn't help laughing as I grabbed his arm and dragged him to a nearby bench. Being late afternoon on a Sunday, the beach was nearly empty, so we were free to talk openly.

And we will *be talking about this.*

Out loud.

"It's called somnophilia, you muppet." I cackled, almost losing it when he turned to face me with the most dumb-founded expression I'd ever seen.

Living up to the names of Shock and Awe.

"What?" I continued, more than happy to drop some knowledge on this sweet summer child. "You thought you were cool enough to *invent* a kink? *Puh-leeze.*"

Gabe chuckled self-deprecatingly. "Okay, so it's a thing, got it. I guess I'm just surprised it's *my* thing, ya know?"

"I'm not," I confidently replied. When he gaped at me again, I clarified. "You *need* this form of release since you always seem to have a lot of things on your shoulders…"

Things you don't share with me.

Gabe stared at me for a long moment, and I wondered if he would have the balls to call me out on my salty subtext—maybe even finally *tell me* whatever I suspected he was hiding. But then he simply puffed out a breath and gazed out over the waves.

"The thought of Theo touching that model right now… of being touched by him…" His voice was barely above a whisper—his hesitant words almost lost in the wind. "It's making me feel some kind of way, Dre."

Because he'd left our connection wide open, I could easily see what he meant. Gabe's focus was scattered, with actual effort being used to keep his mind from snaking its way back to the maximalist mansion we'd left behind. It was exactly how I felt whenever I was away from my twin for too long—as if a physical piece was missing, with the rest of me wandering aimlessly until we were in each other's presence again.

It's how I'm starting to feel about Theo…

Fuck.

He's as unhinged about this man as I am.

I need to get this situation under control.

Deciding to put my twin out of his misery, I quickly tapped in and out of Theo's head—just long enough to see what that kimono-clad whore was up to.

"Theo's alone in the hot tub on his terrace." I reported through our bond. *"Just looking at the ocean."*

In the direction we went.

As if Theo's thoughts had somehow taken corporeal form, I suddenly felt a caress on the back of my neck—the sensation so pointed it made me shudder.

Weird.

Without knowing what powers Theo possessed, I realized we needed to at least *look* like we were doing what we'd said we were going to do.

"Ready to test out our creepy contraptions?" I rose to stand and rubbed my hands together eagerly. "Ready to dose each other with mystery juice?"

Gabe huffed as he stood and fiddled with whatever he had rigged up under his long-sleeve shirt. "I don't know what you put in *yours*. Mine is just water."

Like hell it is.

I grinned—the promise of a brotherly competition lighting me up better than any drug. "Hmm, I dunno, dude," I teased. "I filled *mine* with whatever Theo has in those weird brown bottles in his studio. Thought I'd make it interesting."

Of course, I was kidding. While I had no qualms about creating a 'discreet' dispenser for fuck knows what reason, I wasn't about to offer Gabe or myself as sacrificial lambs.

At least, not in this case.

"Gabe…" My hesitant tone had him immediately paying attention. "You're absolutely, one thousand percent sure you want to get with Theo? That you want *him* to be your… *first?*"

Fuck, this is still kind of awkward.

I expected my twin to share my sentiments—to blush as bad as Butch did whenever Xanny said something out of pocket about their personal lives in front of the rest of us.

Speaking of kinky fuckers.

Instead, Gabe squared his shoulders and looked me dead in the eye—as serious as I'd ever seen him. "Yes, I'm sure. I've never been more sure of anything in my entire life. I want… No, I *need* to sleep in the studio's bedroom tonight. I swear to god, if you suggest I wait even one more day, Imma cut a bitch."

I threw back my head and laughed before holding up my hands in mock surrender. "Okay, okay—whatever you say! I don't wanna end up being the bitch you cut, you horny psychopath."

Gabe chuckled before peeking at me apologetically. "Yeah, I could have approached that better. I was over here sweating, thinking you were going to make me wait until my nuts fell off."

Slinging an arm around his shoulder, I pulled him close —*needing* to remind myself of our unbreakable connection before handing him off to someone else. "I will never *make* you do anything you don't want to. And this is a *good* conversation to have—even if it's uncomfortable. It's important to articulate what you want and need, especially with kink."

A stray thought had me turning until we were face to face again—two deceptively perfect mirrors who were nowhere near as alike as we appeared.

"On that note…" I hesitated only a moment before powering on—determined to practice the clear communication I was preaching. "I know you and Theo already verbally agreed to this, but somno is *usually* enjoyed within a relationship where trust has already been established. What if… what if he…"

What if he hurts you?

Or worse.

I will go full scorched-earth on his ass if anything bad happens.

Unsurprisingly sensing my anxiety, Gabe reached out and grabbed my wrist before moving our conversation back to our mind-bond.

"How about you stay in my head the entire time? That way, if things go south, you can step in?"

I almost choked on the emotion that ripped through me. I'd already been planning on checking in while Gabe and Theo were getting busy—for both selfless *and* selfish reasons—but my twin giving me *permission* to experience this with him was some next-level trust.

Trust I don't deserve.

"Sounds like a plan," I solemnly replied before a smirk of victory twitched my lip. "Lord knows you need *someone* watching your six since you didn't even notice I tagged you with my superior perfume dispenser."

I proudly pointed at Gabe's neck, where a telltale neon yellow paintball mark now graced his skin. Just as quickly, my smug smile faded. A neon orange mark shone brightly on my wrist —the same wrist he'd grabbed a moment ago.

You fucker.

"Looks like we both lost… or won…" He lightly laughed, looking miles more relaxed than he had all afternoon. "But whatev. Let's go find some grub and discuss how things are gonna go down tonight."

I snorted at his choice of words before remembering that one of our favorite pizza shops was near this end of the board-walk. "Yeah, we can grab a slice and waste a few hours before heading back."

To where our prey awaits.

CHAPTER 13
GABRIEL

So much anticipation was thrumming through my veins by the time I crept toward the studio, it felt like I was vibrating.

I need something to take the edge off.

"What you need is to chill, dude." Dre's voice rasped in my head. *"The sooner you get your ass into position, the sooner the games can begin."*

Of course, the idea of getting my *ass* into *position* only heightened my hyper awareness of the situation.

Including that Dre will get a front-row seat.

Oddly, it didn't feel awkward or intrusive. It was like a weight had been lifted by letting my twin into this part of my life—to share my previously hidden desires with him.

"Somnophilia…" I rolled the word over on my tongue as I entered the small bedroom off the studio and shut the door behind me.

Now that I knew this kink had a name, I'd fallen into a bunch of Reddit rabbit holes to pump myself up for tonight. Seeing others casually discuss the exact experience I was after was comforting, and helped me better articulate my reasons. For me, it wasn't just about acting out a consensually non-consensual fantasy, although that was part of it. What I craved most was the promise of temporarily erasing the pressure of my daily existence.

Or the threat of my potential destiny.

It was also weirdly hot to be pursued so aggressively, even if my natural tendency was to dominate whoever was threatening my supremacy. The way I looked meant guys—and girls—hit on me regularly, so I often took over the conversation to make it clear if I was interested or not.

Even if being in control wasn't what I wanted in the end.

Theo hadn't cared if I was interested. In his mind, I'd already been licked and claimed, and the more I resisted, the harder he came at me. Even though I'd acted big mad about it, dude saw straight through my bullshit as easily as if he were a mind reader himself.

So I gave in and gave him permission to do anything he wanted to me.

Anything…

Crap.

"I'll stop him if he tries to fuck you from the jump." Dre's natural calm immediately stopped me from spiraling. *"Unless that's what you want…?"*

I blew out a slow breath as I climbed into the freshly made bed. Supes had a stupidly high pain threshold, so I wasn't worried about my virgin ass. But I'd been so dick drunk off Theo's smooth voice telling me what to do, I hadn't thought through how far I wanted this to go.

"Then popping your cherry shouldn't happen yet." My twin's reply was firm, blessedly deciding for me. *"Just let me take care of things, Gabe. I've got you."*

Maybe it was the knowledge Dre would protect me, or that I was *finally* allowing myself to experience what I'd wanted for so long. But it wasn't long after I got settled that my eyelids grew as heavy as lead—my body turning boneless as I instantly relaxed.

That's weird…

Consciousness eventually returned, although only somewhat. The only illumination to be seen in the small room was from a few slivers of moonlight trickling down through the skylight like falling stars. Just as my senses recalibrated, I realized I was now naked, with a larger body curled over me, and the sensation of lips and teeth trailing along my neck. Someone who smelled familiar.

Theo.

"Fuck," I gasped, and even though Theo had my arms and legs pinned in place, I tilted my hips, hoping to find some friction between us.

Theo hummed against my skin. "Are you having a sweet dream, angel?"

Is this a dream?

It was hard to know. My thoughts were a disjointed jumble of horny longing and vague awareness—and my eyes could barely stay open for more than a few seconds at a time—but I was fine with it.

If this is a dream, it's the best fucking dream I've ever had.

"More," I murmured, turning my head in hopes this intoxicating man would get the hint and kiss me. "But not… everything."

Not yet.

"Whatever you want, angel," Theo chuckled low—his breath tickling my lips as he lifted his head to gaze down at me. "As long as I get to taste you."

"Yes," I whispered, almost *delirious* with need. "Please put your mouth on me."

I knew I was playing a role—just like I'd been doing almost my entire life. Only this time, I wasn't convinced it was acting. It made absolutely no sense to be so insanely attracted to someone I barely knew—someone who my family considered an enemy until proven otherwise—but I was going to enjoy every second of this experience.

"Please," I whimpered, not giving a good goddamn how desperate I sounded. *"Please…"*

I am here for it.

Theo smiled in the moonlight, and the evilness in his expression only made me harder. "I love when you say that word," he murmured before lowering his lips to mine. "So perfect…"

I moaned like a whore as his tongue invaded my mouth. It tangled with mine before somehow forcing its way down my throat, and I blissfully gagged around the intrusion.

I am also here for his freakishly long tongue.

Assuming it even is his tongue…

Before I could question the logistics of what was happening, Theo withdrew and pulled back with a contented sigh. "What a pretty little skinsuit you'd make."

This man can wear me like a skinsuit whenever he wants.

My twin didn't share my enthusiasm, as I felt his power building inside me—readying to strike.

"No, Dre… I want this. Please…"

Apparently, that was also the magic word for *him*. Dre immediately stood down, even as he continued to hover on the edge of my semi-conscious state—mentally assisting while Theo *physically* did his thing.

Joining forces to give me everything I ever wanted.

My cock was rock-hard and dripping precum everywhere, and when I thrust again, I could feel it smearing over Theo's abs.

Is he naked, too?

Fuck, yes…

It was suddenly *imperative* that I see what this man was packing. But Theo was firmly holding me in place as he traveled down my body—kissing, nipping, and caressing me as he went.

Caressing…?

I snapped to attention just long enough to register that *yes,* I could feel Theo rolling my nipple between his fingers with one hand while using the other to lazily trace my hip bone.

While at least four other hands pinned me down.

No… not hands…

"He's changing into his true form, Gabe. I need you to stay relaxed and take it."

Much to my annoyance—and horny confusion—my dick *jumped* at being told to 'take it,' even by my twin.

Dre chuckled in my head, using his power to send me back into a dreamlike state, but not without a closing remark.

"You're such a—"

"…good boy," Theo chuckled, firmly gripping the base of my aching cock before tonguing the slit. "I want to fucking devour you."

Please.

Please consume me.

Wet heat enveloped my cock, making me arch off the bed with a broken sob. The movement caused *whatever* part of him was holding me down to tighten—coiling around my wrists and ankles like vines climbing a tree.

What the hell is *he?*

And why do I not even care?

I should have been terrified. I should have been rallying my power—connecting with my twin to send this fucker into a coma before he got his rocks off. Instead, I gratefully melted into weightless bliss, relishing the sensation of giving up control.

What would it feel like to exist in this space all the time?

Theo pulled off my cock with an obscenely wet sound. "You taste divine, little angel. I'm definitely keeping you now…"

Keep me forever.

A sharp stab of *jealousy* made my stomach clench, and it took my foggy brain a moment to realize the emotion was coming from Dre.

Oh, no…

Even with the possessive thoughts I'd randomly picked up when he let down his guard, it hadn't occurred to me that Dre might want Theo as much as I did. We'd never crossed this bridge before because we'd never been interested in the same person, but this wasn't something I could simply *ignore.* Forget about covert missions—or darkest desires—because I would rather die than ever hurt my twin.

Despite what I've been ordered to do…

Quickly burying *that* traitorous thought, I focused on muscling my way past the mental barriers Dre had constructed between my conscious and subconscious to confront him.

"If you want Theo, we need to talk about this."

"No. We don't."

"Last call for your safe word," Theo cheekily sang as he pressed my thighs onto my chest—exposing everything to him for the taking.

"Just take it, Gabe. I want you to have this."

Fuuuuck.

"I want it," I choked out, taking the permission he was giving. "Please, don't stop."

Never stop.

"That's what I like to hear," Theo replied, as if he'd expected nothing less. "Now, tell me… will I be the first one inside your tight little ass? Is that what you want when you're ready?"

Something—*Jesus, what* was *that?*—ghosted over my hole, and it was all I could do to not demand he fuck me already.

If I don't get him inside me soon, I'm gonna die.

"It's your job to get me ready." My lips were moving, but it was *Dre's* words that emerged. "And you can start by swallowing my fucking cock."

Shit.

Theo froze before a low growl rumbled out of his chest. "Have you forgotten who's in charge here, angel? Shall I remind you?"

"Yes!" I rasped, *actually* vibrating this time with an overwhelming combination of lust and confusion. "Make me yours."

I felt *Dre* freeze, but Theo wasted no time. My dick disappeared down his throat as *something* pushed its way into my ass.

"Fuuuuck," I sobbed as nerve endings I didn't know I had lit up like a string of Christmas lights.

Instinctively knowing this was a dangerous predator, my powers rallied to fight. But unless I wanted to give the game away, I needed to do exactly what Dre had told me to.

Take. It.

I was more than happy to obey. Theo was sucking my cock like it was gonna shoot top-shelf liquor, and he'd now added *another* something to stretch me open as I vainly writhed in his hold.

"Please, please, please," I chanted, tossing my head from side to side as pressure began building at the base of my spine.

Please, take everything.

"Just a little longer, Gabe," Dre coached, his voice strained with mental exertion. *"I'm almost inside him…"*

The idea of Dre *inside* our mark had me arching backward as my cock abruptly pulsed—unloading in Theo's mouth while I gasped for oxygen.

Then, I started *humming.*

It wasn't a sound I'd ever made before, and with my entire body now vibrating like a hive of bees, I panicked.

Until Theo started making the same noise.

"Oh, shit!"

Dre was clearly alarmed, but instead of yanking me back to consciousness and shutting the whole thing down, he booted me into a deep sleep and locked the door behind me.

What the fuuu…

When I woke up again, I was alone in the studio's spare room, still naked, but covered by a soft blanket that definitely wasn't there before.

What. The. Fuck. Happened?

A knock on the door had me sitting up and clutching the blanket to my chest—as if I were a helpless normie and not a supe who could easily make someone's head explode.

Although it's easier with the help of my twin…

The tension immediately bled out of me as Dre slipped into the room and climbed onto the bed. He pulled me close—careful to keep the blanket between us as he did—and I wondered which one of us he was trying to comfort.

"Why'd you do that?" I finally asked after a full minute of silence that he apparently had no interest in filling. *"I don't*

wanna get a bad rep as one of those dudes who falls asleep in the middle of fucking."

Or coming…

My question was supposed to make him laugh, but Dre released a growl instead and squeezed me tighter.

Now I was fully freaking out, and not just because I still didn't know what my twin was upset about. I also had no idea what had happened to Theo.

"You better not have hurt my—"

"Your *what*, Gabe?!" Dre snapped as he abruptly released me and sat up, but then moved the conversation back into our heads.

"What the fuck happened in here?"

Beyond aggravated, I sat up as well, resisting the urge to punch this fucker in the face. I forced myself to be satisfied with delivering an icy glare instead.

"How the hell should I know?! You tucked me in before I could see what Theo is."

Dre gave me an odd look before taking my hand in his and blowing out a shaky breath.

"I only caught a glimpse, and I'm still processing what I saw."

Well, that doesn't sound good.

My twin was *never* ruffled. I'd seen *Wolfy* upset more times than him, and that was saying something.

"But you said you saw him change into something else, right?" I

hesitantly asked, wanting to know more, but worried that whatever he was about to tell me might change everything.

Or nothing…

Which might be worse.

Dre nodded once before dropping his gaze to our clasped hands—squeezing so tightly, I flinched.

"I did…"

"But…"

"But he wasn't the only one who changed."

CHAPTER 14
THEO

It's simply not possible.

I stuffed another bite of Belgian waffle into my mouth, vibrating with agitation as I dissected what had happened last night.

Or... what *appeared* to have happened.

Partway through my enjoyment of Gabriel, I'd started to resonate. This was a phenomenon particular to my kind—with both mates and biological family—but occurred at a frequency other beings couldn't hear. So while it surprised me, I had no intention of letting it stop me from swallowing my angel's perfect cock.

But then *he'd* resonated as well.

Which was. Not. Fucking. Possible.

The Acosta twins were *human.* Their ridiculously rich family may have been mysteriously untraceable, but I'd been subtly poking at them ever since they arrived at my house a week ago. If there was anything *other* in their DNA, I surely would have detected it by now.

Right??

On a lighter note, the absolute control Gabriel had given me over his body had been, for lack of a better word, earth-shattering. I'd barely needed to use my powers to keep him on the edge of sleep. He'd wanted me to take over so badly that he'd hovered in a state of semi-consciousness all on his own.

Somehow…

Regardless, using my tendrils to hold my angel down—invading his throat and ass with my essence while he drifted on the edge of consciousness—was a salacious experience I would covet forever.

Since I'm never letting him go at this point.

Because now I can't…

With an annoyed growl, I took another bite. Hopefully, stuffing myself with the delectable combination of crispy waffle, fresh fruit, and copious whipped cream would somehow blockade my true form from emerging to track down what it now saw as its *match*.

Distasteful.

I couldn't comprehend this turn of events. In all the centuries I'd been gallivanting around Earth—fucking countless humans for both fun and research purposes—I had never *imprinted* on one before.

This is most inconvenient.

Yes, true mating bonds were possible with my kind—and we called such compatibility a *stellar collision*—but it wasn't needed for reproduction.

Even if we are required to reproduce at least once in our lifespan.

Centuries ago, on my home planet, I'd dutifully located a suitable Stellarian for this very task. We both temporarily exited the vessels we were inhabiting and combined our essences to create a single offspring 'for the glory and continuation of our species.'

Gross.

Then, I'd hurried off to enlist in the next outward-bound expedition.

For Stellaria!

Well… for me, *really.*

Not only did I possess no desire to form romantic bonds, I had less than zero interest in familial ones. Luckily, Stellarians were singularly focused on colonizing other planets—as most alien races were. So after fulfilling my duty, it was easy enough to use our collective mission as an excuse to star hop away from anything that threatened to tie me down.

And yet… here we are.

Resonating for a goddamn human.

An insistent knock on my bedroom door had me quickly turning on the TV. Anything to disguise the fact I'd been sitting here in uncharacteristic silence, contemplating my entire existence.

So incredibly distasteful.

It was my longtime housekeeper who banged into the room, laden with cleaning supplies. True to form, she immediately fixed me with a knowing *look* that had me bristling.

"Out with it, Lupe," I growled. "You know I prefer candor over the judgmental murmurings you'll be otherwise emitting in two sec—"

"Why are you hiding in here like a frightened child, *Tay-Tay?"* she interrupted—her customary term of endearment only rubbing salt in the wound.

This must be what having a meddling mother feels like.

Thanks, I hate it.

"I'm not hiding," I haughtily replied, even though it was precisely what I was doing. "I needed to catch up on pertinent business without unnecessary distractions."

Like the uncontrollable desire to breed *my mate.*

Lupe performed an exaggerated turn toward my plush seating area, and the 85-inch screen mounted on the far wall.

Which was currently playing highlights from the last season of *Bored Trophy Wives of Awakener's Bay.*

Sigh.

"I see," she deadpanned and faced me again. "So this"—she gestured toward the breakfast-in-bed Jensen had prepared for me, *without judgment, I might add*—"has nothing to do with the beautiful boy sitting at the kitchen island? The one pretending not to wait for you like a sad, lost puppy dog?"

MY MATE NEEDS ME!!!

Countless tendrils shot out of me, nearly upended the lacquered food tray onto my blood-red satin sheets before snaking down the hallway to spy. Just as Lupe had reported, a disgustingly heartbreaking mix of sadness and confusion was radiating from the area surrounding the kitchen's breakfast bar.

Alongside recognizable anger.

I see someone else is equally displeased with this turn of events…

What a surprise.

Andre had made his disapproval of my pursuit of Gabriel abundantly clear. I highly suspected he'd been the reason my angel took days to obey when he clearly wanted to submit immediately.

But I prevailed in the end.

All at once, I realized I'd almost missed the opportunity to antagonize Andre by openly flaunting my victory.

Forget these pesky… feelings.

The show must go on!

All trepidations forgotten—at least, swept under the rug, for now—I gleefully hopped off my bed and strutted into my spacious walk-in closet to change into something more presentable. Then I glimpsed the tiny hot pink sleep shorts I was wearing in the full-length mirror and promptly changed my mind.

Who needs to be presentable?

"And what's on the breakfast menu for my pretty little interns, Jensen?" I cooed, breezing down the hallway with my rose gold kimono flapping open behind me like a superhero's cape. "Something sweet, I hope?"

As sweet as Gabriel tasted last night.

More than used to my dramatics, my long-suffering personal chef simply rolled his eyes and pointed toward the fridge. "Your charcuterie board is all prepped for lunch, T. I even rustled up some prickly pear jam, since you mentioned living off of it during your time in Argentina."

I felt Andre's eyes boring into me, but my attention was stubbornly fixed on my angel. On how he was looking at me.

On how my body was responding to him.

Practically resonating.

Gabriel's gaze was like a physical caress, and goosebumps broke out over my exposed skin as he slowly drank in my bare chest and abs before fixating on the noticeable bulge in my shorts.

Which is growing more noticeable by the second.

Jensen muttered something under his breath as he headed for the elevator. But even a nuclear explosion couldn't have distracted me from the sight of Gabriel's pink tongue as it darted out to wet his lips.

"Are you still hungry, angel?" I murmured, unable to stop myself from stepping closer—although I managed to resist reaching for him. "Do you need something to fill you up?"

Like my cock?

Or other appendages?

"I…" Gabriel's beautiful face had gone slack as he made eye contact again. "I need…"

Tell me…

The moment was interrupted as my angel abruptly shook his head, his dreamy expression turning hard and sulky in an instant. "I need some air."

With that, he shoved away from the breakfast bar and stalked onto the terrace. I frowned, my tendrils uncoiling to hesitantly drift after him, trying to determine what had inspired this sudden change in his demeanor.

What did I…?

"What did you do to him?" Andre growled, suddenly standing two inches away.

"Excuse me?" I huffed, continuously annoyed by both twins' abilities to sneak up on me.

I must be off my game.

"Last night," Andre continued, placing his hand on the break-fast bar behind me and leaning in—invading my personal space until I was forced to retreat a step. "What. Did. You. Do. To. Him?"

I scoffed and straightened, closing my kimono and cinching it tight. "Only what he asked for, *demon.*"

Andre scowled, his brow furrowing in thinly veiled irritation. "He didn't ask for—"

"He did," I curtly interrupted. "Your tasty little twin *begged* me to take what I wanted from him—no matter how conscious he was."

Deal with it.

It was the truth, and I was in no mood for Andre's insinuations. This was my most attractive skinsuit to date, and with my latest incarnation as an eccentric artist with limitless connections and money, there was no shortage of humans wanting to pleasure me.

Even if my focus has drastically narrowed to two humans in particular.

The expression on Andre's annoyingly symmetrical face morphed into a smug satisfaction that was equal parts fasci-nating and unnerving.

"Begged, hmm?" he hummed, somehow looming over me, despite being a few inches shorter. "Have *you* ever begged for something, Theo?"

What the…

This was highly irregular. Not a moment ago, I'd been imag-ining Gabriel kneeling for me, but now *I* was the one whose knees—and resolve—felt unsteady. Andre's proximity was short-circuiting my instincts, flooding my receptors with the addicting scent of whiskey, raw cedar, and almond mixed with something metallic.

Like a pristine box of exacto knives.

The strangest part was that this visceral onslaught had my body *relaxing* alarmingly.

What is he *doing to* me?

My easy prey on the terrace was temporarily forgotten in favor of the insidious threat before me. Quickly retracting my tendrils back inside, I reared back, caging in the man cornering me—poised to strike.

No.

Not to strike…

I could only watch in horror as my tendrils undulated rhythmically, giving me only a second to prepare before I produced the humming sound Stellarians made when our resonance matched another.

Noooooooo!

My only saving grace was that Andre wouldn't be able to register my humiliating song. There was still no explanation for why Gabriel hummed along last night, but I was officially going to chalk it up to coincidence and my overactive imagination.

I'm sure some no-strings-attached fucking will get it out of my system.

"What the *fuck?*" Andre hissed, clutching his chest and squinting at me accusingly.

He opened his mouth again, but instead of the vitriol I was expecting, he emitted a sound that had my borrowed blood running cold.

A perfectly resonant note.

WHAT THE FUCK IS HAPPENING HERE?!

Andre clapped a hand over his mouth, his eyes rounding as he struggled to contain his outburst.

Or whatever else is trying to escape…

The mental fog I was battling immediately cleared, leaving razor-sharp focus in its wake.

I think I know what's going on here.

My people were a symbiotic race—parasites, if you will—and once we claimed a body, our DNA melded so seamlessly with theirs that even a trained geneticist wouldn't be able to detect us. Perhaps the reason I'd failed to detect anything *inhuman* in my new houseguests was because they'd already been claimed by my fellow Stellarians.

Which means they've finally come for me.

To hold me accountable for my crimes.

Maybe…

I didn't want to be hasty. My current identity had been painstakingly curated to my liking, and the idea of starting from scratch again made me stabby. Not to mention, if I was wrong and the Acosta family was as well-connected as their money implied, then I didn't want to risk incurring the sort of wrath that could ruin me, anyway. I needed to be absolutely sure about what I was up against.

So I'll proceed with caution.

For now.

"I propose a ceasefire!" Clapping my hands together, I beamed—fully prepared to kill this young man with kindness if need be. "I'll be out of town tomorrow for a business meeting, but I would simply *love* to have your family for dinner later this week."

Andre's gaze widened the tiniest amount, but contrary to my choice of words, I wasn't planning on consuming anyone.

At least, not like that.

For the moment, I meant exactly what I said. It was high time I learned who I was doing business with—both with Ward's 'inside man' at the Salahs and the supposed humans I'd allowed into my home. I may have been hiding who I was, but that didn't mean anyone else was allowed to.

Hmph.

"Our parents are dead," Andre slowly enunciated, mistakenly thinking that would be the end of it.

I thoughtfully tapped my bottom lip, loving how he tracked the motion. "Gabriel mentioned an older brother—one who's taken care of you since your parents' untimely death."

Andre's eyes narrowed. "Yes… but I doubt he'll—"

"…want to miss meeting the *infamous* Theo Coatl," I crooned, determined to take back control of the situation. "Especially as I would like to offer both you and Gabriel more *permanent* positions."

On your knees.

Or dead.

My little *demon* was back to his signature impassiveness, but I'd seen enough to know the idea of me meeting his older brother unnerved him.

Good.

"Fine," he replied, his gaze briefly flickering to where his twin stood hunched over the terrace with his eyes on the ocean a few blocks away. "We'll see if… Wolfgang can fit dinner into his busy schedule."

And now I have a name.

"I'm sure he'll manage," I lightly laughed as I turned and headed for the stairs, ready to channel my wild cocktail of emotions into creating something dreadful. "Please pass along to *Wolfgang* that I'm simply *dying* to meet him."

And time will tell if he feels the same.

CHAPTER 15

ANDRE

What the fuck?

What the fucking fuck?

Everything had been going to plan. Gabe was 1000% on board with being the bait. Theo was falling right into our trap. And Wolfy had no clue I'd gone rogue.

But now everything has gone to shit.

Last night had felt like a fever dream, even with me being the one behind the wheel in my twin's head. While my end game had been to figure out what kind of creature we were dealing with, I was serious about making it the best possible experience for Gabe.

To show him that what he wants isn't weird.

Even if things got weird…

Indirectly *bottoming* for Theo—while holding Gabe on the edge of consciousness—was a trip, but nothing compared to when our mark began to *glow*.

From the inside out.

It looked like pinpricks of light passing through a shrapnel-damaged surface—hairline optical fibers that emerged from his skin with a purpose and moved in a way that suggested sentience. Mesmerized, I could only gape through my brother's eyes as these illuminated tendrils thickened and reached for him—for *us*—before producing a humming vibration that was achingly familiar.

Like a childhood lullaby that I've forgotten…

Although no one's ever sung me a lullaby before.

Before I could place the melody, a low buzzing sensation started building in my twin's chest. This vibration intensified before morphing into something else—something that felt *alive.*

Something that was answering Theo's song.

Like a goddamn mating call.

My immediate reaction had been shock, then fury. Then I refocused on how to stop this monster from claiming my twin… only to realize Gabriel was *asking* to be claimed.

Not on my watch, bro.

That's when I'd shut the whole thing down, sending Gabe into a deep sleep as I rallied to strike. But my opponent surprised me yet again. Instead of taking advantage of his prey's supposed helplessness, Theo had simply licked my twin clean like an animal before grabbing a blanket from the closet and tucking him in.

Almost… sweetly.

Even weirder was how Theo seemed as confused as I was about the whole thing, since he'd stared at my sleeping brother for a solid minute before leaving. Even though the freaky deaky light show was over, and Gabe was thankfully still in one piece, as soon as I heard the stairwell door close, I raced into the room to make sure my other half was okay.

To make sure *I* was okay.

I'm not okay.

Since then, my twin had been understandably freaked out, especially because I *still* hadn't explained what I saw.

Because how the fuck do I explain something like that?!

Especially now that I've joined the mating call chorus.

What. The. Actual. Fuck?

This entire situation had veered off the rails, and I needed to get things back on track before this became a goddamn train wreck.

Especially now that Wolfy's been invited to dinner.

I'd left it up to Gabe to invite our brother. Not only was I too rattled by what had happened, but I assumed their *extra special bond* would soften the news that our mark had all but commanded The Hand of Death to visit his home.

The larger issue was how I was going to handle Wolfy's presence. As confident as I was in my ability to protect Gabe, I could admit—to myself—that I probably should have run my plan by the supe who'd been playing the game for way longer than I had.

Although he would have shot down my idea from the jump.

Because it was mine.

Familiar resentment bubbled to the surface. If Wolfy had just taken me under his wing in the first place—as he had with Gabe—then I might have the skills needed to plan this operation. Instead, I was perpetually left in the dark with things I *should* have been included in.

What is his problem?

What is his problem with me?

My phone buzzed in my pocket, breaking my salty spell. While I would normally ignore it, I was curious who thought they could get a hold of me through a *phone call,* of all things, so I glanced at the screen.

Luca Meier.

Thank fuck.

Seeing my mentor's name was like a shot of calm straight into my veins. Luca was so much more than just the villain who'd helped hone our powers in Switzerland every summer at our parents' request. He was a legendary inspiration, yes, but also a father figure—not just to Gabe and me, but to the other Suarez kids who passed through his doors.

Especially Wolfy.

But right now, he's all mine.

"Hey, *Sensei.*" I forced my tone to sound light. "What's up?"

Luca didn't reply at first, but that tracked. As The Kinetic Assassin, his powers involved moving objects with his mind, but I'd long suspected there was more to it than that. And as someone who knew how easy it was to invade someone else's brain if they hadn't built up their defenses, I covertly tightened the locks on mine and patiently waited him out.

Knowing him, this could be a test.

"I'm in Big City," he finally replied in his thick Swiss accent. "And Wolfgang mentioned a dinner at the home of your... employer later this week."

He was carefully wording things, and it wasn't just out of concern for who might be listening in. Luca was a long-standing member of the supe council in Geneva, which meant he *had* to remain neutral with the petty squabbles of our kind. This meant there were things Wolfy inevitably kept from him, but my stomach still sank to wonder how much my mentor knew about my fuck ups with this mission.

How was I supposed to know any of this would happen?!

"Would you like for me to accompany him to your dinner?" Luca smoothly asked, and I could have wept with how badly I wanted exactly that. "As your… long-lost uncle, perhaps?"

I choked on a laugh. Luca was one of the palest mother-fuckers I'd ever seen, but Gabe and I had more of our mother's Icelandic skin tone than most of our siblings, so it could work.

And it sounds like Theo's focus will be on Wolfy, anyway.

Thoughts and prayers.

"Yeah, I would appreciate you being there," I replied before familiar bitterness crept in. "But I guess it's up to our big bad leader."

Luca was silent again, and I sighed, annoyed with myself that I couldn't just let my childish jealousy go—especially in front of someone I deeply respected.

"There are reasons Wolfgang needs to lead your family," he softly explained, although the decisiveness in his words left no room for argument. "And I need you to *trust* me on that, Andre. Can you do that?"

I don't know.

"Yes," I replied, with as much conviction as I could fake. "I trust you."

That last part was true, at least. Luca may not have been related to me by blood, but he was someone I trusted with my life.

And I would lay down my life for him in return.

"Well done," he murmured—and I puffed up at the praise. "I will explain to your brother why I will join him for dinner. The main reason being that I would love to see you boys while I'm here."

My gaze drifted out the window of the Uber Black I was taking to The Refinery—alone. I'd half-heartedly invited Gabe, but he must have picked up on my mental state, because he turned down the offer. If Theo hadn't been out of town on business, I would have dragged my twin along, anyway. But since our mark was gone, there was no problem with leaving him behind.

Truth be told, I was looking forward to an evening alone with my thoughts.

And whoever wants to kneel for me.

"Thank you, Luca," I whispered, referring to more than just his offer to come to dinner.

"Always, *schätzli,*" he replied—the only person I would ever put up with giving me a cutesy nickname. "And remember, *mastering others is strength, but mastering yourself is true power.* Enjoy the club, Andre."

"Fuck," I swore as the line went dead, once again suspecting Luca's powers were closer to ours than he let on. But I was thankful he'd called. Being calm and in control was where I needed to be to enter a scene, and just a few minutes of talking to my mentor had achieved that.

I've got this.

I just need to let out some steam.

Then I'll fix the Theo situation.

Simple.

"Fay," I nodded at the hostess before meeting the gaze of the figure by her side—her partner in business and in life. "Madam."

Sinistre cocked their head, noting the way I addressed them by honorific instead of with our usual first-name familiarity. "I see you've arrived in a mood. There's someone here I'd like to introduce you to, Andre. Come."

Exhaling in relief, I allowed Sin to lead me to one of the private rooms reserved for gold card members like me. It was the one I preferred—the one decorated with cold, modern furnishings and equipped with toys for inflicting pain.

And rubber play sheets for easy cleanup.

Sin left me inside and I sat in the leather armchair before helping myself to a glass of water from the carafe on the side table. Then I let the blessed silence wash over me. My mind was still open to Gabe—as always—and I quickly checked in as I prepared to shut him out.

"You're still alone at the house, right?"

"Yup. Jensen just left for the night. I'm out on the terrace enjoying the view, so you can stop worrying, Mom."

I chuckled—not only because the idea of our deceased mother ever giving a shit was laughable, but also because I knew for a fact 'enjoying the view,' was Gabe-speak for firing up a fat blunt packed with the strongest weed known to man.

He better save some to share after I'm done here.

As if on cue, the door to the playroom swung wide without so much as a knock, and a slim man a few years older than me strutted in as if he lived here.

It looks like we have a brat on our hands.

Well done, Sin.

"Hi… oh…" He wrinkled his nose at the rubber sheets. "What's with the plastic? Are you planning on murdering me?"

Hopefully not.

"I'm Andre." I smiled in what I hoped was a pleasant way, considering my nerves were shot. "Why don't you take a seat so we can get to know each other?"

I gestured toward the armchair on the other side of the table, but my new friend only frowned. "You don't want to just get to it?"

Excuse me?

It was my turn to frown. "No. I prefer to negotiate before we play, so I know your limits."

So I don't murder your dumb ass.

With a flippant wave of his hand, he flopped into the seat. "Fine. My name's Shane. He/him. And I like pain. Mistress Sinister, or whatever, said to come talk to you."

I take it back.

What the fuck, Sin?

Madam Sinistre knew I enjoyed brat taming, but also repeatedly mentioned—along with Fay—what a good educator I would make. It was suddenly clear this little meeting was less about a scene and more about me making sure a baby submissive didn't lose his way.

Too bad there's only one sub I care about mentoring.

Making a split-second decision, I reopened my mind to my twin before leaning forward with my elbows on my knees. "Pain, hmm? So you want me to hurt you, Shane?"

"Yes." Raw lust flashed in his eyes, and I knew without a doubt that this man would be down to fuck, no matter how compatible we were from a kink perspective.

It is tempting…

Maybe we *could* have had fun together. Maybe I could have delivered some of that pain he was hoping for—pain I was *desperate* to unleash on someone. Unfortunately, Shane here mostly wanted to get dicked down by a Dom, just to say he did, while I had no interest in wasting my time.

"What about marks?" I continued—more for Gabe's benefit than this idiot—smiling when I felt my twin perk up at the question. "Can I leave marks on you anywhere?"

Shane's brows furrowed in confusion. "Well, I'd prefer none that can be seen. Actually, none at all. I don't want you to spank me *that* hard…"

As if a spanking is the worst I would do.

All at once, I felt Gabe slam shut our mental connection, but I didn't worry about it. He was most likely assuming things were about to get serious here and wanted to give me privacy.

Too bad he's dead wrong.

I took another sip of my water, mentally deciding exactly how many standard negotiations on my checklist I'd torture Shane with before letting him down easy. The problem wasn't his inexperience, that Sin had sent him in unannounced as a potential student, or that he fell short of being a hot as fuck silver fox in a ridiculous kimono with an attitude problem that bordered on psychopathy.

Okay, maybe that last bit is part *of the problem.*

In the end, I would have respected every hard limit Shane gave me and enjoyed making him explode all over the rubber sheets while he sobbed through his mild spanking.

But *I* would have left unsatisfied. If tonight had accomplished anything—besides demonstrating some healthy negotiations for my twin—it was to remind me that normies couldn't handle everything I wanted to give.

None of them can…

CHAPTER 16
GABRIEL

"Waiting for me under the stars, angel?"

Shit.

I slammed the door shut on my mind-bond with Dre before hastily stubbing out my blunt and toeing it over the edge of the terrace to the street below.

Turning, I found Theo casually leaning against the open doorway, looking like sin incarnate. He was dressed in a suit similar to what he'd worn to The Refinery, only this time, it was in a strangely tame charcoal gray. The jacket was off and slung over his forearm, with his crisp white dress shirt rolled up to his elbows—allowing his pricey watch to catch the moonlight.

And for my dick to catch a boner.

I didn't know *who* he'd been with, but it was safe to assume they'd left the meeting knowing exactly who was in charge.

Dude looks intimidating as fuck right now.

And it's so fucking hot.

"You're back early!" I blurted out before realizing Theo had never specified *when* he'd be returning.

Because why would he need to?

It's not like we're a couple…

As much as I didn't want to admit it, this obsessive uncertainty probably explained *why* I'd chosen to sit out here.

Hoping for this exact scenario…

But with more porn music playing in the background.

"I hope it's okay that I was hanging out on the terrace," I awkwardly added, because I was kind of high, and already half-chubbed thinking about kink negotiations and chance encounters.

Because why not make things weirder?

"It would have been better if you were in my hot tub," Theo replied. His gaze was locked on me with an intensity that would have been alarming if I wasn't secretly way into it. *"Hanging out.* Naked."

Not helping!

With a smirk, he tossed his suit jacket on a nearby rattan sun lounger, clearly amused that I was blushing like a goddamn schoolgirl.

Okay, this is ridiculous.

"I dunno, dude." I scowled, annoyed that he had me so twisted—that my chest was tight with what could only be described as *longing*. "It would be kind of weird if I just rubbed my nutsack all over your hot tub while you weren't home, don't you thi—"

My words broke off as he stalked closer. "I disagree," he murmured, lowering his mouth until his lips were only centimeters away from mine. "Especially as I've already seen you naked… already tasted you…"

Is he going to kiss me?

Fuck, I hope so…

Ugh, I'm such a slut for this man.

As if to illustrate my point, I parted my lips in a blatant invitation for him to shove his tongue—*or whatever that was*—down my throat again. Before we made contact, Theo abruptly changed his trajectory, dragging his nose along the column of my neck instead, inhaling deeply. Making me shudder.

Making me *whimper.*

Jeeeesussss…

"What's the matter, angel?" He chuckled, his breath tickling my skin in the cool night air. "Too impatient to let me breathe you in first? I promise, we have plenty of time to play—especially with Andre gone…"

How does he know Dre isn't here?

And why would it matter…?

Ohhh.

In my horny haze, I'd forgotten all about how my twin was playing the role of the possessive protector.

Although I don't think he's playing.

I'm one to talk…

Me playing the role of a desperate ho begging to be fucked by *whatever* this man was packing—no matter how conscious I was or how dangerous he was—had already dangerously drifted from acting into reality. I *needed* Theo's skin on mine—

needed him stuffed inside every hole I offered. I needed to be so full of him we became one singular being.

One collective tangle of star stuff…

I *knew* this was delulu—that if Dre was in my head right now, he'd already be in an Uber, on his way here to pack our bags and get me the hell away from whatever was scrambling my brain. But I'd shut him out before he could realize Theo had returned, and assumed he was busy at the club anyway, so this porn scenario was just for me.

Just me, myself, and my menty b.

To add to the surreal vibe, my body was *buzzing* again—alive with millions of bees trying to fly up my throat and out into the starry night. I was drinking in Theo's proximity like a dying man while also being hyper-aware of my rock-hard dick obscenely tenting my gray sweatpants.

And how I wasn't wearing anything underneath. Again, probably by subconscious design.

I'm such a fucking slut.

"Your scent…" Theo hissed against my neck—almost angrily. "You smell like… like *mine.*"

Yours…

The thought of belonging to this man had me groaning pathetically, and I couldn't help lowering my face to his throat, breathing him in as well. Theo smelled like the air during a thunderstorm—a crisp, pungent aroma charged with electricity and an unexpected hint of sweetness.

I need…

"I need…" I gasped, wishing I didn't have to ask but understanding why I did.

Because negotiations are important for setting limits.

Because Dre would kick my ass if I got myself killed over some dick.

"Tell me," Theo growled with his lips—*finally*—on mine. "I want to hear you beg for it."

Because negotiations can be sexy as fuck.

He roughly pulled me closer, chuckling smugly as my dick jabbed against his muscular thigh through my sweats, leaving no doubt what effect he was having on me.

We out here at this point.

"Please," I choked out, feeling the pressure in my chest lessen at his closeness—allowing my body to go limp in his hold. "Make me your toy."

Make me.

"So perfect," Theo praised, understanding exactly what I needed as he shoved me to my knees and reached for his belt. "The perfect toy for me to play with."

Overcome by my dream scenario coming true, I watched in a daze as this ridiculously attractive man pulled down the zipper of his dress pants with a mouthwatering purr.

Make me yours…

But the sound of footsteps approaching made both of us freeze.

"So *this* is why you haven't returned my calls?" a ragged voice sobbed, and I turned my head to find a well-dressed, but disheveled, woman standing just inside the doorway leading back inside.

Whut?

She was pointing a compact Glock at Theo with an anguished expression on her mascara-streaked face. "Because you've been *cheating on me* with some… some *RENT BOY?"*

Fuck.

"Marguerite," Theo cooed, zipping himself up and gracefully moving so his body was between me and the armed intruder. "I was wondering why I hadn't seen you at any of my parties recen—"

"BECAUSE YOU FUCKED ME THEN NEVER SPOKE TO ME AGAIN!" she shrieked, and I immediately felt a change in the air.

I might not have noticed if my supe senses hadn't been cranked way up, but I registered Theo as *moving*—even though he appeared to be standing still. It was the glint of *something* traveling in the space between him and the unhinged woman. Something that shouldn't exist.

What the hell was *that?*

"Is it not universally understood that my parties are hedonistic affairs with no strings attached? Or that everyone who attends signs a waiver acknowledging as much?" Theo's voice had taken on a threateningly frigid tone that had my dick rallying all over again. "So, how did you get the mistaken impression that our *casual fuck* was anything more than that?"

Burn.

"It was *implied!"* Marguerite croaked, gripping her gun with both hands in a failed attempt to hold it steady. "You s-said you were looking for a muse…"

"I was." Theo turned the full weight of his stare to where I was still kneeling for him. "But the search may be over. *Twice* over."

Well, shit.

This was not at all what Wolfy had sent me here for, *or* what Dre had coaxed me into accomplishing, but I no longer cared. When Theo looked at me like this—like I was every star in the universe shining just for him—I felt simultaneously weak and invincible.

Like I could take on anyone.

Starting with anyone who thinks they'll come between us.

A broken sob brought my attention back to the unfortunate normie doing exactly that, and my vision went red. I wasn't worried about either of us being shot. A tiny little Glock wouldn't do shit against a supe, and I assumed the same was true for whatever Theo was.

But I still did *not* like this bitch pointing a gun at *my man.*

She's already dead.

"What's happening…?" Marguerite's rage turned to confusion as her arms uncontrollably shook and blood began pouring out of her nose.

I smirked.

Oops.

That mysterious glint flashed in the air again, and I could only gape as she inexplicably rotated her wrists until the gun was pointed at her own face.

Wait.

I'm *not making her do tha*—

I flinched as the trigger was pulled, spraying a combination of blood, brains, and skull fragments all over Theo's expensive wooden floor.

Dang.

"Well, *that* was most unpleasant." Theo wrinkled his nose at the mess before gazing down at me again with unmistakable heat. "I truly hope this clearly unstable woman's inevitable end hasn't ruined the mood… What do you say, angel? Do you still want to play?"

I stared up at him in astonishment. This unknown creature— our mark—had just 1000 percent made a random normie unalive herself, without appearing to have touched her at all.

Yet, here he was, still casually hoping to facefuck me.

AND I AM HERE FOR IT!

"I don't see a problem," I breathlessly replied, reaching for the zipper of Theo's pants with shaking hands. "And I still want—"

My words were punched from my lungs as my back was abruptly slammed against the ornate railing.

"You're taking this gruesome death rather well," Theo hissed, burying his hands in my hair and yanking my head back to look up at him. "Most *humans* would be terrified."

My heart was racing, my dick was throbbing, and the object of my obsession was looming over me with murder in his eyes.

Murder aimed at *me.*

Shit.

CHAPTER 17
GABRIEL

What if he attacks me?

Will I be able to finish the job?

"She was going to... hurt you..." I swallowed thickly, keeping my gaze locked on Theo's so he could *see* the sincerity of my words. "That bitch got what she deserved."

Even if I wish I'd been the one to kill her...

It was official. My method acting had turned into my full-blown identity. I was completely gone for this eccentric psychopath, and despite the 'rules' hammered into my head since birth, I would kill countless normies—countless *supes* —if it meant protecting him.

I am a murderous slut for this man.

Even if he might want to murder me...

Theo's gaze softened and sharpened all at once. "What are you made of, angel?" he murmured, releasing my hair to glide his fingertips along my jawline before brushing his thumb over my lips. "What *are* you?"

There was only one answer to that question. "I could be yours," I whispered, knowing Wolfy was going to kill me for saying that—if Dre didn't beat him to it. "Please…"

Please, let me be yours.

"How could I say no to such a perfect creature?" he sighed as he unzipped his pants. "Such a perfect little cockslut."

That last part was growled so menacingly, my hair stood on end, but I still melted under the heady mix of praise and degradation.

And the sight of his massive cock.

I'd expected something unusual to get pulled out of his pants, but besides the size—which was proportionate to his enormous frame—it looked like your average dick.

Why the hell is that disappointing me?

I mean… I'm not that *disappointed.*

Theo smirked at my blatant thirst before slipping his thumb into my mouth and prying open my jaw. He placed the fat head of his cock on my tongue, but instead of immediately sliding down my throat, he paused to observe me. Coolly.

"No one's ever been *mine* before—and some have died trying." He glanced offhandedly at the corpse bleeding all over his floor. "But I'm suddenly… *intrigued* by the idea. Shall we explore this together?"

Fuck. Yes.

I nodded enthusiastically, then moaned as Theo fed me his massive cock, inch by glorious inch. He bottomed out and pressed his groin against my face—holding me captive against the railing with my jaw straining, my airways cut off, and tears streaming down my cheeks.

But fuck, I've never been happier.

"Just so you know, being *mine* means you will be my muse *and* my possession," he absently spoke as his scent washed over me—adding to my daze. "And any… misplaced loyalties you arrived here with will need to be set aside for the only master you'll obey from now on." His gaze bore into mine and my vision grew spotty around the edges. "Me."

"Yes," I gasped when he finally withdrew. Wiping a hand over my spit-covered chin while I caught my breath, I breathlessly added, "I'll do anything you say."

Just let me worship you.

I was no longer in control over the shit coming out of my mouth or the unhinged direction of my thoughts. If accepting communion at Theo's altar was my only purpose in life from here on out, then I would die a happy man.

Hopefully, not anytime soon.

"My angel." Theo sighed contentedly before abruptly slamming into my mouth again and starting up a punishing rhythm. "You were made to be mine. Both of you were…"

Made to be yours.

Both of us…

Despite knowing he was going to be *pissed* about how far off script I'd gone, my blissed-out thoughts drifted to my other half.

I wish Dre was here…

It was thanks to him I was finally allowing myself to experience what I'd craved for so long. And if Theo wanted us both, our bond was in no danger of breaking.

We could have it all.

Without losing anything.

I reopened my mind to Dre, consequences be damned. Blatant *shock* immediately shot through our bond in response—so much that if my mouth hadn't been stuffed full of cock, I might have laughed—but I *wanted* him to see how happy I was.

How grateful.

"Shall I fill your throat or cover your face, angel?" Theo asked as he withdrew once again and took himself in hand. "How shall I mark you as mine?"

I almost wept hearing him say the words I'd been hoping for, even if Dre went eerily still on the other end. "Both," I rasped. "I want you everywhere. Fill me completely. Make me yours."

Make both of us yours.

Dre growled, and Theo smirked. "That's the plan," my dream man breezily replied, hovering his dick over my tongue and beginning to stroke. "Palms on your thighs, angel. I bet you could come without even touching that perfect cock, hmm?"

I hummed in agreement, letting my eyes flutter closed as Theo took over. His dizzying proximity, the salty, sweet taste of his precum, and knowing I was officially being *claimed,* all converged to drag me toward oblivion.

I want to exist in this space all the time…

It didn't take long for Theo to release a guttural groan, pulling back so his load coated my tongue, cheeks, and chin before obscenely dripping down my neck. I moaned at the flavor—at the degradation of it all—before opening my eyes so I could meet his smoldering gaze with a single word on my cum-covered lips.

"Yours."

The look on Theo's face was an intoxicating mix of awe and ownership, and I preened under the attention. I was so high from the experience that it took me a good minute to realize Dre had shut the door to our connection at some point.

Shut and locked it tight.

I'm in so much trouble.

Better make it count!

Scrambling to stand, I pulled my tee over my head before kicking off my sneaks and shoving my sweatpants down my legs. I held back my super speed, but was still naked in record time, shuddering in anticipation.

"Do you want me to taste you again, angel?" Theo's gaze dropped to my dick before returning to my face. "Or is there something else you had in mind?"

Tell him what you want, Gabe.

Negotiations are important.

I blew out a slow, shaky breath, but forced myself to maintain eye contact. "I want you to fuck me. Just prep me first with your…"

Thanks to Dre being weirdly tight-lipped about the whole thing, I still didn't know *what* I was dealing with here. But my request was less about pain management and more about wanting to experience *whatever* Theo had stuffed inside me again.

Whatever had made me whole.

Because it felt like home.

Theo cocked an eyebrow in challenge. "With my *fingers,* you mean?"

I shook my head, knowing I was playing with fire but wanting *all* of him—not just the parts fit for normies. "No. I mean, whatever you... really are. I-I know you're a... supe or something, and I promise, I won't tell anyone. I just need to feel you again..."

Need to feel this.

Theo's lips twisted in amusement as he approached. "You believe I'm a supe, hmm? What does that make *you?* A cape chaser?"

Bruh.

"Maybe." I laughed self-deprecatingly and rubbed the back of my neck, suddenly feeling naked as fuck. "I've never been called that before—"

Theo hummed as he crowded me, lighting up every nerve ending where his suit roughly rubbed against my bare skin.

I wonder if I have a suit fetish?

Fuck, I am not *gonna psychoanalyze that one...*

"If you tell anyone what you *think* I am, I'll have to kill you," he murmured, capturing my lips with his. "I hope that's all right."

"Yes," I sighed—because I would rather die from this than die without ever having experienced it.

Bye, self-preservation!

Being threatened by Theo Coatl while enveloped in his man musk with his tongue invading my mouth was worth risking everything. It was enough to make my dick jump where it was trapped between us, leaving no doubt about how gone I was.

He chuckled at my reaction, backing up a step to look me over. "Very well. Would you prefer your room, or the one off my studio? Or my bed, perhaps?"

The idea of Theo drilling me into *his* infamous mattress was tempting, but I already knew exactly what I wanted.

It's a need, not a want.

"Right here," I rasped, lowering myself to the terrace floor before laying back and planting my feet wide. "Under the stars."

The predatory gleam in Theo's expression was momentarily replaced by something that looked suspiciously like vulnerability. Just as quickly, it vanished, and he began unbuttoning his dress shirt—his signature smug smile firmly back in place.

This is affecting him just as much as me…

"How romantic," he cooed, although the bite in his tone was noticeably absent. "I can't wait for my long-suffering neighbors to hear the moment I take your virginity."

Take everything.

My body felt like it was *vibrating* again. I needed this man to fill me up immediately, even if I still wasn't sure *what* he'd be using to do so.

Show me what you are.

"You remember your safe word?" he asked as he cast aside his dress shirt and undershirt—exposing his broad chest and beefy abs to my thirsty view.

"Shock," I whispered, swallowing hard as I tentatively invited Dre back in, only to be stubbornly ignored.

"Please don't shut me out."

"I expect you to use it if you need it," Theo growled, joining me on the ground and roughly spreading me wider. "Otherwise, I'll continue to assume I have free rein to use your body, however I please."

"You do," I croaked as a spurt of precum dribbled onto my stomach. The fact Theo had left his pants *on* to fuck me was making it hard to concentrate, and I had to grip the head of my dick to stop myself from exploding.

"Uh, uh, uh," he tutted, batting my hands away. "Hands off that gorgeous cock. It belongs to me now, as does every one of your orgasms."

I huffed even as I obediently placed my arms above my head. "Dude, I can't promise I'll last long, but my refractory time is unmatched."

Supe perks.

"Mine too!" Theo's grin turned wolfish before his expression hardened. "How coincidental... But you *will* wait until I've filled you with my cum—multiple times—before you find release."

I opened my mouth to retort when I suddenly felt something wrap around my frenulum—similar to whatever had held me down in the studio bed—and *squeeze.* Ignoring my squeak of surprise, Theo smoothly entered me with another sinuous appendage, and I quickly realized this was probably the same feature he'd used to pull the trigger on his stalker's gun tonight.

Oh, my god…

WHY IS THIS SO HOT?!

I was *desperate* to see—as if a visual on *him* would somehow validate my entire existence—but Theo roughly gripped my chin and held my head in place.

"Eyes up here, angel," he chuckled darkly, hovering his face over mine. "I would hate to ruin the mystery."

"Fuck," I choked out as he rubbed against my prostate—ruthlessly stretching me while I writhed. "I just… I need…"

Please, please, please.

"Say it," he hissed, shifting his hand so his fingers tightened on the sides of my neck.

"Please, fuck me," I rasped, hoping he was about to cut off my air again. "Fill me up like the cockslut I am. Make me yours. Please. I *need* you inside me, before I…"

Before I fucking die.

"As you wish." Theo smiled in a way that had me shivering before removing his *whatevers* from my ass and notching his miraculously lubed-up cock against my opening. "I would love nothing more than to be inside you—taking control of every inch. Owning you."

"Yes!" I cried out as he slammed home. "Fucking *own* me! I'm yours…"

"Say that again," he growled, lowering his lips to mine so our breath became one. "Don't stop saying it until I'm done with you."

I obeyed, chanting *"yours, yours, yours"* with every thrust. My back arched as he pummeled into me, and I struggled in his hold.

Even though I never want him to let me go.

The same mysterious appendages that were alternating between stroking my cock and squeezing the life out of it were also pinning my arms in place. Combined with the scent of blood in the air, I was *feral* for it. Theo was owning me completely, using me like a fucktoy as he emptied into my ass so many times I lost count.

More, more, more.

I was delirious, my gaze on the night sky as my mouth fell open—allowing the stars themselves to pour down my throat —awakening something inside me that had been dormant for twenty-three years.

Since time began.

"Are you ready, angel?" Theo's voice drifted into my limited consciousness from… somewhere.

For some reason, I couldn't *see* him anymore, even as his cock continued to lazily pump—ensuring everything he'd unloaded stayed locked inside.

"Yes," I whispered. My tears were making the stars go blurry, but they surrounded me—holding me tightly in their oddly comforting embrace. "I'm ready to go home…"

I *felt* Theo hesitate, but only for a moment. His vine-like grip on my dick twisted, flicking my oversensitive glans and causing my vision to whiteout as an orgasm rocketed through my entire system.

"Fииииии…" I sobbed around *whatever* was still lodged in my throat, while a bucket load of cum coated my chest and abs. Theo fucked me through it, only stopping his movements after every drop had been wrung out of me.

I'm going to sleep for days.

My eyelids drifted closed as he withdrew, and I was vaguely aware of how *empty* I felt.

How alone.

"Theo?" I whimpered pathetically, blindly reaching for him.

I heard him murmur something in reply the same moment I felt a warm cloth being wiped over me.

No.

That's his tongue.

Jesus Christ, I can't go another round…

Luckily, both my dick *and* this mysterious sex creature understood playtime was over for the night. And even though I wasn't entirely sure my corpse wouldn't be joining the one lying only a few feet away, I somehow felt as *safe* as I'd ever been.

As safe as Dre makes me feel…

My thoughts were unsurprisingly on my twin as wrecked exhaustion claimed me, and the last thing I heard before I drifted off was Theo confirming what I already knew.

"Mine."

Yours.

CHAPTER 18
ANDRE

I hadn't been back to the Teal Coast neighborhood in two days, and I was having some seriously annoying feels about it.

At first, I'd stayed away because the idea of setting foot inside Theo's mansion made my skin crawl. But the longer I sat with that, the more I questioned whether *not* returning was to blame for my unease.

*This was **not** how this shit was supposed to go down…*

Of course, my absence hadn't gone unnoticed. To avoid someone coming after me like the Repo Man, I'd sent both Gabe and Wolfy one-word replies to their initial texts, but only our clan leader remained satisfied by that proof of life.

As if on cue, my phone buzzed.

Brain Drain: *Me again [waving hand emoji]*

Case in point.

Brain Drain: *Why haven't you come home?*

I scoffed, not least of all because Gabe was now apparently referring to Theo's maximalist hellscape as 'home.'

He's probably lounging around in his very own kimono by this point.

My jumbled emotions had settled down enough for me to realize I was triggered by more than just my twin getting comfortable in our new digs.

Brain Drain: *Are you mad because Theo and I are fucking now?*

There it is.

Asshole.

That text almost had me re-opening our mind-bond just so I could tell Gabe what a douchebag he was. But that was exactly what he wanted, and if anyone was well-versed in how to handle bratty behavior, it was me.

Ignore, ignore, ignore.

"Don't tell me that's *Shane* who's texting you?" Sinistre's soft but commanding voice had me lowering my phone before I did something stupid—like reply. "I was certain you'd either scared him straight or frightened him away from the scene for good."

My eyes narrowed. "You know, Sin. The only reason I haven't mentioned that stunt you pulled at the club the other night is because you and Fay have always been nice enough to let me crash here."

Like two angels in my time of need.

Theo calls Gabe his angel…

Sin chuckled in such an evil way, there was no hope of me continuing to play mad. "Oh, but the threat of your famous death stare was worth it to see that *tourist* flee from the room like you were coming after him with a bullwhip."

I scoffed. "There's no bullwhip in that room. Unfortunately."

Sin hummed thoughtfully as they sat beside me on the crushed velvet sofa that matched their Hollywood Regency decor. "And yet, I've never seen you use a bullwhip on a sub —or any tools that could leave lasting damage if handled incorrectly… Why is that?"

My jaw grew tight as I gritted my teeth. "Because bullwhips aren't my thing."

"I find it hard to believe *you* don't want to whip someone until they're covered in a gorgeous visual reminder of the pain you gave them." Sin's tone had gone low and sultry— lulling me into hanging on every word. "Like a *gift.*"

"Careful, Sin," I growled, hating how much I sounded like Wolfy, but *needing* them to stop calling me out so accurately.

Even though it feels good to be seen.

True to form, the Madam knew exactly what I *actually* needed. "Is it because a good crack from a bullwhip could break the skin—making them *bleed?* Are you afraid that might happen… or worried that it won't?"

Fuck.

My phone buzzed again as Gabe simultaneously tapped on my mental walls.

So, of course, I looked.

Brain Drain: *I can feel how upset you are right now. Let me in, dude.*

Brain Drain: *Please…*

With a slow exhale, I set down my phone once again and secured another lock on my brain blockade.

Imma let that boy cook.

To be honest, our separation was killing me. This was the longest I'd gone without having my twin in my sight or my head, but I needed to work through my shit first.

If Gabe was in danger, he'd tell me.

Right?

"Trouble with a submissive?" Sin gestured toward my phone.

I wanted to be annoyed by their prying, but Sinistre was the closest thing I had to a friend outside of my family. The urge to tell them *everything* was strong, but there were rules— harsh divides between supes and normies—to protect my kind from being doxed.

Although they used to say the same thing about heroes and villains…

"Yes, but not *my* submissive," I huffed, flipping over my phone again just to see Gabe's name on the screen. "My brother's going through a sub-awakening and I'm—"

Oh, no…

"You're helping guide him?" Fay's excited voice chimed in from where she'd miraculously appeared in the doorway— just in time for tea. "Seeeeee! We always knew you were mentor material."

Ugh.

"He's my *brother,"* I muttered, even as I made room for Fay to squeeze onto the couch beside me, secretly loving being surrounded by so much annoying support. "What was I supposed to do—just let him fumble his way through this on his own?"

Besides, he's already found someone to dom him.

Someone I'd kill to dom…

"Your *identical twin,* you mean? Funny how you failed to tell us about this valuable asset of yours," Fay scolded, although there was no heat in her words. "As if The Refinery couldn't use two hotties like you to heat up our demos—and otherwise."

"Cupcake…" Sin warned, their tone loving but firm. "Not all twins exist to fulfill taboo romance dreams."

Fay huffed. "It would be easy money, is all I'm saying."

I laughed, knowing she was legitimately thinking about their business since she was completely uninterested in men. "Sorry to disappoint you, Fay. Gabe and I are close, but not *that* close, so… keep dreaming."

"Make both of us yours."

I scowled at the memory of Gabe's dick-drunk thoughts. Besides being *our mark,* Theo had made it clear he only wanted my twin, so the idea of us somehow *sharing* the guy was ridiculous.

Even if I'd totally be game.

Sin's hand on my forearm brought me back to the present. "We can find you the perfect sub… a masochist who will gladly take everything you can give—"

"No," I interrupted, my shoulders slumping as I hung my head. "You can't."

Talk about a dream…

They were silent for a good minute, and I wondered if the famously patient Madam Sinistre would finally tell me to go fuck myself.

"Andre." My gaze snapped to Sin's face at the commanding tone. "From the moment you walked into my club—on your eighteenth birthday—I knew you were made for this. Never mind how your naturally dominant qualities leave every unattached submissive in the room panting like a dog. You've also *done the work to do this right.* I have no doubt that whoever ends up being yours will be treated well. So why are you so afraid?"

"I'm not," I growled, feeling my powers roiling beneath the surface, ready to lash out at the perceived threat.

Causing Gabe's powers to answer mine in alarm.

Just tell him you're fine.

I'm not fine, though…

"You don't trust *yourself!*" Sin barked, and I realized I'd never heard them raise their voice before. "And you need to tell me why this instant so we can *help* you. As your *friends.*"

Goddamn tears were stinging my eyelids, but I stubbornly held Sin's angry gaze. As if realizing her softer energy was needed, Fay gently laid a hand on my opposite shoulder—grounding me while still allowing this standoff to play out.

Jesus… It's like facing off against another supe!

Fuck it.

I'll tell them everything I can.

"I *don't* trust myself," I confirmed, feeling my heart rate increase the same way it might have before battles I'd never been allowed to fight. "And there are *reasons* for that. Things I'm not allowed to tell you. I'm not… I'm not a *normal human,* Sin. Do you understand what I'm saying? That *what* I am is… dangerous?"

Sin's eyes widened as my words landed. They hesitantly removed their hand from my forearm, making my chest tighten.

Now they're as afraid of me as I am.

I closed my eyes but reopened them a moment later as Sin's smaller hand tucked into mine and squeezed.

"Understood. Thank you for telling me… for telling us." Sin gestured to Fay with their free hand. "And don't worry—club rules apply. What happens here, stays here, and as there are no policies stating supes aren't allowed at The Refinery—"

"There should be, though," I huffed, gratefully squeezing their hand in return. "If I'm not careful, I could *kill* someone, and I… I wouldn't even have to touch them to do that."

"I see," Sin murmured thoughtfully, quickly glancing at Fay before returning their full attention to me. "And therefore, you don't feel like it's possible to find someone who can match you. Is that it?"

Oh, I've found them.

"It's complicated…" I murmured as my gaze drifted to my phone again, wondering if Theo knew Gabe was texting me. "There's so much about my world that makes something like *this* messy as fuck."

Not least of all that who I want is the enemy.

I didn't bother trying to elaborate, as it was nearly impossible for normies to understand the larger picture. Until recently, 'heroes' were completely off-limits, but my fellow villains weren't much better. *Every supe* was considered a threat to one's clan until proven otherwise, so unless an alliance was already established—or an arranged marriage set in motion—you had to be extra careful about who you let into your bed.

It's why so many of us moonlight as normies on the Bangers app.

Or join kink clubs.

Or just wait until our inventus drops into our lap…

My thoughts must have drifted to my eldest brother a little too hard, as my phone chimed with the unmistakable sound of the Wolfy bat signal.

Sigh.

Darth Handsy: *Luca is looking forward to seeing you at dinner tonight. I assume you'll have found your way back to Theo Coatl's by the time we arrive.*

Assholery just runs in the family.

My self-pity shifted to anger in a heartbeat. The lack of anything resembling a question or concern in Wolfy's text tracked, especially since he and Gabe had most likely been in contact since my disappearance. Hell, they'd probably *agreed* Luca was the perfect bargaining chip to get me to slink back to Theo's.

Assholes, all of them.

Except Luca.

With a grumble, I had to admit their leverage was solid. Seeing my mentor was a huge draw, not least of all because it provided me with the perfect excuse to show up while still maintaining a shred of dignity.

And I'll just deal with the Gabe and Theo situation after.

After I've had a few drinks.

"You know… it's weirdly *comforting* to know supes are also fumbling their way through life," Sin absently mused, and I tensed.

Oh, fuck.

I just showed weakness.

But… I didn't die.

My brain was still whirring with this unexpected intel when the Madam peered past my shoulder with an amused expression. "Although I should warn you, *this* revelation far exceeds the twin one—at least in the eyes of a certain cape chaser in our midst…"

I turned to find Fay staring at me with eyes so big that she looked like a goddamn anime character.

"You're never getting rid of us now," the little cupcake whispered, almost reverently, before shaking herself out of her stupor. "But don't worry, Dre. Your secret is safe with us. And this changes nothing about our friendship… besides the millions of questions I'm going to have for you!"

My phone chimed again, reminding me I hadn't replied to Wolfy's text.

And I won't be, thank you very much.

Even if I have no choice but to obey.

I sighed and scrubbed a hand down my face, feeling simultaneously lighter and heavier. "Well, I appreciate that—for real. And I'll answer anything I *can*, but right now, I need to get ready for a family thing."

Fay noticeably perked up, making Sin and me laugh.

"Sorry to disappoint you, Fay, but it's just dinner. Supes also do boring everyday things on top of epic battles." I chuckled as she pouted—clearly disappointed by the lack of violence and gore in my immediate future.

Although, this dinner could go either way...

CHAPTER 19
ANDRE

Sharing a bedroom with Gabe meant both of us were skilled at finding somewhere else to be when the other brought home a fuckboy. He usually headed to the Suarez family compound outside the city, but I would've rather slept on a park bench.

Of course, Sinistre would never allow that.

I'd crashed at Sin and Fay's so many times over the years that the closet in their extra bedroom was well-stocked with my clothing. Besides being convenient for my current circumstance, it had worked out well on the countless nights I hadn't felt like going home after the club.

Gabe called Theo's house our 'home'…

That's gonna go over well with Wolfy.

I grimaced. In the end, it had been *my* idea for Gabe to distract Theo in this way, so I needed to at least *appear* to stand by the plan we'd set in motion.

Even if I am weirdly bunched up over who my twin is fucking.

Without me…

Fuck.

I was so distracted by the direction of my thoughts that I ended up grabbing the same white suit I'd worn to Wolfy and Simon's wedding. The angelic look would be a ridiculous choice for tonight—not least of all because Theo had offhand-edly called me 'demon.'

But why not add more chaos to this clusterfuck?

Deciding to go all in with the black sheep of the family vibes, I let Fay apply some artful black eyeliner before smudging it into slept-in chic. My favorite black boots completed the look, and I couldn't help thinking how pretty Theo would look spit-shining them for me.

I really need to get laid.

Needing to soak up some calm before the storm, I rolled down the window on my Uber ride over—allowing the ocean breezes and neon lights of Big City to wash over me like a baptism.

This *is home.*

This city.

And Gabe.

So why do I still feel like something's missing?

Pausing outside Theo's front door, I took a deep breath before slowly blowing it out—quieting my mind in the way our mentor had taught us to.

I can do this.

"Salü!" Luca's achingly familiar voice had me spinning around like an excited puppy.

"Hey, *Sensei!"* I replied, unable to stop the wide grin stretching across my face as he approached.

Despite it being *July*, dude was wearing a thin cable-knit sweater—although his classic Scandinavian looks made it casually cool instead of preppy.

We get enough preppiness in this family with Butch and his polo shirts.

Shudder.

"My *schätzli.*" He laughed, drawing me into a hug that made me feel all warm and fuzzy and shit. "I've missed your face."

"You literally *just* saw Gabe and me after graduation," I teased. "For the big, fancy grand opening of the Berlin gallery, remember?"

The gallery Wolfy bought us.

Which was probably more a gift for Gabe than me.

Realizing I needed to acknowledge the man lurking next to Luca like an ominous shadow, I nodded at my eldest brother.

The leader of the formidable Suarez clan.

The infamous Hand of Death.

"Good evening, Dre." Wolfy coolly looked me over, clasping his gloved hands in front of him in the way that made Simon inexplicably swoon.

They are so weird.

"Wolfy," I replied, equally cold. "Come to see if we're behaving?"

He sighed and dragged his gaze over the building in front of us—and I was secretly pleased to see he seemed as disgusted by the architecture as I'd been.

The man does have good design sense, I'll give him that.

"Well, we already know *you're* not," he murmured before snapping his focus to me again. "Is there a reason you left your brother alone on the job for days?"

"There is," I replied, my lip curling in a snarl. "But it's not really any of your business, so—"

"Everything you do is my business!" Wolfy hissed, moving into my personal space so fast it took all my willpower not to stumble backward instinctively.

I stood my ground, despite knowing a centimeter was the only thing separating me from death.

What a fucking asshole.

"Wolfgang," Luca warned, and my fury ignited as my brother showed *him* respect by standing down. "Now is not the time."

"Very well," Wolfy retreated half an inch and smoothed his hands down the front of his customary all-black suit. "Although we *will* be continuing this conversation, Dre. It sounds like you need a reminder of your place in this family."

At the bottom.

I didn't know what bothered me more—that Wolfy didn't see me as enough of a threat to put me in my place now, or that he still wouldn't hesitate to kill me in the future if he thought I was a danger to the clan.

To him, specifically.

"Fine," I gritted out, suddenly eager to step inside the very place I'd been avoiding like the plague. "Let's get this over with…"

My words trailed off as I found the door *locked* for the first time since Gabe and I had arrived.

What the…

"Oh, hello, demon! I forgot to tell you I had new locks installed!" Theo's chipper voice called down from the fourth floor terrace, sending my already dark mood into pitch-black territory. "Well, I *would* have told you if you hadn't been playing hide-and-seek the past few days. Just use the app on your phone to get in. See you at the top!"

There better be some hard liquor waiting for me up there.

"You let him install apps on your phones?" Wolfy hiss-whispered as I led them into the garish entryway. "He could be *tracking* you through it. What if you'd come to the compound…?"

Highly unlikely.

To my petty satisfaction, the decor immediately caused Wolfy to lose his train of thought. This allowed me to focus on mentally berating myself for putting the entire clan at risk.

"That is a problem Xander could easily rectify," Luca smoothly intervened as the elevator doors closed and we ascended to hell. "You will contact your brother tomorrow to look at your phones, yes?"

It took me a moment to realize Luca was addressing *me*—that he was allowing me to take responsibility for my mistake and fix it.

Thank you, Sensei.

"Yes." I smiled at Luca before returning my gaze to the glowing numbers—wondering why my body felt like it was vibrating the closer we got to the top. "I'll take care of it."

Wolfy scoffed as the elevator slowed. "Why does Luca get an answer like that, yet you give me a hard time?"

I smirked. "Because he's not an asshole."

My brother chuckled, which relieved *some* of the tension, but before he could reply, the doors opened, revealing…

A crime scene?

"What the *fuck* is this?!" I demanded, striding across the space for a closer look at the carnage. "Is that… *blood?*"

Gabe was at my side in an instant, and any leftover tension I was carrying immediately evaporated. "Yeah, well, if you'd gotten back to me, I could have *told* you we'd had an… incident with an intruder. That's why there's a lock on the front door now…"

Dumbfounded, I could only stare at the crusted bloodstain darkening a corner of one of Theo's Persian rugs. The body was gone, and the area—including the chalk outline on the expensive wood floor—had been neatly roped off by crime scene tape.

Like a velvet rope at an art exhibit…

"Yes, it was a truly unfortunate incident." Theo appeared in the terrace doorway, and I was struck with déjà vu from the first time I laid eyes on him.

The moment he became the bane of my existence.

While Theo wasn't wearing a signature kimono—*thank Christ* —his ridiculous fashion sense was still shining through. Billowy peach-colored linen pants were belted high on his waist, paired with a chain-print Versace blouse. This was unbuttoned completely—no doubt to reveal his pristine A-shirt and tasteful chest hair beneath.

It's giving Robin Williams in the Birdcage.

Wolfy was dead silent—his gaze flickering between the decor, the bloodstain, and Theo's outfit as if deciding which shock to his system to address first.

Felt.

In the end, he chose the easiest one to deal with. "You… *killed* an intruder?"

It *looked* like he was addressing Theo, but I knew what he was *really* asking—and who.

He wants to know if Gabe blew up our spot by revealing his powers.

Theo pressed his hand to his chest and glided into the room. "Me? Oh, no, no, no. This highly disturbed individual— lovesick stalker, if you will—tragically took her own life after discovering me with what appeared to be her replacement."

Gabe looked like he wanted to melt into the floor as Theo pulled him close, leaving no question why his supposed stalker would make that assumption.

"B-but why not have Lupe clean this shit up?" I interrupted, desperate to redirect Wolfy's death glare away from my twin. "And where's the fucking body?"

WHAT THE FUCK HAPPENED HERE?!

Theo gave me an odd look. "The police came and did their…" —he fluttered his hand toward the scene of the crime—"thing and then took the body away for the medical examiner. That's what one does when there's a death, correct?"

Wolfy, Luca, and I simply stared back at him. That was not what *our* family did. Not at all.

Oh, fuck.

That means Gabe was probably questioned by the cops.

Back when Biggs Enterprises was running the city, the higher-ups in the police force had access to every supe who'd been registered with the United Super Nations. Therefore, it was universally understood, if you had powers, you didn't want to end up anywhere *near* any crime scene.

Especially one involving a normie.

> *"What did you* do, *Gabe?!"*

My twin visibly flinched at hearing my voice in his head for the first time in days, but his outward attention was wisely fixed on Wolfy.

Like a man staring down the firing squad.

"If the police have already been here, why not have this cleaned up?" Luca calmly asked—as unwavering as a light-house in the middle of this shitstorm. "Isn't that what one does when there's a... death?"

Unsurprisingly, Theo was unruffled by the piercing blue gaze of The Kinetic Assassin. "Why, I thought you'd never ask!" he exclaimed, releasing Gabe and circling the bright yellow tape until he was facing his captive audience.

Here we go.

"I was going to have it cleaned, but then realized there was a natural harmony found in the composition of the chalk in relation to the soiled rug. Add to that the effortless commentary it provides on the futility of unrequited *love*... Well, how could I *not* leave it as a decaying performance piece to be enjoyed at my next gathering? I have decided to call it..."—he spread his arms wide with a flourish, a diva fully in his element—"Obsession!"

Who needs a drink?

CHAPTER 20
THEO

"Don't you think it's time to introduce yourself to your *guests*, T?" Jensen's no-nonsense voice drifted over from the kitchen island—interrupting my manifesto.

Rude.

His gaze was lowered as he meticulously plated our dinners, but I could plainly hear the familiar exasperation in his tone.

I suppose I'll behave.

For now.

"Theo Coatl!" I beamed at our *guests* as I strolled closer with my hand outstretched for shaking. Or kissing. "Even without this being a *family* dinner, I would have known you were related to my boys. The resemblance is uncanny."

So at least that *was the truth…*

I was determined to uncover what Andre and Gabriel were hiding from me and assumed this informal meeting, disguised as a social call, would shed some light on the unusual situation.

Expose the cracks.

So I can break them further.

The strapping blond Norseman in our party gracefully stepped into my path. "Luca Stjärna. It is a pleasure to meet you, and thank you for inviting us into your home." He shook my hand briskly before gently steering me away from the other man.

The one who could only be…

"Wolfgang." The deliciously imposing 'big bro' nodded politely, although he kept his oddly gloved hands to himself. "And forgive me if I don't shake hands. Personal preference."

Fascinating.

"No offense taken," I breezily replied, before gesturing toward the dining table. "Lord knows where my hands have been."

And just because I knew it would make *everyone* uncomfortable, I gave Gabriel's perfect ass a cheeky little pat as he walked by.

To illustrate my point.

"Jesus, Theo," he muttered, although he still took his usual seat to the right of mine at the head of the table. "Could you tone it down?"

No.

I cannot.

"So, how is the internship going?" Wolfgang asked as he took a seat—his judgmental gaze sliding from Gabriel to me. "Since that is what my brothers are here for." His focus broke for a moment as Jensen brought out the plates, and I immediately realized why.

Wolfgang was intensely *aware* of the space between him and my longtime chef—carefully shifting his body so there was no chance of accidental contact. He'd also taken the seat as far away from *me* as possible, although he seemed unconcerned about the fact Luca had sat directly next to him.

Well, now I have *to touch him.*

Jensen said his goodbyes and headed out for the night, which was all the permission I needed to start misbehaving again.

"Your brothers are doing a fabulous job in all things… including as my interns," I crooned, slicing into my rare steak with enthusiasm. "Consenting adults that they are."

This earned me a snort from Andre, and Wolfgang's eyes narrowing only seemed to amuse him more. In contrast, Gabriel looked to be attempting to slide low enough in his chair to hide beneath the table.

If you end up under there, a demonstration shall commence!

"In fact!" I continued, pointing my bloodied knife at Wolfgang for emphasis. "I would like to offer these two handy helpers *permanent* job opportunities—complete with room and board, of course."

My bed is quite large.

Wolfgang began cutting into his steak with the skill of someone who could handle a blade. "It's unclear if you're asking for my permission or not…" he calmly began, making me bristle. "But that is something I would need to discuss with both Dre and Gabe privately. Even with them being *consenting adults,* I am the only parent they have at this point, and it's my responsibility to protect their best interests."

Luca turned to give Wolfgang a *look* of some kind, but unfortunately, the angle I was at hid it from view. Andre, however, had no issue voicing his reaction aloud.

"Well, *I'm* interested in the opportunity," he bluntly stated around a mouthful of Cobb salad. "I mean, what the fuck else am I doing with my future?"

My cock unexpectedly thickened at his challenging tone. In the interest of conveying a united front, I dragged Gabriel's chair a few inches closer and took a slow sip of wine before watching this exciting standoff unfold.

Let him have it, demon.

To my disappointment, it was Luca who answered. Even more disappointing was how this immediately caused Andre to relax.

Just as things were getting exciting.

Again, rude.

"I'd like to remind you that you and Gabe already own a wildly successful gallery in Berlin." Luca smiled warmly at Andre. "And according to Erich, almost all the pieces on display have been sold."

Wait… what?

"You talk to Erich?" Wolfgang looked genuinely surprised, but I didn't care *who* the fuck Erich was or that Luca sounded slightly embarrassed as he replied, "We met at the gallery opening and have kept in touch, yes."

That wasn't what caught my attention at all.

"You own a gallery where you sell your work?" I sputtered, looking between the twins in confusion. "Why the fuck wouldn't you put something like that on your resume?"

Or, more importantly, in your social media bios?

Gabriel shrugged sheepishly and shoved an enormous bite of steak into his mouth. Andre huffed—leaning back in his chair and crossing his arms over the unexpectedly *white* suit he was wearing.

This night is full *of surprises.*

"*Wolfy* owns the gallery. And our fine art portfolio wasn't relevant to the job we were applying for," he deadpanned, as if I didn't have years of experience with curating pretentious CVs.

B-but… the prestige!

Not much shocked me, but the idea of any up-and-coming artist *not* using this impressive asset to wedge their foot in the door of opportunity was astonishing.

Everybody in the art world knew that success mostly came from your connections rather than hard work. These two had the means to establish themselves as the who's who that *others* would want to know… yet they didn't seem to care.

How bizarre.

Puzzling behavior aside, I was still fixated on how this pair of stiff industrial designers were hiding unleashed fine artists beneath their all-black-clad exteriors.

"Describe your art to me," I quietly requested.

Begged, rather.

I was incredibly invested in the answer—not least of all because it was killing me to know there was a side to *my* twins I had yet to see.

Because, yes, they are mine.

So, therefore, I need to know everything about them.

"Their art is beautiful," Wolfgang replied, snapping my attention back to him. "It's mixed media on enormous canvases—

always framed in black—an absolute mess of color and texture that feels like… tangible emotions…"

He chuckled self-deprecatingly. As if what he'd said hadn't made perfect sense—as a description, but also to explain *why* I was so drawn to these two enchanting creatures.

Why my tendrils *are so drawn to them, that is.*

Which gives me an idea…

Unleashing a single tendril, I snaked it behind Andre and Luca—headed straight for Wolfgang.

Let's see what you're made of, big bro.

"DON'T!" Gabriel's hand was suddenly gripping my forearm so tightly that I felt actual pain beneath the customary spark that contact between us ignited.

Well, this is interesting…

My tendril was poised mid-air—only inches away from his older brother—and apparently, my angel didn't like that one bit. At first, I assumed it was a flare-up of possessive jealousy, since Gabriel and I had fucked on nearly every surface of this house over the past few days.

Including the table we're currently eating on.

Bon appétit!

However, the way he was looking at me now—with pure *terror* in his eyes—went beyond a knee-jerk reaction.

Aww… he doesn't want me hurting Wolfgang.

No, that's not it…

The pieces were falling into place. Gabriel didn't want me touching his brother… the same brother who supposedly didn't shake hands…

Something else is *going on here.*

Realizing his error, Gabriel snatched his hand away as a villainous grin stretched across my face. "What's the matter, angel? Are you worried there might be a repeat of what happened here the other night?"

His perfectly symmetrical face drained of color as he glanced toward what remained of the doomed Marguerite.

Gotcha.

Gabriel had just confirmed he could not only see my tendrils —which no *human* had been able to before—but that he knew I'd killed our intruder.

But I don't believe I accomplished that alone…

"Speaking of the crime scene elephant in the room," I cackled, pulling my phone out of my pocket. "Just this afternoon, I received the official coroner's report from my agent. He needed my approval before we sent a press release, but I noticed something *odd* on the report. Something… unexplainable."

"Do tell, Theo," Andre drawled, throwing back the lowball of whiskey Jensen had poured for him before he left. "The anticipation is killing me."

It just might!

To be honest, I was having trouble finding the motivation to kill the Acosta twins. Gabriel was proving to be the perfect plaything, and Andre was calling to me like a siren's song. Thanks to whatever mixed up signal my true form had zeroed in on, I was actually feeling more *possessive* of them than anything. Perhaps even… attached.

I'll still be able to kill them if need be.

I think…

"Apparently, my lovesick stalker suffered from an *aneurysm* only moments before turning the gun on herself," I mused, letting my gaze land on every person seated at my table. "Yet… There was nothing in her medical history to suggest anything like that was likely to occur. So *incredibly weird,* right?"

Everyone at the table had tensed, and I let my question echo in the silent room while I soaked up the fraught emotions flavoring the air.

Along with a minute pulse of power.

Ooh!

Someone's *having a hard time holding back…*

But who?

I was also still trying to determine *what* I was dealing with here, as the twins—and our guests—seemed to be unusually skilled at appearing human.

Yet they're anything but.

Based on their appearances, they *might* have been supes, but it was more likely that they'd all chosen their super-sized vessels for maximum intimidation—just as I did. Plus, most supes were fairly bad at hiding their power from a sensitive being such as myself. Not to mention, there was absolutely no reason either heroes or villains would be circling *me* and my research.

Not yet anyway.

The Salahs are smart enough to protect their investment.

Since they know they'll go down with the ship.

And that sniveling lesser supe, Joshual Preek—known as Minor Influence, apparently—passed the test when I star hopped to Sunrise City earlier this week. His hatred for supes was so thick I could taste it, which immediately erased my concern that he was a mole for the other side.

Our meeting concluded with me feeling confident that my dealings with Ward and the resistance would remain a secret. But since I knew the value of controlling *everyone* involved with everything, I also insisted on exchanging direct contact information with our 'inside man.'

In case I decide to kill Ward.

Before we parted ways, I left Preek with specific instructions on how to redirect all shipments from my middleman perfumery to *me* should shit hit the fan.

Which is highly possible now that Blunt Force is joining the Salah clan…

I banished the thought, as whatever Big City's infamous villain family was up to wasn't my present concern.

The threats in front of me are.

CHAPTER 21
THEO

Despite what some close-minded humans believed, countless species existed in the galaxies, with many possessing deceptively humanoid forms.

Some, literally…

Case in point—the four sharing my table.

Even though my kind had many natural enemies, the only logical explanation *here* was that I was facing down a squadron of Stellarians sent to collect me.

Or worse.

Along with my unit, I'd been sent to this planet with a clear mission—to research *why* the *Lacertus* had chosen to breed with Earthlings. But then I went rogue and decided to test the theory for myself, not least of all, because fucking in human form felt incredible.

And it wasn't as if I was the first Stellarian who'd thought of it.

Unfortunately, the others I'd arrived with took our mission a little too seriously. So, as soon as I realized there were more enjoyable ways to conduct research, I quickly disposed of anyone who opposed my ideas. Then, I'd slowly disposed of any Stellarians already infiltrating the population with their offspring.

It's survival of the fittest, after all.

This may have seemed barbaric, but it was how my kind operated. At least, to anyone we perceived as a threat.

Just… usually not our own species.

Oops.

Yet, despite my crimes—and the bombshell I just dropped about the coroner's report—no one at the table was making a move to attack me. Stranger still, when my gaze landed on Gabriel again, I was startled to find an almost *pleading* look in his pretty blue eyes.

What is it, angel?

What are you made of?

My phone chimed the same instant Wolfgang's vibrated— which broke the delicious tension—and the email from my agent was temporarily covered by a text preview.

Preek: *I think your test subject suspects something.*

I frowned. Zion Salah might have been his clan's heir, but he was also a meathead athlete who played some ridiculous, never fully explained sport called Deathball. Between his violent profession and the strength of what we'd been dosing him with for years, it was a wonder he had enough brain cells remaining to formulate a suspicious thought at all.

Create a distraction. Perhaps involve him with the wedding planning?

Preek: Oh, he's involved himself. I might lose my job thanks to him and that idiotic villain—

Wolfgang cursed under his breath across the table, so I placed my phone face down on the table to return my full attention to my guests.

And their weaknesses.

"What's the matter, Wolfy?" Andre snorted. "Is Simon telling you to get your ass home and into your kennel already?"

Simon, hmm?

Wolfgang didn't seem the least bit offended by Andre's implications, which only made me more interested in uncovering this family's secrets.

It sounds like Wolfgang is someone's dog.

So who's truly in charge here?

"No, Simon's at the spa tonight," he muttered—concentrating on his phone as he typed up a response to whoever had interrupted. "But apparently, your brother is behaving idiotically enough to warrant a Google alert."

"You have another brother?" I turned to my twins, once again feeling *covetous* over any scrap of intel I could gather on them.

Purely for survival reasons, of course.

"Two more brothers and a sister," Gabriel quietly spoke, tentatively resting his hand on my forearm again—lighting up my nerve endings in a most disturbing way. "Maybe you can meet them someday?"

What?

"What?!" Wolfgang snapped, tucking his phone into his suit jacket pocket as he glared in our direction. "That's it. A word, Gabe. Outside."

Big bro seems rather uptight.

"What about me, Wolfy?" Andre chuckled, pouring himself a fresh glass of whiskey from the bottle Jensen had apparently left for him as well. "When do I get to be involved in your top-secret pep talks, huh?"

"Never," Wolfgang growled, rising from his chair so fluidly that my tendrils retracted in alarm. "Gabe?"

Then he snapped his gloved fingers.

And I growled.

That's my *toy, dog.*

The smile that lazily crept across Wolfgang's face had me reconsidering my decision to flaunt my plaything in front of him.

Because now he knows my *weakness, too.*

To my dismay, Gabriel scurried to obey his brother, and I had to forcibly restrain my tendrils from encircling Wolfgang in a lethal squeeze as they headed for the elevator. Before they disappeared, Gabriel shot me a small smile over his shoulder —perhaps to reassure me things were fine.

Most likely to stop me from adding to the crime scene.

All at once, I recalled how the fear in my angel's eyes hadn't been for his brother's safety, but for *mine.*

Even knowing what I could do, he protected me…

Perhaps I have this situation all wrong?

"He doesn't mean that, *schätzli.*" Luca's words had me snapping out of my reverie to refocus on the best dinner theater I'd watched in ages. "Wolfgang simply has a lot on his shoulders now that he's head of the family—"

And how did that happen?

"How did they die, Andre?" I interrupted, determined to make everyone as unsettled as I was. "Your parents, I mean."

Both men gaped before Luca spoke again. "I… don't believe that's an appropriate question to—"

"He killed them," Dre murmured, his eyes on what was left of his—*second? third?*—glass of whiskey. "Wolfy killed them so he could ascend the throne and boss the rest of us around until the day we follow them to the graves. Or until he kills us next."

Oh, this is getting good…

"Andre!" Luca raised his voice, and from the way my demon flinched, it didn't happen often. "Why would you say such things about your brother, especially in front of your…" the Swiss' words trailed off as he eyed me shrewdly.

Probably trying to figure out if Andre and I are fucking as well.

The answer is a pre-emptive yes.

"Because I'm tired of his shit, and I don't care who knows it," Andre grumbled in reply, even as he kept his tone respectful. "I wasn't born to be a follower, Luca. You *know* this."

Luca hummed thoughtfully, and the resonance of the sound had me cocking my head—like an animal catching a hint of prey.

Or a fellow predator…

"I do know," Luca calmly replied, his gaze briefly flickering to me, monitoring my reactions. "But *you* know that simply doesn't work in this family—"

"Well, maybe being a part of this family doesn't work for *me!*" Andre barked as he rose from his seat so abruptly that the chair almost toppled. Just as quickly, his shoulders slumped. "I'm sorry, *Sensei,* I didn't mean to snap at you… I just… I just need some air."

Andre stalked to the terrace without so much as a glance in my direction—as if he was embarrassed to have shown weakness in front of me. This was typical male posturing to disguise vulnerability, but oddly, I didn't want to capitalize on it.

I wanted to *comfort* him.

Well, that's inconvenient.

My attention drifted away from Andre to find Luca staring at me with so much coldness in his eyes that I involuntarily shivered.

"One big happy family, hmm?" I joked, grinning broadly to hide my wariness.

"Too many alphas under one roof," he flatly replied—his unblinking gaze burrowing into my soul. "Do *you* have any children, Theo?"

It wasn't a casual question, which only added to my suspicions. "Not that I know of," I cheerfully replied, curious if I could lure him out with enough antagonizing. "*You* know how it is, I'm sure."

From one breeding alpha to another.

My comment struck a nerve, but not how I'd expected. Instead of rising to the challenge, acute *sadness* momentarily flashed over Luca's features. Before I could drag his odd reaction back into the light, the whiskey bottle Andre had been pouring from fell over.

As if something knocked it aside.

Was that… him?

"Ready, Luca?"

The unexpected sound of Wolfgang's voice was the only reason I didn't unleash my tendrils to attack—even if I was now eyeing Luca in an *inhumanly* predatory way.

But we're all supernaturals here, aren't we?

"If you insist," Luca murmured, not appearing threatened at all as he smiled at the other man. "I was enjoying myself."

I bet you were.

Wolfgang snorted. "Well, I now need to clean up this publicity nightmare, so if you could tear yourself away from the *fun,* I'd appreciate it."

Luca rose from his chair as gracefully as Wolfgang had, and although I kept my gaze locked on him, I couldn't resist poking for more intel.

"Any press is good press," I chuckled. "Especially in the art world."

"That's right, Wolfy!" Andre called from outside—listening in even as he leaned over the terrace railing with his back to us. "Take some notes for *your* gallery."

"The gallery is in your names, Dre!" Wolfgang snapped back, and I glanced over to find him pinching the bridge of his nose. When he caught me watching, he straightened and smirked. "If he keeps up with this attitude, I might just leave them both here permanently."

My lip curled in return, as now familiar possessiveness roiled beneath the surface again. "That's the plan," I crooned. "With or without your permission."

Run along home, little dog.

Wolfgang's gaze darkened threateningly, but Luca was already carefully herding him—with no contact—into the elevator. "As enlightening as this dinner was, I agree that it's time to go. Theo." The Swiss gave me a curt, almost *respectful* nod before following the other man into the cab. "It was a pleasure to meet you."

Likewise.

To add to the strangeness of the evening, I *meant* it. I couldn't remember the last time I'd been around another creature who could legitimately intimidate me, and even if I couldn't be completely sure what Luca *was*, the familiarity of the encounter had almost… settled something inside me.

I think I'm growing soft in my old age.

All familiarity aside, my tendrils had still registered Luca as a potential threat, so his connection to Andre and Gabriel…

Gabriel!

For a moment, I panicked, thinking Wolfgang had packed my angel's bags and was disappearing with him into the night.

I sighed in relief when my tendrils located him on the third floor—even if he wasn't waiting for me in the studio bedroom. He was in the studio proper, seated at his usual workstation, with his jumble of emotions focused on what-ever he was working on.

Seeking a creative outlet.

Respecting that process enough to leave him to it, I turned my attention to the other twin. The one radiating *fury* out on my terrace. The one I was aching to touch.

Like a moth to the flame.

"Ahh, it's good to have you boys to myself again," I purred, draping myself against the railing beside him so I could see his face. "Without meddling *family* to ruin the party."

The party in my pants.

A hint of a smile twitched Andre's luscious lips, and I took that as a win. "I can't believe you *growled* at Wolfy, dude," he huffed with a shake of his head, but the *admiration* behind his words made me puff up with pride.

I shrugged, playing it cool even if I was still slightly wary. "Well, he thought he could order Gabriel around, not realizing your twin belongs to me."

As do you.

Andre tensed, but he kept his gaze fixed on the lights of the pier as he carefully replied. "Yeah, you guys are what now… dating? Casually fucking? Are you planning on passing him around like an hors d'oeuvre at your next gathering?"

The idea of anyone so much as *looking* at Gabriel during one of my parties had me leaning forward so my face was inches away from Andre's.

"You misunderstand, *demon*," I scoffed. "Gabriel is *mine*. As in, no longer available for the enjoyment of anyone else."

Ever again.

He smirked—not intimidated by me in the least—which, oddly, made my cock twitch. "What about *you*, Theo? Are you still available to be enjoyed by others?"

205

A delightful shudder danced over my skin. The alpha in me had wanted nothing more than to show Wolfgang and Luca that this was my territory, yet when *Andre* challenged me, I simply wanted to play.

How can I not be drawn to this pair?

"No," I replied, slightly horrified to realize this was true. "Well… except by one other person, but he's been playing hard to get."

Andre moved so fast, I barely had time to react before he was on me—crushing me against the stone railing with his hands locked on either side of me. Caging me in.

With his hard cock rubbing over mine.

By Stellaria!

"Are you talking about *me*, brat?" he hissed in my ear—his breath on my skin and his scent in my nostrils immobilizing me. Like prey. "You think *I'm* here to be *your* plaything?"

I can't think of anything I want more…

"Didn't your twin tell you? I want a pretty little matched set," I rasped, not at all sounding unaffected by what was happening.

What IS happening?

Andre hummed. Then—without warning—sunk his teeth deep into my neck.

I cried out, arching backward as white-hot pleasure burst behind my eyelids, and so much precum pulsed out of me that I wondered if I'd just climaxed. Before I could gather my thoughts, Andre swept his tongue over the wound and unceremoniously released me.

What. The. Fuck?

"In your dreams," he breathed, ghosting his lips over mine—streaking them with my blood.

By Stellaria…

Then he spun on his heel and strode back inside, leaving me to raise a trembling hand to my throbbing neck while his parting words drifted back on the evening breeze.

"And mine."

CHAPTER 22
GABRIEL

I awoke with a start as a plate of bacon and eggs landed next to my head.

"Finally! Some color…"

Blinking the sleep out of my eyes, I lifted my head from the worktable to find Theo gazing down at me with an unusually fond expression on his handsome face while wearing his most ridiculous kimono yet.

It was leopard print. As in, printed with actual leopards prowling through the jungle—reminiscent of how he'd been stalking me.

Fuck, this man can. Get. It.

I couldn't even pretend to play it cool. My hungry gaze traveled over the satin material—mapping the way it clung to his impressively well-sculpted muscles. It didn't even matter that whatever supernatural witchery he was hiding under there was to thank for holding the entire carnival ride together.

Don't care.

I'm still gonna climb aboard.

I was absolutely ravenous for this man. It was as if I'd never had sex before, because all I could think about was his mouth on mine, his mouth on my dick, his mouth and hands on my skin… his fingers—or whatever else—inside my ass… stretching me so he could pound into me with his cock and…

What I glimpsed last night…

Why won't he show me what he is?

"Hungry?" Theo purred, gripping my jaw and forcing me to look up at him.

"Starving," I rasped, unable to stop my gaze from dropping to his tasty bulge taunting me from beneath the silk.

Fucking feed it to me.

I now knew from experience that Theo wasn't actually naked beneath his robes. He wore either swim briefs or shorts so he could dip in and out of his hot tub multiple times a day. I wasn't sure if these soaks were related to *whatever* he was, or if it was just part of his routine, but I coveted the knowledge. Just like I coveted the tiny mole in the crease of his inner thigh, or the way the morning light fell on his face during breakfast. Or the way it felt to be so filled by him I no longer knew where I ended and he began…

Fuck.

I don't think I can walk away from this.

"Color looks good on you," Theo chuckled, gently tilting my head before swiping his thumb over my cheek.

When he withdrew his hand, I saw it was covered in a rainbow smear of chalk pastels—reminding me of what I'd been up to until the early morning hours.

What I'd fallen asleep doing…

"Oh, fuck," I swore as his amused gaze drifted to my crumpled project and the pile of half-broken pastels next to it. "I… um, I just needed to… you know. And I didn't bring any of my supplies, so I went digging until I found… I hope you don't mind…"

Theo was silent—studying the smudged 8x10 piece of cartridge paper on the table as if it were a gallery piece instead of the desperate result of late night eMOtioNs.

This is so embarrassing.

"I don't mind," he quietly replied, looking surprised by his own answer before continuing. "Are chalk pastels what you prefer to work in?"

My face was aflame, and I wished the studio floor would open up and swallow me whole so I didn't have to answer. Fine art was *not* what Dre and I did. It wasn't what the very snooty art school we went to expected from us.

We were two minor cogs in the industrial design machine, whose sole purpose was to create objects that were useful, with beauty as a secondary goal—if at all. *"Form follows function"* was a famous phrase in our field, and it essentially meant that our job was to invent items that would fulfill the destiny they were intended for.

Exposing the truth to the materials.

Why won't Theo show me the truth?

I suddenly realized he was waiting for a reply, and even though my *hobby* was the last thing I wanted to discuss with him, I knew he wouldn't let it drop until I did.

And maybe I don't really mind so much…

"Yeah, I like chalk pastels," I mumbled, snatching a nearby wet wipe to awkwardly clean off my face. "Charcoal, acrylics, inks, graphite… pretty much everything that's not oil paint because I'm too impatient for that shit."

Show me, show me, show me.

Theo hummed as he pulled his phone out of his pocket. "Well, then I'll buy you a little of everything."

Wait…

"Wait, what?" I squeaked. *Fucking squeaked.* "Dude. You don't… you don't have to *buy* me art supplies. I have a bunch of stuff at home. Well, at Wolfy's house, since that's where we'll be going after this internship ends—"

"No." Theo's tone was a low growl that had my toes curling in my sneaks as he gripped my chin again—roughly this time. Possessively. *"This* is your home because this is now a permanent position, regardless of what Wolfgang *thinks* he has a say in. That's what you want, isn't it?"

Holy. Fuck.

My body was vibrating in response to the agitation I could feel—*feel?!*—pouring off the man towering over me. And to the command in his tone.

There is no way in hell I can walk away from this.

I didn't want to "keep my dick to myself and do my fucking job," as Wolfy had so eloquently instructed after pulling me aside last night. There was nothing I wanted more in life than a permanent position as Theo's rent boy fucktoy instead of my current role as a good little soldier for the Suarez clan.

And my supposed destiny as the next in line for the throne…

All I could think about at the moment was leaning forward and burying my face against Theo's silk-covered muscles— just breathing in his weirdly addicting electricity scent until the day I died.

But I can't.

I can't, I can't, I can't.

However, I knew better than to reply with "I can't," so I tried to explain it in another way without revealing too much. "It doesn't matter what I want, Theo…"

"Bullshit."

I swiveled on my stool to find Dre leaning in the studio doorway—making me wonder how much he'd seen.

Ugh.

"You're actually gonna crawl back to the compound after this?" my twin growled, his tone dripping with venom—none of it meant for anyone in this room. "Instead of staying here with me?"

Wait, what?

"You're staying here?" I choked out, almost falling out of my chair from the mix of shock, envy, and relief that rocketed through my veins. "W-what about Wolfy?"

"Fuck Wolfy!" Dre scoffed, and I couldn't help noticing the way Theo turned to grin at him.

Which revealed the *bite mark* on his neck.

"WHO FUCKING BIT YOU?!" I snarled, standing so abruptly the stool toppled to the floor with an echoing clang.

I was ready to go to war. Whoever had touched what was *mine* was already six feet underground in the Suarez family burial site in our backyard—they just didn't know it yet.

And I'm going to take my time sending them there.

"Dude. *Dude.* It was me." Dre was suddenly at my side with a hand wrapped around the back of my neck—instantly settling me. "I'm sorry, okay? You know how Wolfy gets me going. I just needed an outlet and, well"—his gaze slid to Theo, almost accusingly—"brats were bratting."

Fuuuuck.

The idea of Dre *dominating* Theo with his teeth in his goddamn neck had me practically punching a hole through the zipper of my jeans. I suddenly *needed* to see this dynamic play out like I needed air, and I didn't know what that said about me, but I was done giving a shit.

Let's make a motherfucking sammich, bro.

My twin grimaced, probably mistaking my reaction as hurt feelings. "We can talk about it later. Right now, we gotta go meet up with Xander."

We do?

"Who's Xander?" Theo growled, and I had to laugh at how fucking ridiculous we were all behaving around each other.

Like a bunch of dogs protecting their food.

Stifling a smile, I laid a hand on Theo's forearm, relishing how *good* touching him made me feel. "Another brother. You'd actually like this one." A sudden thought had my eyes narrowing as I turned to Dre. "Why are we meeting Xanny? What happened to 'fuck Wolfy and following his orders?'"

Dre cackled, moving around Theo to pack up my breakfast to go for me. "This wasn't a directive from Wolfy. It's actually something Luca asked me to take care of."

"How exactly are you and Luca related?" Theo asked—the dangerous edge in his voice making both Dre and me freeze.

This wasn't jealousy or possessiveness. This was one predator recognizing another as a threat.

Is he… worried about us being around Luca?

Why is that so fucking cute?

"Related?" Dre muttered as he came back around to join us. "Are you blind, Theo? Luca is an old family friend of our parents. I *wish* he was our actual dad, but he's more like a… mentor."

"Is that right?" Theo mused, with an almost *gleeful* smile on his face. "Just a mentor, you say?"

He was sizing up my twin with what I now recognized was his version of our mental probing. Only I'd concluded Theo used his tendrils to *taste* the air around his subjects—knowing that no one could see.

No one except me, apparently.

Wait…

Dre's gaze had lifted to stare at a shimmering tendril hovering directly over his forehead.

"Can you see *that, Dre?"*

"Sure can. Saw it the first time you two got busy with each other, too."

What?!

"Don't say anything! He might attack—"

"You know, Theo…" my twin drawled, and I tensed, bracing for whatever grenade he was about to throw. "I've been thinking about the coroner's report you mentioned… How that stalker lady supposedly suffered an aneurysm before turning the gun on herself? I'm no expert, but I have a weird fascination with brain stuff, and I don't think there's any fucking way she would have had the motor skills needed to accomplish that in the middle of a major neurological event."

Theo's tendrils retracted back into his body in a mesmerizing way as he cocked his head and icily replied. "What's your point, demon?"

I would have folded like a goddamn chair in this situation, but Dre only smirked. "All I'm saying is that shining a light on the aneurysm doesn't work if you're trying to spin a tale about a spurned side piece showing up and painting your floor with her brains. So you might wanna leave that part out of the press release. Not unless you *also* want to mention how it wouldn't have been physically possible for her to shoot herself. Ready, Gabe?"

Then he handed me a makeshift egg sandwich—where he'd apparently used two thick slices of bacon as bread—and winked at Theo before strutting from the room. Leaving no crumbs behind, all around.

Dang.

Theo frowned in the direction my twin had gone and my anxiety skyrocketed.

Gotta soothe him.

Gotta comfort my…

My what?

"We won't be gone long," I murmured, although I didn't even know what this errand was even about.

All I understood was that the idea of spending more than a few hours away from Theo sounded worse than death. And part of me—a frighteningly large part—wanted him to be as torn up about our separation as I was.

"Good," he replied, turning his attention back to me with an indulgent smile that made my chest feel like it was full of bees again. "I'd actually like both of you to accompany me to a meeting later today with my business associate. He wanted an update on the perfume dispenser, so why not have him meet the geniuses behind the prototypes he'll be testing?"

I knew *this* was exactly the type of thing I needed to run by Wolfy, and that he would most likely forbid us from going.

The fewer of Theo Coatl's associates who see our faces, the better.

But then I caught the *pride* in Theo's voice, and all I could think about was how I wanted more of it. I also wanted to get a visual on who *he* was in business with—in case things went south.

In case I needed to protect him.

I am in delulu la la land over here.

But knowing counts for something, right?

"We'll be there," I whispered, tilting my head to deposit a soft kiss directly over Dre's bite mark—drinking in Theo's shiver like the air I needed to breathe.

Lalalalala.

"Good boy. Six pm at Ars and Invenio. By the USN…" he whispered back, like he was telling me a secret. "Don't be late, angel. And make sure that demon twin of yours joins you."

I hope he does.

In every way.

"Aye-aye, *Capitán!*" I laughed. Grabbing my jacket, I ignored one brother's voice in my head, and chased after another—feeling all giddy and almost in *love* or something.

Stranger things have happened!

CHAPTER 23
ANDRE

"Honestly, I don't know who's giving Wolfy more gray hairs —you two sluts or Balty."

It's nice to see you too, Xanny.

I rolled my eyes at the shadowy figure lurking under the pier next to a bobbing WaveRunner. "Why is it news that Balty was rolling around in the mud with Zion Salah?" I scoffed. "Those two idiots have been doing this dance for the last decade."

It was Xander's turn to roll his eyes as he stepped into the light, revealing his signature wetsuit and even more signature smirk. "Yeah, but did you *see* the photos on SNZ? Baby Hulk looks like he can't decide between punching that lizard dick or riding it."

I shrugged. "Again. Show me the tea."

Gabe glanced between us, adorably confused. "But Balty's not gay…"

You're cute.

Xanny and I made eye contact, and it was all over. We started howling, and we didn't stop until Gabe gave both of us a petulant little zap to the brain.

Brat.

All this did was make me *ache* for the real brat we'd left behind. The one whose blood I could still taste on my tongue.

Fuck, he loved being bitten.

I wanna do it again.

Harder.

"Watch yo'self, little mind-melter," Xander chuckled. "Don't forget, I have that Uno Reverso power. I can zap your brain right back!"

I rolled my eyes so hard this time, I almost saw the brain in question. Yeah, our brother might be the *inventus* of Captain Masculine, but he hadn't even known he *had* powers until last year, so he could eat a dick.

Although, he'd probably enjoy that.

"So Luca wants you to look at our phones." I put a stop to the showboating by getting down to business. "To make sure no one's tracking us."

Gabe glanced at me sharply.

"You think Theo's keeping tabs?"

"I dunno. But Wolfy flipped when he realized we had apps that unlocked the doors, so I promised Luca I'd have Dorky Antihero here check it out."

"Stop talking about me with your creepy twin thing," Xander huffed. "But yeah, I'll fix your phones…. iiiiif I can take DNA samples from both of you."

Everything's a negotiation.

He turned to grab a lab specimen box from the back of his WaveRunner as I scowled. "Why do you need samples from us again? Didn't you just get some after the whole Simon heritage discovery?"

The entire reason we're slumming it in the Teal Coast neighborhood.

Potentially with Simon's father…

Oops.

When Xander turned to face us again, he had a swab in each gloved hand and a scientific gleam in his eye—which told me there was no escaping this. "Yes, well, as mentioned, that was before you two sluts started fucking the missing link to my research."

I huffed. "Only Gabe is fucking…"

Wait.

In almost comical slow motion, I turned to face my twin, finding less shock and awe on his face than I was expecting.

Pun intended.

No. The person who I was closer with than anyone else on Earth was glaring at Xanny like he'd just spilled tea he was not supposed to be pouring.

*Which is why we call him **The Mouthy One.***

"I fucking *knew* it!" I barked, pointing an accusing finger at a guilty-as-fuck looking Gabe. "You and Wolfy and your goddamn secrets. Am I the only one in this family who doesn't know why we're *really* on this job? Why not just fucking *TELL ME* what's going on?!"

Why am I an outcast in my own clan?!

Gabe's face was stricken. "I don't *know,* dude… I mean… I *do,* but—*FUCK!* We shouldn't be talking about this out in the open—"

"I DON'T FUCKING CARE!" I shouted, beyond done with this shit. "You're gonna tell me right now why Wolfy treats me differently than you, Gabe, or I am shutting you out of my head for good!"

Don't think I won't!!!

"IT'S BECAUSE HE DOESN'T TRUST YOU, OKAY?!" my twin shouted back, although his voice cracked, annoyingly pulled at my heartstrings. "But I don't know *why*…" His entire soul seemed to deflate as he puffed out a breath. "I'm so *sorry,* Dre. I wish I could tell you more, but I-I can't…"

Can't or won't?

Does it even matter?

I was so furious I couldn't form words. Having my deepest suspicions confirmed stung like a bitch, but that wasn't what hurt the most. Knowing Gabe had been forced into a position of conflicting loyalties for his entire life made me see red.

Especially knowing who put him there.

I swear, it's like Wolfy wants *to be my nemesis*…

But I refuse to let him come between us.

"It's okay," I sighed, pulling my other half into a hug that soothed both of us. "It's just one more fucked up situation in our fucked up family—"

"Suckahhhs!" Xanny sang as he snuck close enough to yank a chunk of hair from each of our heads, like a goddamn psychopath.

MOTHERFUCKER!!!

"What?" He shrugged when we both spun to glare at him. "You two dummies let down your guards—too busy crying over a supe mistrusting his own family. A *clan leader,* of all things! As if that's not business as usual. Lest you forget, Wolfy tried to *kill* me when I was barely out of diapers. That's how he knew I had powers when no one else did."

You're just proving my point, dude.

Rubbing the top of my head to ease the sting, I side-eyed our older brother as he carefully packed our hair into his specimen box—debating if testing his Reverso powers was worth the risk.

I could totally take him…

"What I'm getting at is don't take it personally, Dre," he sighed, snapping off his rubber gloves with the efficiency of someone who used them for work *and* play. "Wolfy might be a controlling asshole, but everything he does is because he loves us… in his controlling asshole way—"

Xander's phone buzzed, abruptly silencing his yapping. When he glanced at the screen, his amber eyes went wide.

"Speak of the devil," he murmured. Another buzz. "And he wants me back at the compound immediately." Xander paled before he squinted closer. "Oh, right… It's *Balty's* funeral today, not mine. Well, shit, I'm definitely not missing that!"

This family is full of fucking vultures.

Peering around the deserted beach, Xander pulled his mask out of his wetsuit pocket before pulling it on and stepping back into the shadows. "I gotta fly. Can you two trouble-makers drive my WaveRunner back to my lair?"

I shot his favorite toy—*besides Butch*—a judgy look. As if I *wasn't* low-key excited to take out my aggression on some waves. "What's in it for us?"

Xander grumbled, which sounded ridiculous as it filtered through the voice distortion feature of his supe mask. "You get to hang out *at my lair*. It's not like you kids didn't love hunkering down at the coolest place on Earth when we all thought Apocalypto Man was back from the dead. Oh fuck! Lemme do the phone thing before I go…"

The nerdiest Suarez of them all held out his phone and hovered it near ours until all three made a futuristic trilling sound. Then he gave us an even nerdier salute and took off into the sky, clutching his creepy box of stolen hair and clan secrets.

Pay our respects to Baby Hulk, slut.

I walked to Xanny's WaveRunner and swung my leg over the side before firing it up. "C'mon," I called over to Gabe. "Let's ride."

Ride or die.

He shuffled closer, gnawing on his bottom lip as he eyed me warily.

"Doc and Xanny think whatever Theo is might help explain the evolution of supes…"

Waving the white flag, I see.

"Oh? Am I cool enough to be in on the intel now?"

Gabe huffed and closed the distance between us before climbing on behind me. Then he wrapped his arms around my waist and laid his cheek against my shoulder blade—officially thawing my cold, black heart by going hard with the sweetness.

Asshole.

"Wolfy only mentioned it because he wanted Theo kept alive for… testing. So he asked me to make sure you didn't —"

My twin cut himself off, but I knew where he was going with that statement.

To make sure I didn't kill him.

Jesus…

Is that how this entire family sees me?

Or just Wolfy?

With a growl, I went full throttle and drove us straight into the sea. After jumping a few waves, my anger settled, and I focused on following the coastline south. While it wasn't completely unfounded to worry that I—or any supe—might kill someone we saw as a threat, the pointed accusation was pissing me off.

It wasn't only because I had barely any kills to my name, especially compared to some of my other siblings, or that unaliving someone during a scene was a genuine fear of mine. Something else was bothering me here—something specifically about… Theo.

I don't know if I can kill him.

Can't or won't?

That startling thought was front and center as I steered us into the drainage tunnel that served as the emergency exit for Xander's warehouse lair. But I brushed it aside for now in favor of my favorite thing.

Judging my older siblings.

Especially those lame enough to have a lair.

The idea of villains scheming in secret lairs was such an old-school concept, I wasn't even sure many did it anymore—at least not in our clan. The newly rebuilt Suarez family compound served as Wolfy and Simon's hideout, and Vi was never far from Wolfy's side. Gabe and I always had our dorm rooms, which were discreet enough for us. Meanwhile, Xander had his ultra secure Big City apartment *and* this top secret warehouse that he primarily used for research and saving the marine wildlife of Awakeners Bay.

How villainous.

Balty was barely raised as a villain outside of his job, kicking ass in the Supremacy Games for our side. But his celebrity lifestyle meant he was on tour most of the year or out at the clubs before ending up in some cape chaser's bed.

I can't believe that idiot's getting married…

To the wrong Salah, too.

As if on cue, an unmistakable blast of Baltasar-flavored anxiety pummeled against our mental walls.

"Fuck," Gabe muttered, fumbling his phone out of his pocket as I used the keys plus my fingerprint to gain access to the warehouse. "Baby Hulk is going through it right now."

I sighed and glanced around Xander's lame ass lair before tossing the keys on the kitchen island—mostly because I knew he preferred them hanging by the door.

What does he expect from the apparently unstable Suarez?

"Yeah, well… it's not healthy to keep that shit locked up inside," I grumbled, salty about all the things. "Maybe this will be good for Balty, you know? Being forced to confront the obvious *thing* that's always been there between him and Zion."

Gabe walked over to join me—his eyes on his phone as he rapid-fire texted our brother the same thing he always did when we felt one of his panic attacks coming on.

Cute cat videos.

"You really think Balty's gay?" he murmured quietly as he slipped his phone back into his pocket.

My heart softened yet again, knowing Gabe was finding parallels of his own with Balty's journey. "I mean, I'm not jumping to slap a label on our boy, but you've seen how he chases Zion on the field… and how Zion chases him off it." I smiled. "Kinda like how Theo's been chasing you."

Gabe lifted his identical gaze to mine. "And how *you've* been chasing Theo?"

Well, fuck.

There was no judgment in his expression—no accusation or even concern. If anything, there was… hope.

Okay, let's discuss.

I *thought* I knew what he was getting at, but also knew I needed to address this carefully. "Do you—"

"Yes!" Gabe blurted out, reaching across the island to paw at my sweatshirt desperately. "I want to share him with you. *Please!*"

Oh.

My stomach had officially dropped into my nuts, leaving me painfully aware of exactly how hot I found the idea of sharing Theo with Gabe.

Fucking smash.

One thing at a time, though.

I cleared my throat. "Okay. Hold that thought. What I was *gonna* ask was if you thought there was more going on here… between you and Theo. Something *serious*. Like what Xander and Butch have. Or Wolfy and Simon."

Especially Wolfy and Simon.

"I-I don't know," he choked out, his chest heaving. "All I know is that when he's inside me, filling me up… *NO!*" he huffed when I wrinkled my nose. "I mean, when his *light* is filling me, I feel… complete. It's the same as when you're in my head. It feels like someone else is taking the wheel—guiding me… Guiding me *home.*"

My heart felt like it was going to beat clear out of my chest. This didn't sound like how our brothers and their significant others had described their *inventus* bonds. Not at all.

It sounds like possession.

The thought didn't freak me out as much as it probably should have. For one, I didn't believe Theo was actually controlling Gabe's mind or body.

If anyone's been doing that, it's me.

It was a terrifying trick I'd realized I was capable of during one of the few times our parents used us for a job—before Wolfy put a stop to it. Yes, Gabe could combine his power with mine to amplify the effect, but I actually didn't need him to accomplish it.

And now I want to do it to Theo.

Fuck.

This is exactly what everyone's afraid of!

"Hey, hey, it's okay…" Gabe was suddenly behind me again with his arms wrapped around my waist—just like he'd done on the WaveRunner. "Talk to me."

"I…" My twin deserved an explanation, especially if we were planning on navigating this throuple situation together. "I think I should tread carefully with this sharing thing."

The problem was, I didn't know *how* to explain it—not without scaring him.

Just tell *him, Dre.*

Taking a deep breath, I opened my mind to him in the same way he did for me when he needed to talk about the hard stuff. The stuff he didn't dare say out loud.

> *"I want to hurt him—more than I've ever hurt anyone before. I want to hurt him in ways that would kill a normie… Because I'm into that."*

I braced myself for judgment, even though it wasn't what we did. Even though I'd scolded *him* for daring to think I'd ever judge him for liking what he liked.

"He'd be into that, too," he immediately replied, squeezing me tighter. "Especially from you."

It's not that easy!

When I simply gritted my teeth and let out a ragged breath, Gabe released me and walked over to the enormous TV before flopping onto one of the oversized bean bag chairs.

"Wanna play *Endless Ocean* for a while?" he asked, picking up a Wii controller. "And then eat everything in Xanny's fridge? Just you and me?"

Nodding numbly, I crowded onto the same bean bag instead of taking the other one—wanting to be as close as possible to my other half. As usual, his proximity quickly brought me back to baseline, but it took me a while longer to realize "just you and me" was no longer the only thing I needed.

CHAPTER 24
THEO

I had everything I needed.

Well, almost everything.

Ward was seated across the booth—looking scared shitless, thanks to me regaining control of our business arrangement— and the waiter had just delivered the bloodiest steak I could hope for.

Practically still breathing.

Just how I like it.

Unfortunately, what was still missing were two things. Two possessions of mine that had somehow become so vital to my very existence, I was having trouble maintaining my corporeal form when they weren't around.

How embarrassing.

"Your meeting with Preek went... well?" Ward ventured, taking a shaky sip of his lemon water.

I couldn't help noticing there was no sloppy wine drinking tonight or drunken harlot convulsing on his fingers, but that was most likely because *I'd* chosen the location. There wasn't a glass on the menu here under fifty bucks, and whatsher-name would have never made it past Chantal at the door.

Ward's lucky he's with me.

"It did." I grinned, slicing into my steak with a satisfyingly wet sound that reminded me of disemboweling someone with my tendrils.

I should do that soon.

It would take the edge off.

My dinner companion was clearly waiting for me to elabo-rate, but I had no intention of doing so. I'd simply told Preek I would triple whatever Ward was paying him to continue spying on the Salahs. All he had to do was stay the course and not say a word about how our meeting had gone, because I *wanted* Ward to sweat about it.

How I love playing with my food.

In the end, I didn't believe for a second that my business associate had simply *forgotten* to mention Preek's existence. But exactly *why* he'd wanted to keep his spy a secret was baffling—especially if all the lesser supe was doing was being our eyes and ears on the ground.

A human wouldn't dare betray me.

Would he…?

My tendrils were writhing angrily beneath the surface— agitated by all the recent additions to my watchlist.

Speaking of which… where are my twins?!

Even as I now assumed that Andre and Gabriel were some-thing inhuman—although *what* remained unclear—I couldn't bring myself to see them as a threat. This made no sense.

Of course, it makes sense.

They're your mates.

Gross.

With my appetite ruined, I set down my fork and glanced around—seeking distraction in my surroundings. Ars and Invenio had an extravagant 1920s speakeasy vibe, and the tufted high-back booth we were seated in offered us privacy, but that wasn't the only reason I preferred to dine here. The discretion the restaurant's staff provided to its patrons was unmatched, making it the ideal location for supes to unwind. Specifically, *villains.*

So I fit right in.

Along with some of the more recognizable normie faces.

"Shit. Is that… is that Sylvano Ricci?" Ward hissed, attempting to positively identify the Deputy Secretary-General of the United Super Nations without being overt.

While being quite overt.

"Yes," I replied, amused and unsurprised by the cameo as I calmly sipped my cabernet. "The USN is only a few blocks away, so he comes here often."

Ward glared at me accusingly—as if I would do something as risky as putting a leader of the resistance in the same room as the man who tirelessly fought for supe equality.

Okay, I would totally do something like that.

I was about to continue taunting Ward when someone caught my eye.

To be more specific, someone caught *Sylvano Ricci's* eye.

Two someones.

The twins.

Interesting…

Andre and Gabe had stopped at the hostess podium to check in with Chantal, but she looked to be giving them no trouble at all. This was despite my demon's scowl and the fact my angel was still in the same rumpled street clothes he'd fallen asleep wearing.

All the attention they were getting could have been because they were young and beautiful, and because their presence naturally enhanced the atmosphere of the venue. Or it was because Ricci and the staff here were trained to sniff out the supernatural, and my twins were practically *glowing* with otherworldly energy.

Glowing just for me.

Because they're mine.

All at once, I wanted to gouge out the eyeballs of everyone who was watching them cross the room to join us. This included Sylvano Ricci, who was now doing his best to look everywhere *except* at the twins.

Even more interesting…

"Here we are," Andre announced upon reaching the booth, for no other reason than to piss me off.

"Yes," I gritted out. "But as it is now an hour later than I'd told you to be here, we started without you."

"Yes," Andre parroted, amusement dancing in his eyes. "But since we're not old men who eat at Early Bird Special time, we're here *now.*"

Unsurprisingly, Ward was watching this disrespectful exchange with his jaw on the table. I could practically see all the work I'd done to reinforce his fear evaporating before my eyes.

Perhaps I can find it in me to kill Andre, after all.

Of course, my sweet angel tried to smooth over the situation by turning his brilliant smile toward my business partner. "Hello, I'm Gabriel Acosta, and this is Andre. We're currently interning for Mr. Coatl and have been working on the proto-types you'd request—*AHHH!*"

I suddenly had no control over my limbs. The instant Ward reached for Gabriel's outstretched hand, I grabbed *my* mate by the waist and dragged him into my lap.

Mine.

"What the fu… What are you *doing,* Theo?!" Gabriel hissed. He blushed deliciously as he wiggled out of my lap and onto the bench beside me—scooting toward the wall in a futile effort to reclaim some decorum.

Too late.

"I don't want him touching you," I growled. My gaze was fixed on Ward, who was once again eyeing me with a healthy amount of fear.

Good.

"It's called a handshake, you lunatic," Gabriel muttered, but then he leaned his weight against my side, and the agitation I'd been feeling settled exponentially.

All is as it should be.

Almost.

My gaze shifted to where Andre was still standing next to the table, staring me down. His arms were crossed, which made his biceps strain enticingly beneath his—*surprise!*—black sweatshirt.

Everything would be easier if he wasn't so aggravatingly attractive.

"I hope you don't think *I'm* ending up in your lap next, Theo," he chuckled.

"That depends," I cooed. "Are *you* going to make the mistake of shaking Ward's ha—"

"Because, if anything," he continued, as if I hadn't spoken. "You'll be in *my* lap. Face down."

Fuck.

My body responded so viscerally to Andre's words that Gabriel had to dig his nails into my forearm to calm us both down.

Both?

Yes. For some Stellaria-forsaken reason, I could *feel* how turned on my angel was by his twin's words—which was then feeding *my* desire like some sort of mindless horniness loop.

What the fucking fuck?!

Ward cleared his throat and began to awkwardly slide out of the booth. "I can take those prototypes and go, Theo, if you—"

"SIT!" I barked. This caused more than a few pairs of curious eyes to flicker in our direction, including Sylvano Ricci, who appeared to be saying his own goodbyes.

Which gives me an idea.

Despite the traitorous way my body was behaving, I had no intention of losing more control—especially not when I could kill everyone in this restaurant in two seconds if I chose to.

So there.

"Can I sit too, Theo?" Andre asked, although he wasn't truly *asking*. He was eyeing the space next to me in an obvious command for me to move over and make room.

So I did.

Again, because I had no control of my limbs.

Shameful.

"Very good," Andre whispered in my ear as he gracefully eased into the booth like a king claiming his throne.

Before I could destroy *all* my credibility by begging him to bite my neck again, Andre turned his attention across the table. "It's nice to meet you, Ward." His voice was cool and professional. I wanted to hear it in the bedroom. "Theo's told us so much about you."

I absolutely had *not* and was about to say as much when I realized what my demon was up to. He was utilizing similar methods to mine—keeping his prey in the dark about how much he did or didn't know in order to control the situation.

Clever boy.

Ward frowned. "Well, Theo hasn't told me shit about you, so how 'bout you enlighten me?"

I bristled at his disrespectful tone, but Andre snorted, more than capable of handling himself. "Nah… I don't think I will. Especially not on an empty stomach." Then he calmly turned and caught a waiter's attention before indicating that he wanted two more of what I was having delivered to him and Gabriel.

Extra bloody steak.

I am so turned on right now.

Sylvano Ricci started to walk by our table on his way toward the exit, so—naturally—I chose that moment to slide the prototypes across the table.

"Here are the top secret dispensers you wanted developed and, *oh!* Aren't you the Deputy Secretary-General of the United Super Nations? Sylvano Ricci, correct?"

Everybody froze. Sylvano Ricci froze in that awkward way one did when a complete stranger talked to you, and Ward looked as if he were expecting Captain Masculine to immediately descend and incinerate him for his crimes.

Most interesting was how the twins froze—not just in the way one did when bracing oneself for embarrassment.

They froze in the way supes did.

Gotcha.

Yes, I'd already determined they were supernaturals, even if I wasn't convinced they were Stellarians. I'd still been considering another intergalactic species with symbiote or mimic-like abilities, but the way Sylvano Ricci's gaze swept over them now confirmed something else entirely.

He knows who they are.

Which means he has files on them in his silly little facility.

"I'm sorry, have we met?" The diplomatic normie smiled politely once his gaze met mine—knowing full well that if I was dining *here,* I was somebody important.

Or, a nobody who's with *somebody important, in Ward's case.*

"Oh, *we* haven't." I breezily laughed, grinning wider when Gabriel shifted uncomfortably. "Although, I *did* choreograph a week-long performance piece outside the USN when all that 'heroes and villains are the same' drama happened earlier this year. It was titled 'Muscle for Hire.'"

Ricci cleared his throat. "Yes, the uh, public nudity certainly attracted a crowd."

"Uh-uh-uh." I waggled a scolding finger. "What you meant to say is the stark display of the human body as a representation of the *shameful* mistreatment of supes attracted a crowd. Your slip was understandable. I wouldn't expect a corporate stooge to grasp the ethereal concept of art when concrete data is the only god you pray to."

To my surprise, the very man I was insulting looked like he was stifling a smile. "My apologies. I'll admit, art is *not* my forte. Perhaps the USN should bring in someone like the infamous *Theo Coatl* to get more involved in our organization—to *humanize* our boring data for public consumption?"

Well, color me surprised!

It was my turn to freeze. Not only did this stuffed shirt apparently know exactly who I was, but he'd just invited me right through the front door.

This can't be that *easy…*

Can it?

"I would relish the opportunity," I purred. "Especially as I'm currently finishing up a cosmetics project with my dear business associate here—Mr. Ward R. Davidson of 88 Cherry Blossom Lane. Won't you say hello to Sylvano Ricci, Ward?"

When all Ward could muster was a curt nod and what sounded suspiciously like, "fuck you, Theo" under his breath, I went in for the kill.

"And these two unicorns are my new full-time employees, Andre and Gabriel Acosta. I'm sure you haven't heard of them as they are shockingly humble. But don't be fooled by their tragically black wardrobes. They are both artists with extremely robust portfolios, despite their talent being inexplicably wasted on industrial design. Although… that skillset could surely come in handy for a partnership between the USN and Coatl Industries, no? How does tomorrow work for the three of us to swing by for a tour? Let's say, late morning or early afternoon?"

The amused smile on Sylvano Ricci's face had melted into something closer to dazed horror. Yet he obediently pulled out his phone to check his calendar and magically fit us into his busy schedule.

As one does.

After the steamrolled Deputy Secretary-General extracted himself from my clutches and left the building, Ward slithered away with his prototypes. Then two more steaks arrived at our table.

Now, I have everything I need.

"Aren't you going to move to the other side of the booth to give us room?" I grumbled at Andre, even though I secretly *loved* the feeling of being crushed between their hot little bodies.

I truly need to move them into my room already.

"No," he replied, in that indifferent tone that made my cock hard. "I'm going to sit right here and eat my steak, and you're going to do the same. You're going to clean your fucking plate, like the good little slave you are."

Fuck!

"Fuck…" Gabriel whispered, immediately getting to work on his steak, even though the directives weren't meant for him.

My angel wanted to be a good boy, but I did not. And if anyone should understand this, it was Andre Acosta.

"No," I sassed, knowing I was going to immediately regret my words and positively *aching* to find out how.

I didn't have to wait long. Further proving just how inhuman he was, Andre struck. Moving faster than I could register, he reached between my legs and gripped my balls through my pants—hard enough to make me release a humiliating little squeal.

Like a stuck pig.

"Very well," he hissed in my ear. "Then you can focus on feeding *me.* Once I'm done, I'll give these back to you. Now get to work."

CHAPTER 25
THEO

The pain was almost blinding.

My entire body was shuddering and tears were blurring my vision—turning the occupants of the dimly lit restaurant into a kaleidoscope of planetary bodies.

Like a stellar collision.

Oh, fuck…

Please don't tell me that's what this is.

The reality was that I could have star hopped away from Andre at any time. I could have simply flitted away and back too fast for the eye to see, but long enough to make him lose his grip. Just enough to turn the tide in my favor.

But I didn't.

Because I fucking love this game.

I loved it for the same reason I'd remained on this planet for so long—why I'd gone rogue from my original mission and killed any Stellarian who stood against me. I loved feeling human, not for the emotions—although those had been creeping in more and more lately—but for the *sensations* that danced across this overly receptive surface of this sensitive skinsuit.

Especially the pain.

"Theo…" Andre haltingly spoke, his grip loosening enough for my vision to clear. I blinked to find an almost *guilty* expression on his face. "Quick. What's your safe word?"

I stared at him dumbly, already missing the anguish and wondering if I should simply star hop the three of us into my bed.

Someone needs to be fucking somebody at this point!

"It's Stellaria," Gabriel rasped, sounding like *he* was the one with his balls in a vise. "And he loves what you're doing to him."

Exactly *how* my angel knew this was a mystery, but he was absolutely correct.

"No. I need to hear it from *him,* Gabe," Dre scolded before looking at me—searching my face almost desperately. "Is *Stellaria* your safe word, Theo?"

I whimpered—the name of my home on both sets of their lips making me dizzy. "Yes. It's Stellaria." I gritted my teeth. "But you'll never hear me say it."

Since nothing here can kill me.

Now Andre shuddered, his intense blue eyes briefly fluttering closed while he seemed to struggle to regain control of himself. When he reopened them, his expression was unreadable once again. Cold. Almost cruel.

Fucking perfect.

"I'm still hungry, slave," he growled, squeezing my already tender balls and giving them a twist that had me doubling over. "Chop chop."

"Yes, demon," I murmured before picking up his knife and fork with shaking hands and beginning to cut. When I glanced up to find his icy gaze narrowing once again, I quickly realized my misstep. "Yes, *Demon.*"

"That's better," he chuckled warmly. Dangerously. "Usually, I'd prefer 'Master,' but we both know it means the same thing in this context."

Double fuck.

I'd always hated answering to anyone, which made life difficult for a creature born into a militaristic society, such as myself. It was another reason I'd found it so satisfying to dispose of my entire squadron, starting with our abusive leader.

Apparently, I'm a slut for abuse elsewhere.

What was most concerning about my present situation *wasn't* that the twins could be working with intergalactic mercenaries. It was that the idea of kneeling for the man I was currently feeding cuts of bloody meat sounded weirdly appealing.

And we can't have that.

Maintaining my obedient facade—since Andre *did* have me by the balls—I covertly unleashed a pair of tendrils.

Aimed for my sweet, unsuspecting angel.

Gabriel's shirt had inched up as he leaned over his plate, exposing the pretty tanned skin of his lower back. Thrumming with anticipation, I left a trail of goosebumps in my wake before slipping into his pants.

And directly between his bouncy little cheeks.

"Theo?" Gabriel whimpered as I pressed inside him—as if there was anyone else in this place with the ability to pleasure him with self-lubricating star stuff.

Or anyone as powerful as me.

For a moment, I faltered, remembering the strange tap on my brain I received the day I showed them to their room.

Was that one of them?

Maybe I should figure out what I'm dealing with here…

Oh, fuck it, I'm too horny.

"Theo," Andre warned as my angel moaned—the same moment I shoved a second tendril into Gabriel's tight ass.

"What?" I blinked owlishly at him, hovering another piece of meat in front of his tasty lips.

"Oh, *fuck,*" Gabriel whispered raggedly, pushing his plate away and laying his palms and face down on the table. *"Jesus Christ…"*

Andre's eyes narrowed while my smile broadened. Gabriel had already confirmed he could see my tendrils—even if I limited what he saw—and I suspected my demon was equally perceptive. But he and I were still doing a dance.

Where both of us are trying to lead.

"Perhaps something he ate didn't agree with him," I continued absently as I carved out a new piece of steak. "Like my cock."

"Yes…" Gabriel hissed. "Give me your cock."

My demon's impassive facade cracked, his gaze sliding to where I was using his willing twin like a toy. Gabriel's pretty eyes were closed—his face slack and dreamy as he lost himself to the sensation of me rubbing circles over his p-spot. He was so close, I could feel his impending orgasm as if it were my own.

"Stop. It," Andre growled, giving me a warning squeeze.

Oh?

"Stop what?" I asked, calmly setting down the knife and fork and clasping my hands on the table, even as I internally shivered with anticipation.

"Don't stop!" Gabriel cried—loud enough to call attention our way again.

Andre swore under his breath, shifting his body to hide his brother from our fellow patrons. This caused me to notice the light sheen of sweat on his upper lip and how his breathing seemed more labored than usual.

Is he… also feeling Gabriel's pleasure?

Or just really pissed off at me?

Either way, I love everything about this.

"Such a tricky position you're in, hmm, demon?" I teased, giving my tendrils a hard twist inside Gabriel just to see *Andre's* eyes cross. "You want to take away my toy… except he's not just *mine*. He's *ours*. And you take care of what belongs to you—isn't that right?"

Despite how close they were, there wasn't anything overtly sexual to the twins' relationship—*much to my disappointment, I might add.* But Andre was clearly the more experienced of the two, and given his more dominant traits, it made sense he would take on a protector role.

Gabriel made a quiet keening sound that almost had me giving him the cock he was begging for, but the gauntlet had been thrown.

"So what'll it be?" I asked absently. "Will you take away your twin's pleasure when you can *feel* how close he is? Or will you let him make a mess of his pants like the needy, *helpless* little slut he's always wanted to be?"

Decisions, decisions…

"Dre…" Gabriel whined, cracking open his eyes to watch our standoff, although that seemed to be the extent of what he could say.

Don't worry, angel—I've got this.

"You wouldn't believe how exquisite he looks when he comes," I continued mercilessly, even as Andre tightened his grip on my balls again. "How *grateful* he is when I take control. Do you know how addicting that is?"

Andre was seething, his jaw clenched as he growled low with every panting breath. I was surprised we weren't attracting *more* attention with our collective display, but it now almost seemed as if everyone in the vicinity had magically forgotten about us.

How oddly convenient.

"Yes," Andre hissed as his other hand lifted to wrap around my throat. "I *do* know, but we're not talking about good boys like Gabe. We're talking about brats like *you,* Theo, and how you need to learn to fucking behave."

Yes, I do.

"Yes!" Gabriel gasped, drawing our attention back to him. His body was loose and pliant as I slowly fucked him—his submission a palpable, beautiful thing. "Dre, I-I'm so close. Please… *make him behave.*"

Oh.

Oh, I truly love everything about this.

248

Andre's eyes widened as rare uncertainty flashed across his face. Then—just as quickly—he buried it again as his grip on my throat tightened and his knee replaced the hand between my legs. I choked on a silent yelp as my demon's full weight landed on my most sensitive parts, but he simply squeezed the sides of my neck until air was nonexistent and my vision started to fade.

"It sounds like our good boy wants *you* to be a good boy too, Theo," he chuckled against my trembling lips. "Will you be a good boy for me?"

Well, there's only one right answer to that.

"No." I barely mouthed the word before shoving one more tendril into Gabriel's tight ass to illustrate my point.

Andre smiled, then bit down so hard on my bottom lip, it was a blessing I *couldn't* make a sound. All I could do was arch beneath him as blood dripped down my chin, but my demon simply lapped it up and brought it back to my mouth to share.

Absolute perfection.

"*Nnngh…* fuck, yessss…" Gabriel groaned, tightening around me as he prepared to detonate.

"Don't you *dare* come," Andre hissed in my ear, his free hand gripping my hair painfully—forcing me to stay present. "I swear to god, Theo, if you do, your nuts will be under my boot next."

Don't threaten me with a good time.

Then, he crashed his lips to mine, and it was all over. Unsurprisingly, Andre owned every inch of my mouth, battling back my tongue until I let him devour me with nips, licks, and warning growls. To my horror, I felt myself *relaxing* in his hold—allowing him to grind himself over me while I whimpered like dying prey.

This entire experience was unreal. It was one thing to get a little rough with my guests during a party, but whatever was happening here didn't feel like a little hedonistic drunken fun to write home about. This was us behaving like animals in human clothing, seeing what we could get away with in polite society. I never wanted it to end.

How will I ever be happy fucking boring old humans again?

Andre's warning about not coming floated to the surface of my consciousness and I almost laughed. I didn't even care about release, but it was absolutely imperative that I got these men to explode. Gabriel was almost there, and I assumed if I made Andre angry enough, it might push him over the edge as well. That would be enough for me.

What have I become?

"Careful," I finally choked out as I tore myself away from his grasp and sucked in a breath. "Being under your boot might be just the thing I need to decompress."

"Brat," Andre muttered, although there was an air of victory on his blood-streaked lips. "It almost sounds like you *want* to be good for me."

With a growl, he sunk his teeth into my neck again—directly over the same sore spot he'd mauled earlier—and every borrowed cell in my body lit up like all the stars in the galaxy.

"Fuckfuckfuckfuckfuuuuuck…" Gabriel chanted under his breath as he convulsed his way through an orgasm that had *my* eyes rolling back in my head.

His deliciously tight little hole clenched around my tendrils as he emptied into his pants like the messy slut he was, leaving me barely holding on. I was feral, clawing at Andre as if he was a lifeboat in a stormy sea, desperate to follow his orders and not join Gabriel in release. To obey.

Seriously… What have I become?

"See," Andre murmured—his lips ghosting over mine again as I returned to Earth alongside my angel. "You *want* me to own you… To crush you until you break. You're gonna love it."

Fuck.

It's true.

"Not if I kill you first," I whispered drowsily, not at all as threateningly as I'd hoped.

My *Demon* hummed thoughtfully as he helped first me, then Gabriel from the booth. "Mmm… we'll see about that." Then he expertly guided both of his *good boys* out of the restaurant —past the oddly *un*interested staff and patrons—and into the cool night air. "Let's go home."

I was so grossly elated by him referring to my house as his *home* that I forgot to reply with some sass. In fact, I was so comfortable in the Uber ride there—snuggled between two men who could still possibly be my enemies—that I fell asleep, and for the first time in what felt like centuries, dreamed of the home I knew before.

Of Stellaria.

CHAPTER 26
GABRIEL

I woke up in the same place I had almost every morning since the night I lost my virginity to Theo on the terrace.

In his bed.

I'd been so fucked out the first time he'd carried me here, I'd barely noticed. After that, Theo had simply *informed* me I'd be in his bed from now on—without giving me a chance to argue. The moment he said it felt like another weight lifted from my shoulders.

But today felt different.

Because Dre came home.

And he's not here with us.

I'd *always* shared a room with my twin. The only times we slept apart were if Dre stayed out late at the club or if one of us had a fuck buddy who was also a sleepover buddy—but that was rare.

And now that my twin was back in the house—and my mind again, *thank fuck*—to not be able to roll over and *see* him was not sitting right with me.

But I also didn't want to leave Theo's bed.

This is the worst.

"Is something troubling you…" Theo murmured—nuzzling his face against my neck, causing his beard to tickle my skin, making me squirm.

When Theo had these unexpectedly schmoopy moments— usually first thing in the morning before he'd totally woken up—I swooned. I still did my best not to point out the behavior, even though I was *here* for it.

I am weak for this man.

Unfortunately, I knew he'd pull away soon enough, leaving me pathetically pining after him until he inevitably manhandled me again. I didn't think he was doing it to fuck with me or to play mind games. It seemed more like my man was a player who'd caught feelings and didn't know what to do with them.

At least, that's what I hope is happening here.

I thought back to how Dre had asked me if I thought something 'serious' was going on here—like an *inventus* bond forming—but I didn't know how to answer that.

So why not dig for intel?

By… communicating and shit.

"How do you know something's bothering me?" I asked as casually as possible, even as every nerve in my body felt like it tensed in anticipation.

Theo lifted his head to stare down at me with an unreadable expression. Then my jaw *dropped* as dozens of starry tendrils appeared—seemingly out of nowhere—to cocoon around us, like a twinkling trellis.

Oh, my god.

He's showing *me who he is!*

"I can *feel* emotions… with these," he calmly explained as two tendrils broke from the pack to caress me with a featherlight touch—down my face and neck before landing on my chest. "Although I usually need to be actively seeking them out."

Fuck, he's so beautiful.

Focus, Gabe…

My mouth was bone dry as I swallowed thickly. *"Usually?"*

"Usually," he repeated, his expression still weirdly blank. "But for some *strange* reason I've yet to decipher, I can now feel every little thing you feel—regardless of if my tendrils are out or not."

Oh, shit.

I froze, and his head cocked with interest, proving his point.

"Can you…" I didn't know why I thought he'd answer this truthfully, but figured I'd shoot my shot. "Can you read my thoughts, too?"

If so, we're fucked.

To my relief, that only made him throw back his head and bless me with a laugh—which was one of my new favorite sounds in the universe. "Unfortunately, I cannot hear all the dirty things you think about me, angel. Although, that would be fun, wouldn't it?"

My face went up in flames as my mind immediately went to *all* the dirty things I'd been thinking since the first moment I laid eyes on him.

It's not as fun as you think…

"Get over yourself, old man," I scoffed in a weak ass attempt to hide my embarrassment. "I have better things to think about."

Psych.

Theo smirked in that slow, filthy way of his that would have bricked me right up if I wasn't already there. He knew it too, as he then pulled down the sheet—exposing exactly how hard I was for this old man.

My *old man.*

Jesus, I'm such a fucking simp.

He hummed knowingly as he took in the glaring evidence. "Oh, do you like that, angel? Do you like being corrupted by an extremely attractive older man?"

"*Fuuuuck…*" I grumbled, feeling my face get redder even as my dick somehow got harder. "I mean, yeah, that's part of it, but it's… more than that. It's…"

I didn't know how to articulate what I was trying to say, so I went for a visual aid.

Assuming he'll let me…

Slowly—so as not to startle him—I lifted my hands and brought them to hover over the tendrils resting on my chest. Theo tensed, holding his breath as I cautiously brushed my fingertips over the glittering matter. It didn't feel like much of anything at first, but then his tendrils grew more substantial beneath my touch—thickening to become more… *corporeal.*

Ohmygodohmygod.

The tiniest "oh" escaped my lips, which was funny, since my entire body was vibrating with excitement.

HE'S LETTING ME TOUCH HIM!!!

This felt huge. This felt like some enormous fucking step in this… well, whatever you called a relationship where one person was supposed to be spying and the other wasn't even a person at all.

Fuck.

This is fucked.

Stubbornly refusing to believe this wasn't possible, I powered on. "I-I like this part of you, too… whatever it is. I like *all* of what you've shown me so far…"

Please, please, *show me more.*

Show me everything.

Theo snatched his tendrils away so fast, I gasped—not least of all because of how *vulnerable* he looked. It reminded me of when I asked to be fucked under the stars for my first time.

Are the cosmos within you, *Theo?*

Just like before, his unusually open expression was replaced —only this time, a truly villainous smile stretched across his face.

Which, again, is doing nothing to discourage my boner.

"You like me sharing my secrets, don't you?" Theo purred, using two tendrils to spread my legs wide while another wrapped around my leaking cock. "But what if I told you nothing about me is how it seems?"

I groaned as another tendril brushed over my nuts and taint before caressing my hole. "Mmm… don't care," I mumbled, planting my feet on the bed—ready for him to do whatever he wanted to me. "I don't think there's anything about you I wouldn't like."

The moment I said it, we both froze, but even if I *could* have taken it back, I wouldn't have. I had never meant anything more in my entire life, and even though that scared the absolute shit out of me, it also felt weirdly calming.

"Keep your dick to yourself."

Too late.

Might as well throw my heart in there, too.

With a low growl, Theo shoved a tendril inside my ass—causing me to arch off the bed as he practically punctured a lung. "Such a sweet sentiment, angel, but an ill-informed one." He chuckled, expanding his tendril as he dragged it out of me, then plunged it in again. In and out, slow and deep, making my eyes roll back in my head. "Shall I enlighten you?"

"Yes!" I choked out—feeling the buzzing sensation in my chest traveling outward to my limbs. "Tell me everything."

I want to know you.

I want you to know me.

He faltered momentarily—which I probably wouldn't have noticed had he not been inside me—but then continued thrusting, almost angrily.

"Very well," he snarled. "Let's start with how old you think I am. Because, let me tell you, my sweet little Earthling, I am as old as this universe you call home."

But this isn't my home…

"Tell me more," I croaked, forcing my blissed-out gaze to stay locked on his—to stay present for *this*. "Tell me, tell me, *pleeeeeaaase…*"

Let me in!

Dre's words about how hot it was to get into someone's head when your dick was inside them—or vice versa, in my case—drifted to the surface. But that wasn't what I wanted. I didn't *want* to sneak into Theo's head and steal his secrets. I wanted him to willingly share them.

I want him to trust me.

Even though he shouldn't…

Theo's eyebrows furrowed. "None of this is surprising or frightening to you, is it? And why *is* that, angel? Why would a supposed *human* not be terrified to meet a creature like me?"

"I'm not afraid!" I cried, desperately riding his tendrils as I chased my release. Desperate for it—for everything he wanted to give me.

Give me more.

Actual tears were blurring my vision, but I refused to look away as pinpricks of light started emanating from his pores, filling me with a sense of longing. "I could never be afraid of you."

I meant it with my whole chest, even as I knew what saying *that* did to creatures like us. How it would immediately be seen as a challenge to be proven wrong.

Theo didn't disappoint. If I'd thought any of his smiles were villainous before, nothing compared to the pure evil now displayed on his handsome face. "Is that right? Well, then let's move on to these tendrils of mine you seem so fond of—the ones that give you so much pleasure."

To illustrate his point, he shoved another inside me and twisted, pummeling my p-spot, making me cry out in mindless pleasure.

More, more, more.

"I'm ready," I croaked, literally vibrating for whatever he was about to show me.

I've been waiting my whole life.

Theo growled inhumanly, making me clench around him before he lifted two more tendrils and hovering them between us. "Would you like to see what else my tendrils are capable of?"

I rapidly nodded, then watched in morbid fascination as his starry tendrils morphed into solid shapes resembling long blades—like *katanas.*

Oh, my GAWD!

He's a goddamn T-1000!!!

"That's right, angel." He continued his threatening theatrics—completely oblivious to the fact that absolutely *none* of this was drying up my thirst for him. "You have no fucking idea who you're dealing with. Those same tendrils filling your tight ass could just as easily be used to tear you apart."

Fuck. Yes.

Tear me the fuck apart.

To further prove he had no fucking idea who *he* was dealing with, Theo then lowered his sexy Samurai swords and sliced shallow lines down my chest and abs—bringing blood bubbling to the surface and causing me to immediately blow my load all over both of us.

FUCKINGFUCKINGFUUUUUUCK!!!!

I legit blacked out as I came. When I regained consciousness, Theo had his teeth buried in my neck and both our dicks in his hand—shuddering as he added his release to the mix of blood and cum already decorating my skin.

Holy fuck.

Yeah, I'm definitely not keeping my dick to myself.

Sorry, not sorry, big bro.

"You are the worst thing that has ever happened to me," Theo muttered into my neck. "You and that twin of yours."

His words *might* have stung after such a mind-blowing experience, but it was hard to take his grouching seriously when he snuggled closer and began licking his bite mark like a schmoopy intergalactic animal.

So he's just a big grumpy alien…

Who's apparently as old as the galaxy.

And a terminator.

Hotttttt.

A familiar knock on the door had me snapping out of my psychotic daydreaming—reminding me that Dre had just 'witnessed' what went down through our now open-for-sexy-times bond.

Why didn't he come join us?

Before I could wrap my head around the crushing disappointment of my twin *not* wanting to share whatever *this* was with me, Theo lifted his head.

"Come in!" he cheerfully called out.

"Wait!" I yelped, scrambling for the discarded sheet, but my twin was already swinging the door wide and waltzing into the room with his usual swagger.

I managed to cover my dick—*thank Christ*—but Dre's eyes locked on the bloody mess on my chest, and his expression turned murderous. His knuckles were as white as bone and his jaw was clenched so tightly, I thought dude might chip a tooth.

Is he worried about my safety?

Or… Theo's?

Instead of addressing the mess on my chest—or the bigger mess between the three of us—Dre cleared his throat and shifted his gaze to Theo.

"Jensen wants to know if we're eating lunch here today, *T,"* he calmly asked, his expression smoothed out once again. "You know, since you masterminded a little field trip to the USN…"

Oh, right.

It's time for a family trip…

What could possibly go wrong?

CHAPTER 27
ANDRE

I was *vibrating* with nerves.

Or… something.

Either way, my senses were on high alert. My palms were sweating and my chest felt tight—my body responding as if I were under attack—all because I'd finally met a brat who could match me.

So why not take Sin's advice and claim him?

That exact question was bouncing around my brain as we Ubered to the USN, effectively drowning out my twin's attempts to comfort me through our mind-bond. I kept turning him down because I needed to process this on my own, especially after everything that had happened over the past twelve hours.

Both with and without me.

The battle at the restaurant had felt like a pissing match between two supes, and I'd barely come out on top. This was partly because *experiencing* Gabe's orgasm made it hard to concentrate, but also because most of my effort had been going toward forcing everyone around us to look elsewhere.

Mostly so no one would call the cops.

While Theo had allowed me to inflict an incredible amount of pain on him—which I could weirdly *feel*—he'd continued to brat me the entire time. I normally lived for this dynamic, but if our situation was going to work, I needed him to submit to me completely. There could only be two choices for a creature as powerful as Theo.

Take the knee.

Or die.

But what if I can't kill him?

Can't or won't?

Can't.

Fuck.

It was time to admit that I'd lost my edge the past few days while sulking at Sinistre's—because Theo's unpredictable behavior continued to catch me off guard. When things went south in Theo's bedroom between him and Gabe a little while ago, I was almost forced to turn that alien fucker into a mindless vegetable. It was only thanks to my twin's absolute *certainty* the psychopath wouldn't hurt him I stood down.

How was he so sure?

And why was I so ready to believe him?

The only silver lining to the stressful clusterfuck—besides my twin still being alive—was the intel I got rummaging around in Theo's head while he was busy villain monologuing. Stranger still was that what I discovered wasn't at all what I expected. The first challenge was finding his brain to begin with. As soon as I breached Theo's skull, I realized what we were dealing with here wasn't simply a shapeshifter.

It was *parasitic symbiosis.*

With the unfortunate host long dead.

Every bone, nerve, and internal organ belonging to whoever this hapless human once was had been replaced by whatever Theo was.

Which looked like… *stars.*

Millions of stars.

After my initial shock had faded, I realized his countless parts resembled glowing synapses—and that neurotransmission seemed to be exactly how he operated.

So he's one giant brain taking a stolen body for a ride.

Cool.

Weirdly, it didn't make me find Theo any less attractive. I hadn't been lying when I told him I had a fascination with brain stuff—although it was more like an obsession. When you were born with the power to control the control center of another person, you naturally learned *everything* about what made that organ tick.

So discovering that Theo resembled the very thing I was already obsessed with only made me *more* determined to figure out how to dominate him. Even if it killed me.

Fuck, I hope it doesn't kill me.

Or Gabe…

My twin knocked again on my mind barriers—insistently— and since I felt like I'd calmed down enough to put on a good front, I let him in. After a quick rundown of Theo's inner workings, I shared what he'd been thinking about while threatening my twin with his Jedi star sabers.

Argentina.

That alone wouldn't have set off my Spidey Sense, especially as Jensen had mentioned Theo traveling there at some point, but the odd overlay of memories caught my attention. Flashes of the jungle and various caves combined with the little brown bottles from Theo's studio to create an unsettling aesthetic collage.

Dude's mind—if you can call it that—is as chaotic as he is!

"Is something troubling you, demon?" Theo's smug as fuck voice brought me out of my thoughts. "You seem a little… *tense.*"

I sighed and turned to face him, doing my best to ignore the dozens of starry tendrils he'd unleashed to hover around me —like an annoying sibling playing the 'I'm not touching you' game.

My gaze flickered to the Uber driver, forcing him to briefly glance at us in the rearview before calmly turning his attention back to the road.

So normies can't see his tendrils.

And Theo knows Gabe can see them.

Great.

"Just thinking about how I need to get laid." I matched Theo's shit-eating smirk as he frowned before getting right to the point. "Why are we going to the USN?"

Theo shrugged as he retracted his tendrils back into his creepy-hot skinsuit. "I've always been mildly curious about the place. Then, with all the *salacious* drama earlier this year, when everyone finally realized all supes are the same, I wondered what sort of secret they'd been hiding behind closed doors all these years. And now"—he slung his arms over our shoulders on either side, drawing us closer—"I have *two* reasons to learn everything there is to know about supes."

He is the worst.

"I don't know what the fuck you're talking about, but okay," I muttered, shrugging him off. Even more annoying was when I immediately *missed* his proximity.

THE WORST.

"Dre…" Gabe sighed, as if it *wasn't* a big deal that this killer alien from outer space—who we'd been sent here to monitor—knew we were supes. "Do we really need to do this?"

I huffed and crossed my arms before turning to face both of them. "Yeah, we do. Kimono Karen here is already on my last fucking nerve, and the last thing I need right now is to be accused of being a supe with no evidence."

Moving with supe speed himself, Theo gripped my chin, forcing me to look at him. "You're going to look me in the eye and tell me you're human?" he hissed under his breath, allowing that terrifying as fuck *static* to pass over his face again—revealing the inner workings beneath.

His true self.

Which he's not sharing with me either.

Theo was looking for a reaction—daring me to cower like the human I was claiming to be—but we both knew I didn't have it in me.

Instead, I maintained eye contact as I practically spat out my reply. "You haven't *earned* anything different. Now get your fucking hand off me before I remove it from your body."

Even if you can just find another one.

To my surprise, Theo looked almost *hurt* by my words, but he obediently removed his hand and placed it in his lap. And to my annoyance, Gabe slipped his hand into Theo's to give it a squeeze—while also giving me the middle finger in my head.

He's so cock-whipped.

Tendril… whipped…

The car pulled up in front of the USN, and I immediately swung open the door before clambering out of the car. I cursed under my breath as I stumbled, wondering why I hadn't let these two idiot lovebirds do the tour themselves.

"Ah, Andre Acosta. Welcome to the United Super Nations! Or are you Gabriel?"

I turned with a smile to greet Sylvano Ricci—more than happy to play this little charade with the man who knew exactly who I was down to my birth chart. "It's Andre, Mr. Ricci. Thank you for hosting us on such short notice. And my apologies in advance for how Mr. Coatl will behave today."

Might as well give him the trigger warning up front.

"I resemble that remark!" Theo huffed good-naturedly, appearing at my side in a flash of red.

As if to taunt me, he was in the same suit he'd worn for the lame sex party he'd hosted the night we arrived—and looked no less devilish in the light of day.

"Sadly, Andre is absolutely correct, Mr. Ricci," he continued, making my eye twitch. "I am not known for good behavior, but any complaints should be directed to *him* for distribution of appropriate punishment."

What?!

I choked on air as Sylvano laughed heartily. "It's quite all right. I could use some excitement around here since the case has closed on The People vs. Biggs Enterprises. Although… Now that the trial has wrapped up, we were hoping to rekindle my father's supe DNA research project. That's where I'm hoping *you'll* come in."

For a moment, I thought he was talking to *me*, since we both knew it was my family who was funding the goddamn research. But the Deputy Secretary-General's hopeful gaze was fixed on Theo.

The alien in human clothing smiled coldly. "What exactly do you think you'll find in *my* DNA?"

My guess would be nothing.

"N-nothing," Sylvano stuttered, furrowing his brow. "We need a marketing campaign created. Something to really wow the public."

"Oh!" Theo brightened. "Now *that* I am more than happy to put out some feelers for."

I'll bet you are.

"Wonderful!" Sylvano clapped his hands before gesturing toward the door across the courtyard. "Now if you'll just follow me insi—"

The rest of his words were lost as a bolt of agony shot through my head, and I gripped my temples to steady myself through the unpleasant sensation.

A quick glance at Gabe confirmed he was experiencing the same phenomenon. This wasn't something we had to deal with often—and not since Wolfy tried to sacrifice himself for all of us in Iceland. It meant one of our siblings was about to be in danger.

Baltasar.

CHAPTER 28
ANDRE

"Are you boys all right?" Sylvano was suddenly standing directly in front of us, doing his best to shield Gabe and me from Theo's gaze.

As if that fucker isn't feeding off every second of this.

"Yup," I gritted out, gesturing at Gabe who was fumbling his phone from his pocket. "We just need to make a phone call. Family emergency."

Sylvano was savvy enough to know the drill. "Understood. I'll leave your names at the front. You can join us in my office when you're ready. Come, Theo. Let's give them some privacy."

Stuffed shirt wingman for the win.

Gabe moved closer and took my hand—his touch grounding me as we sat on a nearby bench to take in our incoming vision.

"Ready?"

"Ready as I'm gonna be."

We were now *inside* Balty's thoughts—enough to know he and Zion were poking around in a home office in the Salah's East Coast mansion. They definitely weren't supposed to be in there, judging by the cloud of stress swirling on top of our brother's baseline mountain of anxiety.

Someone needs to teach this dude some hippie breathing exercises.

Next came a separate glimpse of Zion's mother—the formidable hero known as Lady Tempest—stalking down the hallway in our brother's direction. It was unclear if her destination was the office they were in, but it was understood if she found them there, a chain of events would be set in motion that would not end well for either of our clans.

No fucking pressure or anything.

Luckily, my twin had already brought up Balty on speed dial. "What's up, losers?" I heard Baby Hulk's dumbass voice on speakerphone, but I concentrated on maintaining my hold on his sight.

What are those two idiots looking for in there?

"Get the fuck out of that room and start walking east," Gabe hissed. "Leave the lizard behind to do his thing. You're playing the distraction."

"Do it, Balty," I growled, turning on the Dom in my tone to get this clueless sub to hop to it. "Move your ass."

Our brother murmured something to Zion before leaving the room. Then he glanced around in a panic before sighing in defeat. "Which way's east, dudes?"

"Fucking hell," Gabe groaned.

I suddenly had a choice to make. While Gabe and I could easily join forces to infiltrate someone's head long enough to *see* through their eyes, I wasn't sure if he knew I could do it on my own. Or that I could also use this connection to map out their surroundings.

Oh, well!

"Walk toward the judgy bust at the end of the hall," I replied, watching my twin closely as I gave Balty perfect instructions.

And now I'm gonna make things worse…

"Lady Tempest is headed his way, Gabe. She knows something about Argentina."

My twin didn't outwardly react, but I felt the tiniest flare of surprise through our bond. Some small petty part of me was thrilled I'd hidden something from *him* in the same way he'd hidden so much from me with Wolfy.

How's it feel, dude?

Balty cracked some stupid joke, and Gabe sighed before bringing us back to the task at hand.

"Stop walking," he commanded—snippier than usual with the Suarez sensitive flower. "All right, listen up, asshole. When she rounds the corner, pretend to hang up, but keep the call connected when you put the phone back in your pocket. Ask her about a trip she took to Argentina. Say you heard the staff talking about it or some shit."

Hooooo… He is SALTY.

"Who?" Balty mumbled, with his signature confusion. Dude didn't have too long to wonder, as Lady Tempest rounded the corner and came into view. "Okay, talk to you later," our brother squeaked out as he slid his phone into his pocket— still connected, like we'd asked.

It's showtime.

I could *feel* Gabe seething beside me, but I ignored him in favor of zeroing in on Lady Tempest's resting bitch face. Balty started stuttering out some questions and I focused on jumping from his head into hers.

Another sneaky trick.

Again, how does it feel?

For a moment, I wondered how a creature like Theo took over a body in the first place—if the person had to be dead first—and if it was like what I could do with my mind hopping.

Xander called him the missing link to his research…

"…when you went to Argentina…" Balty's voice drifted from the phone and I sharply inhaled as I jumped from his head into Lady Tempest's memories.

Surprise!

> At the last second, I dragged Gabe along for the ride— whether to be moral support or as an olive branch, I couldn't be sure. The next thing I knew, we were both standing in the Argentinian cave we'd seen countless photographs of in our family's secure archives. This was the same cave currently supervised by the normie anthropologist Dr. Lorenzo Torres-Maldonado and under the sole protection and benefaction of the villainous Suarez clan.
>
> But that wasn't who was there with us now.
>
> Or—rather—*then.*
>
> We'd definitely gone back in time, as I could *feel* how much younger Lady Tempest's body was as I gazed

out from *her* eyes to the now familiar cave paintings depicting the original supe alien ancestor invasion.

"A lot of politicians on both sides of the aisle have paid hefty sums for this information, but they still don't 'own' all the pieces to the puzzle. That's what's kept me rich—doling out crumbs to the vultures."

Whoever was speaking caused fury to bubble up inside Lady Tempest, and her—*our*—gaze shifted to fall on an unfamiliar man to her left.

A guy named Richard Cabrera, according to her memory.

He was in his early to mid-sixties and wearing the telltale khakis and protective gear of an archaeologist. Unbeknownst to him, Lady Tempest was imagining showing how useless that gear was by flaying him alive with her wind power.

A sudden flash of the future—still the past from present time—revealed she'd done exactly that in retribution for this normie leaking the truth about supe heritage to Capitol Hill for his own gain.

RIP, Dick.

"Mmm… Wouldn't it be more fun to *also* use this information to our own advantage?" a vaguely familiar voice echoed strangely from somewhere out of sight— like an itch I couldn't scratch. "Release this grenade when the time is right?"

I wanted Lady Tempest to turn and show me who was speaking, but her predatory gaze was fixed on the archaeologist. "Agreed." She backed up the mystery man's statement. "And I suggest you fall in line, Richard."

Richard With a Death Wish snorted with the air of someone who did *not* realize he was outclassed. "I don't take orders from women, but sure, sweetheart."

Wrong answer, dude.

Lady Tempest started to turn toward the other man in the cave, but then Balty's foghorn voice ripped me back to the present.

Nooooo!

"Wait! Do you know an anthropologist named Dr. Lorenzo Torres-Maldonado? He studies ancient civilizations in South America and I was hoping to… apply for an internship with him. Yeah. You know, after the Games are done."

Present-day Lady Tempest's irritation morphed into pure confusion. "An *internship?* What on earth would someone like *you* do for an anthropologist?"

"Lift heavy things," Baby Hulk deadpanned, and I couldn't stop the snort that snuck out of me.

Might as well roast yourself before someone else does!

A little girl's voice joined the conversation on their end, which broke *everyone's* concentration. I glanced over to find Gabe glaring me into an early grave.

"What the fuck kind of witchy woo was that?"

> *"You've done that with me before, Gabe. Chill."*

"Um. WITH you being the key word. And not even close. What else can you do on your own?"

"This is your *grandchild!*" Balty hissed—AT LADY FUCKING TEMPEST—almost Hulking out in the process. "How about you find the time to treat her like a part of this family—which she *is.*"

Whoa.

When did little big bro grow a pair?

Gabe and I dropped our drama to focus on possibly rallying to Balty's defense, but—*shockingly*—the famous hero stood down. Even more shocking was our brother protecting some random Salah kid.

What the hell is going on over there?

"BALTY!" Gabe shouted in the silence that followed Lady Tempest walking away with the little girl.

"Yeah, yeah, I know, I fucked up," Balty snapped directly into the phone, and sounding way snippier than *he* usually did. "The only thing I got out of Lady Tempest was her thinking I'm a bigger freak than she already does."

"What are you talking about, Balty? You kicked ass!" I laughed—even if I *was* slightly disappointed we wouldn't get to fry Lady Tempest's brain. "We got that shady lady on lock, thanks to you."

"What are you talking about?" he sputtered, sounding muffled. "I didn't get her to say anything about Argentina. She denied it all."

Have you not figured out how this works by now, dum-dum?

Gabe took over with our slower-than-most bro. "Yeah, but the minute you mentioned Argentina, her mind went to

Argentina—to the cave Doc's working on. She's *been* there, Balty. Tempest knows about the paintings and our history."

"So, she knows Doc?" he whispered, like the overgrown, excited puppy he was.

"No, she doesn't," Gabe replied, his eyes narrowing as he zeroed in on me again. *"That* she was being truthful about, at least."

Unlike me.

How. Does. It. Feel?

"Good idea to ask if she knew Doc, though," I piped in, if only to keep Balty on the line and make Gabe wait to confront me. "Genius."

I popped back into Balty's head in time for him to reenter the office and find Zion triumphantly waving a photograph. When he—*we*—reached him and glanced down, he saw a sepia toned image of a much younger Lady Tempest outside the Argentinian cave, standing next to the same man from her memory.

But who was taking the photo?

Then Balty focused on a memory of his own—one that involved being chased down in the woods by Zion earlier today. So I hightailed it the fuck out of his filthy little head. Plus, I needed a minute to process what I'd 'seen' through Past Lady Tempest's eyes.

Why did that other man sound so familiar?

She doesn't know Doc…

"...dang, bro. Did your balls get bigger since you left home?" Gabe spoke loud enough for Zion to hear. "You almost went full Hulk on Lady fucking Tempest."

Zion's voice got all low and sultry. "Yeah, you did. You defended my little girl. *Our* little girl."

Wait…

Zion Salah has a kid?

And these two idiots are official like that *already?!*

I really needed to get laid, as I couldn't stop myself from grumbling. "Everybody's shacking up around here. It's weird." Realizing I was showing myself, I quickly switched gears. "Hi, Justice! Heard you're gonna join the family."

"Hello, Shock and Awe." Zion chuckled, throwing our supe names back at us like a Deathball pass. "Thanks for being our wingmen."

Anytime, Godzilla.

"No problem at all," Gabe smoothly replied, knowing as well as I did that buttering up the Salah clan heir was the right political move. "Thank *you* for delivering dirt on your family. Our bloodthirsty leader will be most pleased."

"Wolfgang?" Zion asked, and I didn't need eyes on the ground to know his grin was the shit-eating kind.

Dang.

Everyone has Wolfy's number.

With prophetic disaster now averted, we hung up, but the tension between us was *thick.*

Let's get this over with.

I awkwardly rubbed the back of my neck. "Listen… Gabe, I—"

"Is *that* why Wolfy doesn't trust you?" my twin quietly asked, his expression almost… fearful.

He better not be afraid of me!

"I doubt it," I scoffed. "I've never been able to get into Wolfy's head. You know that. Someone taught that fucker how to lock that shit down tighter than Fort Knox."

A certain Swiss Sensei, if I had to put money on it.

Whatever Gabe was about to say was interrupted by an incoming text. We both glanced down to find Balty had sent two images. The first was of the photograph I'd just seen, while the other looked like it was the back of the photo, blank except for a faded pencil scrawl in the bottom corner.

"Zoom in," I instructed, as if my twin wasn't doing just that, to reveal the words, 'At the site with Richard and T.'

Richard Cabrera and…

No.

No fucking way.

Gabe and I locked eyes as my blood ran cold. "You don't think…" he began, although his expression told me we were on the same page, even without the mind-bond.

Even if we might not want to believe it.

I blew out a slow breath as a snippet of Theo's recent rambling resurfaced. "What did he say in the Uber on the way over here? About the Masculine-Antihero drama… 'when everyone *finally* realized all supes are the same…' Does that mean *he* already knew about our shared heritage?"

"And is he working with Lady Tempest on… something?" Gabe barely whispered. His stricken gaze fell to his phone. "W-what do I say to Balty? I… I don't want anyone coming for my… for our…"

Fuck.

Neither do I.

"Just tell him the guy in the photo is who Lady Tempest was thinking of in Argentina," I muttered. "Then send it to Simon with the name 'Richard Cabrera.' Other than that, we don't know shit."

My other half practically melted into the pavement before obeying my instructions and tucking his phone away. "Done." He glanced up at me hesitantly. "But… *I* want to know more."

"Yeah," I growled, grabbing his arm and dragging him toward the front entrance of the USN. "So do I. And we're gonna find out exactly what the fuck is going on here."

CHAPTER 29
THEO

If there was one thing I was sure of, Sylvano Ricci was completely human.

Well, at least someone around here is!

"How closely were you following The People vs. Biggs Enterprises trial, Mr. Coatl?"

I retracted the tendrils I'd left hovering near the twins in a begrudging attempt to give most of my attention to the man seated across from me. The *only* reason I did was because the startling pain and strange second-hand anxiety I'd felt pouring off Andre and Gabriel had lessened exponentially.

What in Stellaria happened *out there?*

They'd acted as if a family emergency had come up, but hadn't made their phone call until *after* experiencing a visceral reaction to… something.

I don't like secrets.

Except my own, of course.

Most upsetting was how my usually non-existent protective instincts had gone into overdrive when I'd thought what was *mine* was under attack. And that Andre was also included in this assessment.

Even though he's been behaving like such an ass lately.

His insistence on *pretending* to be human was insulting enough, but then to say I hadn't *earned* the right to know if he was a supe…

How DARE he!

"Mr. Coatl?" Sylvano Ricci gently repeated.

Everything about Ricci was gentle. Calm. His mannerisms reminded me of someone who'd stumbled upon a wild animal in the woods, and while this animal might not be known for unprovoked attacks, the man in charge of the United Super Nations was smart enough not to push his luck.

Especially since he doesn't know what I am.

But he definitely knows what the twins are.

Tamping down the irrational urge to kill him simply for knowing more about the objects of my obsession than I did, I dutifully refocused on our conversation.

Try to act human, Theo.

"I only followed the bits of the trial that interested me." I smiled broadly—flashing the pearly whites I'd worked so hard to perfect. "Specifically, the flawlessness of Captain Masculine's physique."

Sylvano Ricci nearly spit out the water he'd been sipping. "Well, he was bred to be flawless—and via less than noble means."

That piqued my interest. "Less than noble, you say?"

Maybe I should have paid closer attention to the trial…

He nodded. "Yes. His mother—Smoldering Siren—had Captain Masculine through an arranged marriage with Vortexio. Unfortunately, her heart was already taken by another—"

"Was it *you?*" I teased, more out of boredom than believing this milquetoast man in front of me could win the heart of a legendary superhero.

The last thing I expected was for Ricci's face to go up in flames. "I'm talking about *before* B-Captain Masculine was born… when Siren met the villain known as Iron Axe."

This sounded vaguely familiar, only because Captain Masculine's sad little origin story was all the gossip sites covered for *months* earlier this year. I'd had to throw a particularly hedonistic gathering on the pier that warranted not only police involvement, but the National Guard in order to get back on top.

Right where I belong.

Except with Andre, apparently…

Swallowing the growl trying to build in my throat, I refocused yet again. "And I bet that got everyone's panties in a bunch when it happened, hmm? A beloved *hero* falling for a *villain?* How scandalous!" I leaned back and scoffed. "Not nearly as scandalous as learning that both are biologically the same."

With the way the man seated across the desk was gaping at me, I wondered if perhaps I'd spoken out of turn. With how the citizens of Big City had swooned over the Captain Masculine-Doctor Antihero pairing—and how quickly the USN responded by overturning the laws forbidding marriage between heroes and villains—I'd assumed this *obvious fact* had all come to light during the trial.

Right?

"Right." Ricci cleared his throat. "That's… exactly why Iron Axe—Franco Marisi—first reached out to my father after he founded the USN. Not only to switch sides, but to help *prove* all supes were the same, through that DNA research program I mentioned…"

"Yes! Let's discuss your marketing needs," I quickly interjected, eager to redirect from revealing too much about what I knew to the goddamn Deputy Secretary-General of the USN.

This distraction is making me lose my edge!

Ricci smiled sweetly—instinctively reverting to his feral animal whispering. "I first need you to understand the history of the project, Mr. Coatl, and why it was originally shut down."

I was unsure why he was wasting my time with this buildup when the big reveal was probably just some politician swooping in with red tape.

Since it's always been in the humans' best interests to keep the supes from joining forces against them.

Which is exactly the paranoia I wish to play with…

When I simply raised my eyebrows expectantly, Ricci continued, "Soon after Iron Axe was announced as the face of the DNA research project, he disappeared. It turned out that Vortexio murdered him so he could claim Smoldering Siren for himself."

Okay… plot twist.

But, still…

I shrugged. "Is that not how survival of the fittest works? Especially for supes, who barely behave better than animals with such things? Mind you"—I held up a finger when I noticed his jaw clench—"I do *not* mean that as an insult. It's simply the way it is."

It's certainly how it is with me.

The hint of anger that had been brewing on Sylvano Ricci's face evaporated, replaced by a shrewd assessment. "Iron Axe was Smoldering Siren's *inventus.* Do you know what that is?"

Something buzzed beneath my skin. Something suspiciously like the recognition that accompanied a mate-based resonant note.

Shoo.

"I do not," I stated, willing it to be so.

Ricci continued to observe me carefully. "It's when two super-naturals of equal power form a bond—combining their abilities to become nearly unbeatable. They can sense the other's presence and emotions, and being apart for even a short amount of time can feel torturous."

Kinky.

"So Vortexio eliminated a potential threat to his safety and a rival male in one fell swoop." I yawned, baffled once again how these Earthlings lived among supes, yet didn't seem to understand them in the slightest. "While also securing a mate to co-create the perfect little war machine for Biggs Enterprises—"

"While also *killing* Siren's soul in the process!" The Deputy Secretary-General of the USN unexpectedly banged his fist on his desk, and something told me that did *not* happen often.

Andre warned *you about dealing with me, human.*

He blew out a slow breath to regain his composure. "Even though it wasn't until recently that Iron Axe's body was found, Smoldering Siren *knew* the moment he died. She told me it felt like…" Ricci took a shaky sip of water before continuing. "Like someone removing her heart from her chest with a rusty spoon. She *still* wakes up nearly blinded by the need for revenge most days, but with no one to inflict vengeance on, she can do nothing but swallow her rage."

You know… this inventus business sounds a lot like a stellar collision…

Suddenly, all I could think about was how I hadn't seen Andre or Gabriel in at least ten minutes, which made me irrationally anxious. Something could have happened to them while this suit was blathering to me about shit that had nothing to do with me.

Where ARE they?

"Why are you telling me this?" I gritted out, doing everything in my power to keep my tendrils from exploding out of me.

If something *had* happened to them, I would snap the necks of every person in this stupid fucking facility until I found out who'd hurt my precious, aggravating treasures.

WHERE THE FUCK ARE MY TWINS?!

As if summoned by *my* nearly blinding rage, a crisp knock on the door told me Andre had arrived—no doubt with Gabriel in tow.

Thank FUCK.

The door swung wide, and the immense relief I felt at having the twins in my sight again made it painfully obvious that this random human had identified my inexplicable *double* stellar collision before I did.

That's a problem for Future Theo to worry about.

"I'm telling you this because I need you to understand what this project means to those already involved," Ricci continued, waving the others into the room. "Humanizing supes will be an important step in any outreach we do—especially as we were *just discussing* how all supes are the same."

The twins both snapped their attention to me in a predatory way that made me simultaneously harden *and* go on high alert.

"Mmm…" Andre hummed as he leaned against the wall while Gabriel took the seat beside me. "I'd forgotten that was common knowledge."

Okay, so I fucked up.

Outwardly, I was calm as ever, but my true form was poised to strike—assessing the twin threats in front of me.

"A funny choice of words—*humanizing*," I crooned. "Since apparently we *all* know supes are anything but. So why bother? What's the goal of this DNA project, anyway?"

Ricci sighed, accustomed to enough supe posturing to ignore the tension *crackling* in the air. "The goal is *answers,* Mr. Coatl. For all sides." He jerked upright, as if a thought suddenly struck him.

Or was given to him…

"On that note." He cleared his throat. "Everyone involved in the project has already donated their DNA to the database—with Captain Masculine and Doctor Antihero being the most notable. It's your choice, of course, but doing so would demonstrate your belief in our mission."

You think you're so sly, don't you?

"I'd be happy to!" I exclaimed, slapping my hand on the desk—causing the one human in the room to startle. "Take a sample now. Go nuts."

Catch me if you can.

"O-okay..." Sylvano Ricci stuttered, fumbling open a drawer to produce rubber gloves and a specimen collection kit—suspiciously prepared for this very circumstance. "I have release forms for you to sign—"

"One of these two can simply sign for me," I snapped. "Since they're my handlers."

And I hate how much I resemble that remark...

"Consent is important in every situation where power is exchanged, Theo," Andre spoke, infuriatingly calm. "Why don't you tell us what you know?"

I felt a strange change in the air pressure—similar to what I'd experienced the first day I'd allowed these two terrors into my home. Then, someone entered my head to get more specific.

"Tell us what you know about Argentina."

"Which one of you is doing that?" I hissed.

"Doing what?" Andre smirked as Gabriel looked between us, clearly on the edge of panicking.

So it's Andre, then.

Sylvano Ricci cleared his throat. "Must I remind everyone in this room that the United Super Nations is a legally binding neutral zone, prohibiting altercations between any supernaturals identifying as either—"

"Well, since I identify as *neither,* your silly little laws don't apply to me, now do they?" I growled at Ricci, although I kept my gaze locked on the smirking demon across the room.

I will fucking kill you, stellar collision or not.

"Theo..." Gabriel cautiously spoke. "We just want to know you—"

"Oh, but *I* haven't *earned* the right to know *you,*" I snarled, my borrowed heart feeling painfully—annoyingly—tender.

Why the fuck do I even care?

"A supe's identity is sacred," Sylvano Ricci evenly interjected as he slid a release form and pen across the desk toward me, his demeanor now that of a diplomat. "But perhaps the same could be said for your kind as well?"

"Perhaps," I gritted out as I scratched my priceless artist signature across the bottom and held out my finger. "Perhaps I'll simply take my secrets with me when I go."

"Don't!" Gabriel grabbed my arm again—just as he did when his family came to dinner. His touch simultaneously soothed and enraged me, but his next words sealed his fate. "Please don't leave me…"

Good idea.

"Very well, angel." I chuckled, low and dark, waiting until the useless blood sample had been extracted before laying my hand over his. "I'll just take you with me."

And then, I star hopped the two of us far, far away.

CHAPTER 30
GABRIEL

"GA—!!!"

Dre's alarmed voice echoed in my head, but I could barely suck in a breath before the subsequent one was stolen from my lungs.

Sylvano Ricci's office blurred into nothingness, and the next thing I knew, Theo and I were hurtling through the ether—so fast, I thought I was going to puke up Jensen's delicious breakfast.

What the FUCK is happening!

We stopped moving as abruptly as we'd started, although I still couldn't see shit. It was so cold I was full-body shuddering, and the sweat pouring off me wasn't helping the situation. The only reason I wasn't completely panicking was because I could feel Theo's arms around my waist—his presence calming me despite *causing* my fear.

"Theo?" I haltingly said.

Or... I *tried* to say. I opened my mouth and formed the words, but no actual sound came out.

What the FUCKING fuck is happening?!

I half-expected Theo to say something ominous—*and totally hot*—even if I couldn't. Instead, he uncurled one arm from around me to point into the distance, toward what looked like a glowing blue orb. Too stunned to do anything but obey, I rapidly blinked until the object came into focus, and a sound-less yelp left me as I recognized what I was looking at...

Earth.

THIS MOTHERFUCKER TOOK ME INTO SPACE?!!!

Now I was terrified beyond belief. I twisted in Theo's hold to wrap myself around him like a monkey in a goddamn tree—burying my face against his neck, and gulping in breaths in a literal last gasp attempt to calm myself.

This can't be happening. This can't be happening. This can't...

Theo tensed before tightening his grip around me and smoothing his hands down my back. Before I could get back to baseline, we'd teleported again, and landed on the roof of the old Biggs Enterprises building.

Imma hurl.

"How the... how the *fuck* were you able to *breathe* up there?!" Theo hollered, unceremoniously dropping me to the tarred surface. "What in Stellaria's name *ARE YOU?*"

I slowly rose from the ground and held up my hands placatingly. Before I could reply to this crazy—*but still hot, goddammit*—asshole, Dre's voice was screaming in my head.

"GABE! Holy fuck. I lost contact with you completely! Where are you right now?"

"We're on the roof of Biggs Enterprises, but I don't know how long we'll be here. Dude took me into space first."

"Okay, I'll be there as soon as I ca—wait, WHAT? That fucker took you to—"

"Are you telepathically speaking to that twin of yours?!" Theo was suddenly standing in front of me with his hand wrapped around my throat—cutting off my airway.

And giving me a massive boner.

Jesus CHRIST, now is not *the time!*

"I don't know what you're talking about," I croaked, refusing to use my super strength to throw him off me.

Despite all signs pointing to this being an actual hostage situation with actual danger to my well-being, I couldn't bring myself to injure this maniac. In fact, the idea of causing Theo any harm made me sicker than the teleporting did.

It's because he's my inventus.

"No, Gabe! Your inventus wouldn't hurt *you. Listen to me. Get him villain monologuing again—whatever you need to do to stop him from moving locations again until I get there."*

I wanted to ask why he didn't just use the USN's Bat-Signal to get Butch to fly here in two seconds. But then I realized Dre had probably made Sylvano swear up and down not to tell any of our siblings or significant others what was happening.

To maintain control over the situation.

This is such a fucking mess.

But it's our *mess.*

"Theo, *please…*" I choked out. That must have been the magic word as he abruptly released me, although he didn't back away. "Please, just explain what you're upset about."

"What *are* you?" he repeated, looking weirdly close to tears. "Or are you going to repeat that 'supe's identity is sacred' bullshit, so you never have to tell me?"

"I want to tell you!" I cried. "But it's not my decision alone to make. I would have to talk to Dre… and I'd also have to make sure my family was safe—"

Theo laughed derisively. "Your *family,* hmm? Like Wolfgang and *Luca?* Tell me, Gabriel… Since we both know you can inexplicably see these." He unleashed some tendrils to dance around him, gorgeously catching the light. "The *real* question is, have you ever seen them before meeting me?"

What?

I was beyond confused by the direction this conversation was going. "Wh… No. I-I think I'd remember seeing something as wild as th—"

The rest of my words were lost as—yet again—Theo grabbed me and our surroundings blurred. When I opened my eyes again, we'd somehow landed in the middle of a kaleidoscope of color. It reminded me of something out of a Dr. Seuss book, with towering structures made from glowing crystals, streets paved with glittering mica, and trees that looked like neon cotton candy. Wherever we were made Theo's maximalist home look like a calming zen spa.

Maybe Jensen slipped something into my scrambled eggs…

"Whatever you do, don't scream, angel," Theo murmured in my ear—implying we'd at least landed somewhere with an atmosphere. "I don't think the Stellarians would be happy to see *either* of us lurking about."

Stellarians…

Oh, my gawd!

"Stellaria?" I asked, although I *knew* in my bones that's where we were. "This is your home?"

Our home...

Wait, what?

Theo tensed and drew me closer. "It hasn't been my home for a very long time, but yes... this is where I originated from."

I simply nodded and peered out from the dark alleyway where we were hiding. Alien creatures in every form imaginable wandered the streets. Some were humanoid while most weren't even close—but none looked like the man beside me. Dre had given me the rundown of what Theo was beneath his hottie exterior, so I assumed these were all stolen vessels from other planets.

But what do they do if there's no skinsuit to steal?

My question was potentially answered when a group of armored figures marched toward us in unison—especially judging by how Theo immediately growled at their presence. They looked like goddamn Mandalorians, which did nothing to discourage how hard this situation was making me.

Space Daddy boner.

"Is... that armor what you use when there's nothing else available?" I dared to ask—desperate for him to just tell me everything about himself.

Please...

Unfortunately, I must have struck a nerve, as Theo roughly grabbed me and the world blurred once again.

Nonononononooooooo!

My back hit a plush surface, and I gasped in surprise to find we were now in the spare room off of Theo's studio.

Why would he bring me here?

"It doesn't seem fair that *you* know so much about me, yet aren't returning the favor…" Theo snarled as tendrils shot out of him to wrap around my wrists and ankles, pinning me in place.

Of course, all this did was make my hard-on painfully harder —especially once he stretched my limbs to the point of pain. "It's time to talk, *Gabriel Acosta… if that's even your real name.*"

"It's not," I rasped, beyond overwhelmed by the cocktail of emotions I was feeling, mixing with what I was picking up from Theo *and* Dre.

I…

We were all a complete wreck over each other—and this situation—and I honestly didn't understand why I couldn't just *tell* Theo we were supes. He'd already figured it out on his own and it wasn't as if we didn't have leverage on him as well.

Dre's power was building—trying to combine with mine to take out Theo—so I rallied what I could to *block* him, even if just temporarily.

Even if I've never attempted to face off with him before.

But I can't let Theo die before I tell him who I am…

"Don't you fucking DARE tell him, Gabe! Just let me—"

"You can tell me anything, angel…" Theo kissed his way up my neck as he curled over me, rubbing his cock over mine and sending sparks of pleasure shooting through my veins as the familiar humming in my chest kicked in.

I no longer saw any reason I *shouldn't* tell the man I was in love with everything about me. He'd just taken me to his *home planet* for Chrissake, and had repeatedly shown me his true form while fucking my brains out. It was the logical next step in this twisted relationship to share more…

Like a really intense get to know you phase…

Via torture.

"My name's Gabriel Suarez," I calmly replied, ignoring Dre screaming in my head to shut my goddamn mouth. "And my supe name is Awe."

Please trust me.

Theo pulled back to stare down at me. "So you're a Suarez," he flatly spoke as dozens of tendrils appeared around us, caging me in. "One of the infamous villain clan who rules this city with an iron fist. Or, I should say, with a *Hand of Death.* What *was* big bro's plan the other night, hmm? To drain my power and use it as his own?!"

No!

"Theo, please!" I cried. "That's not even how Wolfy's power works. And it's not… That's not why we're here. He sent us here to—"

"Ah, yes." Theo laughed bitterly, the raw *hurt* radiating off him making my heart feel like it was cracking in two. "Wolf-gang *sent* both of you here with a purpose, didn't he? Two pretty little distractions to keep my attention away from the *real* threat at my table. The one sent to collect me for the crimes I committed against my own kind!"

What the fuck is he talking about?!

"DUDE, YOU NEED TO LET ME IN HIS HEAD RIGHT NOW SO I CAN SHUT HIM THE FUCK DOWN!"

"I love you!" I sobbed, tears blurring my vision so badly I couldn't even see how Theo reacted to my ridiculous words.

"And I know it's too soon but I *feel* things for you that make no fucking sense and I am so fucking sorry that we came here under false pretenses, but please just let me explain, please, I…"

"HE'S GOING TO FUCKING KILL YOU!!!"

No.

He won't.

"I'm going to kill you now," Theo calmly interrupted, sounding almost *sad* about it, and my vision instantly cleared to zero in on the threat before me.

He wouldn't…

Would he?!

My heart felt like it was about to shatter for real as Theo slid off the bed and once again raised two tendrils shaped into razor-sharp *katanas*. All at once I understood that this was *not* his usual showboating, and that if I didn't act now—either physically or mentally—then I was about to be dead.

But I can't hurt him.

Can't or won't?

Can't.

Because he's my…

Inventus no longer seemed like a strong enough word for whatever Theo was to me—not after what he'd shown me today. If I was going to die by his hand, so be it. There was only one thing I'd try to make this stop.

"Shock…" I whispered—letting my power fade in favor of calling upon both my safe word *and* the only other being who meant more to me than life itself.

Please…

Theo froze with his shimmering blades poised inches away from my exposed throat. "Fuck. You truly don't play fair, angel," he huffed as the murderous expression on his face shifted to mild annoyance. "You're lucky you're my…"

Your??

Theo's expression changed once again—to confusion, then terror, then vengeful fury. *"WHICH ONE OF YOU IS DOING THIS?!"*

WHAT?!

Neither of us had to wait long for an answer. A dark chuckle I knew well echoed from the doorway a moment before Dre appeared behind the man looming above me.

"What a naughty boy you've been, Theo…" he purred—sliding his hand around Theo's throat like a loving caress. "Did you really think you could take Gabe away from me?"

"Fuck you, *demon,*" Theo gritted out, with considerable effort, and it was only then that I realized he was completely frozen in place.

Is… is Dre *doing that?*

Oh, my god…

"Mmm… wrong again," Dre tsked, gliding away from him to easily unclasp the tendrils wrapped around my wrists and ankles—somehow in complete control of the situation *and* Theo. *"I'm* going to be fucking *you,* but only once you've sat in time out for a couple of days…"

He can hold him like this for DAYS?!

Holy fuck.

How powerful is *he…?*

"You'd better never let me free, Andre," Theo snarled as my twin straightened and turned to face him again. "Because as soon as you do, I *will* kill you—"

"No. You won't," Dre calmly replied, cupping Theo's cheek almost sweetly. "Not only because you're feeling the same crazy shit we feel for you, but because you *know* you've finally met your match."

My twin leaned in close and brushed his lips over Theo's, whispering his next words like a prayer. "I can't actually kill you, but the things I want to do to you will make you wish I could. Doesn't that sound like fun?"

Theo only growled in reply, and even though he had decided not to kill *me—thank fuck—*the sound set my survival instincts on high alert.

I am way out of my league here…

With both of them.

Satisfied with that animalistic response, Dre turned to where I was still cowering on the bed. "C'mon, idiot," he grumbled. "You and I need to talk about some shit while our sammich filling thinks through his big feelings."

Nodding dumbly—and more than a little freaked out—I took my twin's outstretched hand. Rising on shaky legs, I followed him from the room, leaving the imprisoned, and extremely pissed off, alien seething behind us.

CHAPTER 31
THEO

At first, all I felt was rage.

I knew the twins were supernatural—despite *lying* about being human—but after centuries on Earth, I never dreamed I'd find a lowly supe who could match me.

"Doesn't that sound like fun?"

Recalling how goddamn smug Andre had been made me want to yowl my displeasure into the quiet of this empty room.

But I don't want to give him the satisfaction.

Although that villain is probably enjoying the show, anyway...

It appeared not only could the twins communicate telepathically, but their powers could infiltrate the brains of others as well.

Including their memories.

Andre had asked me about Argentina in Sylvano Ricci's office. This probably meant he'd accessed my past and current business concerning the caves by digging around in my head.

How much do they know?!

And if he could hold me captive—*inside my own vessel*—that meant he'd also figured out what made me tick.

Panic bubbled to the surface, but I stubbornly swallowed it down. Just because this abnormally powerful supe had conjured up imprisonment methods known only to fellow Stellarians did *not* mean he knew how to kill me.

Don't think about it. Do NOT think about it—

"I have no intention of killing you, because I take care of what belongs to me, remember?"

"GET THE FUCK OUT OF MY HEAD!" I shouted, while tears of frustration welled up in my eyes—adding to my humiliation over this entire ordeal.

"Not until you start acting right," Andre calmly replied before he was gone again—clearly not even breaking a sweat.

Why is that so goddamn attractive?!

When Andre had led Gabriel from the room, they'd first gone to their bedroom down the hall. I'd assumed they were packing to leave—which would have been wise—but then I'd heard them rustling through my studio and walking around on the floor above me.

Meanwhile, my rage only grew.

I wasn't worried about them taking anything of value—especially as they could *steal* my mental secrets anyway—but I hated feeling so powerless. To not only give up control but have it *taken* from me was a novel experience, and an extremely unpleasant one at that.

And not one I would classify as fun…

My fury only fueled me for so long before exhaustion took me under. When I awoke again, the house was completely silent, and the only way I had any concept of how much time had passed was from the stars visible through the skylight above.

How was Gabriel able to breathe up there?

Sigh.

I think I know why…

Not being able to unleash my tendrils to investigate my surroundings was driving me mad. The only reason I hadn't already gone insane was that I could still feel the twins nearby.

My *twins.*

With another growl—one with far less vitriol than I'd previously displayed—I realized I still saw them as *mine.*

Fuck.

I may have fucked up.

It took the human body several—extremely painful—seconds to fully succumb to the effects of space, and these fragile creatures passed out fairly quickly during the ordeal. Since Gabriel was supernatural, I knew he'd last longer than most, and had only planned to bring my angel into outer space long enough to remind him who was in charge. To sample his fear.

Just to get a taste…

But then he'd *clung* to me—sought comfort from the very creature who was terrorizing him—and I'd started panicking right along with him.

It had finally dawned on me at that moment that not only did I not know what I was dealing with… I didn't know what I was doing. All I understood was that the idea of causing the man I'd kidnapped actual *harm* made me feel untethered and unworthy.

I definitely fucked up.

The instant the thought occurred to me, the hold on my frozen limbs lifted, and I collapsed to the floor with the groan.

Then I growled and rose to stand.

I'm going to kill—

A hard flick to my goddamn *brain* almost sent me back to my knees.

"No." Andre's stern voice simultaneously enraged and aroused me—which only enraged me further. *"But if you're ready to apologize, come find us."*

APOLOGIZE?!!!

With my indignation firmly back in place, I flung open the door and stormed through my studio and into the hallway. As I'd suspected, the twins' room looked as uninhabited as before they'd moved in, and the *terror* that shot through me at the possibility of them being gone was the most devastating thought yet.

"You're getting warmer…"

Oh, shut up.

I somehow *knew* they were upstairs, although just why they hadn't fled to wherever their villainous clan holed up was beyond me.

"You know why we stayed."

"STOP FUCKING TAUNTING ME!" I bellowed as I stomped up the service stairs, even if most of my anger was directed inward.

Stupid supe making me contemplate ALL THE THINGS!

Neither Jensen nor Lupe were anywhere to be seen in the common area of the fourth floor, and it didn't look as if they'd been in today at all. This implied the twins had told them to steer clear of this fiery showdown, and that was probably for the best.

There may be no survivors.

A familiar vibration built in my chest as I stalked down the hallway toward my bedroom, drowning out my righteous anger. This sensation morphed into a low humming that bordered on resonance, but I stuffed it down—stubbornly intent on finding revenge, *not* romance.

"Oh, but now you're getting colder…"

I flung open my bedroom door so violently a few priceless paintings fell off the walls, but my focus was on the bed.

On the two men waiting there for me.

Mostly on the one who *dared* to think he could control me.

"Stop," Andre's infuriatingly unruffled voice commanded the same moment my body froze in place again.

"What's the matter, *demon?"* I snarled, glaring at him with every ounce of hatred—or whatever—I was feeling for him. "Worried I'll tear you apart if I get too close—starting with your cock?"

"I don't give a *shit* how much you wanna act out with me, Theo!" Andre's impassive mask actually wavered, as a fury to match my own flared in his blue eyes. "But you need to address what you did to *him…"*

Ah, fuck.

I followed the path of Andre's finger to observe the man beside him—the one wrapped in my favorite flamingo-and-palm-frond kimono, with his legs pulled up tight against his chest, and tears gathering in his eyes.

Tears I put there.

Just… fuck.

I'd be the first to admit that—even with how long I'd been alive—I'd never cared about another being as much as I cared about myself. But watching a tear slide down Gabriel's cheek to land on his plump, *trembling*, lower lip, I suddenly felt like the biggest piece of shit in the entire universe.

"Bingo."

"I…" I began, although I didn't even know *where* to begin.

"Here's what we're going to do," Andre gently spoke out loud again, and if he hadn't been holding me in place, I may have collapsed in relief. "If you promise to *behave,* I'll release you, starting with your human form. Then you're going to fucking *crawl* across this bed and apologize to the person who means more to *us* than anything."

If I hadn't already felt terrible, Andre's voice *cracking*— whether from rage or sadness, it didn't matter—was the final nail in my coffin of self-loathing. I *wanted* to get closer to Gabriel, but I still hesitated.

Because I don't deserve whatever they're offering.

"Don't you?"

My gaze snapped back to Andre's face, but instead of the disgust I was expecting, I found patience and a whole other mess that was too much for me to contemplate at the moment.

Not today, Demon.

"C'mon, little starshine." His lips twisted in a barely contained smirk. "Why don't you crawl over here to where you belong?"

Not even the threat of death would have made me acknowledge the *warmth* that flooded my veins at his words. Regardless, the fight bled out of me and, a moment later, I felt Andre gently lift my invisible bonds.

He's trusting me.

Even after what I did…

With a heavy sigh, I removed my cosmic dust-sprinkled suit jacket and tie, then tossed both to the floor before kicking off my shoes to join them. It didn't escape my notice that Andre was stretched out with his big black boots on my expensive comforter, but I graciously decided that was a fight best left for another day.

Today, I need to crawl.

And crawl, I did. Bravely keeping my gaze on Gabriel, I slowly approached my angel—hating myself a little more the closer I got, but still hoping *he* wouldn't hate me when I got there.

"I'm… sorry," I stumbled over my words, extremely unaccustomed to admitting when I was wrong. "What I did was unforgivable," I added, in case Andre was no longer hanging out inside my head to hear my apologetic thoughts.

It would be easier to say this in there.

"Were you… actually going to kill me?" Gabriel asked, barely above a whisper, and my stolen heart officially shattered.

"No!" I rasped, reaching for him in desperation.

"Theo," Andre warned—mentally tugging on my true form before I made contact. "It should go without saying that if you ever threaten my brother again, I am trapping your tendrils inside you permanently."

Snatching my hands away from my prize, I nodded, beyond ashamed of everything I'd done.

How can I make this up to him?

To both of them…

Cautiously, I peeked at Gabriel. "Angel, I swear, I had no intention of truly hurting you. I was just so *angry* about the secrets you two have been keeping from me. I star hopped us into space because I *needed* to taste your fear—to remind myself I was the one in control…"

Ugh.

That doesn't sound good, does it?

To my immense relief, Gabriel laughed. "Star hopped, huh? Well, I have to admit, we understand feeding off fear more than the average person. And I *like* you being in control… usually…"

I bristled. My angel was trying to make *me* feel better—at the expense of his own comfort—even though he'd been close to *crying* only moments ago.

This simply won't do.

"I frightened you, Gabriel," I huffed. "And while I greatly enjoy being in control, I like *you* being happy more." The instant I said it, I realized it was the truth, which surprised no one more than me. "I *want* to show you how sorry I am, but I need my tendrils back first, sooo… it would be fantastic if that could happen…"

The last bit was entirely aimed at Andre, and while I knew my tone was demanding, I figured my demon could simply punish me later for my attitude.

"Oh, I'm planning on it."

His threat sent a delicious shiver down my spine, which was only magnified when my true form was released from bondage. I sighed and stretched as my tendrils tumbled out of me, but then Gabriel hissed in a breath and I froze, feeling worse than ever.

Even the sight of my tendrils scares him now…

After a tense moment, he smiled shyly and reached for me, and that was all the permission I needed. I dove into his arms, cocooning him with as many tendrils as I could to touch as much of him as possible—uncaring how pathetic that made me seem.

I'll simply play it cool again later.

"All right, I'm gonna let you two kiss and make up," Andre chuckled as he slid off the bed.

"Where are you going?" I snapped, redirecting a few tendrils to greedily reach for him.

Andre batted them away. "To make myself a snack since I told Jensen to take a hike for a few days. You need to focus on part one of your groveling, but remember… I'm still lurking in here"—he tapped his head—"like your worst nightmare."

You mean my wildest dream?

He made it to the door before the rest of his words landed. "Part one?" I asked, licking my lips in anticipation.

Andre turned to grace me with a smirk. "That's right. Once you're done here, I expect you to come out and join *me* for part two. That's when you're really gonna learn what it means to crawl."

I didn't give him a reply, and Andre didn't insist on it before he closed the door behind him. We both knew I'd obey.

Probably not without a fight, but… still.

My present priority was the man crushed beneath me, however, wrapped in colorful satin.

Like a present just for me.

"You look so pretty in my clothes," I purred, snuggling closer again. "Please tell me you're naked under there…"

Gabriel huffed, even as he wrapped his arms around me. "You're such a dirty old man. I just wanted something that smelled like you. I hope that's okay?"

I couldn't help it. A perfectly resonant note hummed from my core, almost immediately answered by one from him.

"Fuck," my angel gasped, releasing me to clutch his chest. "Sorry. I don't know why that keeps happening…"

He truly doesn't know what's going on here.

"We call it resonance," I whispered against his skin before pulling back to better look at him. "It's something that happens between… Stellarians when they match."

"Match?" Gabriel gazed up at me so hopefully, I knew there was no getting out of this conversation.

And my angel deserves to know what he is.

At least… what I think he is.

"Yes," I replied, gently caressing every inch of him with my tendrils—shocked beyond belief that I was *enjoying* feeling this connected to another creature. "It's a similar phenomenon to what Sylvano Ricci was describing with the *inventus* bond."

Gabriel nodded as he absorbed my words, his wide-eyed gaze fixed on me like I held the secrets of the universe.

Apparently, I do.

"What do Stellarians call this phenomenon?" he whispered.

"A stellar collision," I whispered back.

"Is that what you think this is?" he asked in my head this time.

Sweet angel.

Obviously, this would be the time for me to shut this down—to extract myself from a potentially messy situation with two infamous villains and cut ties with Earth altogether.

To simply let the world burn without me.

But I no longer wanted to drift through this universe like a wandering star—not when I could have two perfect beings to call my own.

I'd rather watch the world burn together.

"Yes," I replied, ignoring every ugly self-serving instinct that flared up, telling me to flee. "That's exactly what this is."

With the most adorable little cry, Gabriel wrapped his arms and legs around me—yanking me down with a surprising amount of strength.

Strength he'd clearly been hiding from me.

Tricky little angel.

"Thank fuck," he wetly rasped against my neck. "Dre too?"

I could *feel* Andre tense in my mind, which betrayed his stance on the matter far more than he probably intended.

I see you, demon.

"Perhaps," I airily replied, strengthened by Gabriel's proximity to become bratty once again. "I suppose it will depend on who comes out on top during 'part two' of my groveling world tour."

Gabriel shook with silent laughter before shoving me off so he could grimace up at me. "Old man… you in danger."

Don't threaten me with a good time.

Shrugging nonchalantly, I flopped onto the bed beside him, although I continued caressing him with my tendrils— soaking in every point of contact. While I was still determined to figure out what my mates were made of, for now, I was simply going to enjoy them, inside and out.

Because they were *mine,* and no one was going to take them away from me.

My twin stars.

My stellar collisions.

CHAPTER 32
ANDRE

Stellar collisions, huh?

Calling this situation a 'collision' was perfect, as it operated just shy of a train wreck most of the time. Which wasn't a bad thing. Even with how I preferred control, Theo's brand of chaos made me hot.

Except when he teleported Gabe away from me.

I had never known true terror until the moment my unbreakable connection to my twin was severed—leaving nothing but dead air on the other end.

Something murderous must have shown on my face when the others disappeared, as Sylvano immediately sprang into action. He was up and out of his chair in an instant, but not to reassure me. Nope. Dude was already fumbling his phone out of his pocket—no doubt intending to call in the Suarez squad to diffuse the ticking time bomb.

Meaning me.

Since he'd *probably been warned about me, too.*

Sylvano was actually one of the good guys, and truly wanted what was best for *all* supes. But the situation was volatile, and

I needed time to regain control of it before Wolfy swooped in like a goth mother hen to take over.

So I used my powers to freeze the Deputy Secretary-General of the United Super Nations.

It was another dirty trick of mine—and broke pretty much every law the supe council had put in place to protect normies and organizations like the USN—but I was done giving a fuck. My other half was *gone* and the batshit crazy alien who'd taken him needed to be taught a lesson. Preferably by *me*.

Which got me way harder than it should have, given the seriousness of the situation.

To my credit, I only froze Sylvano for a moment—just long enough to scramble his memory of the past twenty minutes. Now, all he remembered was that his pleasant meeting with Theo had ended with a casual plan to reconvene on the DNA research program marketing campaign.

Along with a reminder to test that blood sample.

"See ya around, Sylvano!" I'd called out, forcing cheer into my tone as I swung open the door and ran into the hallway. "Be sure to send Theo's sample results to Xanny!"

As curious as I was about Theo's genetic makeup—or lack thereof, since he was a goddamn *body snatcher*—I was too busy focusing on *not* panicking as I raced for the USN's main entrance.

Luckily for everyone in my path, Gabe came back online to report he was alive and on the roof of the old Biggs Enterprises building. And by some miracle, our Uber was still waiting for me outside. But then, Theo vanished with him again before I could even finish climbing into the car.

At that point, I'd almost broken down and called Butch and Xander for help.

Since Gabe is more important to me than my pride.

That's when *Luca*, of all people, had texted me.

Kinetic Kenobi: *You'll be able to intercept Theo at his house. Stellarians always return to the nest with their mates.*

There had been *way* too many red flags in Luca's message for me to deal with on top of the shit show I was already experiencing. So I simply chose to blindly trust the man I'd trusted my entire life.

Even if he eventually has some explaining to do.

My *Sensei's* uncanny intuition was freaky enough, but it was even harder to ignore the eerie way traffic parted—with every light turning green along the way—allowing my Uber to reach the Teal Coast neighborhood in record time.

In the nick of time.

Back in the present, I slowly blew out a breath as I spread fancy as fuck fig jam on the mini toast crackers rich assholes seemed to love—willing myself to calm.

I need to get back to baseline for when Theo comes out here.

Because he was lucky that I couldn't *end him earlier.*

Now that my rage had settled, I didn't believe our chaotic alien would have actually *killed* Gabe. But it sure seemed like he was going to at the time.

Maybe he was just scared…

It seemed ridiculous to consider that this unfathomably powerful creature would be afraid of anything. But he'd seemed legit upset about my twin and I not telling him we were supes—as if us keeping him at arm's length meant it would be easier to leave him.

Sweet baby psychopath.

It was nothing personal…

As I'd half-explained to Sinistre and Fay, there were so many laws in place surrounding a supe's identity—mostly to protect the best interest of their clan—that deep personal relationships outside of our families, marriages, and business arrangements were almost nonexistent. With the added complication of Gabe and me being sent to Theo's home under false pretenses—*and this entire thing being a stellar collision*—and it was no wonder everyone's emotions were raw.

Emotions we can all feel as if they were our own…

My head snapped up as I heard the door to Theo's bedroom open down the hall, followed by his footsteps traveling in my direction.

Well, that was quick…

"You alive in there, Gabe?"

"As if you weren't lurking like Big Brother the entire time."

I smirked and began cleaning up my nosh, not in the least bit embarrassed to be called out. Gabe had made it clear he didn't mind me 'lurking' during playtime—had *asked* me to. I'd also realized that if it involved Theo, I was a greedy asshole who coveted every piece of him I could get.

Which reminds me…

"Do you… want me to leave the door open for this? It's been a long time coming, so I'm probably not gonna play nice."

Such an intense jolt of raw lust shot through our mind-bond that I almost doubled over the kitchen island.

Jesus!

"Sorry. Um… yeah, I do. I-I really like watching you own his bratty ass. Is that… weird?"

I couldn't help the laugh that bubbled out of me. We were twin supes in a throuple relationship with a skinsuit-wearing alien our family had sent us to spy on. An alien who was also possibly the father of our Mafia Queen, involved in some shady ass business with the Salahs, *and* seemingly on the run from his fellow Stellarians. Enhancing my pre-existing code-pendency with Gabe by openly sharing someone we were both crazy about was one of the more rational decisions we'd made in this entire situation.

Because in no universe would my twin and I have eventually settled down and gone our separate ways. And if we *had*, we would have been all up in each other's business on the daily —to the point of driving our poor partners away, if not insane.

So why not stick someone equally psycho in the middle and make a murder sammich?

"All right, demon!" Theo announced as he came into view—doing a sassy little twirl for good measure. "Here I fucking am."

Oh, this is gonna be fun.

"Not weird at all." I finally replied to Gabe, because I could *feel* him spiraling in the other room—thinking he'd somehow offended me by wanting to pull up a chair. *"Just sit back and enjoy the show."*

Because this brat's gonna learn.

Schooling my expression into a mask of indifference, I strode from behind the counter to the dining area. Grabbing *Theo's* chair at the head of the table, I spun it to face outward before lowering myself to sit—relaxed, with my legs spread wide.

Hint, hint.

Time to crawl.

Of course, Theo either didn't catch my drift or—more likely—chose to ignore it. In signature bratty fashion, he crossed his arms and cocked a hip before staring me down. I stared back, drinking him in, in all his currently unblemished perfection.

Because he won't look like that for long.

He'd changed into one of his countless kimono robes—*big surprise*—and I forcefully had to stop myself from smiling at the cats-driving-spaceships motif.

The man does have a sense of humor, I'll give him that.

I was surprised he hadn't just teleported himself from the bedroom now that the space-cat was out of the bag. But then I smirked, realizing he probably hadn't bothered because he assumed I could suppress that ability as well. The truth was, I didn't know if I could, just like I wasn't sure if I could kill him.

But I have no problem keeping him on his toes.

"What's so funny?" Theo scowled, still waiting for me to play a role he could easily hate.

Since that makes it easier for him to push me away.

Not this time.

"You're not a very good brat, you know," I drawled, *loving* how he bristled. "Why wear such a pretty little kimono when you know I'm just going to tear it off you?"

Theo straightened at that, immediately rising to the challenge. Glaring at me imperiously, he slowly untied his belt and slid the robe off his shoulders before letting it pool at his feet in a puddle of silk.

Revealing the goddamn banana hammock he had on underneath.

I take it back.

He's a very good brat.

There was no other way to describe the bright yellow monstrosity stretched around his junk. And when he spun— revealing how the back was little more than a string of dental floss shoved up his ass crack—I nearly used my powers to send him to his knees.

But that's not how I want this to go down.

"Cat got your tongue, demon?" he purred, strutting closer as I concentrated on not openly drooling at all the hard muscles on display. "My guests had *plenty* to say about this little number when I wore it for the hot tub party I hosted over the summer. It was so much fun to see just how many people I could fit inside… my hot tub, I mean."

Oh, is that how you wanna play?

I couldn't stop the possessiveness that raged through me like a wildfire—cutting down everything in its path as my vision went red. Faster than even I could register, I reached up and grabbed Theo by the hair before slamming him to his knees at my feet.

"You are such a fucking whore," I growled. That strange buzzing sensation that might have been resonance started up in my chest again, but I was too pissed off to know for sure.

Fuck… I can't…

Right now I *needed* to get myself back to baseline—even if I could tell we were both hungrily feeding off this wild energy shift.

I can't let myself lose control…

"Yes, I am." Theo grinned up at me like Satan himself, fanning the flames. *"Your* whore."

That snapped me out of my dangerous spiral. Grounded by the clear distinction of our roles, my panic subsidized and my focus sharpened, although I didn't loosen my grip.

"Fucking *right,* you're my whore," I hissed, yanking him closer. "You're my goddamn *slave.* You can flounce and flirt all you want in your daily life, Theo, but your only purpose behind closed doors from now on is to take my cock and give yours to Gabe. Because the three of us *belong* to each other now. Do you understand?"

I need you to understand.

I need this just as much as you do.

Please…

My twin hummed in approval of my words—both spoken and unspoken—but Theo was rendered speechless for possibly the first time in his entire life. Then a slow, filthy, deliciously *bratty* smirk spread across his face, and I knew he was ready to play.

Ready or not.

"I'm not sure I do, *Demon,"* he murmured. "Perhaps you should repeat yourself."

Here we go.

CHAPTER 33
THEO

I may have gone too far.

If I hadn't been inches away from Andre, forced to kneel at his feet—albeit *willingly*, but he didn't need to know that—I may not have noticed the subtle shift in his expression. But the instant I challenged him, the lovely gemlike light I often admired in his blue eyes flattened to a lifeless gray.

It looks like my time is up.

How delightful!

"How fast do you heal?" he gritted out, his hand flexing in my hair—almost as if he was steadying himself. "Because by the time I'm done with you, you're going to look like you were mugged down by the pier."

I couldn't stop the full body shudder that ran through me, not least of all because he hadn't *asked* if he could beat me within an inch of my life. We both knew the thought of it made me hard—as evidenced by the threatened integrity of my thong —so I focused on answering his actual question.

"Instantaneously, if I so choose," I replied, only a little smugly. "As I'm sure you've figured out with your snooping,

I'm effortlessly controlling every cell in this skinsuit, so cosmetic adjustments are simple. No one will ever need to know you like to play rough with your *whore.*"

Fuck, I like being called that.

I like the idea of being… his.

"No." Andre growled, moving his other hand to my throat and squeezing so tightly my balls throbbed. "I… *want* my marks on you somewhere, Theo. You're going to need to leave some on you so I can…" He swallowed, his expression turning vulnerable for a moment as he searched my face. "So everyone knows…"

I hissed in a breath, practically coming on the spot. I'd always had a penchant for pain—especially in this oversensitive form —but most humans couldn't deliver what I could take. But Andre could. The idea of him feeling so possessive that he needed to mark me up in *ownership* instantly settled my turbulent emotions, leaving blessed *silence* in its wake.

Like the infinite vastness of space.

"You want everyone to know I'm yours," I stated, smiling in satisfaction when *Andre* settled as well—back to that impassive calm I found as attractive as his bursts of insanity. "Well, you know my safe word. I say do your worst."

Wreck me.

The smile that stretched across my demon's gorgeous face was deliciously evil, and I thanked my stars that a true villain had found me.

A match made in heaven.

If there was a heaven…

"Oh, I will," he murmured before his gaze shifted over my shoulder. "And I think I'll take care of your decorating problem while I'm at it."

Decorating probl—?

Before I could ask what problem he could possibly have with *perfection,* Andre lifted me by the throat and hurled me across the room.

An unholy shriek escaped me—more from surprise than anything—which turned into a laugh as I landed flat on my gold-columned coffee table in an explosion of glass.

Ohhhh… so this *is how my Demon likes to play!*

I could have easily picked myself up from the mess and fought back, but the sheer exhilaration of this consensual abuse was making me dizzy. I'd also nearly come from the first round alone, so—to prolong the experience—felt it was best to simply enjoy the sensation of countless shards piercing my delicate skin.

This is bliss.

Andre's black boots crunched into view on either side of me. "Fuck, you look good," he mused, his gaze running over my bleeding body like I was a work of art. "And this table has never looked better."

"Careful, Demon," I taunted with a shaky smirk, tasting blood. "My mouth still works."

His gaze darkened. "Is that right?"

I moved to rise, but Andre grabbed me by the hair—*dragging* me through the mess of shattered glass and splintered debris before slamming my lacerated back against the seat of my blue velvet wingback chair.

"Do you remember the first night Gabe and I were here?" he asked, pinning me in place with his legs as he slowly unbuckled his belt. "When you hosted that lame ass gathering, lording over everyone from this chair just to show off for us?"

How dare he?!

"You mean the night I watched some worthless human slobber all over what's *mine?*" I hissed, feeling shockingly raw and exposed. "And then had to *feel* you get your dick sucked by someone who wasn't me?!"

I was dangerously close to tears for the second time in only a handful of hours. But the visceral memory had now been uncorked, so Andre would simply have to deal with the overflow.

Here I fucking am!

My demon froze with his hand inside his boring black boxer briefs before withdrawing—sadly, empty-handed. Then he slowly crouched over me, cupped my face in his hands, and rested his forehead against mine. I was raging inside, but he didn't speak for several minutes. Instead, Andre simply ran his thumbs rhythmically over my cheekbones, his breath ghosting across my lips until I relaxed again.

Is this another one of his superpowers?

Forcing me to contemplate and *calm?!*

"The only reason I kissed that random himbo was because I saw you sitting in this chair looking fly as fuck with some rando about to give you a blowie. I fucking saw red…" He sighed and brushed his lips over mine—achingly gentle compared to the violence of a few minutes prior. "I can't even remember who ended up on my dick—only that I wished it were you. And the only reason I even got off was because

Gabe forgot to put up his mental blocks, so I had a front-row seat when he thought about *you* owning his subby ass while he painted the sheets in the studio bedroom."

Wait a minute.

"Have you been… *involved* every time I've been with Gabriel —through some witchy mental bond?" I gasped in faux horror, although I was anything but horrified. The idea of having both my twins at once made me *feral* and had me reaching down to free my cock from its confines.

Before I snap a string…

Of course, Andre was having none of it. He grabbed my wrist —bending it backward until something twinged painfully— before chuckling low.

"I told you, Theo. We're a package deal." Then, he cocked his head and grew momentarily distant, all but confirming that my angel was a voyeur in the current scenario. "Gabe knows I like watching you own him, just like he gets off on watching me own you. *Fuck.* We are both so hot for you, you crazy fucking alien. So can you *please* just get over your bullshit and open wide so I can feed you my cock already?"

Mmm, that doesn't sound right…

I hummed thoughtfully. "I'm not sure I'm ready yet, *Demon.* I was enjoying your interior decorating input—"

My sass was lost as Dre abruptly flipped me onto the nearby fainting couch so violently the walnut legs buckled. I was about to complain—as I *did* enjoy the orgy positions the couch allowed—but Andre straddled my head and shoved his cock down my throat before I could do anything more than gag.

"Such a good little cockslut," he praised, using the curved arm as leverage to shove himself in deeper. "I knew you'd submit to me."

SUBMIT?!

A growl rumbled in my chest. Or perhaps it was resonance, but I was much too annoyed—or vulnerable, goddamnit—to tell the difference. Regardless, my shameful instinct to flee suddenly reared its ugly head, and I tensed, readying to star hop and escape.

"Oh, no you fucking don't." Andre pulled out and slapped me across the face so hard I saw the stars, anyway. "If you need to safe out, do that, but you are *not* running from this. Do you understand?"

"Fuck you," I spat, simultaneously wanting to hide from him *and* burrow into his arms, like I had with Gabriel.

But that's not how Andre shows his love…

Wait.

Does he love me, too?

"You should know the answer to that," he muttered as he dragged me off the collapsed couch and back to the pile of shattered glass. "But apparently you need a reminder of where you belong, and *who* you belong to."

I cried out as my knees landed on the glass—sending dozens of signals for both pleasure and pain to the core of my being.

More.

"I'll always give you more." Andre smirked as he rubbed his cock across my battered face—mixing precum with the blood already decorating my split bottom lip. "I'll fill you up until you *think* we're done, but then I'll keep giving, because we both know you can take it. Do you understand?"

My shoulders slumped as my eyes drifted closed. I could no longer look at the man before me. Resonance was building in my chest, and my tendrils were *aching* to emerge and touch what was mine, but I… couldn't.

I couldn't accept what Andre was offering. Not only hadn't I *earned* it—just like he'd said—but I never would.

I don't deserve any of this.

"Little starshine…"

Andre's voice in my head was like a beacon in the night sky, coaxing me to open my eyes—forcing me to *look.*

Forcing me to stay.

When my gaze locked with his, he gently pried open my mouth and began pushing his cock inside. I moaned at the silky feel of him sliding over my tongue—at the salty taste and the way my jaw strained around him.

More, more, more.

"When I said you hadn't *earned* it, I was only talking about my supe name—which is Shock, by the way." He wrapped his hand around my throat so he could feel himself filling me up. "But you'll never have to earn how I, or Gabe, care about you. Never that."

As soon as he uttered the words, I *felt* my angel agree, courtesy of a mental push filled with affection and desire.

I want it all.

From both of you.

Andre gave a hard thrust that made me gag, but also provided an excuse for my eyes watering.

Because all this crying is terrible for my reputation…

Since Andre couldn't let me get away with anything, he gently trailed his thumb over my wet cheekbone, even as he forcefully fucked my throat. "And when you get scared and think about running, you won't, because you'll know better. You'll know that if you ever disappear on me again, I'll tear this goddamn universe apart to find you. Do. You. Understand?"

Fuck.

There was no hope left for me. Tears were now freely streaming down my face as Andre planted his other hand in my hair and increased his pace.

"So perfect," he praised—his normally even tone growing strained. "Such a perfect whore. Just for me."

That.

That's it.

The last stronghold of my stubborn resistance melted away, replaced by a bliss I didn't think was possible. Andre didn't expect me to change who I was at my core or to obey him unquestioningly. He only wanted me on my knees like *this*—for *him* alone. He wanted me to accept the exquisite pain he *needed* to give until we were both satiated and ready to fight for dominance all over again.

That does *sound like fun…*

My tumultuous thoughts smoothed out until the only things that existed were my Demon's cock fucking my throat raw, my angel chasing his own release in the other room with his 'mental blocks' open for me to see, and the knowledge that I didn't have to run from this. Everything I wanted was right in front of me—being offered freely and without condition.

Give me everything.

Unable to wait for permission, I released a few tendrils to burrow under Andre's shirt, feeling the chiseled planes of his abs contract as I slithered higher.

"Fucking hell!" he gasped as I reached his nipples and gave them both a rough squeeze—relishing how his pain cycled back to me through our pleasure loop.

My Demon probably wanted to reprimand me, but he was already coming—curled over me with his hand wrapped so tightly around my throat, if I'd needed air to breathe, I would have been shit out of luck.

Absolute perfection.

I still moaned like the whore I was and took advantage of Andre's weakened state to wiggle just enough to catch most of his release on my tongue.

Because I still want to devour what I can.

"Such a fucking brat," he huffed as he straightened and withdrew—delivering another slap across my face that was disappointingly much gentler than before. "You did that just so I'd punish you later."

Guilty as charged!

"Maybe." I shrugged, making no move to remove my tendrils from beneath his shirt as he zipped himself up. "Maybe I just like touching what's *mine.*"

Andre's lip twitched as he helped me rise. Then he delivered the softest kiss before backing up a step to look me over. I could only imagine the bruised and bloody mess he saw, but the way his eyes flared in approval had me preening.

"You can touch me all you want," he murmured, reaching out his hand and leading me away from the wreckage. "Now let's go fit all three of us into your big, slutty bathtub so we can figure out which marks are the ones that will stay." He glanced over his shoulder with a challenge in his eyes— daring me to argue. "Because you're *mine* too, you know. *Ours*. Do you finally understand?"

"Yes." I smiled, uncaring that I'd somehow fallen into the very trap I'd run from for my entire life. "I understand."

I'm yours.

CHAPTER 34
GABRIEL

He's ours, he's ours, he's ours!

I was the definition of a goofy, lovesick fool, but I couldn't even be mad about it. After Dre *finally* got his playtime with Theo—and I came all over myself listening to them redecorate the living room—my twin and I squeezed into the hot tub with our man.

Our man!

It somehow managed to not be weird, even though Dre and I hadn't shared a bath since we were kids. Just like he'd explained to Theo earlier—it was about our mutual obsession with *him.* I ignored my twin's dick, and he ignored mine, and we just enjoyed cleaning up our wrecked hottie until the water was filthy and it was time to get out.

Because he's ours and this is happening!!!

"Dude, I'm gonna hurl if you keep pumping out these schmoopy feels," Dre grumbled as he poked through the pre-made meals Jensen had left for us in the fridge when we gave him the week off. "Who knew you were such a sap?"

I blushed, but still grinned like a lunatic. "Deal with it, asshole. You're totally in lurve, too."

He straightened and shut the fridge before turning to face me fully.

"How do you know you're in love?"

Dre asking this question in my head, coupled with the infamous Suarez stare, meant he was *serious.* I was so floored by him coming to *me* for advice that I couldn't articulate a coherent reply.

"I thought… Didn't you tell Theo—"

"I told him he should know how I feel. Because I've been spraying that chaotic alien with so many pheromones, dude's not gonna be able to set foot outside without the world knowing—"

"Where the fuck are you going?" My twin switched to verbal speech so fast, my brain glitched.

Following his glare, I turned to find an uncharacteristically apologetic looking Theo, dressed in another tame dark suit—which meant he was in business mode.

And something tells me it's not about the business of staying home to fuck.

Boo.

Theo cleared his throat. "I need to… go handle a situation that's come up with a venture on the East Coast. I shouldn't be gone long—"

"Does it have to do with whatever you and Lady Tempest discovered in those Argentinian caves?" Dre calmly asked, with balls the size of goddamn Argentina.

Theo's expression turned blank. Not impassive, but unrecognizable—like a blurry photograph. "How much do you know, and where did you get that information?" His voice was the coldest I'd ever heard it, and my heart sank, worried that all our collective schmoop was going up in smoke.

Nooooooo!

"Theo." I raced over to him and placed my palms on his chest —desperate to diffuse the situation. "Listen. Our family already knows all about the caves, and our giant lizard space invader supe heritage."

"Gabe…" Dre warned.

As if he cares about protecting our clan…

"That's actually the main reason we were sent here," I powered on. "We just wanted to learn more about what *you* were so that *we* could understand…"

Fuck, this is hard to explain.

I need to get Wolfy back here—with Simon.

Although, that might make things worse…

Theo's expression came back into focus and softened as he gazed down at me. "So you could better understand what *you* are."

What?

I could *feel* Dre's surprise along with mine, and I realized I could kill two birds with one stone.

Redirect from our Queen and *dig for intel.*

Mostly dig for intel…

"What do you know about us, Theo?" I whispered.

Begged, really.

His gaze hardened again, but only because he refocused on Dre. "You tell *me,* since you can simply sneak into my head and *steal* what you want."

Ouch.

But, fair.

Dre softened this time. "Tell you what, starshine. From now on, I'll stay out of your head unless you invite me in. I want you to trust me—to trust *us."* His gaze flitted to me. "But we *do* know you're involved with the Salah clan somehow—"

"Which we haven't told Wolfy!" I blurted out as Theo tensed. "And we'll help you cover your tracks with whatever's going on tonight. Tempest can take the fall."

She's a bitch, anyway.

"Jesus, Gabe!" Dre choked out, although amused admiration danced in his eyes. "I didn't think you had it in ya to be such a... *villain."*

I do for my stellar collision, apparently.

Theo blinked, clearly stunned by my promise of aiding and abetting. "Doesn't your clan have a pending marriage with the Salahs?" he slowly spoke, as if testing the waters of our loyalty.

Is that *why you're acting so shifty?*

I laughed and bounced on my toes to kiss him. "Don't get it twisted, old man. Word on the street is that our brother's engagement to Atmosphera is off."

Way off.

Although a Salah is still on the bargaining table...

Apparently, that *was* the issue, as Theo grinned broadly in response. "Well, *that's* a relief! And no need to worry about helping me fight this little fire"—his gaze fell to his phone as a text came through—"I have a plan for tonight... for how to wipe my hands of this project completely."

That's not ominous or anything.

But still hot.

"Do you plan on filling us in on any of this orrrrr...?" Dre drawled.

Theo glanced up, back to being unamused. "That depends, demon. Will *you* be coming clean on why you want to know more about Stellarians—or what your interest is in *me* specifically?"

Fuck, he even negotiates like a supe.

So fucking hot.

"Cool it, Gabe," my twin huffed before smirking at Theo. "I'll think about it—maybe discuss it over drinks with our sweet angel at The Refinery tonight while you're busy fighting mysterious fires."

Theo glared at Dre in return, and if it wasn't for the raw lust I could feel traveling back and forth through our shared bond, I might have thought fists were about to fly.

It still could happen...

The only reason their standoff didn't last into the night was because Theo's phone chimed again, breaking the tension.

He sighed and gripped my chin before delivering the softest kiss that ended with a devilish nip. "This won't take long, angel. I'll come meet you at the club when I'm done, so... *be good.*"

The last part was said with a growl that made my toes curl in my leather low tops. "Okay," I replied in a breathy voice. "I'll be good."

Jesus, I am a sap.

Don't care.

"Will *you* be good tonight, Theo?" Dre asked, crossing his arms over his chest and giving our man a *look* that would have put *me* on my best behavior.

But this is Theo we're talking about.

The chaotic alien released me, smoothed his hands down the front of his suit, and raised a single brow at my twin. "No," he replied before vanishing.

"Fuck!" I yelped, stumbling backward in surprise.

"I know," Dre deadpanned. "Imagine how it felt watching him do that *with* someone you care about in tow."

My guts twisted as I imagined the terror he must have felt, but I agreed Theo had probably just been reacting instinctually to a perceived threat.

Although I could have done without being dragged into space…

Knowing we *both* needed a break, I went for a laugh. "Sorry, dude. Sorry you didn't bag a hot psychotic alien who's a *good boy* like me."

Dre cackled. "Yeah, well, I don't *want* a good boy. Not that there's anything wrong with being one," he quickly added.

I sniffed. "Oh, I know. Theo *loves* how good I am."

"He does." Dre smiled softly. "I think he loves *you,* dude."

My heart felt too large for my chest. "I hope so," I whispered. "Because there's no way what I'm feeling isn't love."

Even though that doesn't seem like a big enough word.

I suddenly realized I had my answer to Dre's question from earlier. "And back to our conversation... I know it's love because what I feel for Theo is a care and protectiveness beyond anything I've felt before—aside from my bond with *you*, of course. I would absolutely fucking *crawl* for Theo. I would kill for him. I'd do anything he says. All of this emotion inside me feels... enormous—almost more than I can carry—but I'm already sharing it with *you*, so I'm not afraid."

How ya like that *schmoop, bro?*

I watched, mesmerized, as my normally unflappable brother paled and swallowed thickly. "Oh, okay. Yeah. That sounds about right..."

You are ridiculous.

"I think he loves you, too," I stage-whispered—cackling when he rolled his eyes. "'Cuz, let's be real. That alien ain't kneeling for just anyone."

Instead of the—rightful—smugness I was expecting, Dre looked worried. "What kind of damage control do you think he's up to tonight?"

I eyed him carefully. "You could just check—"

"No," my twin sternly replied. "I told him I wouldn't and I want him to trust me."

I held up my hands in mock surrender. "Fine, fine. Still wanna go to the club?"

Because I definitely do...

Now that I'd tasted the kink scene, and *lived* it, there was no going back. It was everything I hadn't known I was missing. All the areas where I'd formerly felt unworthy and weird in my sheltered life—hiding who I was among normies—were now being filled with unconditional acceptance.

Maybe even… love.

Dre puffed out a breath and ran his hand through his hair. "Definitely. I need a drink and we actually do need to discuss how we're gonna reconcile our original mission with this current"—he waved his hand vaguely—"shit show. But let's grab some pho first."

Oh, hell, yes.

But…

"Ugh, you know the best pho is on the other side of town," I whined. "It'll be annoying as fuck to Uber to Pho Real and then back to The Refinery."

A mischievous gleam lit up Dre's eyes, telling me there was trouble ahead. "Who said anything about an Uber?"

I spread my arms wide. "What are we gonna do, dude? Fly? Ride our broomsticks?"

My twin smirked and moved around the kitchen island until he was standing directly in front of me. Then he took my hands in his and gave them a squeeze.

"Do you trust me?" he murmured, and my stomach dropped.

This does not bode well…

"A-about what?" I stuttered, although I was starting to suspect.

"Do you want to know how I found you back here when Theo took you… star hopping?" Dre whispered as that *resonant* sound began emitting from his chest. *Calling* to whatever lived inside me.

Whatever was inside both of us.

Oh, fuck.

"*Luca* texted me… outta nowhere," he continued, tightening his grip as if I might try to run. "Just to randomly inform me 'Stellarians always bring their mates back to the nest.'"

I swallowed the lump clogging my throat as my resonance hummed in response to his—unsurprising, because Dre was my other half.

Could it be true?

"Now I have no fucking idea how our *Sensei* knew what was going on at the USN, that Theo is a Stellarian, or that we're his mates—but let's forget all that for now…" Dre laughed as the alien in question's multi-million dollar kitchen flickered in and out of focus. "How do you explain this stellar collision business, Gabe, or you being able to *breathe* in outer space?"

I want it to be true…

So fucking bad.

"I don't know," I croaked, my mouth dry as a bone and my heart racing like a jackrabbit.

"Most importantly…" Dre rested his forehead against mine, pressing our chests together—instantly reminding me who I'd always been connected to. "How do you explain this?"

And then we were gone.

CHAPTER 35
ANDRE

Star hopping is elite.

It went without saying that I was never going to Uber again, especially if it meant not dealing with my least favorite thing —Big City traffic.

And especially if I can be my own Uber Eats…

As exhilarating as our trip through time and space had been, the implications of discovering this ability were impossible to ignore.

We were born for this, apparently.

As much as I hadn't wanted to admit it, deep down I knew there were *reasons* we connected with Theo like we did— beyond our raw animal attraction. The Stellarian-specific resonance was a clue, along with what happened during that first night in the studio's spare bedroom. Thanks to my front-row seat of the action, when our alien probed Gabe's throat with a starry tendril, I felt… *something* reach for him in return. Something stirring to life inside my twin.

Inside both of us.

With the evidence piling up, it just made sense that we should also be able to *star hop,* as Theo called it. Knowing what *he* was made of, all I did was imagine the cells of my body traveling from point A to point B—like information being transmitted through synapses in a brain.

Easy.

So even though Gabe and I were dressed more casually than I would've preferred for the club, my belly was full of pho, I'd brought my perfect brat to his knees, and now had a new trick up my sleeve that put my existing powers to shame.

I felt like a god.

"Well, look what the cat dragged in." Fay tittered as we breezed into The Refinery's foyer. "Of course, the Acosta twins could make a couple of burlap sacks look hot, so I'll let the streetwear slide... this once."

"Much appreciated, Fay." I flashed my most brilliant smile, knowing damn well she would have let us in wearing burlap sacks. "We were in the neighborhood and wanted a drink... but *also* required an expertly curated atmosphere, so here we are!"

The Madam's sassy little 'cupcake' rolled her eyes good-naturedly as she walked out from behind the podium to greet us. "I'm already letting you in, Andre—you don't need to butter me up. May I suggest grabbing spots at the bar near the hammered Rat Pack wannabes?"

Oh?

Something in the normie's tone caught my attention, but when I searched her eyes for clues, she was gazing back at me serenely, as if telling us where to sit wasn't totally weird.

I could just pop into her head and poke around...

No.

"Sounds good," I carefully replied, even as my Spidey Sense tingled. "And can you please tell Theo Coatl where to find us when he gets here?"

Fay's on fleek eyebrows nearly flew off her head at the name drop, before she nodded—clearly intrigued about who I'd bagged. "Right on, Dre. I'm happy for you."

"Thank you," Gabe gushed, choosing that moment to completely blow up our spot. "We're all very happy."

I grabbed my twin by the elbow to steer him through the curtain and away from our thirsty cupcake. "Oookay… thanks for the heads up about open seats, Fay! Byeeee…"

"Don't you go turning into a brat on me," I hissed in Gabe's head as I dragged him toward the bar. *"Now she'll* really *turn into a cape chaser…"*

Oh, fuck.

"Hold up. She knows we're supes? When did that *happen?"*

I sighed as we claimed two barstools next to the handful of obnoxiously loud men wearing off the rack suits, complete with extra shiny sharkskin sheen.

Wolfy would probably put his hands on them for that crime alone.

"Yeah." I signaled for the bartender to deliver two of my usual whiskeys, neat. "When I disappeared for a couple of days recently, I was holed up at Fay and Sin's place. I crash there a lot, but this time I got all up in my feels about how frustrated I've been over our… situation, and some other truths might have come out…"

Gabe nodded thoughtfully as he gnawed on his bottom lip. "Is it because you were angry at me?"

"What? No!" I hiss-whispered as our drinks were delivered, although I really didn't need to worry about being quiet.

The Rat Pack contingent was currently competing over who could drunkenly talk the loudest, so you would have needed supe hearing to catch our conversation. My brother still looked unconvinced, and I realized it was time for *me* to be as honest about my kink journey as I'd expected from him.

Since we're beyond open-door now.

The door has been blown off its hinges at this point.

"It was more that I thought everything I'd ever wanted was being dangled in front of me with no hope of it ever being *mine.*" I took a sip and peered around the crowded main area. "You gotta understand… I've been searching for a sub for a long time, dude. That's why I joined the club in the first place —even though I knew I wouldn't find what I needed here. Not with the way I wanted to play."

A jolt of lust had me rolling my eyes and turning back to my twin to level him with a *look.*

Behave.

"Sorry," he cackled, although that wannabe brat didn't look sorry at all. "You and Theo wrecking the place was hot."

"It sure was," I agreed, sending some of that raw lust down the line for our chaotic alien to taste—wherever the fuck he was.

Out fighting fires.

Starting *fires, more likely.*

Gabe sobered and picked up his drink. "I get it, though. All the things I wanted… I never bothered asking anyone to give it to me. I was embarrassed, but also… I just knew how disappointed I'd be with some lame ass butt pats when I really wanted to be choked within an inch of my life."

I had *not* expected that to come out of my twin's mouth, and unfortunately, mine was full of whiskey when it did. Barely stopping myself from spraying Sharkskin Sinatra next to me, I swallowed and coughed out a laugh.

"Dude, you are such a pain slut," I chuckled before warmth filled my chest. "Not as bad as our man, but still…"

Gabe placed his hand over mine on the bar and gave it a squeeze—grinning like an idiot while he did. *"Our* man! I can't believe we get to share him."

My lips twisted at how ridiculous he was—not that I was one to talk. "We do."

I'm happy too, dude.

His smile faltered, and he swallowed thickly before switching to our mind-bond again. *"I-I want to share him with you… more."*

Oh?

Of course, I knew what he was asking, but Gabe needed to learn how to advocate for what he needed.

"Out loud," I commanded—cranking up the Dom tone so he'd know I was serious. "You don't need to ask or beg. Just tell me exactly what you want."

My twin licked his lips and nervously glanced at our drunken neighbors before meeting my gaze again. I snuck my hand out from under his so I could put mine on top, reminding my other half I was here.

"You can tell me anything."

Gabe gave me a pained look before gathering his courage. "I-I want Theo to fuck me while you're fucking him. So I can feel him inside me while you're inside him. I want…"

His gaze grew glassy and distant as he teetered on the edge of subspace—the place where he'd always belonged but never allowed himself to exist. I wanted him to stay present for this conversation, however, so I brought my other hand to the back of his neck and gently squeezed.

"You want to feel what *Theo's* experiencing while we do it, right?" I prompted. "You want to turn him into a sloppy, shaking, drooling mess… With me?"

"Fuck…" my twin choked out, dropping his other hand to my knee for balance. "I feel like I might blow just thinking about it, so… yeah. That's what I want. *Jesus…"*

What a good boy.

"Was that so hard?" I teased, shooting a glare over his shoulder at a group of women at a nearby low top watching us with lecherous interest.

Wrong tree, little doggies.

A tiny tap on their horny brains had them looking elsewhere for conquests, and Gabe's slow exhale brought my attention back to him.

"Do you think Theo would be into—"

I didn't even let the idiot finish his question before releasing his neck to give him a firm flick to the forehead.

For real?!

Gabe chuckled and smiled sheepishly. "Yeah, okay… that was a dumb quest—"

This time when his voice trailed off and gaze went distant, I knew it was for an entirely different reason. Because I saw it too.

Rows and rows of the same little brown bottles we'd first seen in Theo's studio were coming into focus— neatly packed in half a dozen boxes scattered around a dank basement space, illuminated by flickering fluo- rescents.

"This is the stuff for the attack?" an unfamiliar voice mumbled—wannabe gangster style. Only it wasn't completely unfamiliar, as it matched one of the shark- skin morons drinking beside us in real-time.

We must be accessing their memories…

"Yeah," another cheap-suited dummy replied. *"Ward says fuck the dispensers. Chugging it will get the job done just the same…"*

Ward?

The sound of a glass being slammed down on the bar snapped us out of our vision, and Gabe and I both groggily blinked as the Rat Pack regatta stumbled away.

"What the hell was that?" he rasped, looking greener than usual.

I didn't feel so hot either, and wasn't sure if it was the combi- nation of star hopping, whiskey, and slimy lowlife visions, but I needed to lie down, stat.

"No clue, dude," I choked out, stumbling off the stool and steadying my twin before heading for the club entryway. "We should probably mention it to Theo later, but right now, we—"

"Hey, you're okay. We've got you." Sinistre was suddenly at Gabe's side to support him. Fay appeared beside me—looking unsurprisingly excited that her evil seating arrangement plan had outed us.

Here it comes.

"I fucking *knew* it," Fay excitedly whispered in my ear as security cleared a path for her and Sin to hustle us toward the private rooms. "Not to fangirl with *shock and awe,* but if you don't think I have every Suarez trading card…"

"Not now, Fay," I groaned, but she was a rabid cape chaser with a bone, and I wasn't recovering from this vision as fast as I normally did.

What is wrong with me?

"I'm sorry, I'm just so excited!" she continued, tucking her tiny ass body under my armpit—as if she could hold up my weight if I collapsed. "And when you're feeling better, I actually want to talk to you about getting a certain *handyman's* autograph. I paid five grand for that trading card on the dark web."

"FIVE GRAND?!" I barked as we reached the room, then immediately regretted it as my head swam from the effort. "I swear to gawd, you better tell me ours cost more."

Even Wolfy's cards *are stacked against me.*

Fay grimaced as the hulking security guards helped Gabe and I stretch out on the waterproof rubber sheets of my favorite playroom. "Ehhh… not quite. And they came as a set…"

Drag me to filth, why don't ya?

"Dre," Gabe blurted out, blindly reaching until he grabbed hold of my hand. "Another one's coming. I-I think it's Balty…"

Fuck.

Now was *not* the time for one of Baltasar's panic attacks—especially not on the tail end of getting sucked into some randos' memories—and I could already tell this one was going to be a doozy.

"We'll be fine, Sin," I croaked—since *they* were eyeing us with concern, as opposed to the morbid curiosity of their girl-friend. "Just… make sure Theo knows where to find us when he gets here…"

"Of course, Dre." Their even tone temporarily soothed the external anxiety barreling our way like a runaway freight train. "There's water on the side table. Take however long you need…"

I vaguely heard the door close just as a wave of *terror* swept over me—so intense, it almost eclipsed what I'd felt when Theo disappeared with my twin before my eyes.

This is bad.

The tsunami of Balty's jumbled emotions swept over me, along with the panicked visuals of a warehouse on fire, a crying child I didn't recognize, more of those brown bottles—shattering into shards of glass amidst the sound of gunfire. Our older brother was screaming something about his *inventus* as he was tackled to the grass by someone who *felt* like Theo… but wasn't.

What the fuck is happening?!

Before I could help direct our power toward whoever was hurting Balty, millions of stars filled my vision—causing my grip on Gabe's hand to loosen as I fell into an unnatural sleep.

CHAPTER 36
ALL ABOARD

Gabriel

The first thing I noticed when I woke up was how groggy I felt, with my head still clouded by sleep and sprinkled with stars.

The second was that a hot, wet mouth was wrapped around my dick.

"Fuuuuck..." I groaned, sleepily thrusting as Theo's familiar petrichor scent hit my nostrils.

Just wake me up like this every day, m'kay?

"That's the plan, angel," he murmured as he slid off my cock with a loud pop and pressed my thighs against my chest. "I simply wanted to check whether I should wake your twin or keep him slumbering for when I fuck you. Which do you prefer?"

I glanced over at Dre's sleeping face the same moment Theo circled my hole with his tongue, and suddenly, all I could think about was being fucked while one—or both—of them kept me asleep and *fuck...*

Now I'm gonna come in about two seconds.

Wait.

"Wait!" I gasped, and to his credit, Theo immediately stopped —releasing my thighs and propping himself up on his elbows to give me his full attention. He was still wearing his suit pants and dress shirt, although the jacket was gone, and I noticed the fabric was streaked with ash.

Like from a fire…

Waitwaitwait.

Momentarily ignoring my throbbing dick, and that I was already naked—*thanks to Theo, I'm sure*—I focused on getting a read on Balty.

Because whatever went down last night was fucking intense.

I sighed in relief as I located my older brother in downtown Sunrise City, seemingly unharmed and more content than he'd been in a while.

And apparently about to enjoy some morning sex of his own with a roughed-up looking Zion Salah.

OKAY, I'M OUT!

That accidental voyeurism instantly cleared the lust clouding my head, and I narrowed my eyes at the man between my legs.

With his mouth inches away from my cock.

Focus, Gabe!

"Where were you last night?" I growled, determined to get him to talk before he distracted me—

It was too late, as Theo chuckled, flicking the V on the underside of my cock with his tongue while a tendril took over with teasing my hole. "Oh, I do love your angry voice. But let's leave the stern Daddy act to Andre, shall we? I much prefer *you* soft and submissive… and *breedable…"*

Holy. Fuck.

Whatever boner percentage I'd lost by mentally walking in on Balty's sex life—*because what the fuck was going on with Zion's lizard dick?*—came back with a roaring vengeance. Now that Theo mentioned it, I *also* preferred being soft and submissive for him, although I'd never in my life considered—

"Fucking *breed* me," I moaned, because apparently I was totally down with getting my ass mpregged by this crazy alien.

The growl Theo released made my hair stand on end and my dick twitch—weeping precum. I didn't even try to silence the pathetic whine that escaped me when he backed off, because good lord, I was here for it.

Give it to me.

"All I've been thinking about for hours is being inside you," Theo murmured as he quickly removed his clothes. "And all the carnage only made me harder…"

My hungry gaze dropped to his fat cock as it sprang free and, suddenly, my priorities shifted. All *I* could now think about was choking on him and I may have legit drooled when I licked my lips and grabby hands reached for him.

Because, yes, I'm willfully ignoring the carnage comment…

Or maybe it's making me *harder.*

I am unwell…

"Oh, no, angel," Theo tsked, lubing two thick fingers before pushing them inside me—eyes riveted to his work as I whimpered at the momentary discomfort. "If you want to be bred, it's your ass I'll be taking. Now present yourself like a good boy." When I didn't immediately obey, his gaze shifted to my face. "Spread yourself like a good little slut."

That'll do it.

With a *very* slutty moan, I placed my feet flat on the bed and spread myself wide.

"And you never answered my question," Theo casually continued as he notched his cock against my twitching hole. "Do you want Andre awake while I fuck you? You both should get comfortable sharing my bed, since neither of you will leave it ever again."

Fuck, I love it when he gets all threatening like this...

Another pulse of precum dribbled out of me. "Yes!" I was half delirious with lust, but I somehow replied. "We already talked about sharing you. He was down with... *fuck—*" I groaned as Theo forced his crown inside me before hooking my ankles behind his massive thighs. "We both want to fuck you at the same *tiiiiime...*"

My words ended with the sluttiest sound yet as Theo bottomed out with a satisfied growl.

And chose that moment to wake up my twin.

———

Andre

The first thing I saw when I woke up was Gabe, naked as the day he was born. His head was thrown back, and dude was arching off the bed so intensely, he looked like the possessed girl in *The Exorcist*.

The next thing I registered was Theo plowing into him with his monster cock.

JESUS FUCK!

"Jesus fuck!" I shouted, scrambling off the bed—nearly falling onto the floor as I slipped on the rubber sheets. "Couldn't you two horndogs wait until you were alone to head to Pound Town? Fuck."

"That's the plan, demon—*fucking.*" Theo chuckled, grinning mischievously as Gabe blushed and half-heartedly tried to cover his dick. "Although we saw no need to wait. Your brother mentioned how group activities were unanimously approved—"

"Our brother!" I shouted again, as the terrifying visions from last night came flooding back. "Shit. Gabe, get off Theo's dick for a mo'… we need to check that Balty's ok—"

"Your brother Baltasar is safe," Theo drawled. I tried to focus on his words, but waves of secondhand pleasure were washing over me from both of them—making me sweat. "I made sure of it before I burned down a building that belonged to me, anyway. Not that I have any idea what the fuck he and the *Lacertus* were doing there in the first place."

Lacertus?

"Yeah… Balty's fine," Gabe blurted out—trying so hard to be coherent while Theo slowly took him apart. "I j-just checked in. He's in b-bed with Zion—"

That comment actually made Theo pause his torment long enough for Gabe's toes to uncurl. "The *Lacertus* escaped? I wonder how that happened…"

Hold up.

If he's talking about Zion Salah…

"I take it *Lacertus* is what you call the giant lizard aliens that originally invaded Earth." I carefully observed Theo as I spoke, wondering just how much he knew about our heritage.

It would be so easy to just…

No.

I promised him I wouldn't dig around in his head.

It sucked to not *take* what I wanted—and experiencing Gabe's horny bliss was making it hard to concentrate. But I needed the basic facts of what happened last night before I could let myself dive into temptation.

I gotta be responsible and shit.

"And you tried to… *kill* Zion Salah?" I gritted out, quickly losing the battle with my will.

This is not good.

"Not exactly," Theo scoffed, trying for nonchalance, but sounding guilty as fuck as he slowly pushed his way back inside my twin. "I simply left him behind in my efforts to destroy the evidence—just as Gabriel suggested. Isn't that right, sweet angel?"

"Yeah," Gabe breathily replied, absolutely dickmatized as he rocked beneath him. "But just a heads up, Zion is Balty's *inventus,* so he gets family protection too."

Waitwaitwait.

When was that *announced?*

Theo's rhythm faltered, but he stubbornly avoided my gaze as he smoothed out his pace—effectively shutting up my twin with his magic cock.

Dude was probably on his last brain cell, anyway.

I was annoyed both these horndogs had insider knowledge they were only feeding me in small doses. Moving closer to the bed, I balanced my knee on the mattress beside Theo—crowding his space. Reminding him who owned him.

"What. Evidence. Did you destroy, Theo?" I enunciated.

What did you do?

"Oh, just the remains of a silly little DNA project I started a few decades ago," he breezily replied, before *finally* turning his head to grace me with a haughty look. "Your family isn't the only one who's been interested in the supe origin story, Andre. The Salahs have been harnessing their heir's dormant *Lacertus* genes since birth—hoping to claim more power for their clan. Meanwhile, Stellarians have been circling for millennia, trying to figure out why *this* rock and its lowly inhabitants were appealing enough for one of our greatest enemies to conquer…" His gaze returned to where my twin was writhing beneath him. "And *breed.*"

Theo must have hit the magic spot as Gabe moaned like a whore, and it was all I could do to keep my expression blank with so many sensations racing through my system.

Maybe we can finish this discussion later…

"We should finish this discussion later," Theo eerily echoed my scrambled thoughts as he unhooked Gabe's legs to get them out of my way. "Because my angel *begged* me to breed him right before I woke you up, and that's what I intend to do."

Wait.

Another unexplained detail of the night before surfaced. Just as I'd been about to intervene with whoever had pinned Balty to the ground, I felt myself being forcibly sent to sleep—exactly like I could do with Gabe.

Is that also a Stellarian power?

Before I could demand Theo give me answers—since it was obviously *him* who'd done it—my gaze dropped to his toned ass. He was curled over my twin, pumping into him like a mindlessly rutting animal, and my focus narrowed alarmingly.

Get me in there.

I'd never in my life wanted kids—and a breeding kink had never been my thing before—but suddenly, pumping this brat full of imaginary babies was all I could think about.

What the hell is happening to me?!

Without realizing it, I'd already climbed onto the bed behind Theo, unbuckled my belt, and wrestled myself free. But then *my* last working brain cell insisted I clarify what this crazy alien was up to.

For my idiot twin's sake.

"You're not *actually* impregnating Gabe, right?" I muttered, coating my dick with lube but only giving Theo's hole a cursory dab as punishment. "He's not gonna wake up full of tadpole eggs or with something trying to claw its way out of his stomach, right?"

Theo huffed a laugh as he spread his knees wider for me. "No. If you must know, Stellarians reproduce through a process similar to Earth organisms dividing cells through *meiosis*. But you're catching onto all this has ever been—an arms race of repopulation between two ancient alien races with Earthlings caught in the middle as breeding mares. Or studs, if skinsuits of a different gender are involved. Which happens occasionally."

My brow furrowed. Xander had suggested Theo was the missing link in his and Doc's research, but if what this alien was babbling about was true, it meant *Lacertus* genes weren't the only intergalactic component to our collective DNA.

But how does that explain what Gabe and I can do?

"Eyes on the prize, Andre," Theo teased, arching his back like an animal presenting itself to its mate. "All I want you to focus on right now is your primal desire to paint my insides with your cum." He peered at me over his shoulder with a challenge in his hooded eyes. "Isn't that what you want, *Demon*—to *breed* me?"

————

Theo

I had officially decided there was nothing I loved more in life than making Andre lose control.

Well, besides making a mess of Gabriel.

So why not both?

Preferably at the same time.

I also appreciated my demon *not* rummaging around in my head, just as he'd promised. While I didn't regret what I'd done last night, I *had* allowed a few—*okay, maybe a dozen*—normies to die in the fire at my bottling plant, and wasn't sure how my twins would react to the news.

Especially the one falling apart so beautifully beneath me.

"Pleeeaaassseeee…" Gabriel whined—the combination of his tone and word choice causing my predatory instincts to go haywire. "Please keep fucking me, Theo… *pleasepleaseplease—*"

I chuckled and glanced down to where he was stretched around my cock. "I'm simply waiting for your twin to decide whether he wants to join the fun. Unless, of course, he's not man enough to claimmmmph…"

My words turned into a strangled sound that I chose to immediately block from memory when Andre entered me so violently, it moved both Gabriel and me further up the mattress.

"You were saying?" Andre growled in my ear as he held his hips flush against my ass—buried to the hilt. "As if everything about you doesn't already belong to me."

Oh, you think so?

"To both of us…" Gabriel whispered blissfully, and I could *feel* some of the tension leave the man behind me.

We can't have that.

"Mmm… But who's in charge here?" I teased. I attempted to swivel my hips, only to have Andre immediately grip me so hard I knew there'd be marks—illustrating my point. "Who's fucking who, and why is the answer that both of us are fucking Gabriel?"

He rested his forehead against the back of my neck with a huff. "You are such a brat."

Oh, I know.

"But you have a point," he grumbled before loosening his grip. "We should have discussed this before I got balls deep, but all I can fucking *think* about right now is… *fuck…*"

Again. I know.

I was also having difficulty staying coherent, and the raw desire I felt for both my mates was barely being contained. Even with how much I'd enjoyed spreading my seed throughout the centuries—*something I wasn't feeling proud of at the moment*—I'd never fallen into an actual breeding frenzy before. I'd honestly thought talk of such things was a myth.

But here we are.

"Let us in, Theo…" Gabriel's strained voice broke through my reverie as he cut in for his twin. "I know Dre promised to stay out of your head, but maybe—"

"Yeah," Andre exhaled against my sweaty skin. "Yeah, that's it. We both need to *feel* you, inside and out. Let us take you apart."

I tensed, not least of all because being torn to pieces—cell by cell—was the only way to kill a Stellarian. My twins had no way of knowing that, however, and I knew they would never harm me—at least, not in a way that wasn't enjoyable. The larger issue was I didn't want the only two beings I cared about to *see* what I'd kept hidden in the deepest, darkest recesses of my soul.

Assuming I even have one.

"Starshine." Andre shifted his position to soothingly run his hand over the ribs *he'd* lovingly bruised. "You may be a brat. I may even punish you for how you behave. But nothing you've done can change how we feel about you—or this bond we have. So let us in. Let us see *all* of you."

Exactly *how* he could understand my hesitation, without having access to my thoughts, was a mystery, but the promise of receiving unconditional… *something* was tempting…

Something like…

Love.

"Yes," Gabriel echoed—reaching for me and cupping my face in his hands. "Please show us what we… what *you* are."

Andre hissed in a breath as I froze.

Could it be true?

Of course, I'd suspected—and hoped—they were part Stellarian, but as neither twin had seemed to fully understand what *I* was, I'd second guessed myself yet again.

"We star hopped yesterday," Gabriel said, gazing up at me so hopefully I grew dizzy. "Well… Dre's the one who did it, but I guess that means I could do it, too. Maybe…"

By Stellaria…

"That's right," Andre purred as he began slowly thrusting, sending pleasure rippling through me. "Meeting you woke something inside us, but we need you to help coax it the rest of the way out."

"What?" I mumbled, still too shocked to do anything but allow my hips to move in time with his—to thrust into my angel beneath me. "How?"

"We don't know." Andre ran his teeth over where my shoulder met my neck, reminding me of the marks he'd already left behind. "Let's see if we can fuck it out of us."

Oh.

Okay.

That I can do.

CHAPTER 37
ANDRE

The instant I sunk my teeth into Theo's neck, something shifted. It was a change in the air—like when your ears pop upon takeoff or a bullet train passes by when you're standing near the edge of the platform.

Like when I star hopped my twin across Big City.

Why doesn't he think he can do it, too…?

"Theo…" Gabe whimpered, clutching at Theo's waist and accidentally brushing his fingers over mine. "Please…"

I shifted my position to give him space, but Gabe grabbed my hand before I could escape—apparently needing the connection between us.

Okay, looks like we're doing this.

"What is it, angel?" Theo murmured as he moved between us —fucking himself on me while thrusting into Gabe. "Do you need to be bred?"

Fuuuck.

Something about that *word* just… *did things to me.* For a moment, I forgot all about what I'd asked Theo to show us, because who gave a shit about the secrets of the universe when this man's ass was swallowing my dick?

Must. Breed. My mate…

With a werewolf-level growl, I gripped Theo's waist with my other hand as well and delivered a violent thrust—reminding him who was actually in charge here.

Me.

"Oh, hello, *Demon,*" he chuckled, slyly glancing at me over his shoulder. "Do you want to play?"

My body was vibrating with desire, but Gabe tightened his grip on my fingers, grounding me. "I'm not playing, brat," I hissed against Theo's skin before giving him a little nip. "I'm going to fill your ass until it's dripping out of you, and I'm not gonna stop until we're fucking done. But first you need to let us in."

I slammed my pelvis against his ass again, making Gabe cry out as it forced Theo into him as well. Theo swore and tried to brace himself on the mattress, but the rubber sheets were unforgiving on his sweaty skin.

So he unleashed a few tendrils to stab into the mattress for leverage.

Causing something to stir inside me—like shifting tectonic plates.

Like a memory I can't place…

"More," Gabe croaked, throwing his head back as his chest began to glow. "We need more…"

The air was sucked from my lungs as Theo's mind opened to us in a rush, and I could feel my twin going slack as he tumbled into the vision with me. This wasn't like when I snuck in to poke around while Theo villain monologued to

Gabe. This was our alien *inviting* us in—showing us things he'd probably never told another living soul for as long as he'd been alive.

It began in a world of blinding color and, thanks to my twin being along for the ride, I *knew* what I was seeing was Stellaria. Theo's home planet. While other Stellarians passed by in a rush—mostly in borrowed forms, but occasionally in armored suits—none seemed to have any personal connection to *our* alien.

"Do you not have any family, starshine?"

After a moment's hesitation, Theo showed us a memory of the *meiosis* he'd mentioned earlier, heavily tinged with resentment.

So parenthood wasn't what he wanted…

It was what was expected *of him.*

The process started with him exiting the apparently leather-lined armor he was in to approach another Stellarian who'd done the same. It was then I realized we were witnessing his true form for the first time.

Oh, fuck.

He looks like a galaxy…

Actual tears pricked the corners of my eyes to see him like this—dozens of starry tendrils surrounding a cosmic island of glittering dust and dark matter, held together by central gravity and pulsing with energy and life. It was like being face to face with the beginning of…

Everything.

I *felt* Theo huff in amusement and quickly redirect our awed attention to the rest of his obligatory mating dance. In an almost robotic way, both Stellarians used their tendrils to carefully extract cells from each other, then swirled around the selected pieces until they'd successfully bonded—forming a single Stellarian offspring.

So there's a piece of Theo out there somewhere?

The instant I had this thought, the vision hurriedly changed, and Theo showed us how he'd enlisted in their version of the armed forces before star hopping to Earth the first chance he got.

I guess dude decided to go out for some milk after that.

What came next made my heart ache. The images rapid-fire flashed before us, giving me the impression this was difficult for Theo to share. Abuse at the hands of his squadron leader, followed by Theo's own cocktail of emotions. Deception, anger, aggression, numbness, shock, and relief were followed by centuries of burying his past beneath so much vice, he'd forgotten how painful it had been to betray his own kind.

Oh, starshine…

Theo's body had gone still between us—his glow heartbreakingly fading. His only movement was the rapid rise and fall of his chest and the gentle undulation of any tendrils not buried in the mattress.

He's ashamed.

And worried about how we're going to react.

"Starshine," I murmured, and began kissing my way down his spine. "You did what you had to do—"

"But I didn't," Theo whispered harshly—his face tucked against Gabe's neck. "I didn't *have* to kill my entire unit. I *chose* to because I no longer wanted to play by their rules and didn't rank high enough to be worth listening to. So I did the only thing I could think of to get my way."

No.

To get away.

"You did what you had to do," I calmly repeated. "To be free."

He lifted his head to peer at me warily, so I continued. "We don't always feel like we belong where we're born, Theo. If anyone understands that, it's me." Gabe squeezed my hand, and I squeezed back—reminding my twin *he* was exempt from any judgment I held against our clan. "But you, Theo, will *always* belong with us."

Always.

"Fuck," Theo grumbled as he dropped his head and thrust into Gabe once again—clearly choosing fucking over feelings. "Why do you insist on making me… *get emotional*, demon? Ugh."

Because I see you.

"That's *Demon,* brat," I corrected as I matched his movements with my own—finding a rhythm that sent fireworks down my spine, enhancing the pleasure loop building between the three of us. "And it's because you're mine. *Ours.* We'll protect you from whatever it is you're running from, but you're not allowed to run from us."

Or this.

"Show us what happened last night," I commanded with an insistent tap of my hand against his ass.

Show us everything.

With a sigh, Theo hesitantly reopened his mind to share his memories from the night before. First, he was mildly annoyed over Major Obscurity belligerently yelling about missing shipments. This then turned into surprise at discovering Balty in his bottling plant, before morphing into blind rage as his normie employees enacted emergency protocol to destroy the evidence—with our brother in the line of fire.

So he made them pay for their carelessness.

Fuck.

He killed *for our family…*

"I…" Theo began—the only anguish in his voice being the fear of judgment from us. "I killed them all and don't feel bad about—"

Mine.

Before he could finish, I sunk my teeth into his shoulder, while simultaneously burying my cock deep inside him. If I could have somehow unleashed one hundred tendrils and filled him with those as well, I would have. Anything to seamlessly join myself with this man for all eternity.

All fucking mine.

"More!" Gabe was babbling, completely out of his mind. "I can feel it *buzzing* inside me. It's like it wants to get out and connect with you…"

I wasn't sure which one of us he was talking to, but it didn't matter, since the overwhelming urge to *breed* Theo had taken over my lizard brain again. I loosened my hand from Gabe's so I could grab Theo's shoulders and hammer into him, grunting with every slap of my skin against his.

Mine. Mine. Mine.

That buzzing sensation was building within my chest, and my vision went hazy as my mouth filled with blood. But then I heard my twin cry out.

"It's too much!"

Stop.

I immediately stopped moving and used one hand to hold Theo in place while reaching the other down to cup Gabe's cheek. "Hey, hey… do you need to safe out?"

"No," he huffed. A blissed-out smile spread over his dumb face as he cracked open an eye to peer up at me. "What I *meant* was… It's *so* much. It feels so fucking good, but I-I don't know if I can hold it all by myself."

Ohhh…

I can help with that.

Settling back on my heels, I hauled Theo up into my lap with his back against my chest. His arms and several tendrils were wrapped around Gabe, so my twin was pulled along with him. A tendril captured his wrists—pinning them behind his back—but Gabe just wrapped his legs around both of us and continuing to fuck himself on Theo's cock, as if unable to stop.

I know the feeling.

"It's so close…" Gabe murmured, his eyes closed again as he chased his release—chased the answer to questions we'd never thought to ask. "I just want to… take. I want *everything.*"

"Careful, angel," Theo chuckled, hooking an arm around my neck as he rode me toward oblivion. "You're beginning to sound like a true Stellarian, claiming everything in his path."

"Why shouldn't we take everything?" I gritted out, so close, my *soul* felt like it was vibrating. "Don't we deserve it? Don't we deserve everything we fucking want?"

Don't we?

"We do," Gabe replied to my unspoken declaration.

I cupped the nape of his neck, tangling my hand in his unruly hair as I brought his lips to meet Theo's. My twin's blue eyes opened—glowing with an unearthly light—and I held his gaze while lowering my mouth to Theo's neck, showing him the answer in my eyes.

Yes, we do.

And we found it together.

The orgasm that ripped through me would have sent me to the floor if the others hadn't been holding me up. Theo groaned into Gabe's mouth and my twin's eyes rolled to the back of his head as they quickly joined me in tumbling over the edge.

Wave after wave of pleasure swept over my skin, alternating hot and cold as I shuddered through three sets of seemingly endless release. My vision whited out, but not before I witnessed starry tendrils erupt from both Gabe and me, coiling around Theo's in a possessive embrace—finally illuminating what we truly were.

"How did we never know?"

"I think we've always known…"

That was all the confirmation I needed, and I allowed myself to fully fall into whatever trance I was under—to fulfill my promise of not stopping until my cum was dripping out of

Theo. Not until I was done with him. Not until we'd taken everything.

Everything we deserve.

Instead of emerging as humans from The Refinery's playroom once our frenzy was over, we simply star hopped back to Theo's home—*our* home—and continued to hole up together. A closed circuit of power, a chosen family of three, a trio of celestial bodies orbiting the only gravitational pull that called to us.

Each other.

And Stellaria help anyone who tries to come between us.

CHAPTER 38
THEO

To keep up appearances, we resumed as much of our previous routine as possible over the next couple of weeks. Jensen and Lupe were in and out for their daily cooking and cleaning, the twins handled all incoming deliveries and interview requests, and I even convinced Gabriel to pose naked for me in my studio.

Since apparently, the last model made him stabby.

Cute.

The biggest change to my lifestyle was no more play parties, but I didn't miss the orgy-fueled debauchery, since my mates fulfilled all my physical needs—as well as the emotional ones I hadn't realized I required. For a proudly solitary creature like myself, it was humbling to realize just how lonely I'd been.

Not that I'll ever admit to that.

It was easy enough to use the supposed stalker-suicide incident as the reason for closing my doors, and my agent was ecstatic that my sudden reclusiveness made the value of my art increase.

Humans are so ridiculous.

One of my favorite parts about nesting with my mates—besides the constant fucking—was sharing everything I knew about Stellarians and *Lacertus,* and the history of both here on Earth. This was partly done so they could report enough intel to Big Bro Wolfgang to avoid suspicion, but also because I *wanted* them to understand what they were.

Although they're not exactly the same as me…

We'd realized fairly quickly they were some sort of Stellarian-supe hybrid—able to star hop, resonate, and produce tendrils, yet still permanently attached to their bodies. Their mind control abilities went beyond the basic forced sleep my kind could invoke, although Gabriel behaved as if Andre was the more powerful of the two.

Which makes no sense if they're identical twins…

"Hey, Theo!" Andre called over from where he was responding to my emails. "Sylvano Ricci's asking when you want to meet again about the USN marketing project."

I grimaced. "That's… odd. I'd assumed the offer would have been rescinded. You know, after the whole"—I gestured toward where Gabriel stood in front of an oversized canvas covered in chalk pastels—"kidnapping a supe against his will… thing."

How awkward.

My angel turned to face me, revealing his medium of choice adorably smeared across his forehead. "It was scary at the time, but it still lives rent-free in my brain." He blushed. "Maybe we could play Alien Abductor sometime? That's gotta be a kink, right, Dre?"

Behave.

But also—consider it done.

Andre rolled his eyes. Loudly. "Yeah, I think it's safe to say you're into anal probing, dude." He refocused on me. "Don't worry about what happened at the USN. I erased that part of Sylvano's memory—"

"YOU *WHAT?!*" Gabriel barked, startling me with his uncharacteristically raised voice. "Dre! Do you realize how many laws you broke? What if *Luca* finds out?!"

Oh.

I should probably tell them Luca is—

Gabriel's phone buzzed with a series of rapid-fire texts, and when he fished the device out of his pocket to look at the screen, he paled.

"Or if Wolfgang does…" he added, swallowing thickly.

With a heavy sigh, Andre closed my laptop and stomped over to his twin before snatching the phone out of his hand.

He scoffed as he read over what big bro had texted. "Why the hell is Wolfy freaking out and asking if we're okay? Is he on drugs or something?"

I snorted. "Perhaps he's finally realized he sent two helpless babes into a lion's den to be devoured."

Andre shot me a withering look that made my cock thicken and my tendrils reach for him. But then his brow furrowed as another text came in. "Now Simon's asking about a missing shipment of serum? From a… bottling plant on the East Coast that the Salahs were involved with…" he trailed off as his unamused gaze met mine.

Well, fuck.

"How does Wolfy know about your connection to the bottling plant?" Gabriel clutched at his chest, clearly panicking. "I thought you destroyed the evidence, Theo?"

"I did," I growled. "And no records would have listed me by name."

How is this possible?

"Lady Tempest must have talked," Andre said, so coldly the temperature in the room plummeted. "We should pay her a visit and—"

"No," I interrupted. "Jaqueline Salah only ever knew me as 'T' and the face I showed the Salahs left me untraceable." I waited until both twins were looking at me before reminding them of my ability to glitch out my features. "I always ensured those pompous *heroes* would take the fall…"

So who the FUCK talked?!

"Ward…" Gabriel's voice cut through my building rage, and I saw him exchange a worried glance with his twin. "Because that's what he was using our prototypes for, right?"

"Ward?" I repeated—confused over not only how my angel put the pieces together about the prototypes, but why this normie *nobody* would be our concern. "He's simply a wannabe gangster involved in some silly anti-supe resistance…" I trailed off as the twins' jaws practically hit the floor.

"You've been working with the… resistance?" Andre slowly asked—the careful neutrality of his expression and tone doing little to quell my growing anxiety.

"I wouldn't say that!" I protested, even though all signs pointed to exactly that. "And this was before I mated for life with the two most perfect creatures in any galaxy." Andre visibly softened, and I took that as a sign to power on. "Besides, all Ward got from me were your two dispenser prototypes. He would still need to mass produce them *and* get his hands on the serum, which he won't since *I'm* in charge of all shipments…"

Oh, shit.

Shitshitshit.

I dropped my face into my hands with a groan the same instant I felt the twins materialize by my side and wrap their arms around me.

Preek.

"Tell us everything, Theo," Andre murmured against my shoulder. "So we can help fix it."

I sighed and lifted my head. "Ward recently let it slip he had an inside man working for the Salahs as their publicity director—a lesser supe by the name of Joshual Preek. So I met with him and offered him *more* money than Ward could ever hope to, along with some mild threats. Our deal was that he'd keep his mouth shut to Ward and send *me* any remaining shipments should things go south."

Which they certainly did a couple of weeks ago.

And Major Obscurity was rambling about a missing shipment that night at the bottling plant…

"Angel." I kept my voice steady to disguise my rising rage and panic, determined to focus on the facts. "When was the last time a shipment arrived from the XOLO perfumery in Sunrise City?"

The perfumery was my cover—the on-paper middleman who sent the Salahs their shipments every six weeks, along with an occasional box for me to store in my basement as my personal stash. Yes, I'd given Preek authority with XOLO to redirect the Salah's crate to *me* if needed, but only upon my explicit instructions.

Did that little shit immediately turn around and fuck me?

With his lips pressed into a grim line, Gabriel released me and trotted back across the room to my laptop. After a minute of clicking around, he looked at us warily. "Nothing has been delivered here since the beginning of last month…"

"FUCK!!!" I bellowed as countless tendrils shot out of me, sharpened for war. "How DARE this practically powerless minion defy me? Am I not *TERRIFYING?!"*

I WILL KILL THEM ALL!!!

A false calm washed over me as Andre gently took me to the floor before draping his body over mine like a weighted blanket.

More emotionally supportive tricks.

I'll allow it.

"*Breathe,* starshine…" he murmured against my skin while carding a hand through my hair, petting me into submission. "Gabe and I have lived among normies—and by default, lesser supes—for most of our lives. A lot of them are cool, but they're still the 'have-nots' in this society. That's where the resistance was born from."

I sighed again—an exhale that was so heavy, I was surprised my true form didn't vacate my skinsuit while I was at it.

Perhaps I had a bit of a blind spot…

Stellarians were the most powerful species on this planet, but to any Earthlings barely scraping by, I was simply another supe who'd been handed everything they could only dream of. As obscenely wealthy and legitimately terrifying as I was —*thank you very much*—that meant less than nothing to those who had nothing left to lose.

"Well," I huffed as I allowed Andre to sit me up and then pull me to my feet. "Two weeks is still barely enough time for Ward to have your prototypes mass produced. There's no way their planned attack can move forward."

Especially since we still hadn't decided on the underground route.

"Attack…" Gabriel mused, and I cringed, realizing I truly was digging my hole deeper with my long list of crimes.

I just wanted to bathe in chaos like the gremlin I am!

"Shit…" Gabriel cleared his throat, looking as guilty as *I* felt before elaborating. "Theo, we forgot to tell you about something we overheard at The Refinery… the night you blew up your bottling plant."

Oh?

Andre swore under his breath and swiped a hand down his face. "Oh, fuck. Yeah, this group of wannabe Rat Pack assholes was sitting next to us at the bar. We caught a flash of their memories and it showed your little brown bottles in a basement somewhere. One of them mentioned the dispensers and the 'attack,' but then another said Ward told them to disregard the plan—that *drinking* the serum 'would get the job done faster…'"

Drinking it?

"I…" It wasn't often I was at a loss for words, but I was truly mystified. "The serum I've developed is *topical.* There's no way of knowing what would happen if one were to *drink it.*"

Count on Ward to ruin a perfectly good plan.

"Theo." Andre's hands were gripping my face, forcing me to focus. "What. Does. The. Serum. Do?"

I scoffed. *"Zion Salah* is what it does. He's been soaking in it for the past thirty some odd years—ever since he exhibited strong *Lacertus* genes at birth. His parents figured out the connection to supe ancestry and a not-so-chance meeting between me and Jacqueline Salah in Argentina sealed the deal. While Zion doesn't possess *Lacertus*-specific powers like flying, fire breathing, and power draining—*all of which Stellarians have evolved immunities to, I might add*—he is quite an impressive specimen. Which is why I cannot fathom how this ragtag gang of normies and lesser supes thinks they're going to force full-blooded supes into drinking…"

Oh.

Oh, I see.

My twins were staring at each other—no doubt already planning together in their heads while I slowly caught up to the direness of the situation.

A situation I caused.

When they looked at me again, however, it was with a mix of deep concern and stubborn determination, but zero traces of judgment.

"Cui bono?" Andre murmured, kissing me sweetly before I spiraled. *"To whom is it a benefit?* The dispensers were just a distraction, Theo. This Preek dude was probably sniffing around the bottling plant long before you ever met with him. You just fast-tracked the plan by giving him access to your shipments and creating a *bigger* distraction with the mess at the plant. And Ward was probably playing you from the start. Lesser supes would *never* give more power to full-blooded supes." He glanced at his twin and dropped his hands from

face. "I bet they're gonna drink it themselves. Just to see what happens."

To watch the world burn…

"Well, fuck," I grumbled, kicking at imaginary dirt on my studio floor. "I've made a mess of things, haven't I?"

Andre snorted, but when I warily peeked up at him, he was gazing at me lovingly. "You have and I will gladly spank your ass raw for it later. But right now, we need to divide and conquer for some damage control. Gabe and I will star hop to Ward's home to see what intel we can torture out of him."

"Mr. Ward R. Davidson of 88 Cherry Blossom Lane is about to learn!" Gabe sang from across the room as he quickly cleaned the chalk pastel from his face and hands with a packet of wipes.

Andre smiled evilly and returned his attention to me. "Meanwhile, I want *you* to call XOLO. Try to figure out where Preek had that missing shipment sent. Even if it's the first stop of many, it will give us somewhere to start. You should probably also arrange for any crates of serum you have here to be moved somewhere secure and off the books. Other than that, I need you to sit tight and wait for us to come back." His expression turned stern. "In other words, *don't do anything crazy.* Can you behave for me?"

As much as I loved *mis*behaving, I was more interested in revenge against the resistance. So I nodded… begrudgingly. "I will be on my best behavior."

Whatever that means.

Andre gave me a *look* that only turned me on, but then held out his hand for Gabriel before demonstrating just how well he could star hop. After they disappeared, I made a mental note to coach my angel on embracing his oddly *suppressed* Stellarian powers before getting to work on my assignments.

Look at me following orders again!

I guess I don't mind so much when they come from Andre.

A phone call to XOLO confirmed the missing crate had gone to a shipping company in Big City. Unfortunately, this meant it could have ended up anywhere, but I made the mature decision to wait for my twins for *that* delightful interrogation. Then I used an unlisted account to reserve space at a storage unit across town and grabbed my phone again to call for a pickup from my usual courier service.

Then paused with my finger over Preek's number in my contacts.

What could be the harm in laying a little trap?

> **I'm looking to unload a few local shipments immediately. Ward said you would know where to have them sent?**

I smiled, knowing poor Ward was already too tied up for Preek to check in with first.

If he's even still conscious.

Or alive.

To my surprise, my phone immediately buzzed with a reply.

Preek: *I can collect them myself. What's the address?*

I hesitated, wondering if perhaps I should wait for Andre's input.

Nah, fuck it.

Even if Preek was powered with supe serum, he'd still be no match for me, and any delay in my reply might spook him. So I quickly sent my address and tucked my phone away, pleased with my plan.

And my doorbell rang not two seconds later.

That was… quick.

Sending down some tendrils to investigate, I registered someone standing at my door with barely enough power to be considered a lesser supe.

How boring.

To assert dominance, I took my sweet time getting downstairs to the ground floor. Peeking through the peephole, I'd barely registered an athletic young man with classic, all-American good looks standing on the other side before a hurricane force wind blew my door off its hinges—sending me flying almost all the way to the elevator.

WHAT THE FUCK?!

I rallied my tendrils to strike, but suddenly couldn't unleash them

In fact, I could barely move at all.

"Theo. Coatl. Or… whatever you're calling yourself nowadays…" A honey-smooth voice chuckled as the sound of heavy boots approached across the marble floor.

I raised my head enough to take in the human looming above me—who was looking less human by the second as dozens of Stellarian tendrils slid out from his impeccable skinsuit.

Oh, no…

Worse than this revelation was the *resonance* he was emitting, and how it was as familiar to me as my own.

Because it was my own.

Well, isn't this poetic justice?

"You're not Preek," I croaked out, having nothing else to say as an eerily familiar glowing cube appeared in his hand—further chilling my borrowed blood.

"Preek's dead." The man smiled as he crouched beside me and began tapping a code into the cube, preparing to send me back to Stellaria or… worse. "My name's Ziggy Andromeda. And I've been looking for you."

CHAPTER 39
GABRIEL

I was one of the least violent members of my family, but the scent of Ward's blood was making it hard to keep up the good cop routine.

Since Dre is definitely the bad cop in the situation.

"Where the fuck did the last shipment end up?" Dre growled before slamming his fist into Ward's lower jaw, causing a few teeth to skitter across the peeling linoleum of the grubby kitchen where we were holding our interrogation.

I guess the resistance doesn't pay well.

"Is that the best you can do?" The normie spat blood directly into my twin's face. "I take it Theo didn't hire you pretty boys for the muscle."

If only he knew Dre was pulling his punches.

Otherwise, there'd be nothing left to interrogate.

Dre hummed before calmly walking around the chair our hostage was tied to and grabbing a pair of crusty old scissors from the stained counter.

Ward scoffed as his pinky finger was gently pinched by the rusty blades. "You two are amateurs, huh? Everyone knows you gotta use garden shears for somethin' like *thaAAAAAHH-HH!!!* How the... How the *FUCK* did you just cut off my finger with a pair of goddamn—"

"I work out," Dre deadpanned, as he placed the scissors over Ward's ring finger next. "Now I'm gonna ask you nine more times where the shipment went. The tenth time, it'll be your dick."

"F-f-fuuuuck..." our hostage stuttered—suddenly not so tough, only one finger down. "The serum's already been divided between our strongest lesser supes, so there's nothing left for you to *fiiiiNNNNGHHHHH!!!* Why did you cut off another one? I'm answering your fucking questions!"

"Must be an amateur thing," my twin drawled before kicking the bloodied fingers away. "You should probably start naming names, dude."

I watched one finger bounce under the fridge, distracted by an uneasy feeling nudging against the edges of my consciousness.

Something's wrong...

"We don't do civilian names, you idiots," Ward hissed, sweat pouring down his face as his body started going into shock. "Only assholes like your *boss* are egotistical enough to give their real names to those they shouldn't have underestimated."

I wonder what Theo's Stellarian name is...

At the thought of my *boss*—because *that* was another role play scenario we needed to explore—my awareness absently reached for the Teal Coast mansion we'd left behind.

Only to get a flash of power.

That didn't belong to Theo…

> *"Dre! I think something's happening back at the house."*

My twin paused with his scissors poised over Ward's middle finger, and I impatiently waited as his gaze grew distant—annoyed I couldn't consciously check in on Theo myself.

"I'm having trouble getting a good read on him, Gabe. It's like something's blocking me…"

Or someone.

Dre snapped back to focus, sealing Ward's fate by speaking to me out loud next. "Okay, we gotta wrap this up. I'll try to figure out whoever's creeping around at home, so we know what we're dealing with before we hop back. You focus on scraping this piece of shit for whatever intel he's hiding in there. Don't worry about being neat."

In other words, lobotomize him.

I frowned. "But… I-I can't do that without you."

My twin huffed and tossed the scissors aside. "Yes, you fucking *can,* dude. There's no logical reason you shouldn't be able to do *everything* I can do, and I don't know who told you otherwise."

Who told me otherwise…

Was Wolfy.

> *"Your twin is abnormally powerful, Padawan, which is a threat to our family. If he ever turns on us, I need to know I can count on you to do what's right."*

"What was that?" Dre murmured distractedly, as he directed his focus across town.

"Nothing," I gritted out—slamming the memory back into its locked box, absolutely *livid* as the pieces fell into place. "Just thinking about some old family bullshit."

Dre laughed humorously. "Yeah, well, we have our own little family now, bro."

We sure do.

A cocktail of rage and protectiveness, unlike anything I'd felt before, swarmed beneath my skin. Wolfy's undivided attention had felt like a gift—even when his favoritism caused issues between Dre and me—but now I suspected our eldest brother had been playing me all along.

Dividing to conquer.

He'd always implied Dre might become too power hungry one day, and if that ever happened, I needed to be ready to stand against him—to protect the rest of my family from my twin.

Which would only work if I was as powerful as him…

"No more games," I hissed under my breath as I turned to face the man unlucky enough to be in my line of fire. "You're going to tell me everything you know."

"Who the fuck *are* you guys?" Ward scoffed, unwisely deciding his last words would be salty ones. "And how did two punks like you even meet Theo?"

It was written in the stars.

Before the normie could add any idiotic closing remarks, his expression morphed into a satisfying blend of realization and terror as I began peeling back the layers of his brain for the intel I needed.

Simple.

I cocked my head, smiling sweetly. "What were you saying, Ward? Something about egotistical assholes underestimating those they shouldn't?"

"You're…" he choked out—his basic motor skills already failing him.

"Not human, obvi," I replied. "We're supes. Extremely dangerous ones, belonging to the most notorious family around. And even though you'll sadly no longer be around for my siblings to torture, you've now given me the names of those 'strongest' lesser supes you mentioned. Guess we'll be paying them a visit next to see if they wanna cough up that missing serum for us."

Literally.

I poked a few slow bleeds in Ward's brain on my way out, while adding every name I'd scraped into my Notes app under the heading *Watch List.*

Then I added The Hand of Death to the bottom.

And sent it to **The Rabble** group chat.

That oughta leave no crumbs.

"You're in a mood." Dre glanced at his phone before eyeing me appraisingly. Even as he said this, he held out his hand— offering his unconditional support, as always.

Because he would never hurt me.

And I should have known anyone saying otherwise was full of shit.

I wasn't sure how much our eldest brother knew about what we were, but it was safe to assume I'd been nothing but a pawn in one of Wolfy's schemes. My phone was buzzing up a storm in my pocket, and I could feel Balty's anxiety pulsing like a strobe among Big City's lights, but there was only one star calling us home.

"I'm just tired of secrets," I rasped, allowing my anger to build like a gathering storm. "All I want from now on is you, me, Theo, and the truth."

The truth to the materials.

A slow smile of approval stretched across my twin's face. "Sounds perfect. Ready to get our man?"

Our man.

"Yeah." I took his hand and grinned in return before my smile faltered. "Dre… I need to tell you something. It's about Wolfy —" Before I could come clean, a visual of Theo's front door blasting off its hinges had me gasping in terror.

Theo's in trouble!

The next thing I knew, Dre and I were back in the Teal Coast studio.

But Theo was nowhere to be seen.

Operating on instinct alone, I unleashed a dozen tendrils to snake through the house—just like I'd watched Theo do countless times to 'taste' the air for clues—and what I found surprised me. Another Stellarian was with him. One who felt weirdly *familiar*.

Just like whoever tackled Balty to the ground outside the bottling plant…

Dre was already striding into the hallway, forcing me to hustle to catch up.

"What's the plan, dude?"

"We're gonna do what we do best."

Play human.

Exiting the service stairs, we peered over the zebra print landing to take in the scene below. I couldn't see much of Theo, but clearly, he'd been thrown across the room during the same blast that took out the front door. I assumed the man standing next to Theo's fallen—but thankfully, still breathing—form was the reason splinters of expensive wood littered the marble entryway like confetti. The man who was now watching *us* like a hawk.

Are we dealing with a supe?

Why can't I get a read on him?

The air around the stranger was weirdly shimmering—implying he was masking what he was—and even though he felt familiar, I couldn't place where I'd seen him before. Mostly, I needed him to back the fuck off from the love of my life.

Clutching my chest, I gasped dramatically. "Theo! Holy *shit,* dude. What happened? Are you okay?"

I took the stairs three at a time as I bounded closer—playing the role of the dumbass intern, cluelessly waltzing into danger. Never mind that I had to use every ounce of willpower to not immediately end the meathead-looking asshole looming over my broken *mate.*

Please be okay.

Pleasepleaseplease…

As usual, that was the magic word, as Theo stirred and cracked open his eyes. "Angel… you need to… run…"

Like hell I'm running.

"Why would I do that when I can just call an ambulance?" I pulled out my phone and continued my idiotic charade, even as I blasted Theo with as much comfort as I could. It was only then that I spared a glance at the man responsible. The one who was going to die. "Unless you've already called for help... sir?"

Because you're gonna need it.

The stranger was watching me in the cold, predatory way supes did, as I inched closer to Theo. Kneeling beside my *stellar collision,* I placed my hand over his heart.

I'm here.

"No, I haven't," Theo's attacker replied. "I've waited too long for this to let anyone else take away what's rightfully mine."

Excuse you?!

Dre silently appeared and lowered himself to crouch beside Theo on the other side. "I think you're confused, pal. This is the artist Theo Coatl and you're trespassing on his property. You need to leave before I—"

"Before you *what,* Earthling?" the man growled as the shimmering effect surrounding him sharpened to reveal dozens of razor-sharp tendrils, leaving no question what we were dealing with here.

Why has Theo not star hopped the fuck away from this guy?!

"Stand down, boys..." Theo weakly spoke. "He'll kill you."

Our Stellarian visitor chuckled and glanced down at a glowing cube in his hand I hadn't noticed before. "It's true. You both would have already been dead if not for the contract I just finished signing with your brother not an hour ago."

Fucking Wolfy.

I was nothing but rage. It was a living thing inside me, clawing to get out, and the first casualty was going to be this intergalactic asshole, followed by everyone who was working with him.

Maybe I'm *the one my family should be afraid of.*

"Gabe. Gabe! Stand down. Don't show your cards. We need the facts first."

My brother's words cleared my head as I heard him speak out loud. "Okay, so you know who we are. Congratulations. That means you also know Theo is *our* job, not yours, random Stellarian."

The Stellarian in question looked surprised. "Theo told you what we are? Interesting… Very well. You may call me Ziggy, and my business with your 'job' is not only far from random, but precedes your business by centuries. That's why we are *all* going to hop back to your family's compound. Together. Then—as a *courtesy* to your clan—I will allow you to extract what you need from Theo's head. Once you're done with him, he's mine."

Like hell he is.

"What do *you* want with him?" Dre growled, gripping Theo's arm just as I realized where I'd seen this fool before.

Doesn't he play Deathball against Balty?

What the actual fuck is happening right now?!

"Dude, I don't care what this asshole wants. We need to get Theo out of here!"

"You think I don't know that?!"

Ziggy held up his glowing cube, as if that alone would answer Dre's question. "Theo Coatl, as you call him, is a fugitive from my planet, wanted for the murder of Squadron X7-Coda-B475. This device—technology far beyond what your tiny minds could ever comprehend—is rendering his powers useless while I scan him for traces of the Stellarians he consumed in the past."

"Consumed…?" my twin murmured, obviously trying to get dude to villain monologue to buy us some time.

"Yes," Ziggy sighed, as annoyed by our 'tiny minds' as Xander usually was. "As you clearly know more than the average Earthling about my kind, I assume you know what we're made of. When one Stellarian tears another apart, there's inevitably some cosmic dust left behind from the fray. This will be useful evidence in convicting Theo for execution—"

EXECUTION?!

Our enemy's gaze snapped to me, and I realized I must have blasted him with a warning shot of power.

Too bad.

He can take Theo over my dead body.

"*Gabe…*"

"*You* will be returning to my family's compound. Alone," I growled, feeling my fury rising like a volcano close to eruption. "This is Theo's property, so without a warrant, you have no authority here."

Ziggy's smile was so condescending, it was all I could do not to unleash a tendril and bitch-slap it off his face. "Actually, little Earthling, as a legal representative of Stellaria, I have the power to repossess everything in Theo's name. And as it's doubtful that he's added you two temporary playthings to the deed…"

The deed, huh?

"Gabe! Why are you fucking with this dude? Let's just hop to the club and figure out our next move from there…"

"No. I know where to go. Hold tight."

Because Star Hopper here just gave me a better idea.

"Angel, please…" Theo whispered.

I've got you, old man.

I've got this.

"Good chat, Ziggy." I smirked, tightening my grip on Theo and seeing Dre do the same. "Be sure to tell Wolfy he has a new clan to make a deal with now. Ours."

And with that, I alone star hopped the three of us across the planet.

CHAPTER 40
ZIGGY

Kill.

I'm going to kill him.

I'm going to kill them all.

Killkillkillkill…

I could do nothing but stare at the vacant space where my prey had lain—*finally* within my grasp, after centuries of hunting. To be so close to victory, only to have it ripped away from me by a couple of lowly *Lacertus* bastards…

"WHAT THE FUCK?!!!" I howled, throwing my Celestial Cube against the nearby elevator and severely denting the metal grate.

At least it's good for something.

"Are you here to model?" A decidedly unamused voice interrupted my fury, and I turned to find an older woman who was barely four feet tall, giving me a judgmental once-over.

"What?" I snapped, quickly retracting my tendrils, although I was certain this human couldn't see them.

The woman's expression turned into a shrewd assessment. "I assume you are here for"—she waved a feather duster toward the stairs—"Theo's naked drawing activities. He buzzed you in, yes?"

Her gaze drifted toward what remained of the door and silence followed.

Awkward.

"It was already open," I blurted out before plastering on my most SupeSports-ready smile. "But yes, I'm here for the... naked drawing... activities."

The woman shrugged before handing over a keycard that said GUEST and turning her attention toward sweeping up the mess I'd created into a pile.

How have Earthlings survived for this long?

I cleared my throat. "Where can I find Theo?"

So I can kill him.

She huffed, clearly done with me. "He should be in his studio on the third floor." Then she added, under her breath, "Do I *look* like his mother?"

I have no words.

Staunchly reminding myself that killing an innocent human would solve nothing, I retrieved my cube and stalked up the hideous zebra-print staircase. Using the keycard to access the service area, I then ascended another flight to the third floor—where I was given unfettered access to what was clearly the inner workings of Theo's daily business.

I can't believe it took me this long to locate this walking disaster.

How embarrassing.

In my defense, it was extremely difficult to identify a fellow Stellarian in the wild, especially if you had barely any leads. Our DNA seamlessly blended with what was left of our hosts and we could just as easily star hop to a completely different galaxy as we could to a new vessel.

During the century it had taken for me to even be *approved* for an assignment to Earth, I'd constantly worried Theo would be long gone by the time I arrived.

But luck was on my side.

Not only had I earned my assignment, but I convinced my superiors to reopen the cold case that had haunted my existence for hundreds of years.

Since the day I was created.

And abandoned.

I slumped against the doorway of Theo's studio with a heavy sigh, unsure if I needed a stiff drink or a swift kill to bury the anguish coursing through my system.

How in Stellaria's name did he star hop away from me?

I had him locked down!

My phone chimed in my pocket and I grimaced, assuming it was Wolfgang Suarez checking in to make sure I hadn't murdered his asshole little brothers.

I *thought* I'd understood what I was up against with the mind-reading supes known as Shock and Awe, and so had locked down my memories the instant they appeared on the landing above me. But the instant one of them hit me with a blast of almost unimaginable power, I realized what Wolfgang meant when he explained how dangerous they were.

How nothing—and nowhere—was safe.

I now suspected *they* had been the unexplained *presence* I'd felt at Theo's bottling plant the night of the explosion—the ones trying to save their idiot brother, Baltasar, from himself.

The ones I sent to sleep for interfering with my hunt…

When I pulled out the device to find the name *Micah Salah* flashing on the screen instead, my stomach enacted a strange flipping motion that added another layer to the swirling cocktail of emotions sloshing around in there.

"Yes?" I answered my phone, sharper than I meant to.

True to form, Micah was as stubbornly sunny as always. "Hey, Zig! I know I shouldn't bother you on the job, but I couldn't wait. How did the thing work? You know…" His voice turned into an exaggerated stage-whisper. *"The top secret thing I developed for you?"*

Despite my dark mood, a smile twitched my lips—before I forced it into a scowl. "I… haven't gotten the chance to use it yet."

Since everything went to shit.

The Salah family engineer hummed knowingly. "Something went wrong. Tell me."

I sighed again. Since the day Zion Salah took over, I'd been unexpectedly *welcomed* into the hero's clan by his seemingly countless siblings. The concept of family didn't interest me—for obvious reasons—but a certain clan member did.

Micah.

This was purely because he was a supe known as Exo-Tech, whose powers involved manipulating non-organic matter into anything his admittedly impressive brain could invent. It was a useful skill for creating weapons and other tools for justice—a nice complement to my kind's natural ability to shape *organic* matter.

Nothing more.

It certainly didn't have anything to do with how he somehow smelled like goddamn sunshine. Or that when his glasses weren't in one of their many high-tech work modes, they made his liquid brown eyes sparkle like galaxies.

And it absolutely had nothing to do with the fact he was the one creature who got me to admit when I'd *failed.*

I suppose it couldn't hurt to get his opinion…

Swallowing down my flight instinct, I beelined for a laptop I spied on a far worktable, deciding to multitask while engaging in what Micah often referred to as 'Zig's unbilled therapy.'

Cheeky little shit.

With one last sigh, I began my report. "I had Theo locked in place with the Celestial Cube, scanning him for evidence before I transported him back to the Suarez compound. He was completely immobilized… or so I thought…"

I gritted my teeth at discovering there wasn't even a password on the lock screen.

Truly, this creature has no sense of self-preservation.

But neither do I, it seems.

While dutifully explaining how the scan worked—since Micah went nuts for the technical details—I clicked around Theo's recently closed internet tabs, desperate for a clue to my prey's whereabouts.

XOLO Perfumerie.

Big City Shipping.

Theo's inbox with over five thousand unread emails.

So.

Much.

Porn.

"Okay, so what went wrong?" Micah's voice had me hurriedly closing a window of what was *definitely* twincest fanfic.

Possibly self-published.

"They somehow star hopped away from me!" I barked, slamming the laptop closed.

"They?" Micah prompted, blessedly calm as my agitation bubbled over once again.

"Yes," I huffed. "The Suarez twins have been stationed here for weeks on an unrelated job for their clan. They walked in on the situation and… *defended* Theo. Then the three of them simply disappeared."

Maybe my Celestial Cube is defective.

"I didn't think Shock and Awe could star hop…" Micah mused.

"What? That's not…" I stuttered. "I don't believe that's what happened."

Right?!

Micah's warm chuckle would have made me murderous had it come from anyone else on this planet. "Listen, Zig. You need to understand something about the Suarez clan—especially if you're gonna work with them."

I'm all ears.

His voice lowered as the sound of a door closing filtered through our connection. "First things first. They do not play by the rules. Hell, they make their own rules! And they get away with it—not just because they're *villains,* but because they have connections with the council, through The Kinetic Assassin. Council members are supposed to be neutral—and I'm not saying Luca Meier's *not*—but the man took the Suarez kids into his home every summer for top secret *training...* like some kind of... *Karate Kid* Mr. Miyagi shit."

I had no idea who this Miyagi character was, but made a mental note to investigate—especially if it was something Micah enjoyed.

Purely for research purposes.

"What are you getting at, Salah?" I urged, as gently as possible, despite my impatience. If left to his own devices, the easily excited supe would ramble all day.

And the clock is ticking.

He laughed in that carefree way of his I envied. "My point is... as much as Luca was supposedly an ally of Apocalypto Man and Glacial Girl, *zero* repercussions rained down on Wolfgang for what we *all* know was the premeditated murder of his parents. Luca's interest in that family has always been with the *kids,* and it's pretty coincidental they're all some of the most badass motherfuckers around." When I didn't reply, he laughed again. "All I'm saying is, I wouldn't be surprised if the twins have some extra tricks hidden up their sleeves for *la familia.*"

What. The. Fuck?

Wolfgang dared to LIE to me about their powers?!

"Thank you for the intel," I mumbled, legitimately grateful even as my blood boiled. "It seems to be a rare thing for a supe to be so… transparent."

This time, when Micah laughed, there was a hint of sadness in his tone. "Yeah, well… I'm *fifth* in line, Zig. I'm so transparent, I may as well be invisible. *Nobody* notices me."

I notice you.

"But that means *I've* gotten good at watching everyone else," he continued, already back to his sunny self. "And it's always a good idea to watch the Suarez clan."

I scoffed, annoyed by what sounded like *respect.* "We'll see about that. In the meantime, do *you* want to know a secret about the supposedly infallible Suarez clan leader, Micah?"

"Fuck yes, I do!" he exclaimed with adorable enthusiasm.

I grinned, physically unable to resist his glow. "I'm immune to Wolfgang's powers."

"WHAT!" he shouted before lowering his voice again. *"That* is badass. How?"

"All Stellarians are." I shrugged, even though he couldn't see it. "Power draining is a fairly standard *Lacertus* ability, along with fire, flying…"

I trailed off as a stray thought surfaced. A wild theory. Something that was Suarez clan-specific.

Luca, you sneaky little devil.

"You've thought of something," Micah breathed into the phone.

I grinned. "I have."

"Tell me, *please*," he begged, and I had to suppress a growl at his pleading tone.

No.

My grin grew. "I'll tell you if I'm correct," I replied. "But first, I need to ask Wolfgang a few questions."

And he's going to answer them.

Every. Single. One.

CHAPTER 41
ANDRE

He did it!

He actually fucking did it.

Discovering Gabe had star hopped the three of us to our Berlin gallery filled me with so much pride, I tackled my twin to the floor the moment I blinked open my eyes.

"I *told* you that you could do everything I could, ya fucking muppet!" I cackled, ruffling his man-bun until it looked like sex hair.

Better hair for bottoming—FOR LIFE!

That asshole actually had the nerve to *blush* as he shoved me away. "Yeah, yeah. I was mostly panicking, and this was the only place on Earth that's technically in our names, so…"

You sly dog.

"This is your gallery?" Theo's voice brought my attention to where he was staring at a piece Gabe and I had created together.

A piece called *Starshine.*

The only painting here that's not for sale.

It wasn't as large as some of our other pieces, and at first glance, probably looked like a fairly simple study of the night sky. We'd created it using experimental glazing—adding transparent layers over the acrylics for depth and dimension to bring out the subtleties of hues.

Technique aside, the inspiration for *Starshine* was the reason we would never part with it. Our little night sky study was actually the visual representation of what Gabe and I dreamed about when we left our mind-bond open overnight.

The universe.

Home.

Him…

Our shared stellar collision.

In two strides, I was standing behind our kimono-clad alien with my arms draped around his waist and my face lowered to his neck—breathing him in.

Fuck, we almost lost him…

"You're safe," I murmured, although I suspected I was also reassuring myself. Regardless, I felt Theo relax in my hold, which helped *me* relax. "Thanks to Gabe."

My other half walked closer and wrapped his arms around us. "Nah. It was a group effort. I never would've started questioning everything I'd been told if it wasn't for both of you."

"All I want from now on is you, me, Theo, and the truth."

No one's gonna give us that.

Not unless we take it.

A beeping noise interrupted our moment. Swearing under my breath, I fumbled my phone out of my pocket and hustled to disengage the security alarm—before the police arrived to arrest us for breaking and entering our own property.

Better them than the local clan leader.

Fuck.

"Gabe…" I grimaced, but then quickly chased it with an encouraging smile. "Announcing we're forming our own clan is fighting words. You realize that, right?"

And that I'll stand beside you, no matter what.

I half-expected my twin to get flustered, but he simply nodded once, more confident than I'd ever seen him. "Yeah, I know. And even if Wolfy kills me for it, at least I'll die on *my* terms."

Dang.

"Angel." Theo cleared his throat and wiggled out of our grasp so he could turn to face us. "The Hand of Death *can't* kill you…"

Gabe scoffed. "I wouldn't be so sure, old man. He may be fiercely protective of his siblings, but I pretty much told him to take his protection and go fuck himself. In the group chat. Not to mention…" His gaze slid to me, full of so much anguish, my breath caught. "Now I've made it clear I will *not* be following the orders he's been giving me since I was young… to take out Dre if he ever turned on us."

WHAT?!

My face must have shown my reaction loud and clear, as Gabe reached for me desperately. "I swear, I could *never!* But Wolfy always acted like the reason he tasked me with the job was because I was special—like I was the only one he could count on if things went wrong. And I ate it up… because I'm a fucking idiot—"

"Stop it!" I barked, pulling him into my arms. "You're not an idiot. You were an affection-starved *baby* who looked up to his older brother, and he took advantage of that for his own gain." Gabe sniffled against my chest, so I gave him a minute before I continued. "Wolfy's also not an idiot, though. And I can't believe I'm fucking defending him, but… there was probably a good reason for what he did."

Yeah, I know.

Hell froze over.

My twin tensed and lifted his head to peer at me suspiciously. "You weren't like… body snatched by that Repo Man bounty hunter Stellarian, right?"

Har har.

Theo sighed and shifted awkwardly. "I… should probably explain who that Stellarian was."

"No." I cranked up the Dom in my reply so he'd understand there was no room for argument. "You do *not* need to explain anything right now—not after the shit you just went through. I want both of you to go upstairs and take a nice shower together to decompress. Gabe and I were just here, so there should be plenty of clothes to change into, including some suits of Wolfy's that might fit you." I smirked. "Full warning though—everything's gonna be black."

Theo rolled his eyes as Gabe led him toward the stairs. "The better to blend in with my new clan, hmm?"

My stomach dropped into my nuts at the enormity of that statement, but I stubbornly kept my smile in place. "You better believe there's a dress code, brat. Just leave the clan business to me."

Gabe looked slightly concerned as they disappeared into the stairwell—his confidence already fading—so I sent him a boost.

"I've got this, bro. We've got this."

Never mind that this was an obvious case of fake it 'til you make it. The only upside was that I was about 85 percent sure Wolfy wouldn't swoop in and murder us, especially with what he let Violentia get away with earlier this year.

I hope…

It also helped to know Repo Man Stellarian had a contract with our brother, which meant he couldn't stab us with a tendril. And Gabe's play was a good one—because it sounded like the gallery being in our name meant Ziggy couldn't take Theo away from us while we were here.

But hiding out isn't the best strategy.

Not if we want to play to win.

I texted Erich next to let him know we were here, since I wasn't sure if the gallery alarm being triggered would alert him. That was a gamble. The German was a close friend of Wolfy's, and on the Suarez payroll as our property manager—among other things. I honestly couldn't decide if it would be better or worse to ask the normie *not* to tell Wolfy we were in town, so I kept the text short, sweet, and unbothered.

It's better to act like I know what I'm doing.

Like I'm the one with the biggest dick.

A group of clubbers stumbling by the front window had me tensing, and I realized I needed to take advantage of how early in the morning it was here.

Local warlords have to sleep at some point, right?

Mistress Noir-Rouge had apparently stayed out of the drama between Wolfy and Vi, but I couldn't be sure the same would happen this time. It would be suicide to go up against seasoned clan leaders—especially on the home turf of one of the Suarez's strongest allies—so I needed to approach this diplomatically.

Cue a call to our handy diplomat.

"*Schätzli!*" Luca Meier answered on the first ring, sounding uncharacteristically ruffled. "Are you all right?"

Fuck.

Wolfy already spoke to him.

"I…" My badassery evaporated. Suddenly, all I wanted was Luca *here,* telling me exactly what to do.

"Where are you?" he urged, and I exhaled in relief before opening my mouth to answer his question.

Then snapped it closed again.

What if…

"*Hallo?*" Luca asked, and I heard the unmistakable sound of his Geneva study's pocket door sliding closed.

What if he's not on my side?

I swallowed thickly, quickly weighing the pros and cons of blindly trusting Luca, the way I had my entire life. To my grim realization—aside from star hopping away from the planet entirely—our Swiss Sensei was the best option we had.

"Andre." His tone was firm and commanding and something in it had me immediately straightening. "I guarantee you, Wolfy has tracking programmed on your phones. Tell me where you are so I can get to you before he does."

Fucking Xanny.

I'd never checked what Xander did to our phones when we met him at the pier, but it was safe to assume Wolfy had decided to not only erase any tracking Theo might have installed, but replace it with his own.

It was odd our eldest brother wouldn't have shared our location with Luca when they spoke, but I didn't have time to dwell on it. Instead, I allowed my awareness to briefly drift upstairs, to where I could feel Gabe and Theo enjoying each other in the shower, and I prayed I wasn't dooming us all with my decision.

"We're at the gallery," I gritted out in a rush. "It was the first place we—"

I stopped talking as the sound of wind and static filled the phone. When I glanced at the screen, it said the call had ended.

What…

Then there was a knock at the door.

And my phone lit up again with a call from Luca.

No.

Even though I could have easily walked to the door and looked through the peephole, I brought up the doorbell app on my phone instead.

And found Luca staring back at me.

No fucking way.

I let the call go through to voicemail, but he immediately called back. Meanwhile, I numbly stared at the door and wondered why he didn't just blow it in like the Stellarian who'd tracked down Theo.

The one who feels familiar.

Because he feels like… Theo.

The formerly inexplicable pieces of my life were suddenly falling into place. While my mentor had always been too powerful for me to get inside his head, I'd always felt a connection to him—as if I could *feel* his presence when he was around.

And sometimes even when he wasn't…

Cautiously approaching the door, I took a shaky breath and pressed my hand against the wooden surface. A low buzzing sensation began vibrating my chest—similar to what happened with Theo, but a hell of a lot closer to what happened between me and Gabe now that our true selves had been awakened.

Fuckfuckfuckfuck.

My phone lit up with a text from Luca.

Kinetic Kenobi: *Let me in, Andre.*

I bet you're already in.

> *"That's all this has ever been—an arms race of repopulation between two ancient alien races with Earthlings caught in the middle as breeding mares."*

Theo's words had me freezing in terror, especially as our family motto surfaced in my mind.

Blood is thicker than murder.

If Wolfy's not our brother…

Nothing will stop him from killing us.

Choosing the lesser of two evils—*I hoped*—I flung open the door, simultaneously rallying my supe powers and the tendrils lurking beneath my skin.

Even though I have no clue what to do with them.

Besides… sex shit…

Luca made no move, either to enter or attack. He simply watched me, cautiously—like one might observe a cornered animal who could be rabid.

Fucking hell.

"Don't tell me *you're* afraid of me too…" I choked out, annoyed at the way my voice cracked.

"Oh, *schätzli,*" he sighed and stepped into the gallery, closing and locking the door behind him before turning to face me again. "My little treasure…"

That fucking did it. I dropped my face into my hands and released the ugliest sob, but I couldn't even find it in me to care. This man had seen me cry before. He'd encouraged me to hone my powers, and held me together when those same powers felt like too much. Along with Wolfy, Luca had been one of our strongest advocates in convincing our parents to keep us away from the battlefield.

Even though we probably could have destroyed everyone.

Or… because *we could have.*

Luca Meier had always felt like family—had behaved like more of a father than my own had ever *tried* to.

But he still hid the truth.

"Why didn't you *tell* us what we were?" I harshly whispered, lifting my head so I could glare at him through my tears. "Gabe and I have lived our entire lives as *outsiders*—never fitting it with normies… with our own clan… Apparently, with supes in general."

Luca cocked his head and offered me that sly *Sensei* smile that drove me batty. "Ah, but you should know by now that we are *all* intertwined. Heroes, villains, *Lacertus*… and even Stellarians."

His gaze flickered behind me, and I turned to see the others had reappeared from upstairs. Theo was eyeing Luca warily, but Gabe's brain was working overtime—putting the pieces together for himself based on what he'd overheard.

"Do you want me to bring you up to speed orrrr…"

"Just give me a minute, dude!"

I'll wait.

My twin approached our longtime mentor—impressively unafraid. "Are you… like us?"

Luca nodded, as reserved as ever, even if I could now *feel* the anticipation buzzing beneath his skin. A low humming that called to me—wanting to connect.

He's probably wanted to connect since we were born.

No doubt sensing it too, Gabe tentatively placed his hand on Luca's forearm.

"Are you the reason we are what we are?" my twin asked, staring into our mentor's eyes with so much hope, I realized how badly he wanted it to be true.

Luca swallowed thickly and placed his hand over Gabe's. "I am. And I hope you don't resent me for that."

My twin scoffed. "Are you crazy, *Sensei?* You think we're gonna be big mad you made us into powerful alien badasses? Bruh." He shot a schmoopy glance over his shoulder to where Theo still lurked in the stairwell. "If you hadn't, we would never have found our stellar collision…"

Luca's eyes widened, but I still had questions before this family reunion got too sappy. "Are we just a byproduct of you"—I grimaced—"spreading your DNA around on Earth? Word on the street is that's been the universal *M.O.* since all aliens first arrived."

Theo had the good grace to mumble something apologetic, but Luca looked *horrified.* "What? No, Andre. You boys were no accident. In fact, despite having been here since the initial squadron of Stellarians arrived, you were *my* first creation. Well…" He canted his head. "Technically my second, but it's all related—"

I had about a million more questions for this man—*err… alien wearing a skinsuit*—but before I could spit them out, more unexpected visitors appeared.

Wolfy and Repo Man Ziggy.

Right in the middle of our gallery.

CHAPTER 42
GABRIEL

When Wolfy suddenly appeared out of nowhere like the goddamn grim reaper, it was all I could do to not start running.

Because being drained by The Hand of Death is not *on my bingo card for this year…*

A few things stopped that from happening. First, I wanted to defend Dre and Theo if he attacked, and second, I knew the three of us needed to come across as a united front.

Even if I don't know what the hell I'm doing.

Aside from star hopping across the globe…

But the thing that had me not only standing my ground but taking a step *toward* Wolfy was that my eldest brother looked like he'd just taken a beating.

WHO DID THIS TO HIM?!

For some fucked up, deeply ingrained reason, my first instinct was to defend my clan leader to the death. But Luca grabbed my arm before pointedly sliding me behind him—apparently already taking sides.

Bold move from a supposedly neutral party.

Of course, Wolfy missed nothing, and had no trouble glaring menacingly at Luca, despite his damaged face.

Eek.

"Looking good, Wolfy!" Dre called out cheerfully, even as *he* moved closer to Theo. "The black eyes match your aesthetic. Did you and your new *business partner* have a disagreement?"

Ziggy snorted, although he didn't look triumphant. "We did. The terms of our agreement stated I was to be informed of the full abilities of every supe involved, yet the powers of a certain set of twins were conveniently downplayed."

Wolfy's still protecting us.

But he won't be for long…

"Yes," Wolfy growled—his death glare still firmly fixed on our mentor. "It appears some extremely crucial information was left out of *my* pre-existing contracts as well."

Wait, what?

Dre cackled, drawing my attention back to him. "It also appears your convo with Repo Man here was pretty one-sided."

"Why are you baiting him, dude?! He's gonna fucking drain us!"

"I don't like how he's looking at Luca. And no, he won't. Because he can't."

Say what now?

Ziggy cleared his throat, looking oddly *human* as he grimaced. "My injuries were also extensive, but my kind heals faster than yours does." His gaze snapped to Dre with predatory focus. "I wonder how fast little hybrids like you would heal."

"Try it and see, fucker," my twin replied.

Waitwaitwait…

They had an actual fist fight?

The words of both Theo and Dre suddenly made sense. For whatever reason, Wolfy's Hand of Death powers didn't work on Stellarians, which meant they wouldn't work on us.

We are more powerful than Wolfy.

I'm *more powerful than him.*

This revelation almost brought me to my knees. For my entire life, I'd looked up to my eldest brother—had simultaneously idolized and feared him. Wolfy was everything I wished I could be, and I placed him on a pedestal. Like a golden god.

But he's just a man.

I felt a familiar tendril wrap around my wrist as Theo pressed against me from behind—grounding me while gathering Dre closer with another tendril at the same time.

Making it clear who we belong to.

Who he *belongs to.*

"So it's true," Wolfy spat, still directing his fury at Luca. "The twins are… whatever *they* are."

Confused, I realized our brother was *only* pointing at Ziggy and Theo.

Not Luca.

He doesn't know…

Luca spread his hands beseechingly. "I'm sorry for hiding the truth—"

"What the *fuck* are they?" Wolfy growled. "What did you DO?!"

Moving faster than I could register, he grabbed Luca around the throat with his dangerously bare hand and slammed him against a nearby pillar.

Holy fuck!

Holy fucking fuck!!!

Hierarchy was everything in the supe world. Even with Wolfy being a clan leader, he was expected to defer to the council and its members, or face severe punishment.

Besides that, Luca Meier was our *mentor*. He was the man who'd given us care and attention when our parents treated us with indifference, or worse. Wolfy not only showing Luca disrespect but attempting to *murder* him was something I never would have expected from our notoriously methodical and unruffled leader.

Unless…

He doesn't think he's making it out of here alive.

My stomach twisted painfully as I realized what Wolfy had probably already suspected. He was outnumbered, in a room with his betrayer and four other creatures who were immune to his only chance of survival.

We could easily take him out.

We could kill him and take over our clan.

We could take over every clan on Earth if we wanted to.

Ohmygodohmygodddd…

"Breathe, Gabe," Dre whispered in my ear as he rubbed slow circles on my back—only somewhat soothing my impending menty b. "Let's see how this shakes out."

I might not make it out of here alive, either.

"What are *you?*" Wolfy hissed, his voice thick with uncharacteristic anguish as he stared into Luca's soul from inches away.

"Something *you* can't kill," Luca replied sadly. Then he allowed dozens of tendrils to appear and undulate around him—causing Wolfy's eyes to widen in shock. "And that was one of the main reasons I chose *your* clan as my—"

"As your *what,* Luca?" Wolfy choked out, and my entire world crumbled to dust as I witnessed a single tear trail down his cheek. "Your breeding ground? As your little Earthling experiment? A means to get your hooks in for eventual world domination—just like the *Lacertus* originally planned to do?"

Luca flinched, but held his gaze. "As my *family,* Wolfgang."

Wolfy sharply inhaled, leaping away from Luca as if he'd burned him. "You're not my blood. My parents are dead, remember? I got rid of both Apocalypto Man and Glacial Girl to keep my siblings safe. *That* was our deal, Luca—not whatever the *fuck* you've been scheming behind my back, you fucking Judas!"

His fists clenched—one gloved, one not—and despite knowing his power couldn't hurt me, I shrank against the others as it rallied, filling the gallery space with his fathomless rage.

And his sorrow.

Oh, fuck.

What if Wolfy isn't the bad guy here?

What if we need to step in to defend him… against Luca?

Dre must have tuned in to my tumultuous thoughts, as he subtly slid an arm around my chest and began slowly backing Theo and me away from the action.

"What's the plan, dude?"

"No plan. Just vibes."

So we're fucked.

"Uh, uh, uh," Ziggy tsked, wagging a scolding finger in our direction. "Don't you go disappearing on me again, baby Stellarians. Not only do you have nowhere to run from here, but the outcome of this *family meeting* will determine your fates. Who knows! Perhaps I'll get to deliver *you* to Stellaria for punishment as well."

"DON'T YOU DARE FUCKING TOUCH THEM!" Wolfy bellowed, pointing a finger at Ziggy while still keeping one eye on Luca. "Even once I'm dead and buried, my siblings will still be under the protection of my clan and every single one of my allies—including those who set me up." He rounded on Luca once again. "Because *their* survival and supremacy was your end game all along, right, *Sensei?*"

"Please listen, Wolfgang," Luca rasped, looking as wrecked as I was feeling. "This was never solely about my *biological* children. In the countless millennia I've spent on this planet, I had wanted nothing to do with the pointless breeding competition both Stellarians and our *Lacertus* enemies seemed obsessed with."

"See?" Theo whispered. "It wasn't just *me.*"

Ziggy shot a glare our way, but Luca wasn't done. "I mostly stayed out of it—uninterested in the fate of this planet beyond the data I was collecting. Then came the original trials at the USN, when supes were suddenly being forced to register their offspring… all because of one boy whose unimaginable power frightened everyone."

"Everyone except *you*," Wolfy grumbled, but I could tell he was hanging on Luca's every word.

Same bro, same.

"You're wrong, Wolfgang." Our mentor shook his head with a defeated laugh. "I was absolutely terrified, because in an instant I went from being a casual observer of Earth's inhabitants to feeling so protective over one tiny supe that I would have killed every person in that building—in the entire city— if it meant I could keep him for myself."

Wolfy hung his head, suddenly seeming far older than his 35 years. "Why didn't you do it? Why didn't you save me before… everything that happened?"

We all knew Wolfy's childhood had been hell, even if I'd only been fed bits and pieces of what he'd lived through. And now he'd just discovered he was a pawn in someone else's game. Someone he trusted. Yet he was still standing.

Still my hero.

My newly awakened tendrils were *writhing* beneath the surface, desperate to be unleashed so I could reach my brother. *Needing* to touch him.

Because I can now…

Fuck.

We could have touched him this entire time.

I held myself back—not wanting to interrupt the moment or Luca's eleventh hour infodump.

"The reason I bided my time was because I saw the potential in you, Wolfgang," Luca gently replied. "You were destined to lead, but all great leaders are made, not born. As terrible as your experiences were—as much as it pained me to know all you endured—these trials made you who you are. Meanwhile, I earned your parents' trust, so when the opportunity arose to fully enmesh myself in your family, I knew you would be powerful enough to assist me. A true master in this harsh world."

"Mastering others is strength…" Wolfy sighed.

"But mastering yourself is true power," Luca finished the quote we'd all grown up hearing. "I am deeply sorry for not being completely honest about what I am—what your brothers are —or about your own heritage and my plans. This was partly done because I didn't want you to have any intel your parents could torture out of you, but… mostly… I didn't want you to be afraid of me."

Wolfy released a sound somewhere between a laugh and a sob. "You mean, like how *everyone* else is—including my own family?"

The family he's willing to protect until—and beyond—his death.

I am such an asshole.

"For the record, I was never afraid of your dusty ass!" Dre called out, buzzing with satisfaction when that got the expected eye roll out of Wolfy.

These two fools.

"Yet, I was explicitly told to be afraid of *you,*" Wolfy replied to my twin, but his accusatory gaze was locked on Luca.

What the fuck?

Luca winced. "I told you to keep the twins under your thumb —that they were both volatile and could challenge you for your throne."

What the actual fuck?!

Wolfy was seething, and I didn't blame him. All this time, I'd seen our eldest brother as the master manipulator. While this was still true, it was apparently more a hazard of the job than a desire to crush us beneath his boot.

Since the puppet master has been Luca all along.

When Dre growled, our mentor hurriedly explained. "There needed to be healthy respect on both sides—perhaps, even a little fear. That's 'how the game is played' in your world, no?"

"Sounds familiar," Ziggy scoffed and crossed his arms, although he blessedly seemed to have chilled the fuck out.

I mean, he's no longer threatening to arrest us.

At least, not at the moment…

Luca took a tentative step toward Wolfy, who responded by taking a step away. My heart officially shattered, as I didn't know if this was his usual instinct to maintain physical space between himself and others, or because of everything we'd learned here today.

I'm gonna buy this man a drink.

Assuming we make it out of here.

Our mentor's shoulders slumped in defeat. "More than anything, I trusted *you*, Wolfgang, and knew putting my offspring in your hands meant they would be safe. All three of them."

THREE?!

I could feel Dre's shock echoing mine. But before either of us could open our mouths to demand an answer to *that* bomb-shell, the front door of our gallery was blasted open with familiar firepower.

Now is not the time, Butch!

But it wasn't Captain Masculine who appeared in the smoke, or Xander welding his *inventus'* power.

The figure who strutted through the wreckage like he didn't give a fuck who or what waited for him on the other side was none other than the true terror of our family.

The one who our on-paper leader kneeled for.

Our **Mafia Queen** had arrived.

CHAPTER 43
THEO

Between learning my only true Stellarian offspring had been hunting me, and that my twins were potentially as powerful as I was—if not more so—there hadn't been a dull moment in the day.

And the exploding doors just keep adding to the ambience.

I squinted into the smoke billowing through the gallery space, preparing for whatever new threat had arrived, even as I monitored Ziggy Andromeda and his Celestial Cube. It was a standard issue device for my kind—I possessed one myself... *somewhere*—but Ziggy's had a few attachments I'd never seen before.

Maybe it's the unwanted child upgrade.

I know, I know… boo, hiss.

Have we met?

Of course, I knew abandoning my offspring with no intention of returning wasn't my finest moment, but I'd always despised being told what to do. And while engaging in copious amounts of unprotected sex with the humans of this planet might have seemed counterintuitive to my aversion to parenthood, I'd always seen it as an opportunity to procreate on *my* terms.

I never claimed to make good decisions.

I'd also never dreamed there would be any major consequences for my actions. At least, nothing I couldn't throw money at to make it go away.

Apparently, I was wrong.

"Putain de bordel de merde! If I don't receive an *immediate* apology for your deplorable, inexcusable actions, *SO HELP ME!"*

Everyone froze as we all collectively recounted our many sins. But once the smoke cleared to reveal the tiniest terror that I'd ever seen—dressed in a silver lamé flight suit and brandishing a riding crop—I realized he was most likely talking to me.

Because the resonant signature embedded in this creature perfectly matched my own.

It appears another consequence of my actions has arrived.

This is just rude at this point.

"Is *that* why you were assigned to spy on me?" I hissed accusingly in the twins' ears, even as I possessively pulled them closer against me. "That… small yet terrifying being who's coming this way—"

Save me!

Andre chuckled. "Yes, but he's not coming for you. Yet."

To my absolute shock, the little psycho stopped in front of *Wolfgang* and jabbed a finger into the much larger man's chest.

"How *dare* you pull this shit again, Wolfy!" he screeched. "After what happened in Iceland, why on earth would you think it was appropriate to run off on another suicide mission? Are you *trying* to get spanked?"

Ohhh…

This must be Simon.

Come to collect his dog.

My shock turned into gleeful amusement as Simon brought the riding crop down on the floor with a resounding crack, causing The Hand of Death to flinch the slightest bit.

This. Is. Everything.

"Boss." Wolfgang cleared his throat and—rather unwisely, in my opinion—attempted to steer Simon back toward the door. "Could you… wait outside with Butch? I'm assuming that's who flew you here…"

"Yes! I'm here, I'm here!" The famous supe known as Captain Masculine *limped* into sight, dressed in full gear. "Although, I think I pulled something with Simon *whipping me* for the entire flight. *Sugar…*"

"And *my* arms are tired—from recording it on my phone the entire time!" another man's voice piped in as equally recognizable green and yellow Lycra appeared. Unsurprisingly, it was Doctor Antihero, with an enormous shit-eating grin on his face, and his attention fully focused on his phone.

"New kink unlocked," he cackled. *"Oh, shit!* Hold on… I told the rest of **The Rabble** I'd video chat so they could watch the action."

My gaze drifted to Wolfgang, who looked about twenty years older than he had two minutes ago, and suddenly, I understood why he acted like such a Grade-A asshole.

Who wouldn't after herding these cats?!

"Flip the camera around, doofus!" A woman's voice drifted over from Antihero's phone. "I *need* to see the moment Simon faces off with his sperm donor."

Nononono…

"Vi…" Wolfgang groaned, pinching the bridge of his nose.

Simon slowly turned, like a vintage horror movie monster, until his green eyes were fixed on *me.*

Gulp.

"I see," he calmly spoke—like the calm before a particularly devastating tornado—but then blessedly shifted his attention back to his mate. "So this entire fiasco is because you were trying to locate my father? Am I understanding that correctly, Wolfy?"

"Yes," Wolfgang replied, clasping his now fully gloved hands in front of his crotch.

Probably a wise move with this little firecracker.

Doctor Antihero cleared his throat, and Wolfgang rolled his eyes before elaborating. "We were also trying to gather data on what Theo is, as Doc is convinced there's a missing piece to the supe heritage puzzle—"

"You've been working with Dr. Torres-Maldonado at the Argentinian caves?" Luca interrupted, clearly surprised by the news.

Wait.

"You knew about the caves?" I hiss-whispered to my twins again. "*My* caves?"

No more secrets!

Andre snorted. *"Your* caves? I don't think so, brat. Our family owns and operates that supe heritage site and all related intel." He abruptly sobered as his voice uncharacteristically wavered. "Assuming this still *is* our family…"

As averse as I was toward the concept of *family,* my borrowed heart broke for my mates and the limbo they now found themselves in.

Hopefully, we can fix things…

With minimal bloodshed.

"Yes, Luca," Wolfgang snapped. "After you insisted Simon and I travel to the same jungles in Argentina where I was *tortured,* I took over the project and put Doc on my permanent payroll. I'm sure you understand why I didn't want to involve the council… or anyone *untrustworthy."*

Oooooh.

"Wolfy!" Simon gasped, delivering a brisk slap of the crop to Wolfgang's thigh—making the formidable supe shift awkwardly in place. "Why are you speaking so disrespect-fully to Luca? I'm sure he's here to help." The not-quite-normie peered up at my fellow Stellarian. "You *are* here to help, hmm?"

"Or else" being the subtext.

Luca inclined his head respectfully, although an amused grin briefly twitched his lips. "Yes, but first, I had to come clean about who—*what*—I came from… an alien race known as the Stellarians." He unleashed the tendrils he'd retracted when the door blew in, to dramatic gasps all around.

Including from Antihero's phone.

From **The Rabble.**

"And that, while your *inventus* always knew I sired some of his siblings, I'd still omitted crucial information... despite all he did to protect his family." His gaze nervously flitted to Wolfgang. *"My* family."

The moment of silence that followed was deafening, but it was immediately chased by a cacophony of voices shouting over each other—causing Wolfy to rub his temples in despair.

"Enough!" Simon shouted, and the appropriately named **Rabble** immediately hushed. "One thing at a time." He then turned to Luca again and stared up at his undulating tendrils with a mix of wonder and recognition. "This... is what I am, isn't it?"

Luca nodded. "Yes, although, with the way I assume you were created, you won't be able to produce tendrils or access the Stellarians' natural abilities, like star hopping. However, you've already accomplished what every Earthling with traces of Stellarian in their DNA can do. You've connected with another who possesses a mix of *Lacertus* and Stellarian DNA to form an unbreakable *inventus* bond. Or, as my kind call it, a *stellar collision.*"

Wait a minute...

Before I could butt in for clarification, Doctor Antihero raised his hand, like a child in a classroom. "Um, Luca? Are you saying that the secret to *inventus* bonds has been a *combination* of *Lacertus* and St-Stellarian DNA all along?" When the Swiss nodded solemnly, Antihero immediately added, "More importantly—*you banged our mother?!*"

Okay, I like this one.

He has his priorities straight.

Luca blushed, but cleared his throat and bravely squared his shoulders before replying, "Yes, but..." A chorus of disgusted groans echoed throughout the gallery space, silencing him once again.

How does anyone *get a word in edgewise with this crew?*

"Okay, spill it, *Sensei!*" A vaguely familiar man's voice boomed from the phone. "Which ones of us got dat Swiss mix when you injected your D… NA into Glacial Girl?"

With a grimace, I realized *this* was the same idiot brother I'd saved during the factory explosion outside Sunrise City. Baltasar Suarez. He of the unfavorable Google alerts and canceled engagements amidst scandals. The one now mated to Zion Salah.

Who I've been complicit in pumping full of serum for decades.

Who I didn't bother saving that night at the factory.

No hard feelings, I hope…

"I think you were the first, Balty!" Andre shouted back, and when Luca glanced at him in surprise, he shrugged. "You said there were three of us. I put two and two together."

"W-what?" Baltasar stuttered. "Ohmygawd. I'm… like Alien Rambo?!"

Who the fuck is—

"Perhaps you should try using those oversized ears of yours to *listen,* Blunt Force," Ziggy snapped. "Or are all the Death-ball head injuries I inflicted catching up with you at last?"

"In your dreams, Star Hopper!" Zion Salah called out from the video chat. "Any head injuries worth mentioning came from *me,* spank you very much."

This family is ridiculous.

I love it.

"Watch this," Gabriel murmured. "I know how to get them to shut the fuck up and refocus." Then he unleashed his gorgeous tendrils, causing mine to writhe beneath the surface —aching to join him.

But it's probably best if I keep a low profile…

Andre cackled before unleashing his as well, and both twins laughed harder when **The Rabble** erupted into screams of shock and awe.

Luca clapped his hands to call everyone's attention his way. "Thank you for the helpful demonstration, boys. Now, where were we? As most of you know, when Xander was born, his parents believed he was—for lack of a better word —defective."

"Surprise, motherfuckers!" Doctor Antihero crowed triumphantly as Captain Masculine—Butch—gazed at him like a big, beefy heart-eye emoji.

Luca nodded. "Their *mistaken* disappointment was the perfect opportunity for me to offer my services." More groans arose, but the Stellarian ignored them. "And before anyone asks, *yes,* Apocalypto Man was aware of and approved the arrangement. It was a win-win, as it supposedly gave them favor with the council—"

"While allowing *you* to infiltrate my clan," Wolfy muttered, but Simon delivered another resounding whack with the crop to silence him.

Luca pressed his lips into a thin line. "As I explained to Wolf-gang before you arrived, I'd already imprinted on him as my adopted son, and decided his family—under *his* future rule— would be the safest place for my future offspring. Your parents were simply a means to an end, with their deaths being a necessary evil for my—*our*—plans."

"I mean... they *were* pretty evil," Xander interjected. "So... girl, bye."

Luca huffed a laugh. "So first came Baltasar, who was created in the usual manner."

"What do you mean...?" Baltasar blurted out, before being shouted into silence by the others.

"He means in the same way *I* was created, I presume," Simon mused, nodding thoughtfully. "The only difference being that Baby Hulk's parental combination was a Stellarian wearing a skinsuit reproducing with a supe while mine was with a normie."

Bunny...

All at once, I realized I'd fallen right into Wolfgang Suarez' plan, simply by being mildly threatened—and more than mildly tempted—by a formidable Frenchwoman.

Sigh.

I'm truly not cut out to be a clan leader.

"You don't need to be a leader, *starshine,*" Andre murmured, brushing a tendril over me in a loving caress. "I'll take care of you."

This promise filled me with so much disgusting *emotion* that I couldn't help snipping, "I thought you were staying out of my head, *demon.*"

He shrugged. "What's the point? Luca's out here spilling all the tea, anyway."

Touché.

"That's correct, Simon." I refocused on the larger conversation to find Luca smiling proudly at the little boss. "Unfortunately, your parental combination meant you had no powers of your own—not until you met your *inventus.* Something similar happened with Xander, except his powers were simply dormant until awakened to defend his *inventus."*

"And to defend myself from being drained by The Hand of Death when I was a baby," Xander scoffed before shrugging. "But I guess that's what kept me alive, soooo… no harm, no foul. Anyway, can you explain the rare genetic mutation we Suarez kids have, Luca? Because Sylvano Ricci just sent me some blood samples from *that guy back there"*—he obnoxiously waved in my direction—"and it looks like the twins' new sammich filling has the same unusual DNA as the rest of us."

CHAPTER 44
THEO

WAIT A GODDAMN MINUTE!!!

"That's impossible!" I sputtered, then immediately regretted it as all eyes—including Simon and Ziggy's—fixed on me.

Would it be so terrible if I star hopped us away from here?

"Yes," my twins replied in unison.

Fine.

"We may not possess traceable DNA of our own, Theo," Luca replied to my outburst. "But it would be ridiculous to think our kind leaves *no* evidence behind once we've thoroughly reconfigured the organic matter of our stolen vessels."

"So you're like… creepy symbiotes?" A child's voice drifted over from the phone. "Cool."

"Excuse me, Miss Ma'am," Zion Salah barked—apparently from a different location. "But aren't you supposed to be in bed? Who's in charge over there?"

"Auntie Vi and Auntie Kai!" Miss Ma'am replied haughtily. "And *they* said since this was *family business*, I could stay up past my bedtime to join in."

"Well said, little queen," Simon praised, and I became confused all over again by the hierarchy in this clan.

"Circling back to the truth about supe heritage…" Luca smoothly took charge once again, accustomed to **The Rabble.** "While the Suarez siblings *do* possess these supposedly rare genes—in reality, *all* supes feature small traces of Stellarian in their blood, along with *Lacertus."*

"Gross," I muttered, not at all pleased by where he was going with this.

Luca shot me a glance. "Regardless of whether my fellow Stellarian wants to hear it, our kind has a natural attraction to one of our sworn enemies. In fact, the original supes were created when any remaining *Lacertus* bred with the first unit of Stellarians who'd arrived to investigate. *My* squadron." When everyone simply gaped at him, he shrugged. "We'll call it a classic enemies-to-lovers pairing, but fueled by the need for dominance. Personally, I didn't partake in the breeding frenzy, as I never cared for such things."

"Until my family came along," Wolfy sighed, with far less bite than before. When Luca simply gazed at him sadly, he offered a small smile and added, *"Our* family."

Ugh, these FEELINGS!

All at once, I understood the concept of 'found family'—not only through the bonds of a *stellar collision,* but through the connection found among fellow travelers hurtling through space.

The ones simply searching for their home.

"How were *we* made, *Sensei?"* Gabriel tentatively asked. "Was it similar to how Stellarians are usually created—through m-meiosis?"

Ziggy snorted derisively, but I refused to acknowledge his presence just yet.

Who wouldn't want to delay the inevitable?

There was no question I was guilty of the crimes Ziggy Andromeda was here to collect me for—even if Andre wanted to justify my actions. The Celestial Cube would provide all the evidence needed to convict me, and a Stellarian jury would sentence me to being pulled apart and scattered into space.

"Stop it," Andre hissed, pulling me closer. "I'm not letting him take you away from us."

Luca cocked his head, observing us curiously, but refocused on answering Gabriel's question. "I'd say you and Andre were created more through *mitosis* than *meiosis*… But yes, it was a similar process to how Stellarians divide their cells to create offspring. In my case, without a fellow Stellarian to bond with, I simply implanted pieces of myself into your mother's eggs and hoped for the best. It was an experiment, to be honest, but it turned out to be my greatest one—*two*—yet."

"What am I, chopped liver?" Baltasar grumbled. "I've got Alien Rambo genes, too! No, Alien *Sensei!* Even better, losers. Wait. Holy shiii—ugar. If I'm part Stellarian, does this mean… *I CAN HUG WOLFY?!"*

Wolfgang recoiled, but it was Simon who answered, albeit with a heavy dose of exasperation. "Not unless you want to experience a little death, like I did when Wolfy and I first touched. And I don't mean the fun kind—à *le petite mort."*

Operating as one, the twins loosened their grip on me and retracted their tendrils before approaching their eldest brother. He watched them grow nearer with an almost resigned look on his face, but bravely stood his ground.

Does he believe they're seeking revenge?

I sure hope so!

"For what it's worth," he murmured when they reached him. "I'm sorry for how I managed… how I *manipulated* the situation. I chose my control tactics based on your personalities, and while it was an effective strategy, I realize it caused lasting damage to our relationships. If I could do it all over again, I would choose a far different approach—one that showed you how deeply I care about both of you. Equally."

Gabriel was buzzing with anticipation, but was clearly waiting for his twin to make the first move. Meanwhile, Andre was giving nothing away—staring at his clan leader, unblinkingly.

Sexy.

Even if I suspect I'm about to be disappointed.

Yes, thanks to their awakened powers, my twins could easily eliminate Wolfgang and take the throne. Some might say they had every right to after his deception. However, I was now intimately familiar with the resonance of these two men, and knew firsthand how oddly *empathetic* they were beneath their occasionally murderous exteriors.

And it's time for 'big bro' to stop underestimating them.

For the sake of adding to the drama, I held my breath along with the others—and gasped when Andre struck. Wolfgang also sharply inhaled as he was violently yanked into his younger brother's arms…

For a hug.

Gross.

"You did the best you could with the shitty cards you were dealt, Wolfy," Andre whispered as Gabriel joined him in smothering The Hand of Death in unconditional love. "You constantly took the hits meant for us, and you did this while believing we feared you. In my case, you probably thought I hated you—which I never did. I mean, sure, I think you're an asshole sometimes, but so am I, so it works. But seriously… thank you." He squeezed him tighter, and Wolfy tentatively placed his hands on them in return. "Thank you for protecting our family."

"Putain!" Simon dabbed at his eyes with a monogrammed handkerchief. "I'm so grateful you monsters hugged it out. I would have hated to have to viciously murder you both in a blood-soaked act of revenge."

I'm not certain he means that…

"Speaking of revenge…" Ziggy chuckled low as my body seized up.

What the…

Oh.

With the twins leaving me unprotected, I now found myself caught in a tractor beam from one of Ziggy's fancy Celestial Cube attachments.

Well, fuck.

"LET HIM GO!!!" Gabriel screamed, attempting to run for me only to have Wolfgang grab him by the arm to hold him back. "Theo only did what he had to do!"

Ziggy scoffed. "He killed his own kind indiscriminately. There's no excuse for what he did."

"Is that what this is about? Or is it because he created you, then bounced to a different galaxy?" Andre was using his 'don't fuck with me' voice, and I was suddenly thankful for how frozen I was—even as I felt myself being dragged toward my cube-shaped prison.

No need to get an erection in front of my new family.

Including various abandoned children.

"It's not only about that," Ziggy gritted out—his gaze focused on the cube as he fiddled with the controls. "It's about doing what's right. For Stellaria."

"What about ensuring the continuation of our kind?" Luca calmly cut in. "What about the laws forbidding the separation of a Stellarian and his stellar collision?"

Wait.

There's a law about that?

Perhaps I should have listened more…

Ziggy stilled so completely, I wondered if his cube had back-fired. "Bullshit. There's no way he found his stellar collision in a lowly *Earthling…*"

Luca grinned, although it wasn't a pleasant expression. "He did. In fact, he found a pair of collisions. That's *twice* the opportunity for glorious reproduction, should they so choose."

We will not *be so choosing, thank you very much.*

But Alien Rambo here doesn't need to know that.

Ziggy was vibrating with rage, much to my enjoyment. "The jury won't accept a match between a true Stellarian and whatever… lab rat experiment you've created here, *councilman."*

"They will," Luca replied with such calm conviction, I immediately understood where my *Demon* had learned—possibly inherited—his boner-inducing aura from. "Because that was the original marching orders we were sent here with. To decipher what the *Lacertus* were doing on Earth and thwart their mission in whatever way possible. This included dominating the breeding situation, and—ironically—it appears I have accomplished that. I've taken superior *Earthling* genes and permanently embedded them with my Stellarian essence, thus creating the best of both worlds in two perfect creatures."

I couldn't agree more.

"Excuse me! I'm still here… Alien Rambo Reject Number One…" Baltasar grumbled before his *Lacertus* mate whispered something filthy that *all* of us could have done without hearing.

"You weren't rejected, squirt!" Violentia—*Auntie Vi*—piped in. "You were living the sweet life, rolling around the *dirtball* field instead of getting the actual shit kicked out of you on the battlefield. I'd bet money Luca had a hand in *that* cushy career path, so quit yer bitchin'."

The tractor beam holding me in place abruptly vanished, and it was only through *my* superior genes that I didn't fall flat on my face in front of everyone.

"There has to be a way around this," Ziggy muttered, his tendrils sharpening to blades as he glared at me with so much vitriol, it was like a punch to the gut.

And I deserve every ounce of his hatred.

Much to my annoyance, the distress in his resonance was calling to mine. But I tamped down the nearly irresistible urge to comfort him, knowing that probably wasn't the best idea at the moment.

The sharpened tendrils are a bit of a deterrent.

"*Frérot…*" Simon cooed, gliding over to where Ziggy was seething. "If I may call you brother? Perhaps you're looking at this situation all wrong?"

"What?" Ziggy snapped, although I noticed how his anger cooled somewhat in the presence of my more terrifying offspring.

Thank fuck someone can calm him down.

Since I'm not cut out for fatherhood either.

"Back when I believed another man—a normie—was my father, I wasted years trying to earn his time and attention." Simon absently fiddled with his riding crop as he stared into the middle distance. "The day I finally put myself first again was the same day I applied for a *très mystérieux* position—as an assistant to an equally mysterious Mr. S."

He glanced over at Wolfgang with a gaze full of love, lust, and a shared history that I envied. "And what do you know? Once I stopped begging for love from someone who couldn't even spare me crumbs, I found a man willing to feed me all the cake I wanted."

Is that a metaphor, or…

"This has been my *life's mission,*" Ziggy growled, although there was more defeat than heat in his tone. "What am I supposed to tell my superiors once I return?"

"I'm sure *Miiicaaah* will help you think of something, Zig!" Zion called from the phone. "That little shit was always a pro at getting out of trouble, leaving me and Isaiah to take the fall…"

Ziggy rolled his eyes but tucked away his cube before lifting his gaze to meet mine once again. "Very well. You win, *Father.* You never have to take responsibility for anything you've done."

Ouch.

But… fair.

Andre growled and stepped forward, as if to intervene, but I held up a hand to stop him. "Actually, I've been forced to confront many unpleasant things about myself over the past several weeks, thanks to my *stellar collisions.*" I shot the twins a grateful smile before refocusing on *my* perfect creation. "I'm deeply flawed, and have a long way to go to be worthy of their love, but… I want to try. And while I can't hope you will ever forgive me for what I've done to you—and our kind—I do hope to see you again someday."

Ziggy's eyebrows shot up in surprise, but I'd already placed a hand over my chest. With no effort at all, I simply allowed my signature resonance to build and reach for his—the only other being whose vibrations would ever perfectly match my own.

I'm sorry.

I'm sorry I wasn't the parent you deserved.

My Stellarian offspring clutched his chest as if it pained him, and I almost faltered, realizing he'd possibly never experienced a resonance of his own before.

I hope you find your stellar collision someday.

Shockingly, he maintained this connection with me for a full minute, until I allowed the vibration to peter off. Then Ziggy Andromeda blew out a slow breath and held my gaze with an unreadable expression meant to hide everything I'd done to him.

"I can't promise you forgiveness, Theo, but perhaps we *will* meet again someday on our travels through the universe."

With that, he was gone.

EPILOGUE

"Is this outfit too *much* for the unveiling?"

I removed the shades I'd slipped on to shield the sun's glare off the Bay and turned away from the railing, bracing myself for whatever awaited me.

This is Theo *we're talking about.*

Unsurprisingly, the star of the show was wearing a silk kimono—his infamous 'leopard print' one. While this wasn't the *most* appropriate attire for an art opening, it was on brand for our slutty alien.

If the paparazzi's attention is what he's after tonight, he'll get it.

He can definitely get it…

As much as Theo could pull off a kimono for any occasion, the issue was that all he had on underneath was a tiny pair of hot pink booty shorts.

Breathe, Dre.

"It's not too *much,* no," I evenly spoke, using every ounce of willpower to not give anything away in my expression.

Because that will only encourage him.

451

"Buuuut…?" he sang, executing a sassy little twirl that caused the kimono to flap around him like a cape, revealing his goddamn *ass cheeks* hanging out of the bottom of the shorts.

"It's too *little*," I concluded, unable to keep the growl out of my voice as my vision went red. "Go pick out something more appropriate."

Before we don't make it to the unveiling at all.

Theo rolled his eyes and sashayed closer. "I hope you don't mean something in *tragic black.*" He sighed and plucked at my merino henley as if it wasn't pricey as fuck. "It's an art opening on the gayest beach in Big City, demon. I'm already *overdressed.*"

I had to blow out a *very* slow breath, which did not go unnoticed. My bratty alien's eyes lit up like the stars glimmering into view overhead, and I realized I was falling right into his trap.

Oh, you wanna play before we go?

With a growl that felt like it came from my pitch-black soul, I grabbed Theo around the neck, relishing the little squeak he made when I squeezed.

"How do you see this ending, brat?" I hissed into his face. "Because no way in hell are you prancing around the boardwalk with *my* ass hanging out for everyone to see. So either willingly change, or I'll rip these whore shorts off you so you can never wear them again."

Theo glared haughtily even as I cut off his air. When I loosened my grip with a *look* that told him I expected an answer, he smiled pleasantly.

Too pleasantly.

"Fine. I'll put something else on." He batted his eyelashes demurely. "Be back in a flash!"

What the…

Before I could respond, he deposited a sweet peck on my cheek and glided away, leaving me more confused than ever.

What in the multiverse just happened?

I was about to march inside after him when my phone buzzed in my pocket.

The Rabble group chat.

Fuck my life.

The Mouthy One: *Since it won't be appropriate to discuss amongst the unwashed masses at the art thing tonight…*

The Mouthy One: *I would like to report that the world's hottest hero and I have captured the last of our lizard serum stealing lesser supes. [Celebration hands emoji] [Trophy emoji]*

Lizard Dick: *I don't remember going out on a job with you, Antihero.*

Only Gay for Lizard Dick: *He was talking about Butch, dumbass.*

Lizard Dick: *And I love your dumb ass, B. [Heart hands emoji]*

The Mouthy One: *Is this thing on? [Mic emoji] I said victory is ours! Where is the goddamn praise?!*

Oh, you want praise?

I chuckled and slid in for a rare chat appearance.

Good job, sluts.

The Not-So Token Hero: *Sugar…*

The Mouthy One: *EXCUSE YOU, DRE? You will NOT be domming MY brat!*

> *I was domming YOU. See you later, hater. [Mic emoji]*
> *[Waving hand emoji]*

I put my phone on silent and tucked it away, knowing full well I'd just tossed a grenade into the group chat.

Maybe that chaotic alien is rubbing off on me…

The truth was, a weight lifted from my shoulders to hear the last of Ward's lesser supes had been collected. Even though it had been Theo's mess to start, I couldn't help feeling somewhat responsible, since Gabe and I straight up *forgot* to tell him about the intel we'd overheard at The Refinery.

Yet I still got put in charge…

While the three of us hadn't completely broken away from the Suarez clan, Wolfy had agreed to 'train' me to manage our own branch—known as the Suarez-Stellari. He tried to play it off as if the reason for his decision was expanding the family business beyond this planet, but I got the feeling it was his way of making amends.

Of finally letting us go.

It was mind-blowing to think of how young Wolfy must have been when he and Luca first made plans for *our* future. And that was on top of all he'd suffered to protect the 'little treasures' belonging to his beloved mentor.

I can see why Gabe always saw him as a hero.

And I finally agree.

Ironically, now that Wolfy had loosened his gloved grip, I no longer wanted to fly far away from the Suarez stronghold.

Gabe and I had officially moved into Theo's maximalist hellscape—*with our names on the deed!*—only to immediately redecorate. After bringing in the same interior designer who'd worked on the compound for Wolfy, we found a happy medium that effortlessly married *our* minimalist needs with Theo's thirst to be as extra as *in*humanly possible.

I should go see what that brat is up to…

"Hey!" Gabe suddenly appeared in the doorway, blocking my path. "Did you see? Xanny said they caught the last of 'em?"

I smiled warmly at my—*literal*—other half. It was incredible how far he'd come since embarking on this journey of subby self-discovery—how much happier he was now that he could be his authentic self. I felt the same, to be honest. Meeting Theo had allowed *me* to fully embrace my darkest desires without fear. And without changing my relationship with my twin.

Gabe and I were more intertwined than ever, thanks to Theo. We were a trio of stars orbiting each other in our own private universe—as close as three beings could possibly be.

Although, according to the taboo fanfic on Theo's computer, he wishes that Gabe and I were closer.

Punk.

"Yeah, I saw…" I huffed. "Xanny sure loves the spotlight of **The Rabble** stage." My lips curled into a smirk as I shook my head. "I still can't believe that antisocial asshole is opening an *academy* to train the lessers they caught on how to handle their newfound powers. What a shitshow that will be."

Hard pass.

Gabe cackled. "If it was *just* Xanny, I'd agree with you. But Butch will be the one actually running the joint, and you know how creepily focused he gets when he's in supe mode."

Blade Runner Butch.

Speaking of the O.G. power-sharing pair, Xander and Butch had recently celebrated their one-year *inventus-versary* by *finally* deciding on a date and tropical location for their destination wedding.

The impending arrival of the newest Suarez might have helped move things along.

I bet Kai is ready to escape this family after the baby is born…

That was an adventure for another day, however. "Yeah, well…" I chuckled. "I'm more than happy to let *those* fools handle the Academy of Not So Extraordinary Lesser Supes. We've got enough on our plates, dude."

My twin nodded sagely, mentally tallying our various ventures. We had our Berlin gallery—which Erich was still managing for us, with enthusiastic help from *Luca,* for some reason—along with whatever family business Wolfy sent our way.

One of *my* biggest side-projects was consulting for Madam Sinistre and Fay as they worked on opening a supe-only version of The Refinery… A club where masks, inhibitions, and concerns about accidentally killing normies could be left at the door.

I'm still not gonna be an educator, though.

Fuck that noise.

We'd also fired Theo's agent and transferred the management of his art to Simon. This was partly done because we kept things in the family, but also to force the wayward father and son to have *some* kind of relationship—even if it was just business.

To our relief, the two hit it off, probably because their expensive tastes and bratty personalities were so similar. For lack of a better word, they truly *resonated* with each other, and their vibe made family gatherings even more ridiculously fun—*or just more ridiculous*—than they already were.

Because yeah, I guess I like hanging out with this family after all.

Luca showed up more often now, since he didn't have to pretend to take a plane. At first, I was worried my relationship with him would feel different—now that all our secrets were out in the open. It did, but only because we could connect like we never had before.

By resonating.

Apparently, this was how Stellarians recognized each other in the wild. And while *stellar collisions* produced compatible notes, the resonance you shared with your family was unique and only understood by those who'd been created from the same ancestral line.

*Kind of like **The Rabble** group chat.*

The one glaring absence at any Suarez-Salah-Stellari get-together was Ziggy Andromeda. Theo seemed mostly relieved that his Stellarian offspring never made an appearance, but I suspected that the occasional hints of sadness and shame I picked up through our bond were because of this unresolved conflict.

Whenever Zion or Balty were visiting Big City, I asked about 'Alien Rambo'—since the Salahs saw him regularly. This was partly to be nice, but mostly to make sure that fucker wasn't changing his mind about bringing Theo in for trial.

It didn't sound like there was anything to worry about. The last I'd heard, Ziggy had star hopped back to Stellaria… with Micah Salah mysteriously disappearing around the same time. I would have been frantic, but Zion didn't seem worried at all. He seemed convinced the Salah family genius had his sights set on bagging some alien dick.

Err… should we tell him about the tendrils?

"Better, *Demon?*" Theo materialized beside us, wearing a bespoke, peacock blue suit I'd never seen before.

"Yes…" I warily replied, still unsure why he was being so *cooperative.*

I don't want a good boy!

"Dang, that fit is fire, old man." Gabe whistled appreciatively before plastering himself to Theo like a fresh coat of paint. "We should get to the unveiling, so, uh… we can come home as soon as possible…"

One mind.

Theo cleared his throat, looking oddly *nervous.* "In the spirit of being truthful, I should tell you I may have exaggerated how old I am."

Gabe backed away to give him space, while clearly trying to hide a smile. "So you're *not* as old as our galaxy—or whatever the fuck you tried to scare me with?"

Scared that slut into coming all over himself.

Theo huffed and smoothed his hands down the front of his suit. "No. I'm only about two or three… thousand years old. It's difficult to know exactly when time is relative."

You are ridiculous.

"I dunno, *starshine,*" I hummed thoughtfully. "You might be too young for us now."

The glare he sent me had my cock dangerously filling out my dress pants, and I hoped he *would* brat me more tonight.

Let me wreck you.

I must have sent that thought straight down the bond as Theo shuddered before reaching for both of us. "We should go," he murmured. "It's important that we're not late."

Who is *he right now?*

"Are you feeling ok—" I started to ask, but he'd already star hopped us to 'the gayest beach in Big City.'

Aaaand, it looks like we are *overdressed…*

It wasn't difficult to tear my attention away from the half-naked bodies surrounding us. The reason we were here was to support our man's art, so I focused on the emcee thanking the local companies who'd clambered to sponsor Theo Coatl's first solo show since his infamous 'brush with death.'

Also, since he settled down.

A notorious bachelor like the Teal Coast's Renaissance Man taking himself off the market would have been news enough. But that he'd shacked up with *much* younger, *identical twins* made the gossip sites lose their collective shit.

And Theo continues to milk that press for all it's worth.

"Please, Andre…" The raw vulnerability in Theo's voice had me sharply glancing at him in alarm. "I need you to under-stand what I created here." He gave me a meaningful look before pulling my twin closer. "How I created it for both of you."

Is he… getting schmoopy?

I was this close to checking my alien's forehead for a fever when the emcee switched gears.

"It is my distinct honor and great pleasure to unveil the boardwalk's new permanent installation, created and curated by Big City's own Theo Coatl. I present to you… *Stellar Collisions!*"

Huh?

Because of the project's scale, Theo had been mostly working off-site over the past couple of months. And while Gabe and I had occasionally dropped by to check in, he'd forbidden these visits the last few weeks by claiming we were 'inhibiting his genius.'

What a sneaky little shit.

An army of assistants yanked away drop cloths at the exact moment various spotlights hit the steel sculptures scattering the beach—illuminating swirling reds, purples, indigos, and golds.

Like all the stars in the galaxy.

My heart was so full it ached. Theo had covered the steel surfaces with layers of paint and glaze—mimicking the technique Gabe and I had used to create *Starshine*.

Which now hangs above our bed.

On blessedly white walls.

"When did you do this?" Gabe whispered as the crowd oohed and aahed. "Is this why you told us to stop bothering you…"

"I also may have been less than truthful about how you both affect my genius," Theo murmured—seeming as transfixed by his art as we were. "I hope you'll forgive me for these little white lies."

"Mmm… I don't know, brat," I whispered in his other ear. "I've been dying for an excuse to punish you."

Theo shivered against me, too overwhelmed to give me an attitude. I loved him like this—even if it meant I wouldn't get that excuse I was after—because there was nothing sweeter than when he let us in.

We see you.

Taking advantage of the low lighting, I licked a trail up his neck until I could deliver a nip to his earlobe. "I love what you've created here—for us. Almost as much as I love you."

Because, yeah, this shit is definitely love.

Luckily for Theo and his aversion to big feels, Gabe interrupted before things got too sappy. Grabbing both our hands, he tugged us along with him, leading us to a nearby piece for a closer look.

Not wanting to break the connection.

"Do you like what you see, angel?" Theo chuckled, and I smiled to hear some of his signature sass had returned. "What better way to honor my muses than to create towering tributes to their perfect cocks?"

Welcome back, brat.

"What?!" Gabe choked out, eyes widening as he craned his neck, trying to see what Theo was suggestively suggesting.

"Behave," I warned, nuzzling Theo's neck again, breathing in his scent like it was the air I needed to breathe. "If you're good, I'll feed you *my* perfect cock once we get home."

"Why wait until we get home?" my twin murmured, pressing himself against Theo's other side. "I wanna fuck under the stars."

Breeeeathe, Dre.

Theo hummed, shrewdly scrutinizing the crowd busy admiring his creations. "I have a better idea. Let's make the obligatory rounds, including with any family who stopped by. Then I'll do *better* than fuck you both under the stars."

"Better?" I cocked an eyebrow—hungrily anticipating whatever was about to come out of his mouth.

My bratty alien licked his lips, looking decidedly more demon than angel. "That's right. Why fuck *under* the stars when you can fuck *among* them? Unless… you're afraid of what's out there?"

"Never," I whispered, meaning it with my entire soul. "Wherever you go, we go."

"Anywhere in the universe," Gabe added, like a prayer. "Until the end of time."

Theo took a shaky breath before scowling at both of us. "You both are the worst—ruining my perfectly good come on with… *emotions!*"

We can't have that.

"Calm down, brat," I chuckled as I dragged them to where Xander was obnoxiously waving us toward the rest of **The Rabble.** "After we're done here, I'll fuck you like the worthless whore you are."

"That's better," Theo sighed happily, plastering on his skin-suit's million-dollar smile. "I *do* have a reputation to uphold, after all."

———

The end… boo, hiss! Get your tendrils on that starry sex scene by **subscribing to my newsletter HERE** *(and* **join my Patreon** *for a peek at Theo's taboo fanfic, coming soon).*

While this may be the end of the Supe heritage storyline, we will see our favorite clan again, at Butch and Xander's wedding, in **Rabble: End Game**. *There is no preorder up yet, but* **subbing to my newsletter in general** *and* **following me on social media** *will keep you in the know.*

This also isn't the last we'll explore this universe (multiverse?)— not by a long shot! Learn more in my **Author's Note** *on the following pages and strap in to my spacecraft. We'll be riding this meteor until the end of (relative) time…*

AUTHOR'S NOTE

Multi-Vers SPOILERS Ahead

Well, fuck. Or, as Butch would say… *sugar!*

This little no-pressure side project—starring a sunshiney, but overworked, superhero who meets the Daddy villain of his dreams—turned into something much bigger than I anticipated.

When I first created **Not All Himbos Wear Capes**, it was a **Patreon** serial, and when I decided to publish it, I purposefully ended it where it *could* be read as a standalone… in case it flopped.

Well, it *didn't* flop, and apparently gay/bi/pan/etc supes were a niche nobody knew they needed. I'm not claiming to be the first to write this particular trope, but I do believe my unique special sauce—that no one else can replicate, try as they might—combined with the rabid fervor *you* Suarez stans brought to the Weird-Ho's table, is what made the magic happen.

I'm talking about you lovelies who ship our original beefy Baby and his Xaddy, those who bow down to the boss (**The Mafia Queen!**) and his sweet murder *mon chou* dog, and those who swoon over the two biggest idiots in love (and their little Lizard Queen!). The ones who live for every appearance of **The Rabble** group chat. *You* have helped me create this world, with characters who feel like family—albeit, a slightly dysfunctional one—because who *wouldn't* want to be a Suarez-Salah-Stellari?

I hope you've now also fallen in love/lust with our twins and their chaotic alien, despite (or because of) the risks I took in this book.

Even though I come from a Why Choose romance background (including a duet with TWELVE mates), puzzling out the individual personalities and relationship dynamics of this unconventional throuple wasn't easy. For example, I'd always portrayed Dre as 'shy' through the eyes of others in previous books, with Gabe being the more talkative, leaderly one. Obviously, that didn't end up being the truth, but I've always enjoyed an unreliable narrator. And my brand is chaos, so it works!

Because the *other* challenge with this book was tying up that pesky overarching plot—the one I had to dropkick into high gear in book two once I realized you maniacs demanded a series. As a pantser-style author, operating on vague ideas and vibes alone, I took this wild ride right along with you.

I debated telling you which parts were planned all along vs. what randomly appeared along the way… but I'm a brat, so, nah.

The good news is that this isn't the end of **Villainous Things**, or of this universe (multiverse?). As you've no doubt already noticed, there *will* be a book 5—called **Rabble: End Game**—mostly because I knew you tiny terrors would demand it anyway (and you *are* quite terrifying). It will be set at Butch and Xander's wedding and feature POVs from *everyone* (including Vi and her lady love). Just a fun li'l something something to keep the party going.

Even *that* won't be the end, however. As you also probably suspect (or know, if you follow me closely enough), I have *multiple* spin-offs planned in this universe—which provides many opportunities for our favorite kinky fuckers to show up again.

The next thing you'll see—in the next week or so, if I can get my shit together—will be the first of my **limited edition Villainous Things book boxes**, featuring an extra special Not All Himbos Wear Capes. The rest will follow in the next several months and I cannot wait to reveal the covers, illustrated by my *inventus,* the amazing **lemonade_doodles**! And don't forget the original art prints (and other Villainous goodies) **in my store**, drawn by **biggsboi_**.

There will also be some 'cesty twin fanfic (written by Theo, of course), but that will only be available **on Patreon**. Sorry, not sorry, Dre. Brats gonna brat.

I've also left the door open to follow Ziggy (and Micah) into space, to see our lesser-turned-greater supes learn how to harness their newfound powers (while finding love, duh), and to explore some good kinky fun with supes enjoying all The Refinery 2.0 has to offer. I'm also planning on dipping a toe into contemporary (gasp!) with some tales from the normies who are just trying to live their lives while surrounded by supernaturals.

The only question is, *which will I explore first?* I will probably poll my patrons—as I do—but mostly, I'll be following my muse. That's why you won't see any pre-orders up yet, but if you **subscribe to my newsletter** or **join my patreon**, you'll be one of the *first* to hear when these pre-orders go live.

In the meantime, don't forget to snag the Multi-Vers BONUS epilogue—Among the Stars—HERE!

This Author's Note (and book, good lawd!) has gone on long enough, so one last note to say THANK YOU! I truly feel like

I've found my calling as an author, thanks to *your* unwavering love for this series and characters.

So strap on your Lycra — more super smutty adventure awaits!

XXX
-C

ACKNOWLEDGMENTS

Just a schmoopy page of extra sloppy thank-yous to:

My kinky BDSM consultant Michelle Kardolus of Cliterature 18+ & Michelle's Bookish Meltdowns, who has also recently stepped up as my "Madhouse" PA (although she's ALWAYS been one of my head hype queens!). Thank you for your guidance so I could create something I was truly proud of.

My intrepid alpha readers: Billie, Kailyn, Katie, Kayla, and Kristina, and my long-suffering comma-checker, Lindsay Hamilton. Your real-time reactions (and thoughtful questions) give me life!

My *inventus,* and NEW Villainous illustrator, Lem (lemonade_doodles) and (other long-suffering soul) my original illustrator, Biggsboi_. HIRE HUMAN ARTISTS, PEOPLE!

My lovelies on Patreon who've cheered me on through advanced chapters, N/SFW art, random musings, and even more random questions/asks for input. You make the writing process feel a helluva lot less lonely.

My Patreon Va Ju-Ju Voodoo Queens: Adrienne, Ashley, Charlotte, Ciara, Cora, Danielle, Diana C., Diana S., Elizabeth, Emily, Fawn, Hillary, Jamie, Kaitlyn, Kayla, Kaylah, Kelly, Kimmy, Kristina, Liz, Nat, Rebecca, Shawn, Shawna, Sophia, Stephanie, Taylor, and Wraithy. Thank you for supporting (and continuing to support) my author journey in this way. I can't wait to send you all your complimentary signed paperbacks with extra special goodies!

My fellow smut + plot peddler author friends! I've been burned so badly in this community, but so appreciate the genuine support (and unstructured chaos) in our group and one-on-one chats.

And last, but certainly not least, my ARC and Street Teams and to the ladies at Chaotic Creatives for handling the ARCs (and an influencer tour) this go-round. I appreciate every bit o' hype you loud, proud Weird-Ho's can spare for me and my dirty little books.

Love is freakin' love, y'all!

XXX
-C

REVIEWS

If you have enjoyed **Enter the Multi-Vers**, please leave reviews! It helps other readers find my work, which helps me as an indie author. *Thank you!*

Amazon
Goodreads
Bookbub

But don't stop there: Tag me in your reviews, stories, edits, videos, and fan art on social. I love to share these posts with my followers!

VILLAINOUS THINGS PLAYLIST

Please enjoy the Spotify playlist that inspired the Villainous Things series (and let me know if you have a song to add):

TWINS & THEO PRINTS AVAILABLE

LINK TO ORDER PRINTS ON THE BOOKS BY C. PAGE

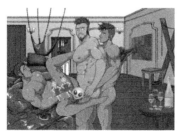

And more!

BOOKS BY C. ROCHELLE

Looking for signed paperbacks, N/SFW art prints, bookplates & other goodies? My store can be found at **C-Rochelle.com/shop** (and **Patreon** members get discounts on art prints and signed books, plus extra swag and personalized inscriptions in their books!)

VILLAINOUS THINGS - SUPERHERO/VILLAIN MM ROMANCE (SLOWLY COMING TO AUDIBLE):

Not All Himbos Wear Capes (*sign up for the newsletter to get the Only Good Boys Get to Top Their Xaddys bonus epilogue*)

Gentlemen Prefer Villains (*sign up for the newsletter to get the Yes Sir, Sorry Sir bonus epilogue*)

Putting Out for a Hero (*sign up for the newsletter to get the Idiots in Love bonus epilogue*)

Enter the Multi-Vers (*sign up for the newsletter to get the Among the Stars bonus epilogue*)

Rabble: End Game (*a just for funsies reunion book, set at Butch and Xander's wedding, and featuring POVs from everyone - including Vi and her lady love. Be sure to **sub to my newsletter** to know when the preorder goes live!*)

Want More Villainous Tales?

Join Patreon (MVPs of DP+) for existing & upcoming bonus content, and **follow the evil author everywhere** to stay in-the-know on various spin-offs!

MONSTROUSLY MYTHIC SERIES (ALSO ON AUDIBLE):

The 12 Hunks of Herculeia (Herculeia Duet, Book 1)

Herculeia the Hero (Herculeia Duet, Book 2) (*sign up for the newsletter for the bonus epilogue: Three Heads Are Better Than One*)

Herculeia: Complete Duet + Bonus Content (*includes Calm Down Monster-Fucker, Three Heads Are Better Than One, & the Thanksgiving*

Special: Get Stuffed, plus UNcensored art)

More Monstrously Mythic Tales:

Valhalla is Full of Hunks (Iola's story)

THE YAGA'S RIDERS TRILOGY (ALSO ON AUDIBLE):

Rise of the Witch

A Witch Out of Time

Call of the Ride

The Yaga's Riders: Complete Trilogy + Bonus Content *(The Asa Baby Christmas Special & the Too Peopley Valentine's Day Special)*

More Yaga's Riders Tales:

A Song of Saints and Swans *(Anthia spin-off novella, which includes From the Depths & the Halloween Special: It's Just a Bunch of Va Ju-Ju Voodoo)*

WINGS OF DARKNESS + LIGHT TRILOGY:

Shadows Spark

Shadows Smolder

Shadows Scorch

Wings of Darkness + Light: The Complete Trilogy + Bonus Content *(Oversized Cupids V-Day Special, The Second Coming Easter Special, & the Sexy Little Devil Halloween Specials Pt. 1 & Pt. 2)*

More from the Wings Universe:

Death by Vanilla (Gage origin story novella)

CURRENT/UPCOMING ANTHOLOGIES:

Snow, Lights, & Monster Nights charity anthology *(featuring The Yule Log: A Valhalla is Full of Hunks bonus tale)*

For 2024: Something gay (featuring normies from the Villainous universe!) and something creepy (with original characters) - *stay tuned for more info!*

ABOUT THE AUTHOR

C. Rochelle here! I'm a naughty but sweet, introverted, Aquarius weirdo who believes a sharp sense of humor is the sexiest trait, loves shaking my booty to Prince, and have never met a cheese I didn't like. Oh, and I write spicy para-normal/monster/sci-fi love-is-love romance with epic plots and dark, naughty humor.

Want More?

- **Join my Clubhouse of Smut on Patreon**
- **Subscribe to my newsletter at C-Rochelle.com**
- **Join my Little Sinners Facebook group**
- **Stalk me in all the places on Linktree**

GLOSSARY

While many people have gone over this book to find typos and other mistakes, we are only human. **If you spot an error, please do NOT report it to Amazon.**

I *want* **to hear from you if there's an issue, so I can fix it.** Send me an email at **crochelle.author@gmail.com** or **use the form** found pinned in my FB group or in my link in bio on TT & IG.

GLOSSARY NOTE: As there are a handful of non-English & scientific words in this one, including bastardized French from our favorite Mafia Queen, I've included a short glossary below for your convenience.

SLANG NOTE: There is always a bit of slang peppered into my writing—**and there is *extra* slang this time, because of how young/ingrained in normie society the twins are.** When in doubt, use Google, or contact me using the methods above if you truly believe it's a typo.

À le petite mort *(French):* Once again, Simon is making things up. This is a combination of *à la* (according/ to the) and *le* *petite mort* (lit. A little death), which is used to describe the post-orgasm feeling of extreme fatigue).

Amygdala *(derived from the Greek, amygdale, meaning almond):* A small section of the brain's temporal lobe, with the main task of regulating emotions—especially fear.

Ars and Invenio *(Latin):* Craft (skilled work, not art) and genius.

Bon appétit *(French):* A wish for someone to enjoy their food.

Capitán *(Spanish):* Captain (masculine).

Carte blanche *(French):* Complete freedom to act however one wishes.

Cui bono*(Latin):* A phrase used to identify crime perpetrators. It asks who would benefit in the situation (usually financially), because that's where you should look.

Frérot *(French):* Brother.

Hallo *(German, Swiss, etc.):* Hello.

Inventus *(Latin):* Find/discover. Perfect passive participle of invenio and the word used to describe supe soulmates.

Katanas *(Japanese):* A single-edged sword that is the longer of a pair worn by the Japanese **Samurai**.

La familia *(Italian):* The family, like The Family (the Italian mafia), like The Suarez clan.

Lacertus *(Latin):* Strength, muscles, vigor, force. Upper arm muscle. In this case, it's derived from *lacerta* ("lizard").

M.O. *(Latin):* Short for *modus operandi,* and used to identify a person or group's habits, to look for patterns.

Meiosis *(Latin root):* A type of cell division that results in four daughter cells each with half the number of chromosomes of the parent cell.

Mitosis *(Latin root):* A type of cell division that results in two daughter cells each having the same number and kind of chromosomes as the parent nucleus. **Note: My proofreader is a science teacher, and suffered through helping me define a made-up process with existing scientific terms. #Bless**

Nouveau riche *(French):* Someone who has recently acquired wealth—typically someone who's ostentatious or lacking in good taste.

Numero uno *(Spanish):* Number one.

Padawan *(Star Wars):* An apprentice Jedi.

Parasitic symbiosis *(Greek root):* A symbiotic relationship in which a **symbiote** lives all or part of its life in or on a living host, usually benefiting while harming the host in some way.

Pho *(Vietnamese, pronounced fə):* A soup dish consisting of broth, rice noodles, herbs, and meat.

Protégé *(French):* Someone who is guided by an older and more experienced/influential person.

Putain *(French):* Fuck (expletive).

Putain de bordel de merde *(French):* For fuck's sake to the max (lit. Shit brothel whore).

Salü *(Swiss):* Hello.

Samurai *(Japanese):* A member of a powerful military caste in feudal Japan.

Schätzli *(Swiss):* Little treasure.

Sensei *(East Asian):* Teacher.

Stellar collision: The coming together of two stars caused by the dynamics within a star cluster, or by the orbital decay of a binary star due to stellar mass loss or gravitational radiation, or by other mechanisms not yet well understood *(love that last bit!)*.

Stellarian: In my many rabbit holes of research, I discovered that Stellarians exist, as a non-binary gender from the *galactian alignment system* (a system created for non-binary people to describe their gender without having to use binary terms), specifically someone who is abinary/unaligned, or neutral-aligned. This felt perfect for Theo (and others of his kind), and I hope anyone on *this* planet who identifies as such knows I borrowed the term with the upmost love.

Stjärna *(Swiss):* Star.

Symbiote *(Greek root):* An organism living in symbiosis with another.

Très mystérieux *(French):* Very mysterious.

Book Club with Luca:

"Mastering others is strength, but mastering yourself is true power."

—Lao Tzu, *Tao Te Ching*

Printed in Great Britain
by Amazon